# INTO
*the*
# STORM

## LISA BINGHAM

D0499591

**DIVERSIONBOOKS**

Also by Lisa Bingham

*The Bengal Rubies*
*Distant Thunder*
*Eden Creek*
*Silken Dreams*
*Silken Promises*
*Temptation's Kiss*

Diversion Books
A Division of Diversion Publishing Corp.
443 Park Avenue South, Suite 1008
New York, New York 10016
www.DiversionBooks.com

For more information, email info@diversionbooks.com

First Diversion Books edition March 2015.
Print ISBN: 978-1-62681-698-5
eBook ISBN: 978-1-62681-699-2

To "Rancy"

Thanks for being my best friend,
my cheerleader, my therapist,
and my big sister.
You taught me to keep trying…and that
most problems can be solved
with an order of bacon.

Dearest J.,

Sadly, I have only one happy memory of my father.

I think I was about five—maybe six? Yes. I was six. I remember distinctly because my younger sister hadn't been born yet and I was leery of a "little stranger" being sent from heaven to live with us.

According to the way Mama tells the story, I was a precocious girl, always getting into cupboards or her sewing box. Worse yet, I had an uncanny knack for escaping without her knowledge. New latches on the doors and a neat fence around the yard made very little impression on my wayward spirit. I didn't want to entertain myself within the confines of the tiny house. As far as I was concerned, the cramped, four-room shack was lacking in imagination. The same was true of the rocky lawn. And the fence? I regarded the neatly painted pickets with the same contempt a prisoner might eye his cellblock bars.

No, I wanted to explore the thick forest that meandered through the valley below the sawmill. There were age-old pine trees and fairy circles as well as squirrels and chipmunks and raccoons. Even better, away in the distance, I could see an enormous emerald pool—an abandoned quarry that had filled with water. I'd been warned countless times about staying away from the old limestone pit, but the mysterious blue-green lake became an obsession. I was sure that something so beautiful must harbor untold magic.

That fateful afternoon, while my mother bent low over her washboard on the front porch, I found a crate in the larder and dragged it up to the back door. Carefully climbing atop it, I leaned forward as far as I could and slipped the hook free from the latch. As soon as it worked free, out I tumbled, coming to a soft landing in the midst of Mama's petunias.

I'm not sure how long I lay there, inhaling their musky scent, my body pulsing with the thrill of being free.

I hadn't been caught.

*I hadn't been caught!*

Quick to finish my escape, I scrambled upright and wriggled beneath the fence in the same spot our dog Lucky had used earlier that week. At a trot, I headed for a forbidden path that wound through the towering evergreens. I would be back long before my mother finished the washing. No one would ever know about the adventure I'd had.

The trail was easy to follow, the ground cocoa-brown against the new spring grass. Birds chattered from the trees overhead—fat chickadees and vibrant jays. Squirrels darted in the shadows, chirping angrily at me for disturbing their idyllic afternoon, their bushy tails flipping and twitching indignantly in their wake. Following them, I left the path and wandered deeper into the woods.

I don't know how long I explored. It could have been minutes or maybe an hour. But gradually, I realized that my surroundings had become completely unfamiliar. I stopped, making a slow, complete circle as my enchantment evaporated. Shadows cast by the pine trees crept ominous fingers across the ground. The familiar noises of the forest faded, overlaid by the guttural croaking of frogs and the incessant creak of crickets. More ominous still were the rustling sounds coming from the undergrowth.

The hair on my arms stood at attention and I was swamped with foreboding. I had disobeyed my mother and she would be cross. And my father...

I didn't even want to consider his anger.

Too frightened to try to find my way back home, I climbed atop a large rock, sitting with my arms wound tightly around my knees. Hugging myself for warmth, I watched the stars blink on, one by one.

Soon, the moon rose high enough over the mountains to cast

its sickly glow and I began to cry in earnest, huge heartrending sobs that exhausted me even further. I'd been a wicked girl and this time I deserved to be punished. My father would see to that.

Yet even as I shivered at the thought of what he would do in order to "drive away my disobedience," I discovered I didn't care. I would willingly face whatever consequences awaited me if only someone would come and take me home.

I'm not sure how long I lay there or when I fell asleep. A pink light was beginning to appear when a strong pair of arms lifted me into a gentle embrace. Still more asleep than awake, I made a weak show of resistance until I heard my father whisper my name.

I waited for his anger to ignite, for the dire reprisals I knew he had planned. I was completely at his mercy.

But nothing happened. Instead, he drew me close and all thought of fighting dissipated like dew against a summer sun. I nestled into the warmth of his body, my nose pressed into his shoulder. His beard was as scratchy as steel wool against my cheek, but oh, so welcome. That beard and the scents of pitch and pine shavings were as familiar to me as my own name.

As relief crashed through my body, sleep threatened to swamp me again. But I felt my father's arms tighten in a desperate hug. A sob snagged his breath—and when he kissed my hair, I felt his tears.

Stunned, I remained motionless in his arms, hardly daring to breathe lest I break whatever spell hung over my father. For the longest time, I'd been sure that he didn't like me much. That he'd resented the fact I hadn't been born a boy. But at that moment, as he hugged me close, I felt... cherished.

Close on the heels of that thought came a desperate panic. Instinctively, I knew that if my father realized I was awake, this unfathomable outpouring of tenderness would vanish and his anger and indifference would return. So I feigned sleep, thinking this could be a new beginning for us.

It was not to be. In the years that followed, his affection would prove more elusive than gold. Unable to comprehend why he found me so unlikable, I struggled to please him, fruitlessly trying to recapture the emotions of that night. But it was as if the depth of emotion he'd felt had boiled dry. My very presence would fill him with a jittery anger that was impossible to control.

If only I could have known early on what lay ahead, the utter fear and emotional darkness into which I would be plunged in my search to recapture that sense of belonging. Maybe if I'd known how difficult such a search would prove, the memory of that distant event wouldn't linger in my memory like the searing heat of a brand upon my soul.

RueAnn

# Chapter One

Washington D.C., U.S.A
September, 1939

Charles Tolliver crossed to the front desk of the Merrimac Hotel and tapped his fingers restlessly on the marble counter. A few yards away, a nattily dressed clerk with an Errol Flynn mustache finished speaking on the telephone.

Charlie checked the tickets he'd tucked into his pocket earlier that morning. Less than twenty-four hours remained before he would be on a train for New York. Mere hours after that, he'd be sailing for London.

So where the hell was Jean-Claude?

Finally, the clerk placed the receiver on the cradle and turned to Charlie.

"May I help you?"

"Room 406, please."

The man turned toward a wall of cubbies, light from the crystal chandelier gleaming from an excess of Brylcreem in his hair. When he returned, he offered a placid smile and slid the key across the richly veined marble along with a small bulky envelope.

"This was left for you earlier today."

Charlie felt his gut tighten, but he kept his features neutral. "Thank you."

Dropping the packet into his trouser pocket, he jingled it carelessly with his spare change as he moved toward the bank of elevators against the rear wall. Eschewing the open car with its buxom operator, he dodged into the stairwell and took the steps two at a time.

Mere moments before reaching the door to the third floor, he paused, peering down over the spiral banister, then up. Backing out of the line of sight, he ripped open the envelope and tipped it sideways.

A gold lighter fell into his palm, causing the hairs at the back of his neck to prickle. The edges were worn, the etchings smoothed away to near extinction.

Jean-Claude's.

Lifting the lid, he examined the mechanism, and then the inner cavity, finding a slip of rolled up paper.

Taking a pen from his inside pocket, Charlie coaxed the paper free, unfolding it.

*Being watched. Second location. 1800.*

Muttering an expletive under his breath, Charlie pocketed the lighter and took the last flight of stairs at breakneck speed. Within five minutes, he'd gathered his belongings and stood at the window, fingering the curtain aside so that he could peer down into the street below.

If Jean-Claude were being watched, that meant it was only prudent to assume…

His gaze fell on a figure who sat on a bus bench at the end of the block. Dark hat, dark trench coat. Had Charlie seen him before? The set of his shoulders, the slouch looked…overly casual. Much like a gentleman in a sweater who'd taken a seat behind Charlie and his companions at the movies last night.

"Bloody hell," he muttered under his breath. With only hours to go, he couldn't afford to miss Jean-Claude, but meeting him now would be more difficult. He could only be grateful that they'd set a backup meeting place early on.

Scanning the street, he grew still when his eyes landed on a construction fence plastered with dozens of posters that proclaimed:

*Come See Glory Bee Hallelujah and Her Diplomat Angels!*

Dropping the curtain, he grabbed his suitcase and his hat and made his way back to the lobby. Strolling as casually as possible, he returned to the front desk.

"My bill, please."

"Of course, sir. I hope your stay was satisfactory."

"Very." Charlie offered him what he hoped was a sly grin. "I've merely managed to find more…pleasant company for my last evening in town."

The clerk's smile was all-knowing. "Very good, sir."

Donning his hat, Charlie approached the shoeshine stand, then, at the last minute, altered his path to the side door. Stepping into the sunshine, he strode north, away from the figure he'd seen watching the front entrance. Carefully, he wove through several side alleys, retracing his steps twice, until he was sure he hadn't been followed. Then, seeing a trolling taxi, he signaled to the driver.

Glory Bee wouldn't be at the theater yet so he would go to her apartment. She was bound to let him borrow her car—and with luck, Charlie would be able to finagle the companionship of one of her roommates as well. A drive into the countryside, a seemingly innocent errand to the Maryland shore…

What could be simpler?

\* \* \*

"RueAnn, there's a phone call for you."

RueAnn barely glanced up. Her needle flashed in the dim light as she repaired the beaded hem of Glory Bee O'Halloran's costume—a strip of fabric worn sarong style during an exotic rendition of *Flying Down to Rio*. RueAnn had been sewing since sunup, making the necessary repairs to the damage that appeared after each performance to the dozens of outfits used in the burlesque review. She still had three ripped seams and a sleeve to reattach. Then it would be time to wash and iron shirts and reset the wigs. If she could get everything finished by noon, she could spend the day exploring the Smithsonian until wardrobe call at six that evening.

"RueAnn, did you hear me?

She made a final knot and bit the end of the thread free.

"Are you sure the telephone is for me?" she said absently, searching for her yellow thread. No one knew she was in Washington other than the performers who were her roommates—and their apartment didn't have a phone.

One of the women who worked in the front office leaned into the doorway. "She said her name was Astrid...Astral..."

RueAnn's head reared up. "Astra?"

"Yeah, that's it."

Her fingers grew suddenly clumsy, the needle pricking her finger and drawing blood. If Astra was on the line, it could only be bad news. Phone calls were next to impossible to arrange in Defiance, West Virginia—especially if Astra wanted to keep her conversation private. Using the pay phone at the company store would have aroused too many questions since the Boggs children were forbidden to use such a "tool from the devil." That meant Astra had hitched a ride to Money or Slaterville in order to get a message to her.

Heedless of the costumes in her lap, RueAnn jumped to her feet. Stepping over the puddle of satin and sequins, she rushed to the stage where a phone had been bolted to the wall near the stage manager's desk. The receiver dangled from its cord, swinging like an oversized pendulum, marking the time it took for RueAnn to wend her way past the carpenters and grips who were readying the theater for this evening's performance.

"Astra?"

There was an audible sob on the other end of the line. "RueAnn, Pa knows where you are!"

"What?"

"Pa knows you're in Washington. I-I don't know how he found out. I swear I didn't say anything. I swear it!"

RueAnn's gripped the receiver so tightly, it creaked. Dear God. Just a few nights ago, she thought she'd seen Clive Meade—one of her father's buddies from the sawmill—on the street outside the theater. But when she'd paused to take another look, the man had disappeared and she'd brushed off the incident as an example of her growing paranoia.

Her younger sister was crying openly now, the piteous

sound made even worse by the distance that separated them.

"Astra, shhh. It's okay. I think I know how he found out," RueAnn offered, nervously wrapping the phone cord around her wrist as her thoughts scattered like buckshot.

"RueAnn, you've got to get out of there," Astra urged, echoing her thoughts.

RueAnn stammered, "I-I can't leave right now. I've got a job. And friends. Last night I went with Glory Bee to the—"

"RueAnn!" Astra interrupted forcefully. "Pa didn't go to work today."

"What?" RueAnn braced her back against the wall.

Her father never missed work.

Never.

"Please, RueAnn, you've got to go. Pa and Gideon took the truck and disappeared late last night. Both of them were mad, RueAnn, really mad. I didn't find out until this morning that they were headed for Washington. It took me forever to get a ride into Money so I could warn you."

"You're sure?" RueAnn breathed. Yards away, the flickering exit sign tapped out its own mayday signal.

*Flick, flick, flick...flash, flash, flash...flick, flick, flick.*

"Yes!" Her sister paused then added, "RueAnn...he took the shotgun with him and..." Astra was crying openly now. "And...and the box from the pulpit."

The phone cord biting into RueAnn's wrist had caused her fingers to turn purple. It was that color, that sickening, unnatural shade that jolted RueAnn out of her disbelief.

She'd been so careful this time. No letters home, no phone calls, nothing. She'd merely slipped away one night, hitching a ride out of Defiance, and heading for the bus station. Emptying the bag of coins she'd been stashing for over a year, she'd asked for a ticket that would take her as far away as her money would allow. Then she'd boarded a bus for Washington D.C.

How much time did she have left? The bus ride to Washington D.C. had been about eight hours, but they'd stopped at least a dozen times along the way. In a truck, her father would have the advantage.

"Where will you go?"

RueAnn scrambled for an answer, but her brain stuck in the same groove, like a needle hitting a scratch in a record. If Jacob Boggs had discovered she worked in a burlesque theater...

There would be no reasoning with him. He would beat her senseless then haul her back to Defiance by the roots of her hair.

Come hell or high water, she would not go back to that life.

"Miss Boggs, have you finished those repairs yet?"

RueAnn started at the costume mistress' call. Glancing over her shoulder, she flashed what she hoped was a natural smile.

"I'm almost finished, Ma'am."

"Very well. I'll see you later this evening."

As soon as the woman disappeared in the wings, RueAnn hunched over the phone. "I've got to go, Astra."

"Be careful. Get away from there as soon as you can."

"I will. I..." She swallowed hard, injecting a light note into her voice that sounded false even to her own ears. "I'll be in touch. Don't worry. I'll find a way to let you know I'm safe and sound."

Very carefully, she replaced the receiver on its cradle. Then, as if the bottom of her world hadn't dropped out beneath her, she made her way back to the narrow room dubbed the "costume closet."

More than anything else, she regretted that she would have to leave Mrs. Bixby in the lurch. The woman had given her a job when no one else would. If RueAnn hurried, she could finish her sewing then explain to her...

What? That despite being a legal adult, she was running away from her father?

Panic made her stumble as she ran the last few feet to the costume closet. Hastily, she gathered her possessions and the mementoes she'd gathered in her short time here—her comb and mirror, scraps of pure silk velvet she intended to sew into a pillow for Astra, and a photograph of the costume crew laughing and pointing at the marquee outside the theater. Shoving them all into her pocketbook, she draped her coat over her arm and planted her hat on her head, stabbing a pin through the brim.

Last of all, she scrawled a hasty note on Mrs. Bixby's "To Do" list, explaining that she'd been notified of an emergency at home and she needed to leave. If all went well, RueAnn would return as soon as she could.

If only that were true. If only she could come back.

She knew that her father would consider them all evil— the comedians, the musicians, the animal handlers…and yes, the strippers. But she'd received more kindness and acceptance from these "sinners" than she'd ever felt from her father's congregation in Defiance.

Aching with the injustice of it all, RueAnn took one last look at the cramped room stuffed to the gills with two sewing machines, fabric bolts, boxes of trims and buttons, and gaily colored threads. Then she dodged for the exit.

RueAnn was so intent on making her escape that she didn't see the figure that stood just outside. The door swung wide, hitting him in the shoulder, and then rebounded to slam against her, sending her pocketbook flying. As her purse landed on the ground, the contents slid wildly over the paint-spattered floorboards, the scraps of silk gleaming red and blue and gold in the midst of the kaleidoscopic mess.

"Hold on, there!"

The man gripped her arm, steadying her just as a resounding slam ricocheted through the theater. From somewhere near the stage, voices rose into shouts.

Every muscle in RueAnn's body strained to hear the cause of the commotion. When she heard a string of curses, followed by the familiar strident commands of the lighting designer. No. It was just Mr. Murphy yelling at his crew.

RueAnn relaxed infinitesimally. She still had time.

"Are you all right?" the man asked.

The world swam back into focus and she found herself staring into the concerned features of a stranger.

No.

Not a stranger.

It was Charles Tolliver. He'd come to visit Glory Bee after her performance last night. Then he'd invited Glory and all her roommates to the movies and dinner.

RueAnn flushed, forcing herself to look away. From the moment she'd been introduced to Charlie, she'd been curiously enthralled by him. As they'd dined on a Blue Plate Special of pot roast and mashed potatoes, she'd hung on his every word, loving the way his accent turned even the most mundane conversation into poetry. And his eyes…they'd continually met hers over the course of the evening, their gray-blue depths sparkling with an inner mischievous light as if he were privy to an unknown punch line. Later, when he'd somehow arranged to be sitting next to her at the movies, she hadn't been able to concentrate on the screen. Instead, she'd been infused with warmth, acutely aware of the way his arm pressed against hers whenever he shifted in his seat.

"Are you hurt?" he prompted again.

RueAnn eased free from the heat that had already begun its sinuous journey through her veins. "I'm sorry, I…I wasn't looking where I was going." Dropping to her knees, she scrambled to gather her things, but in her haste, she only made things worse.

"Here, let me help."

He crouched on his heels and began to scoop up her makeup and personal items with the careless efficiency of his sex, dumping them pell-mell into her pocketbook. He was so clumsy—yet so willing to come to her aid—that she involuntarily laughed, her distress easing.

"Charlie isn't it?" she said with forced casualness.

"I've come to take you to lunch," he replied without preamble.

RueAnn paused, startled.

"But Glory and the others are—"

"Not with Glory. Just the two of us, if you're game."

A glow unlike she'd ever felt before began low in her body, spreading upward until it radiated through her body to the tips of her fingers and the ends of her toes. But a bang from the stage shattered the effect and the heady emotions dissipated like smoke.

"I'm sorry, I can't." She quickly cleared her throat so that she wouldn't betray how close the words had come to cracking under the strain of her disappointment. "Really, I wish—"

Charlie grinned at her then. A lopsided grin that made his pale blue eyes twinkle invitingly. He was obviously a man prone to laughter because lines radiated away from his eyes and the creases bracketing his mouth deepened. "Come now. You've got to eat."

In the light of the bulb that hung overhead, his sandy hair gleamed with reddish highlights. She could see the faint echo of a naughty little boy in his face, although there was nothing childish about his appearance.

She glanced at her watch. "But it's only ten thirty."

"True. But I've got some business to see to in Maryland and I thought you could keep me company."

RueAnn rose, looping her bag around her arm. Yet her true attention was centered on Charlie as he straightened to full height. He was tall, taller than her father. But not beefy like Jacob Boggs. This man was lean. Angular. His shoulders so square, they could have been carved from a block of granite. Even in her current state of agitation, she couldn't deny the fluttering deep in the pit of her stomach.

Why? Why had this happened to her now? Why couldn't her father let RueAnn lead her life as she saw fit? Why couldn't she pursue her job, her dreams—and yes, why couldn't she spend time with a gentleman like this one? One who was charming and good-looking and...and...elegantly foreign?

When she spoke again, it was with very real regret. "I-I'm really sorry, Charlie, but..."

She hurried toward the exit, her shoes making dull thudding noises. Like nails being pounded into a coffin.

Behind her, she heard Charlie scoop something from the floor, but she paid him no mind. If something more had fallen from her bag, it didn't matter. She needed to leave. Now.

But if she'd thought to escape him, it wasn't to be. Charlie quickly caught up, leaning around her to push open the door.

After the gloom of the theater, RueAnn blinked against the

sudden morning light.

"Why the rush?" Charlie asked as he joined her on the rickety stoop.

"I'm sorry, Mr. Tolliver, truly I am."

"Charlie."

"Charlie." She scrambled to think of a logical excuse for avoiding his invitation when just last night she would have broken her right arm for a few hours alone with him. "I…I have some important errands and—"

"I'll help you do them later. I've got Glory's motorcar. I can take you wherever you need to go." He pointed to a blue sedan parked in the theater's back lot.

She took a deep breath, before turning to face him. "If you want to know the truth, I'm trying to avoid someone."

"Who?"

She hesitated only an instant before saying, "My father. He's a minister. He doesn't approve of my job and if he catches me here…"

RueAnn couldn't continue, and to his credit, Charlie didn't pry.

"Then come with me," he said gently. "I'll help you get away—for the whole day if you want."

RueAnn opened her mouth to refuse just as she became aware of a disturbance from the front of the theater. Glancing past Charlie's shoulder, she froze as a battered pickup truck screeched to a halt, nearly blocking the alley. An all-too-familiar shape emerged from the driver's seat. Her father stood grim and bullish, his features clouded with anger. He barked an order to the other passenger and her brother emerged, moving toward the main entrance.

*They'd found her.*

"Please say you'll come," she heard Charlie say, his voice seeming to float to her from a million miles away. "'Pears to me like you need some time off. All this work in the theater has left you pale. And if you're with me, your father wouldn't even know where to look. I can take you far away from here."

*Away.*

She looked at Charlie, at the blue Model A sedan parked so close to the exit, at her father's battered pickup.

Distantly, she heard the thump of fists pounding on the front doors of the theater. It would only be a matter of time before her father decided to come down the alley in search of another means inside.

"Come on," Charlie said again.

This time she nodded, hating herself for using this man— this sweet, funny man—in order to make her escape. She had no choice really. She had to leave before her father caught sight of her.

*And she wanted to go so badly.*

"Okay."

"Bravo," Charlie said with such pleasure that a pinpoint of warmth settled in her chest.

He held out his hand, palm up. She stared at the offering, at skin free from the cracked, grease-stained calluses that she'd seen on every male she'd ever known in Defiance. So different. And yet strong and compelling in a way she couldn't completely fathom. Somehow, she knew that if she went with him, she would be safe. If only for a little while.

Numbly, she slid her cold fingers over his and allowed him to lead her toward the sedan.

## London, England

"Please, Susan! You've got to help me!"

Ignoring her twin, Susan Blunt used every ounce of energy she possessed to appear as if she were studying her stenography characters, when in reality she wanted to turn to Sara and demand, "Why? Why did *you* have to kiss Paul Overdone? Why you and not me?"

But pride prevented her from giving even the least sign that she'd seen them earlier—Paul and Sara, huddled together in the upper hall, Paul's arm around her waist as if they'd just shared a passionate embrace and torn away from one another.

Not for the first time, Susan railed at the unfairness of it all. While Susan had been born practical and permanently rumpled, Sara had been gifted with an ethereal femininity that drew men to her like bees to honey.

And Paul Overdone, one of her brother's best friends from University, was no exception.

Susan scowled at her notebook. She'd only just met Paul. Matthew, the oldest of the Blunt children, had brought him along during a weekend visit the day before. From the moment he'd burst through the door on Matthew's heels, Susan had been smitten.

But clearly, he'd been drawn to Sara. Vibrant, effervescent Sara, who attracted men with infinite ease.

"Susan!"

Sara snatched the book from Susan's hands and threw it onto the bed.

"What?" Susan sighed, finally breaking her silence. "Do you have a ladder in your last pair of stockings and want mine?"

"As if *you'd* have an extra pair hanging about."

True.

Sara grabbed her arm. "No, this is serious. I've put myself into a bit of a pickle. With Paul, I mean."

Not something that Susan wanted to talk about, if you please.

Sara stamped her foot like a petulant child. "Are you listening?"

"Yes." Susan couldn't completely hide the belligerence in her tone.

"Paul invited me to the fancy dress party he and Matthew are attending at the Primrose Dance Hall."

Susan ignored a stab of jealousy. "It's a bit of a short notice, isn't it?"

"Yes. Well…I accepted, of course."

Of course.

"But that was before I remembered I'd agreed to go to dinner with Bernard and his mother. I can't back out now. You know how frail Mrs. Biddiwell has been."

Susan rolled her eyes. Dear, sweet, Sara. She was beautiful, kind, and as scatterbrained as the March Hare. It wasn't the first time she'd double-booked herself.

"I know I should simply tell Paul that I've remembered a previous engagement but—"

Sara blushed—she actually *blushed*—making Susan's headache intensify.

"Anyhow, I had this sudden, scathingly brilliant idea." She bit her lip, grinned, and then blurted, "Take my place—just for a few hours—then when I've finished with Bernard, I'll come to the hall and we can switch over."

Susan laughed outright, then quickly sobered when she realized Sara had been completely earnest in her request.

"You want me—" she pointed to her own chest in disbelief, "—to pretend to be you—" she pointed to her twin, "—on an evening out with Paul?"

Sara clapped her hands. "Yes!"

Susan stared at Sara with utter bewilderment. Then, leaping to her feet, she said firmly, "No. No, no, no!" In two strides, she put as much distance as possible between Sara and herself—as if mere proximity to her twin could weaken her resolve. "How could you even suggest such a thing?"

Sara waved away Susan's patent indignation. "You needn't get on your high horse. We've done it before."

"Not since we were twelve!"

Sara clasped her hands together in mute supplication. "Only because we haven't had a serious need to do so," Sara countered, her tone so reasonable, she could have been proposing that they switch places in a grocery line.

"Sara! The man asked you to a *dance*. And you wish to return the invitation by playing a prank?"

"Not a prank," Sara countered indignantly. "Merely a…a… substitution. A *temporary* substitution." Sara grabbed her hand. "If all goes well, Paul will never be the wiser and things can continue on as planned."

*Continue on as planned.* And what exactly did her sister

mean—more kisses in the hall? Intimate dinners? Drives in the country? Why in heaven's name would Susan want any part in such romantic developments?

*Especially since she wanted the man for herself.*

No. She did not want the man for herself. Paul Overdone had already made his attraction to Sara abundantly clear and Susan would not be caught groveling for the crumbs of his affection.

Which was precisely why she could not—*would not*—surrender to Sara's emotional campaign.

As if sensing her sister's stubborn resolve, Sara grasped her hands. "Please, Susan." Her expression became wistful—and therefore so much harder to resist. "I wouldn't do this if… if I didn't genuinely *like* the man. And he'll be returning to University in a matter of days."

Susan opened her mouth to refuse—yet again. For heaven's sake, how many times would she have to say no?

But even as the words formed on her tongue, she was suffused with the ever-present wish that she could be more like Sara. What she wouldn't give to be so relaxed with men, to react to their attentions so effortlessly, so naturally.

*Even if it were only for one night…*

"He'd know," she offered weakly.

Sensing a chink in Susan's will, Sara's tone became even more conciliatory. "It's fancy dress. Any differences he might sense will be easily explained."

"I don't have a costume."

"We have the Spanish dancer ensembles from last year in the trunk under the stairs."

"He'll know…" Susan began again.

"Nonsense. This is no different from all those times we switched classes at school." Sara squeezed her hand. "You'll laugh at his jokes, drink some punch, and dance. You'd only have to maintain the façade for an hour. Two at the most."

One hour with Paul treating her as if she were his girl.

Perhaps two.

"Please Susan," Sara wheedled. "Pretty, pretty, please. Will you do it?"

Susan took a deep breath, knowing that someday soon she would live to regret her response, but finally she whispered, "Yes. I'll do it."

Dearest J.,

I remember so clearly the day my sister was born. For a week before her birth, my mother grew clumsier, alternately clutching her belly to ease the growing weight, or pressing a palm to the mysterious rippling beneath the worn cotton of her dress.

I saw my father watching too. His expressions were difficult to translate, and therefore all the more frightening to me. At times, he stared at her ponderous breasts with a hunger I didn't understand, then his gaze would flick to her stomach and he would look away.

Today, however, there was nothing but a black stare aimed in my direction. Immediately, I cowered in my chair and began to eat my soup, being careful not to slurp or dribble—even though my father ate noisily from his place at the opposite end of the table.

From her chair nearest the stove, my mother pushed her own bowl away, holding the back of her hand to her nose as if the very smell revolted her. Her features were pinched and wan—and I began to wonder if the lump of her belly was like the parasites that grew on the willow trees by the brook. The waxy blossoms were beautiful, but soon, the host tree would die under their voracious need.

My father didn't compliment my mother on her cooking. Instead, he took it as his due. He was the master of this dilapidated castle, and my mother wore herself out trying to please him. This day was no exception. Although he could have reached the icebox by tipping back his chair, he barked an order and my mother scrambled to bring him a cool glass of milk.

My mother handed my father his glass, then gasped,

gripping her belly. A liquid rushed from between her legs, staining her dress, her shoes, and the scrubbed kitchen floor with its pinkish hue.

From outside, the noise of autumn leaves scuttling down the street sounded like dried chicken bones being tossed into the wind. Then my father erupted. "Goddamn, Rachael! Couldn't you have picked a better spot for that?"

I stared at my father, then my mother, wondering how she'd come to wet herself. I received a tanning if I didn't get to the privy in time.

My mother grimaced and collapsed into her chair, panting.

Pa pointed his dripping spoon at her. "We've got no money for a doctor. You know that don't you?"

"I-I know that, Jacob." She glanced out the window. "Don't you fret none. Maisy will come help."

It finally dawned on me that mother was talking about the baby. She'd told me when God was ready to send my baby brother or sister, Miss Maisy Dixon from down the road would tend after me.

"Don't know why you need that busybody here." My father's spoon aimed at me. "You had that one by yourself."

My mother grew even paler. "Please, Jacob. That was different. We were on our way to the clinic in Drury at the time, don't you recall?"

"You made a right mess in the back of the truck, that's all I remember."

I blinked uncomprehendingly.

"Please," my mother whispered. "I'll need help."

He scowled, ripping a piece of bread with his teeth. "Just see to it you have everything done and a hot meal on the table once I get back."

My mother's eyes glittered with tears, but she nodded and pushed to her feet. The pain must have passed because she refilled my father's glass and mopped up the mess on the floor while he demolished a piece of apple pie. Then he drained his cup and stood. Without another word, he jammed his hat onto his head, grabbed the cylindrical bucket containing his dinner, and stomped out the door, letting the spring slam it shut behind him.

He'd barely stepped through the front gate when my mother bent double and gasped. "Hurry! Get Miss Maisy."

Miss Maisy was a widow lady who lived with her sister Ada just west of the company store. The closest real doctor was at the clinic in Drury, eight miles away, and Miss Maisy—who'd lived in Defiance since God was in short pants—had become the next best thing.

My heart was beating like a hummingbird's as I careened through our gate, down the lane, and thundered up to Miss Maisy's front door. I reached high to ring her bell, then waited, counting the seconds.

"One, two, three…"

When I reached thirty, I rang the bell again and pounded on the door. But there was no answer.

The garden!

I rushed around the side of the building, fruitlessly checking each row. My only real hope was the slate I found propped up next to her washboard. Miss Maisy used it to keep track of her orders. I erased the slate with my skirt and printed, "Pleas cum kwick. RueAnn."

Not knowing what else I could do, I left the slate propped against the door and ran back home.

I was several yards away when I heard my mother screaming. The sound was so horrible, I skidded to a halt, clapping my hands over my ears, wondering what could be so terrifying about angels coming with a baby wrapped in a white eiderdown quilt. That's what my father had said would happen.

The anguished cries came again, weaker this time. I moved forward, my feet seeming to be stuck in tar.

The moment I stepped across the threshold, all thought of angels and eiderdown quilts shattered. Ghoulish red stains ran down the length of the hall from my parents' bedroom to the kitchen. The smeared trail gave testament to a struggle that I could only imagine.

Gorge rose in my throat and I gripped the wall, forcing

one foot in front of the other, frowning at the strange mewling sounds that came from the kitchen.

Had a wild animal come into the house? Had my mother been mauled and left for dead?

As I rounded the corner, I could scarcely believe what lay before me. My mother was sprawled on the kitchen floor, her skirt wadded up around her waist, her hips and buttocks gleaming white beneath the bare kitchen bulb. Oddly, I found myself thinking that I'd never seen my mother naked before.

"RueAnn?" she whispered, her eyes half-closed.

She'd propped her shoulder against the lower cupboards, but it was the writhing mass between her legs that filled my chest with a horror. I was sure that I was staring at a monster from one of the fairytale books mama read each night. This was what an evil troll looked like, purple and covered in slime and blood, with squished up features and a gaping mouth.

Dear God, this thing was killing my mother! I could see blood seeping from between her legs, thick and inky and terrifying.

"Maisy…" my mother rasped. Her lips were turning an awful shade of blue.

"Sh-she wasn't there. I-I left a note," I added quickly when my mother closed her eyes and began to weep.

The thing on the floor moved again, its mewl becoming a wail. The noise roused my mother, because she opened her eyes. "H-help me."

Her hand lifted, revealing a length of twine and a gleaming pair of shears. I involuntarily took a step back.

"P-please, RueAnn. Tie the…string…around the baby's cord."

I stared in revulsion at the mass on the floor, taking in the arms that beat ineffectually against my mother's thighs. Repulsed, I saw the long twisting rope that came out of the baby's stomach and disappeared in the bloody thatch between my mother's legs.

"RueAnn…come…here!" My mother's stern reprimand ended in a strangled cry. "Help…me!"

I reluctantly moved forward.

"Tie…the string…near…the baby's…tummy."

She couldn't possibly want me to touch that… creature…

But it was clear she did. Just as it was clear that she was swiftly losing what little strength remained in her quivering body.

I was sure that my mother's instructions were wrong, but I couldn't disobey her. Sinking to my knees, I took the twine from her trembling fingers and wound it around the fleshy cord. It took two tries to make the necessary loop.

"Tighter," my mother whispered. Dark circles seeped into the hollows beneath her eyes. "As…tight as you…can…"

I pulled on the string until my fingers ached, then made a knot.

"Now do it…again…a little…ways away…"

My mother held the scissors toward me, her hand shaking violently. "Cut…between…the…strings…"

I sobbed openly. "No, mama!"

She grabbed my wrist, her fingernails digging into my skin. "Do…it!"

Her eyes filled with fire and remorse—as if she knew a part of my childhood had shattered completely.

"P-please…RueAnn…"

Weeping openly, I took the scissors. They were sticky with blood, but I managed to place the blades on either side of the ropy mass.

"M-mama?"

She'd grown terribly pale, her eyes flickering closed until her lashes lay like black spiders against her skin.

"Mama?"

She didn't answer and I deliberated for several long seconds. If I did this horrible thing, I would surely kill the baby that writhed on the floor. The infant was looking more and more human as a pinkness seeped into her skin. I could see her tiny fingers and toes and the turned-up tilt of her nose. As if she knew I was watching, she cried in earnest, her shrieks rattling the windows.

I felt a tug of regret. She was to have been my baby sister. But I would have to kill her to save my mother.

"I'm…sorry," I whispered. Then I refused to look at her

again as I cut down on the lifeline connecting her to my mother.

The baby screamed even louder, her body shaking with the effort. Her distress was punctuated by my own desperate weeping. Then, just as I wondered what I was supposed to do next, I heard pounding at the door. The squeak of the screen. The clack of heels in the hall.

"Sweet heaven above!" Maisy Dixon cried when she stood in the doorway. "Ada, come quick!"

I stared up at her uncomprehendingly. Then, disgust roiled in my chest and I threw the scissors to the ground before clutching the wriggling shape that was my sister. If she were to die, she would die in my arms.

Maisy and her sister Ada rushed to my mother's aid, dragging her limp body into the bedroom. I could hear them shouting for towels and clean sheets, but I couldn't bring myself to move. Instead, I cradled my sister and cried, waiting for her body to grow cold and stiff. I had killed her as surely as if I'd plunged the scissors into her breast. For that I would burn in hell forever. But it would be worth it, I told myself hollowly. As long as my mother could be saved.

I began to rock back and forth, and soon my sister grew quiet in my arms. I stared down at her, paying little mind to the mess, seeing instead her sweet face and rosebud mouth.

As I reached out to stroke her cheek, rage settled deep in my chest. I'd been told that my sister would be brought by an angel, but that had been a lie. There were no angels. Merely pain, blood and fear.

My father—the person charged with teaching me right from wrong—had lied. If that were the case, could any man be trusted?

RueAnn

# Chapter Two

Maryland, U.S.A.

"So where exactly are we going?" RueAnn asked.

Charlie glanced at the map, then the highway signs announcing they were only a few miles from the shore. They'd been driving for nearly a half hour now.

"We're headed to a place known as Sweet Briar to take a look at my aunt's house."

"Oh?"

"No need to worry. My aunt 'passed on' nearly a year ago. She left my mother most of her estate, including her house."

"I see."

"Although I've been in the States on business for nearly a year, it's taken this long for legal matters with my aunt's estate to be cleared up. So this is my only chance to assess the property and determine what to do with it. Since being recalled to England, I can't put it off any longer."

"Recalled?"

"With all the trouble brewing in Europe and Asia, the company I work with is closing up shop and I'll soon be out of a job. As soon as I return to England, I'll join the military. Probably the Expeditionary Forces."

"But then you could be sent to war, couldn't you?"

He shrugged with as much casualness as he could muster. "It's unlikely that with my flat feet I'd be sent anywhere other than the basement archives."

She blinked and he tried to interpret what he saw—pity, concern?

"Would you have to go where they tell you?"

He laughed, squeezing her hand. "I'll go where I'm needed—even if it's only to fetch a cup of tea for the officers."

Rather than pulling away, he loosely wrapped his fingers around hers. His pulse thumped as he felt her hesitation, her indecision, then softly, almost imperceptibly, she relaxed.

"You'll be careful, won't you?" Her fingers twined even tighter around Charlie's.

"Promise."

"Where is this house?"

"Near the shore, I'm told."

Spotting a petrol station up ahead, he eased the car onto the shoulder. "I've got to get fuel. Why don't we grab something to eat and a soft drink while we're here? Then tonight, I'll take you somewhere special."

"I'd like that."

They bumped into the gravel parking lot. While RueAnn went to fetch the key to powder her nose, Charlie told the attendant to fill the tank, then paid the proprietor a dime to use the phone. An operator quickly made the connection, and mindful of curious ears that could tap into the conversation, Charlie waited until the call had been answered.

"Yes?"

"Douglas!" Charlie offered with feigned exuberance.

"No, sorry. You have a wrong number."

"Dreadfully sorry. I'd hoped to meet a friend for drinks come sundown, but I must have made a mistake in dialing."

"Good luck in your search."

The line clicked and Charlie replaced the receiver, his heart pounding.

"Would you like to make another call?" the rotund gentleman behind the counter asked.

"No. No, I'm fine. Thank you." The message had been received. Come sundown, he would meet with Jean-Claude. Until then…

Grabbing two sodas from an ice chest, Charlie approached the counter. "I'll take these and two of your boxed lunches."

"Fried chicken or ham sandwiches?"

"One of each," he said and gestured to the colas. "Could you open the bottles? We'll drink them here."

Charlie pushed the necessary coins forward, then gathered up their lunches and the two icy bottles of pop.

Walking out into the muggy heat, Charlie saw RueAnn waiting for him by the car. He motioned to a picnic table set beneath the trees a few yards away.

"Shall we eat here?"

After settling in the shade, he set down the boxes and opened the lids. Inside were sandwiches made on thick slices of dark bread, cold fried chicken, crisp dill pickles, apples, and a box of Cracker Jacks for each one of them.

As they ate, they talked of inconsequential things—like the placard on the front window that proclaimed that the proprietor offered additional services as mechanic, barber, and Justice of the Peace.

Charlie didn't realize how hungry he'd been until, thoroughly sated by the good meal and even better company, he leaned back, watching indulgently as RueAnn dug into a Cracker Jack box retrieving a little paper wrapped parcel.

"What have you got?" she asked Charlie.

"Sorry?"

"Each box has a surprise."

"Really?"

"Uh huh." She held up the packet she'd found inside.

Charlie peered into his box, crowing when he found his own prize. "Aha!" Feeling much like a little boy, he ripped the package open with his teeth and shook out the miniature toy.

"What is it?" she asked, leaning over to get a better look at the round object in the middle of his palm.

"'Pears to be a compass." He held his hand flat, twisting the compass to and fro. "Would you look at that? The silly thing works." He nudged RueAnn with his elbow. "What have you got?"

Her unveiling was more leisurely. Bit by bit, she peeled back the paper to reveal a gaudy ring.

"Oh-ho! You've won the real prize, I think. Jewelry tops expeditionary equipment every time."

"You think so?" She laughed, sliding the faux diamond onto her finger, hissing when it pinched. She adjusted the fit, then held her hand up, watching the light sparkle on the paste stone.

His tone became indulgent. "Perhaps these little tokens are meant to tell our futures. I'm off for the great unknown while you are destined for…"

He looked at her.

No, he looked at her lips.

"For what?" she whispered.

"Marriage?"

She shook her head.

"Wealth, then. You'll make millions on the stage."

RueAnn bit her lip. "No. I…I won't be going back. Not anytime soon. Besides, I'm not a performer. I'm…"

He moved toward her without thinking, his lips touching hers, briefly, then lingering.

When she didn't demur, he cupped her face in his palms, returning to kiss her again, more fervently, completely, before tearing away, knowing that to do more might cause her to bolt.

She stared up at him, eyes wide and leery—like those of a doe caught by a beam of light.

Knowing that he had to move carefully, he murmured, "We should go."

She nodded, glancing away.

They returned their bottles to the proprietor and threw away the remains of their lunch. More slowly than necessary, he helped her slide into the car, his fingers skimming down the length of her arm before he shut the door.

He was not an inexperienced man. He'd lost his virginity at fifteen. He was used to women pursuing him—or winning them over with a minimum of fuss. So why did his blood pound out an irregular cadence as he rounded the hood and slid onto the seat beside her?

*Keep your mind where it belongs, Charlie boy.* This wasn't a woman he could kiss and tumble.

"Charlie?"

Her voice was so soft, he almost didn't hear it over the noise of the engine springing to life and the crunch of tires as he made his way back onto the road.

"Hmm?"

"Is it always like that when you kiss someone?"

In an instant, his well-thought-out restraint disappeared, replaced by a crashing sensual heat. And just as he had so many times that day, he found himself looking at her—really looking at her. As if his very life might depend on searing this moment into his consciousness.

Glancing away from his driving, he reached to stroke her cheek with his thumb. Her eyes grew huge with want and she moved into the caress like a cat seeking warmth.

"No," he whispered through a throat gone suddenly tight. "It isn't always like this."

"So this is something special."

"Yes. This is something special. Very, very special."

"I thought so."

Charlie drew her closer, his arm wrapping around her shoulders until her head rested in the hollow of his shoulder. As she settled there with a sigh, her hand resting lightly on his chest, he knew that to his dying day, the scent of sea breezes and warm summer grass would bring with it a crystal clear image of this moment, this embrace, and a needy contentment unlike any that he'd ever experienced before.

Beside him, RueAnn melted into his warmth. For a moment, she closed her eyes, listening to the faint beat of his heart in his chest.

She was being a fool. She knew that. If there was anything that her father had drummed into his daughters, it was that they should beware the evils of the flesh and the cunning nature of man. No decent woman would be caught spending so much time alone with a male, let alone allowing one to kiss her. Add to that, the fact that Charlie had taken her far away from the city and now intended to take her to his aunt's vacant house. A proper woman wouldn't have put herself in such a position.

But as she slid her arm around Charlie's waist, she couldn't remember a time when she'd felt more alive. More at peace. She felt safe with him. Something she hadn't experienced in a very long time. And even though she knew that her actions were foolhardy and reckless.

At this moment, she truly didn't care.

## London, England

Susan had never imagined that being pretty would require such effort. Under Sara's ministrations, Susan's hair had been washed and rinsed in rainwater, her skin scrubbed with sugar and lemon juice, slices of cucumbers placed over her eyes. Her nails were painted a brilliant scarlet and her legs were scoured with a pumice stone until they were smooth and shiny. Using a hot iron, Sara crimped her unruly tresses into exaggerated Marcel waves, then drew the rest of her hair into a severe chignon alleviated only by a single curl in the center of her forehead.

Susan grimaced. "It's not a terribly flattering hairstyle, Sara."

"Nonsense. You look very foreign." Sara lowered her voice dramatically. "Very *exotic*."

Susan doubted that. With her toffee brown hair and the smattering of freckles over the bridge of her nose, she looked blatantly English, in her opinion.

Sara peered at her with eyes narrowed. "If we'd had time, we could have dyed our hair black."

"Heaven forbid!"

"Just a rinse. It would have washed out within a week or two."

Susan stared at her sister in horrified disbelief. "You have the morals of a common criminal, worrying about what color your hair should have been all the while you're plotting to deceive the man you say you admire."

"Oh, pooh," Sara said dismissively before spitting into a little pot of eyeliner.

Susan grimaced. "Really? Is that necessary?"

"I can't very well go to the loo for water, can I? Someone might see. Now hush!"

Sara leaned close to dramatically outline Susan's eyes. Then, using the same brush, she painted a black dot the corner of Susan's lip.

"A beauty spot? Sara, I think you're going too far."

"Nonsense. One simply cannot go *too far* with fancy dress. There's going to be a costume contest, you know, and I don't want you spoiling my chances of winning."

Susan's mouth dropped in horror. "I'm not going to have to...to parade about, am I?"

"I don't think so," Sara said firmly. Taking a brow pencil from the pile of cosmetics on the vanity, she added, "But you might."

Susan scowled, but Sara didn't notice. She had finished drawing a graceful arcing brow over each eye à la her favorite movie actress, Greer Garson. Tossing it onto the vanity, she held a tube of crimson lipstick aloft. "Relax your mouth. You know how difficult it is to correct red lipstick if it's applied improperly."

Before Susan could respond, Sara swiped the color over her mouth, then stood back to admire her handiwork. A slow smile conveyed her satisfaction. "You're going to sweep the man off his feet."

For one fleeting instant, Susan forgot that she was meant to impersonate her twin. She pictured how Paul would react when he saw *her*, when he danced with *her*.

Then, just as quickly, such fantasies were dashed as Sara's eyes met hers in the mirror and she said, "Just remember, you're doing it for me."

"Of course," Susan said quickly. Praying that Sara wouldn't see the wistfulness that had crept into her gaze, Susan jumped from the vanity stool and strode to the armoire for a pair of black shoes. "When do you think you'll be there to switch places?"

Sara frowned. "Not before nine, I'm afraid. It may be as late as ten."

"How will I know when you're there?"

"I'll send a note through one of the wait staff. Then I'll meet you in the ladies."

Susan avoided her sister's eyes as she gathered the beaded pocketbook they'd borrowed from their mother. Inside was a compact with powder—Sara had given her strict instructions to mind the shine on her nose—a latchkey, a few shillings for emergencies, and a handkerchief. All very ladylike, and yet somehow foreign.

Yet, even as she'd collected the last of her things, Susan dawdled. "You're sure we should be doing this?"

Sara grimaced. "Must you worry so?" She handed Susan a pair of black elbow length gloves which Susan struggled to don. Sara's hands had always been a size smaller than Susan's, but the gloves to Susan's original costume had been misplaced long ago.

"They're too tight," she said, hoping that even that flimsy excuse would be enough to make Sara reconsider.

"They'll stretch."

Holding Susan at arm's length, Sara ran a smoothing hand over her hair, then adjusted the rows and rows of flounces which had been added to one of their mother's old nightshifts before the whole thing had been dunked into a boiling pot of red dye.

"What if it rains?" Susan tried one last time. "The last time we wore these costumes it rained, and the red seeped through to my underthings."

"The radio said tonight would be warm and clear."

"But—"

"Enough!" Sara pushed her toward the door. "You mustn't keep Paul waiting."

Susan hesitated, still worried that this whole arrangement could go terribly, terribly wrong. What if she couldn't convincingly portray her sister? Worse yet, what would Paul think of her if he realized he'd been duped?

"Go now before you think too hard," Sara said, opening the door and hiding behind the panels. "I'll be there as soon as I can."

Sara planted a hand at her sister's back and pushed. Susan all but tripped into the hall. Worse yet, Paul and Matthew were making their way from her brother's room at the end of the corridor.

"Are you all right?" Matthew asked.

"Yes," she said quickly, breathlessly. "I must have caught a heel on the runner."

The door slammed shut behind her. The audible *snnnick* of the key being twisted removed Susan's last means of escape.

Matt had the grace to look sheepish. "Is Susan upset that she hasn't been invited? I suppose I could ring a school chap or two—"

"No!" Susan blurted, horrified. Then more calmly, "No. That's not necessary. She's got a bit of a…a headache, actually," Susan rushed to interject. "She said she planned to spend the evening with a hot water bottle and a good book."

Since that was exactly how Susan had intended to pass the time, the words rang true.

"If you're sure."

"Absolutely. *A Tale of Two Cities.*"

The two men stared at her blankly. "What?"

"The book. That she intends to read. It's one of Susan's favorites. Once she begins to re-read it…the world could slip away." She punctuated the statement with an airy wave of her hand.

Matthew continued to stare at her as if she'd gone mad, but he finally pulled himself together enough to stammer, "Ah. Well, then…Shall we go?"

It was Paul who extended his arm to her. He was dressed as a Highwayman with a black kerchief tied over his head to form a mask, jagged holes cut out for his eyes. He wore a billowy black satin shirt, laced at his neck, and a red sash tied at his waist. She laughed when she noted the carved wooden pistols which had been shoved into his belt. She recognized them immediately. They belonged to her younger brother Michael, who was ten.

"How much did you have to offer Michael for the use of his weaponry?"

"Three pence."

"Sheer robbery." Then realizing what she'd said, she laughed and Paul followed suit, his chuckle low and velvety smooth.

Slipping her arm through his, she allowed him to usher her downstairs to the entryway, where, without thinking, she grabbed for her coat.

"Won't Susan mind if you take her wrap?" Matthew said as he grabbed his own raincoat and threw a darker Mackintosh in Paul's direction.

Susan froze. In one unguarded instant, she'd almost revealed herself. But when she glanced at her brother, he was busy trying to fit his executioner's hood into his pocket.

"Susan suggested I take hers since mine is…torn. The lining, I mean. Is torn."

Thankfully, Millicent Blunt breezed into the room. "Here you are, Matthew. Paul." She handed each of them a small cardboard box. "I kept them in the larder so they would stay fresh."

*A corsage.*

Although Mr. Blunt faithfully gave his wife and daughters corsages every Easter, Susan had never been given one by a gentleman caller. It was Sara who received the flowers and the invitations, while Susan…

Invariably stayed home with a book and a hot water bottle.

"Do you need help, Paul?" Millicent murmured delicately.

"No. Thank you, Mrs. Blunt," Paul said, handing the box to Susan. "I'm sure we can manage."

Feeling more of an interloper than ever, Susan opened the lid and gasped. Inside was a beautiful purple orchid, its throat stained with streaks of gold and white.

"It's lovely," she breathed.

There was a florist's card next to bloom. In a scrawling hand Paul had written, *"To a night filled with possibilities."* Then he'd signed his name.

"Thank you so much."

Before she could gather her scattered wits, Paul picked up the flower. It was then that she noted that he had long, slender fingers. Artist's fingers, Sara would have called them.

He removed the pin at the corsage's base, then eased closer, two fingers straying beneath her neckline to ensure that she wasn't pricked.

Heat rose to her cheeks. There was something infinitely intimate about the gesture. Her mother had offered to help him, but he'd insisted on attaching the corsage himself. That had to mean something didn't it?

His head bent close as he made sure the pin had caught her dress and the flower. When he moved away again, Susan could have sworn his lips grazed the top of her head.

"You'd better hurry," Millicent was saying, oblivious to the caress. "I'm sure Ellen is waiting for you, Matthew."

Susan's father strode in from the sitting room. "A picture first," Harry Blunt insisted.

Since he'd been given a Kodak for Christmas, Susan's father had begun taking pictures at every opportunity—parties, celebrations, first days of school, Mayday, grocery store openings.

Knowing that it was best to humor him, Susan allowed herself to be sandwiched in between her brother and Paul. When Paul's arm slipped around her waist, drawing her close to his warmth, she didn't resist. She could have been facing a firing squad at that moment and she still would have smiled as the heat of Paul's body seeped into her side.

Then, all too soon, the photo was complete and Paul was steering her out the door into the warm evening air. His hand remained firm on her back as they navigated the walk and slipped through the garden gate.

And through it all, it took every ounce of will Susan possessed to resist turning to see if Sara watched their progress from the upper window.

## Sweet Briar, U.S.A.

"How much farther to your aunt's house?" Although she had no stake in the outcome of their errand, she found herself eagerly awaiting her first glimpse of his aunt's estate.

"My solicitor gave me directions since my mother never had a chance to visit Aunt Bess here in the States."

"Was she older or younger than your mother?"

"Older. Bess met and married an American during the Great War, then came home with him when he was injured. He died before they could have children of their own. I suppose that's how I inherited the place." Charlie dug into his jacket pocket for the scrap of paper he'd referred to from time to time and double-checked the hand-drawn map.

"As far as I can tell, we're nearly there," he said absently. Then he wedged it beneath his outer thigh and the seat of the car.

"What sort of house is it?"

He shrugged. "I've seen a few photos. Near as I can recall, it's a huge Victorian monstrosity. A neighbor's been paid to check on it now and then to keep the vagrants out. But other than that, I have no idea what I'll find. Eventually, the property will have to be sold, of course. Once I know its condition, I'll have a better idea how to proceed. We'll poke around a bit, then I'll take you back to town for a nice dinner."

Charlie drew to a stop at a crossroads. Since no other traffic was in view, he referred to the map, then the street marker situated in a patch of grass where the road veered into a "Y."

"This is the place."

Turning to the right, he proceeded slowly toward a gravel road ahead of them, following the meandering lane through a heavy copse of trees with a bit more eagerness.

The lane grew bumpy, the trees on either side forming a tunnel of greenery. But as the car topped the rise and rolled out of the stand of oaks, in front of them lay the house.

"Would you look at that?" Charlie murmured in surprise.

RueAnn couldn't remember ever seeing a house so big. It was a huge Queen Anne Victorian painted in what had once been fanciful shades of pink, white and mint green, but its former glory was a memory now. The outer slats were peeling and wind-damaged. Gingerbread moldings decorated every possible angle. Some of the intricate scrolls were broken or hung at crazy angles around high, narrow windows gleaming dully beneath a layer of grime and salt. Nevertheless, with the ocean serving as a glittering backdrop, the edifice rose from its bed of weed-choked lawn like a grand dame in faded finery.

RueAnn gasped. "From the way you were talking, I expected something much more grim."

The car crunched to a stop on a pea-gravel drive and Charlie leaned to gaze through the passenger window. RueAnn caught a whiff of his cologne. No, not cologne. It was the clean scent of soap and man.

"You like it then?" Charlie asked absently. She found herself watching the words being formed by his lips, wondering again what would happen if he leaned closer and pressed his mouth to hers. Would she feel the same explosion of pleasure she'd felt earlier?

"It's the most beautiful house I've ever seen," she said truthfully.

RueAnn wasn't dissuaded by the Victorian's rickety condition. If this were her house, she would enjoy the challenge of bringing the property back to life. A new coat of paint, some millwork, panes of glass, and a shim here and there would do the trick.

"It could be rather quaint, couldn't it?" He shook his head in bewilderment. "Who would have thought the old curmudgeon could have conceived of a color scheme like that?"

"Can we look inside?" RueAnn breathed.

"That's why we're here." Charlie slid from the car and squinted up at one of the Belvedere towers, then grimaced at the sight of missing shingles. Rounding the hood, he opened the door for RueAnn.

Suddenly impatient for what other treasures awaited, RueAnn bounded from the car, grasping his fingers tightly and pulling him more quickly toward the door. Charlie laughed, taking a key from his pocket and sliding it into the lock.

From the moment Charlie opened the door, they became explorers in a treasure hunt of surprises. A parlor, dining room and kitchen. A sunroom. A breakfast alcove.

With each discovery, a better picture of Charlie's aunt began to take shape. The furnishings were spare, clutter and bric-a-brac kept to a minimum. The chairs and tables and settees that graced each room weren't the finest antiques, but they gleamed with a rich polish beneath their dustcovers.

"I believe some of the furniture pieces were willed to other relatives," Charlie said absently. "This must be what's left."

Eager for more, RueAnn drew Charlie upstairs. The second floor was completely empty—four rooms and a small bathroom—so she led the way to the staircase and the third floor. There, they found two small empty chambers, a large bathroom the size of a parlor, and a bedroom. In the center of the room was the only piece of furniture to remain in the upper level, an ornately carved, four poster bed. Obviously from the previous century, it was high and narrow and impossibly delicate, its linens stripped away to leave a bare, lumpy mattress.

RueAnn released his hand, drawn past the bed to the circular space formed by the Belvedere tower. High windows completely circled the room within a room. Below the sills lay a deep, circular bench with cushions, and below that, shelves crammed with books—more books than she'd ever seen amassed together by a single person.

"It's a shame your aunt had no children," RueAnn mused absently, her gaze scanning the titles: *Moby Dick*, *Around the World in Eighty Days*, *Treasure Island*.

"My mother said Aunt Bess was too mean for motherhood, but I had the feeling the feud between the two of them was the result of a beau the two of them fought over. I've never been able to piece together the story and my mother won't talk about it."

"So your aunt lived here alone? All alone?" She wrapped her arms around her waist, making a slow circle. "I can't even comprehend how a house this size could hold only one woman. And this room—" she gestured to the tower where she stood. "There are more books here than the library in Defiance."

She crossed to the window, bracing her hands on either side of the glass, gasping at the view it afforded her of the ocean stretching out, out, into infinity. She watched the waves crashing onto the beach, followed a faint path that carved through the dunes and back to the house to an overgrown lawn and—

"Roses," she breathed.

She suddenly rushed toward Charlie, grasping his hand.

"Come on!"

She took him by surprise, pulling him back down the stairs, through the parlor and dining room to the kitchen beyond. RueAnn inhaled deeply as they walked out onto a wide porch, her gaze riveted on the yard beyond. On the hill leading down to the dunes were dozens and dozens of rose bushes—lavender, white, burgundy, yellow, and pink. The air was laden with their heady, overpowering scent.

Laughing, she wrenched free from Charlie's hand, racing to the copse of bushes.

The flowers were tall and woody—more tree than bush. RueAnn was sure they hadn't been pruned in years, but even their ungainliness held an inexplicable appeal. Scooping clump of blossoms into her hands, she buried her face in the tufts of petals and breathed deeply of their perfume.

"Oh, Charlie, you can't possibly want to sell this place," she exclaimed, lifting her head.

He grinned indulgently, stating the obvious, "But I live in England."

"Then you should move!"

He chuckled, approaching her slowly, his hands shoved deep in his pockets. The breeze gusted at his tie and rumpled his hair, but he didn't seem to mind. In turn, his lack of pretense made her feel comfortable, as if the need to prove herself was unnecessary.

"My aunt made her living by renting rooms during the summer. I really don't think I'd be content with such an occupation."

"So you'd rather—" she stopped, staring at him, a sobering moment as she remembered that he would soon be a soldier.

Her hands dropped to her sides. He moved toward her, slowly at first, then more urgently, until he was framing her face in his hands. Then, he kissed her. Softly, hesitantly. And, when she didn't resist, more hungrily, pulling her tightly against him so that she fit against him, soft to hard.

A rush of desire swamped through her body, flooding all reason. She clung to him, praying that he would never guess how that point of contact had swamped her own sense of being, making her want things she couldn't, *shouldn't* ever have.

Seeming to use every ounce of will he possessed, Charlie broke off their kiss and gazed into her eyes.

RueAnn trembled in his arms, feeling dazed. Was this what she'd been missing? When she'd sworn that she would never fall under a man's spell? Had she been unwittingly denying herself this pleasure?

She gripped his shirt, drawing him closer, rather than pushing him away. He kissed her more leisurely this time, hesitantly exploring the sweetness of her mouth, giving her time to adjust to the intimacy of his embrace. But she was a quick study, countering his movements with those of her own as her body began to thrum with desire.

Slowly, his hands slid around her hips, splaying over her derriere, bringing her tighter against his hardness.

For a moment, she stiffened, frightened. She broke free, taking a quick breath, but he remained absolutely still. Dragging air into his lungs, Charlie waited, watching, obviously wondering what the next few heartbeats would bring. Would she slap him? Wrench free and stalk away?

She touched her lips with her fingertips. They were bruised. Aching. But that ache was nothing compared to her need. When Charlie's head bent toward her again, RueAnn didn't deny him. In fact, she met him halfway. She was tired of ignoring the feelings bubbling inside her. True, her life might have been turned topsy-turvy in the last few hours—and she didn't know yet how she was going to rectify that situation. But right now… this instant…she felt alive and energized and…

Feminine. For the first time, she didn't feel like a dutiful daughter or a scared little girl. She felt…empowered.

Charlie's mouth was hungry against her, his tongue probing

between her lips—and she let him enter. Just as she let him draw her down to the grass so that their bodies could crush together.

When his hand lifted to cup her breast, a spasm of pleasure shot through her, causing her body to jerk so that her hips arched into the hardness below his belt and the womanliness of her breast filled his palm.

There was no real thought or reason. There was only want. A pulsing hungry want that made her grasp at his hair, his shoulders, his hips. Unbidden, she pulled off his jacket, then tugged his shirttails free from his waistband. She wrenched at his tie, his collar.

She didn't know what she sought. She only knew that his hot flesh against her palms was soothing and enervating at the same time. She had ceased to be a person. Instead she was a mass of pulsing hunger. There was no thought of right or wrong or God's judgment. There was only this moment.

This man.

When his head lifted and he gasped, his eyes filled with stunned passion, she refused to let him think about anything but her. *Her.* She wanted to be a priority to someone. She wanted to feel loved and desired. It was as if she'd been wandering cold and forgotten in an icy wasteland and had suddenly been offered warmth. Real warmth that filled her from the inside out and left her glowing in its radiant heat.

"Hey," he whispered against her ear. "We should slow—"

"No," she whispered in return, her voice conveying her desperate longing. "I don't want to slow down. I don't want to stop. I just...*want*..."

His lips crashed into hers then, his fingers plucking at the buttons of her blouse until she lay bared before him. Then he greedily began to suckle and lick, first one and then the other globe, drawing her deep into his mouth. She moaned, dragging him back onto the grass. His hands struggled with the fabric of her skirt, pushing it up over her hips. Then his fingers delved into her knickers to find the sweetness beneath.

Her breath emerged in a quivering rush. It felt good. So good. Better than anything she could remember. Better than escape or freedom or…

Drawing his head back up so that he could kiss her, again and again, she wrestled with his buckle, then the fastenings of his trousers, until she could reach beneath and feel the thing which had always frightened her about men in the past.

But she wasn't frightened now. She was beyond thought, beyond feeling.

Again, he tried to draw back, but she wound her legs about his hips, drawing him to her, to that aching spot that only he could fill. She was so tired of being good. So tired of being alone. And cold. And wanting.

In one thrust, he pushed into her and she cried out, first in pain, then in wonder as her body began to pulse and the world shattered around her into a rose-scented kaleidoscope, pleasure radiating convulsively through her body. She was only distantly aware of Charlie leaning above her, pumping into her, before arching his head back and crying out with his own release.

Then they were still.

Silence crashed around them. Rose petals, loosened by the wind, floated down upon them like pink snow.

And for the first time in her life, RueAnn thought she might know what it must feel like to be loved.

Dearest J.,

My mother changed after Astra's birth. We both changed. While I grew insolent and rebellious, my mother drew into herself, becoming a shadow of the person she had been.

I would never know if it was my sister's difficult birth, the dire loss of blood, or my father's resulting rage when a doctor was summoned, but my mother became somehow…broken. I remember coming home from school to find she was still in bed, staring at the same faded spot in the wallpaper, the coal heater left untended and supper not started. On the bed beside her, Astra would squirm and fret, hungry for human warmth.

Knowing my father would be home soon, I would bully my mother into donning a housedress and combing her hair. Then, with Astra in a basket at my feet, I would sing to my little sister while I chopped onions to throw in the frying pan and fill the room with savory odors that would convince my father that Mama had been cooking all day. After that, I would peel potatoes and set them to boil, cut up greens or snap beans, fry chops or salt pork. If I was lucky, Mama would muster the energy to make a plate of biscuits, and we would both scramble together a meal good enough to satisfy my father.

I truly didn't mind the extra chores. I pretended Astra was my baby and carted her around in my dolly buggy—even dressing her in some of the baby doll outfits brought to me by Santa until she grew too big. And the time with Mama was comforting.

But when my father stepped through the door, those idyllic hours would end as abruptly as the sun being overshadowed by a thundercloud. Since Astra's birth, he'd become more sullen and difficult to please. We walked on thin ice, never knowing what would send him into a rage.

No wonder my mother fled to the sanctuary of her bedroom once the supper dishes had been cleared. I would watch her stumble back to bed, her hand propping her up as she moved those last final feet.

Once she'd left the room, my father would hunch over a glass of bread and milk, his eyes like burning coals against my back as I scrubbed the last of the pots and pans. I wanted nothing more than to crawl to bed myself, but I couldn't. Not without incurring his wrath. So I would dawdle over my task. And after every last drop of moisture had been dried and the dishes had been put away, I would choose the chair farthest away from him, cradle Astra in my lap, and do my homework.

It was difficult work since my father watched me hard, absently ladling sopping wads of milk-soaked bread into his mouth. His gaze was like a rough hand scratching over my face, my neck, and the bare skin of my arms. Only once the glass was completely empty would he stand, scraping the chair back, then stomp into the parlor to read his paper.

As soon as he left, I would gulp air into my lungs. Then I would huddle over my sister, whispering, "He's gone. He's gone."

When it became clear that my mother would not be able to keep up during the butchering season, Rebel Mae Patroni came to help us, sleeping on an old mattress dragged into the cramped bedroom I shared with Astra.

Rebel Mae was one of thirteen children from a family that lived near Beetle Cove, so she was accustomed to hard work. She was tall and gangly with dull brown hair and a face more freckled than fair. When I discovered she would be coming, I relished the idea of having someone to talk to.

But Rebel Mae proved to be dull-witted and slow. She rarely spoke, and when she did, it was a grunted, "Yes'm" to my mother or "No, suh" to my father. Nevertheless, she had strong hands and an even stronger back which would prove valuable to us as my father stalked the high country for game to fill the smokehouse before the winter storms hit.

My only real solace in her arrival was a new variety of food.

She'd been taught well by her mother so our diet was soon augmented by savory stews, cobblers, and cornbread.

For a time, in those awkward moments when my father ate his bread and milk, his hard stare began to wander from me to Rebel Mae. I would see him scrutinize her every move, much the way he tracked a rabbit in the forest before drawing a bead and shooting it in mid-lunge.

If Rebel Mae felt his gaze, she gave no indication. She placidly went about her chores while my father watched her calico dress ripple from the movements of her hands, or the hem rise to expose the backs of her knees when she put away the plates in the overhead cupboard.

I wondered if she felt the same prickling between her shoulder blades as I did on those black, black nights. If she did, she gave no indication. Instead, the kitchen filled with a taut expectancy, like pulling an imaginary string so tightly it threatened to snap.

Soon after, I began sleeping with Astra in the bed beside me, snuggling up to her warmth and drawing strength from her sweet baby freshness. I pretended to be fast asleep each night when the door cracked open and light from the hall spilled onto the floor like a shard of glass. I kept my breathing slow and shallow, clutching at my baby sister for strength and protection...

While on the mattress opposite the door, Rebel Mae slept completely unaware.

RueAnn

# Chapter Three

London, England

Susan wasn't sure what she'd imagined tonight's fancy dress party would entail. Other than a few dances at the local vicarage, she'd never gone to one of the clubs with a boy. So she'd fretted as Matthew collected his companion for the evening.

In her worst moments, she wondered if it would be a grown-up version of the boy-girl mixers organized by Miss Murphy's Dance School. The twins were five years old when Mrs. Blunt dressed them in their best frocks and shepherded them six blocks east to Miss Murphy's for their first "lesson in the social graces." In Mrs. Blunt's opinion, a true lady should be able to sew a straight seam and plan a month's worth of meals. She should keep a journal and compile a neat, monthly list of expenses. She should be polite and poised, well-read in the romantic classics, and graceful. Above all, she must be graceful.

With that lofty goal in mind, Mrs. Blunt had begun the girls' training as early as possible, marching them weekly to Miss Murphy's where they had been paired up with equally uncomfortable boys. There, the children would be taught the "acceptable" dances: the waltz, rumba, and fox trot.

Surely an evening at the Primrose Dance Hall would be a little more sophisticated.

They were less than a block away from the club when Susan realized that her lessons at Miss Murphy's would offer her little expertise. The syncopated beat of swing music seeped through the walls and windows to the street beyond, causing a lightness to her companions' steps that was contagious.

"Do you like to dance?" Paul asked, bending close. There was something intimate about the gesture that caused a tingling to radiate through her extremities.

An answer escaped her. Sara loved to dance—which meant that Susan, who didn't have a clue how to perform the newer steps, would have to do her best to muddle through.

"It's been a while…" she said vaguely.

Since her last dance at Miss Murphy's, if the truth were told. She'd been eleven—no, twelve—at the time.

Some of her dismay must have shown on her face, because Paul chuckled. "Don't worry. We'll take things slow."

His hand was warm around her waist as he ushered her into the club. More than anything, Susan wanted to lean into the embrace. It was what Sara would have done, after all. But she couldn't bring herself to be so bold.

The moment the door closed behind them, they were enveloped by moist, warm air, heavily laden with the scents of cigarette smoke, ale, and perfume. After leaving their wraps with the coat-check girl, they headed to the first empty table they found—one crowded between the dance floor and the bar.

"Would you like a drink?" Paul asked.

Susan opened her mouth, but her mind went blank. What would Sara order?

"Sara has no head for alcohol," Matthew proclaimed archly, ushering Ellen Tibbets into the seat opposite Susan. "One drink and she begins swearing like a sailor."

"Be quiet, Matthew," Susan said, shooting her brother a warning glare. Instinctively, she knew her response was mild compared to the way Sara would have handled their brother. Dear Lord, she would have to be careful or she'd be found out by her own sibling.

"Let me choose something for you then," Paul said.

"Brilliant."

Matthew and Paul disappeared into the crush at the bar.

"I adore your costume," Ellen said, removing a compact from her bag and peering quickly at her reflection. "I'm afraid I had to throw mine together at the last minute."

Susan doubted that. Ellen had come as Marie Antoinette, complete with low décolletage and powdered curls.

"You've certainly captured Matthew's attention."

"Really?" A blush touched the girl's cheeks. "I-I hope so. I mean...Matthew is...Well, he's..."

Susan grinned. "Yes, he's all that and more trouble than he's worth."

The two women were laughing as Paul and Matt returned with glasses of dark ale and something much paler for Susan.

Matthew had barely set the glasses down before he drew Ellen to her feet and onto the dance floor. But Paul was inclined to linger, especially since they were virtually alone. He drew his seat closer to Susan's as he set their glasses down. His gaze was intense. His smile warm.

Nervous, she reached for her drink. "Am I going to regret this?" she asked.

He leaned close to whisper. "Ginger beer."

Susan shivered when his lips grazed her ear.

"I can't have you thinking ill of our time together, now can I?" Before she could respond, he wound his fingers between hers and drew her up. "Let's dance."

She barely had the wherewithal to leave her glass on the table as he led the way through the tables. To her relief, the band had segued into a slower ballad. A willowy brunette cupped the microphone as she crooned the opening lines to Irving Berlin's *Always.*

*"I'll be loving you always..."*

Although they began the dance with a respectable distance between them, it took only a few bars of music before Paul pulled her tightly against him and they were cheek to cheek.

Susan allowed herself only a moment of self-chastisement for taking advantage of the situation. Then she surrendered herself to the embrace. She didn't care of Sara would mind or if Paul would be horrified if he ever discovered their ruse. She refused to think about anything but this night.

This dance.

This moment.

Closing her eyes, she breathed deeply of his scent—Bay Rum and Brylcreem. She might only be allowed an hour or two as Paul's escort, but she intended to live every second as if they'd been meant for her.

Paul was an excellent partner, teaching her the steps to the Jitterbug and permitting her to tromp on his toes without complaint. And during the ballads…

Those were the moments she enjoyed most as she was pulled into his arms, his hand tight against her waist, his breath teasing her hair.

The clock passed nine, then ten, and there was still no sign of Sara. Susan prayed that somehow her sister had been permanently detained because she didn't want the evening to end. Ever.

As the final strains of Benny Goodman shook the rafters and the bandleader announced a fifteen minute break from the music, patrons thronged toward the bar. But when Susan would have returned to their table, Paul pulled her through a maze of corridors, past the Ladies and Gents, to a small door at the back of the building. Cool air hit her cheeks as they stepped outside, and Susan gasped in relief.

He led her down the alley to side street that opened onto a small park. Tugging her hand, pulled her beneath the broad arms of a willow tree, then spun her around as if they were dancing.

Laughing, she closed her eyes and lifted her face to the breeze. But when her back encountered the rough bark of the tree, her lashes opened and she focused on Paul's face as it hovered so close to her own.

His gaze was intent, his breathing labored. But she realized with a start that he wasn't winded from the exertion. Even to an inexperienced girl like herself, it was easy to see the passion in his eyes.

Susan didn't wait for him to speak—or even make the first overtures. Instead, she wrapped her arms around his neck.

His lips covered her own, parting them, his tongue slipping inside to deepen the embrace as his body pressed her more tightly against the tree.

Merciful heavens, she'd never been kissed like this before. For the most part, she'd endured fumbling caresses or pecks on the cheeks on those few occasions when an evening with a boy had demanded more than a handshake.

But it was clear that Paul was no boy. Nor was he content with a mere handshake. He bent into her, his mouth continuing its ravaging exploration while one hand moved with infinite slowness from her waist, up, up, up, until his thumb caressed her nipple through her costume.

She gasped against him, but made no demurs. Rather, her own hands blazed a trail, down his chest and around to his back, pulling him so tightly against her that one of Michael's toy pistols dug into her hips. Then, blushing, she realized it wasn't a toy at all, merely the proof of Paul's attraction to her

To *her*.

Paul tore away, dragging his lips to her ear. "I've been wanting to kiss you like that for ages."

"Really?" The word was a mere whisper of sound.

"Your brother has a family photograph on his desk at University. I can't tell you the number of times I've stared at that picture, at the way you're looking up at the camera laughing. I've wondered for the longest time what you'd be like in person."

"Disappointed?" she offered boldly.

"No." His eyes were intent in the moonlight. "No, not at all."

He framed her face in his hands, his kisses growing less frantic and more deliberate.

"You amaze me," he said as he explored her jaw, her temple, the curve of her ear. "You're so beautiful, so full of life."

For one instant, she felt a wave of shame at her deception, but she pushed it resolutely away. She was experiencing a swirl of emotions that she couldn't have dreamed were possible— excitement, desire, need. Once Sara returned, she would be banished again to her role as an onlooker. And after this taste of true passion with Paul, she didn't think she could ever settle for anything less from another man.

Because she wanted *him*.

She'd wanted him since the moment they'd first met.

His lips moved over hers. His body crushed hers against the tree and she wrapped her arms around his waist, clutching him tightly as if he were the only anchor in a hurricane. She could no longer think, she could only feel—his strength, his adoration, his passion.

When his hand cupped her breast, she gasped, leaning into him, needed more, more. In a few scant hours, he'd become her addiction and she couldn't get enough.

Suddenly, he broke free, breathing hard.

"We have to go back."

She stared at him in confusion. "Go back?"

He laughed softly. "In a minute. Maybe ten."

Susan glanced over his shoulder. Heavens, they hadn't been seen had they?

Paul gathered her against him, more gently his time.

"If we don't go back, among people…" he took a shuddering breath. "We may not be able to stop." When he looked at her, his gaze was rueful. "And much as I want to, I'm not about to make love to you up against a tree."

An unbearable heat flooded her face and Susan quickly covered her cheeks with her hands.

"Come here." Paul dropped his arm around her shoulder and drew her toward one of the iron benches. "We'll sit. We'll talk. Then…when I'm a little more…myself, we'll go dance."

Again, warmth scalded her cheeks. Sex in her family was not something bandied about casually. At sixteen, Millicent Blunt had handed the twins a pamphlet outlining the process and the workings of male and female bodies in only the vaguest terms. Susan had learned more from whispers at school than from her mother. But this evening, she'd been given a crash course in all that she'd only been able to imagine—and she was beginning to believe there was still so much more that she didn't know.

They sat on the bench, but there was a bit of emotional space to their embrace as they gathered their wits about them. For some time, they didn't talk—and to her surprise, Susan found that the silence was comfortable and inviting. With other boys, she'd invariably felt bound to fill any awkward gaps in the conversation. But this…

This was heaven on earth.

"What are you thinking?" Paul asked.

"That I like being with you."

He smiled in a way that was at once reassuring and arousing. "Does this mean that you'll be my girl?"

"Yes," she answered without hesitation, then realized she was speaking not for herself, but for Sara. And Sara already had a gaggle of male friends attempting to woo her.

Before Susan could temper her reply, a sudden whistle pierced the darkness. Startled, she looked up to see Matthew bounding from the alley. Impatiently, he motioned to them with his hand.

"We've got to get home." There was a urgency to his tone.

Susan felt a cold wash of reality flood through her body. Had Sara arrived? Had Matthew somehow seen her?

"They just broke into the music to announce the Germans invaded Poland earlier today."

Beside her, Paul grew still. For a week now, the news broadcasts had been heavily laden with references to Britain signing a Mutual Assistance Treaty with Poland. This could only mean…

England would soon be at war.


## Sweet Briar, U.S.A.


It was some time later when Charlie felt RueAnn shiver beneath him.

Suddenly, he became conscious of the sun that was beginning to set and the gusting breeze that came off the water.

"You're cold," he murmured.

She started to shake her head, but he kissed her on the corner of her mouth. "Come on," he whispered, loath to break the tenuous mood that wrapped around them like gossamer threads. "It's going to get chillier as the sun begins to set."

He kissed her again, softly, sweetly, trying to draw away, then kissing her again until he finally forced himself to put some space between them.

Rolling to his feet, he reached down to pull her up beside him. Tenderly, he helped her adjust her clothing, then surreptitiously fastened his own trousers. Then he wrapped his arms around her waist and kissed her in that hollow between her neck and shoulder.

"Charlie, I…I've never…"

"I know," he murmured.

"I-I'm not the sort who—"

"Shhh," he whispered into her ear. "I know."

Wordlessly twining their fingers together, he drew her back to the house.

"I doubt there's electricity." He reached for the light switch. It clicked ineffectually. "As I feared. But I'm sure we have water and firewood aplenty."

Twisting the tap, he confirmed his suspicions. "We could start a blaze in the grate and rustle up some candles."

Left unsaid was the fact that he was assuming they would still be here once it became dark.

When she offered no protest—and indeed appeared a bit relieved—he pressed the possibilities even farther.

"I bet there's a coal-fired hot water heater somewhere…"

Again, she didn't protest. Instead she asked, "Is there a basement? Isn't that usually where they put such things?"

He led her to a door on the far end of the kitchen where earlier he'd seen a set of wooden stairs. Moving carefully down into the dim space, he was grateful for narrow windows at foundation level that provided faint illumination. As soon as they reached the dirt floor, he saw the squat shape of a boiler furnace and beside it the coal-fed water heater.

"Aha!" he walked through the aisle of homemade cupboards filled with bottled fruit to investigate the heater, its controls, and the small mound of coal still heaped beneath the chute.

"Here, will this help?"

RueAnn handed him a box of matches.

"Where did you find these?"

She pointed to one of the shelves that his aunt used to store home preserves.

"There's a stack of candles and matches over there as well as tinned meats and vegetables."

Charlie rapped the water tank with his knuckles. As near as he could tell, it was full. "See if you can find some kindling."

"I saw a bundle of newspapers over there."

"That'll do."

She brought him the papers and he quickly wadded up a few pieces and placed them in the empty chamber of the water heater. Then he rolled the rest of the papers into tight logs that he placed on top of the crumpled squares.

Touching a lit match to the corners of the papers, he tended the flames, adding little chunks of coal, then larger and larger bits until he was satisfied with the heat being generated.

"It shouldn't take too long," he remarked, brushing his hands off as best as he could. "Grab some of those candles and take them upstairs." Glancing out the window, he felt a pang when he saw the lengthening shadows. "I'll be along in a minute. I've got to get more firewood. I think I saw some next to the tool shed at the end of the garden."

He waited until she had gone before hurrying back outside. After a quick look around, he loped toward the ramshackle building, melting into the shadowy interior as the last few rays of sunshine hissed on the distant horizon.

Squinting into the darkness, he waited for his eyes to adjust until, finally, at the far end, amid moldering piles of clay pots and abandoned tools, was a small, compact shadow.

"Jean-Claude!"

The little Frenchman hurried toward him, his hand extended. "Charles, *mon ami*." He lowered his voice to the barest of whispers. "We do not have much time."

"Were you followed?"

"I do not think so. But I do not want to take more chances than necessary, eh?" He withdrew an envelope from his suit pocket. "My contacts in Europe have collected some alarming information which I have copied down for you here. It is imperative that you deliver it to London as soon as possible." Jean-Claude took a large handkerchief from his pocket and mopped his brow as Charlie withdrew the papers. "The Nazis have been gathering top scientists all over Europe."

"What kinds of scientists?"

Jean-Claude shrugged. "Most are physicists, chemists, and propulsion experts."

"Where are they being taken?"

Jean-Claude pointed to map folded between the papers. "Somewhere here." He pointed to a spot circled in red near the border between Austria and Germany. "Several of my associates have noticed a great deal of activity near the town of Hausburg. That is all I can tell you."

Nodding, Charlie slipped the papers back into the envelope and from there into the breast pocket of his suit jacket. "I'll see that my superiors receive this information."

"*Très bien.*" Jean-Claude hesitated, then added, "I wondered, if I could ask of you a favor."

"Of course."

The man drew another envelope from his pocket, hesitated, then handed it to him. "This is a personal matter. A bit of insurance on my part."

Charlie frowned.

"I have reason to believe that a handful of close business associates are anticipating a day when the Germans may begin amassing against Western Europe."

"Do you really think it will come to that?"

Jean-Claude frowned. "Haven't you heard? They attacked Poland only this morning." Jean-Claude tapped the second envelope. "This list is a copy of six fellow businessmen that I have reason to believe are already forming economic ties with the Germans. I have managed to obtain certain documents proving this to be so."

"Do you want me to pass this on as well?"

Jean-Claude shook his head. "No, no. Not yet. The list

is useless unless war is declared and these men continue to collaborate with the Germans. Keep it safe for now. Until I have further need of it." His eyes grew grim. "It may prove the means to bring my family to safety if need be. But take great care. Not all of these businessmen are French. To be found with these documents could be dangerous for you."

Charlie nodded. "Consider it done."

A sad smile tipped Jean-Claude's lips. "Then I will bid you *adieu, mon ami.*"

They shook hands—and for a moment, Jean-Claude clung to him a moment longer than necessary. Then he released his grip and settled his hat on his head.

Charlie offered him a half salute and began backing toward the door. He'd only taken a few steps when Jean-Claude stopped and called out, "Charles?

Charlie paused, one brow lifting.

"Be quite careful as you return to Washington and begin your journey home, *mon ami.* I was not followed until I contacted you."

"You think you're being tailed?"

"Perhaps. Or perhaps, *mon ami*, it is you."

* * *

A niggling disquiet caused Charlie to pause at the car before returning to the house. Opening the boot of the Model A, he reached into his side pocket, then frowned when he drew out a packet of envelopes tied with a pink satin ribbon.

"What the hell?" he murmured, then remembered. When RueAnn had stormed from the theater, he'd found them on the floor. Eager to catch up with her, he'd thrust them into his pocket until he could give them back to her.

But looking at them now, at the neatly tied ribbon, the ever-so-faint scent of perfume clinging to the paper, he felt an inexplicable stab of jealousy. They were love letters, he had no doubt.

And yet…

She'd been a virgin until today.

Refusing to think along those lines, Charlie unlocked his valise, burying the ribbon-wrapped envelopes along with Jean-Claude's documents deep in the inner pocket of his luggage. Then he relocked everything and returned to the house.

The rooms were eerily silent as he stepped inside.

"RueAnn?" he called out, but received no answer.

Climbing the stairs, he made his way through the second floor, then up to the third. The moment he scaled the last step, he could see a faint glow seeping into the hall from the doorway at the far end.

Of course. The Belvedere tower.

He crossed the remaining distance as quietly as he could, not wanting to startle her—and yes, worried that he might find her crying or unsettled.

Instead, he saw that a fire snapped in the grate, warming the bedroom with its redolent glow. Somewhere, RueAnn had found sheets and blankets and made the bed, dragging another blanket onto the floor where she sat.

"I thought I'd lost you," he murmured.

"No."

Suddenly unsure of himself, he slid his hands into his pockets and stepped into the room.

"I should have known this was where I would find you. A princess in her tower."

She shook her head. "I'm no princess. I'm…me." She smiled shyly. "I hope you don't mind. I took a bath while you were out, then borrowed one of the nightdresses that I found in the cedar cupboard. It was so clean and crisp. I don't think it's ever been worn…"

She stood and Charlie stood rooted to the spot, unable to speak. Her hair tumbled in wet waves around her shoulders—and with the too-large nightgown, she should have appeared childlike and small. But there was nothing childish about her. He swallowed as the light pierced the worn cotton. Her shape was limned so clearly by the glow, she could have stood naked before him. The crocheted yoke slipped down her shoulder, the lattice-like design playing peek-a-boo with one rosy nipple. And when she moved toward him, Charlie found it difficult to breathe at all.

Wordlessly, she reached up, unfastening the buttons to his shirt. His trousers. Then she pushed the clothing away, leaving him naked and trembling.

On fire.

Taking his hand, she pulled him toward the bed.

In doing so, the nightgown shifted again and he hissed when he saw a network of scars crisscrossing her back.

"What's this?" he asked, his fingers trembling as he traced them.

She froze at his touch, then glanced over her shoulder, "War wounds," she murmured

Then, before he could ask her more, she took his face in her hands and kissed him.

For a woman who'd been so innocent mere hours before, she'd learned quickly, plunging her tongue into his mouth, dragging her hands down his back, and pulling him to her. Her skin was warm and damp, smelling of soap and woman and...

*Roses. She still smelled of roses.*

All coherent thought fled, leaving him mindlessly centered on one thought, one need. Making love to this woman.

They tumbled onto the bed together, heedless of whatever lay ahead. There was only a hungry meeting of souls and bodies and mouths.

Charlie couldn't remember ever being this overwhelmed by a woman. There was no conscious awareness of anything outside the velvety texture of her skin and the sweetness of her mouth. For a moment he forgot everything—his upcoming deployment, his submerged fear, his hasty trip to America. There was only this time, this place, this woman.

And then, she was arching against him, begging him for the release he'd given her mere hours before, and he couldn't wait any longer. Settling between her thighs, he plunged into her, again and again, until he felt her begin to implode before allowing himself his own rush of pleasure.

While from out of the darkness came the booming accusation.

"Fornicator. *Fornicator!*"

Dearest J.,

Rebel Mae Patroni had only been in our home a few weeks when there was a shift in her demeanor. She began to assume an arrogance that I wouldn't have thought possible from someone so placid—especially since she came from circumstances far simpler than our own.

The change confused me. Suddenly, Rebel Mae was the one giving orders. She told me when to go to bed, what to wear, how to act. She even began paddling me when I disobeyed, rather than telling my father about my naughtiness when he came home.

Worse yet, she began to treat my mother with an air of disdain. Not that she was outright disrespectful. No, it was more a sly manipulation, such as insisting that Mama rest in bed so often that Mama spent more time in her room than anywhere else.

Once, when I arrived home from school early, I caught Rebel Mae wearing lipstick—lipstick! My father would have tanned my hide if he'd caught me wearing "the mask of Babylon."

But it wasn't the makeup that made me grow to dislike Rebel Mae. No. It was the fact that when she bent to put biscuits in the oven, something flashed gold and red from a chain between her breasts. Catching my stare, Rebel Mae quickly buttoned her blouse and told me to change my clothes for chores—but not before I was sure I recognized the object.

Just as I'd suspected, Mama's garnet necklace turned up missing. It had been a present from a grandmother I'd never met. For as long as I could remember, it had been kept in a box in her top drawer. But when I went to fetch Mama some socks,

I noticed the box was empty.

Secretly, I suspected that Rebel Mae had stolen the necklace—although I didn't dare utter the words aloud. When I asked Mama about the missing piece of jewelry, she grew pale, searching my gaze before turning her head and mumbling that it must have fallen down in the drawer somewhere.

From that point on, I kept my eye on Rebel Mae. I was sure she'd maliciously taken the necklace, but I would need proof before taking my accusations to my father.

Rebel Mae must have sensed my scrutiny because she kept her tops tightly buttoned from then on. Nevertheless, her behavior became increasingly odd. Rather than having me help with the dishes after dinner, she sent me to my room to complete my homework. I would spent the next hour or two concentrating on my studies and playing with Astra, all the while conscious of a house that had grown quiet. Too quiet.

Sometimes, I would tiptoe back to the kitchen, only to discover that Rebel Mae had left the dishes in the sink and had disappeared. Stranger yet, my father was also nowhere to be found.

Soon after the disappearance of the necklace, my mother and Astra came down with the fever and I was given the task of caring for them. Since my father was leery of the illness, I slept in Mama's room while he took the couch.

Astra was especially ill, alternately screaming in distress or spitting up what little food I'd managed to get into her belly. It was a relief, when late one night, her fever broke and she fell into a light sleep.

Knowing that she might wake again, I decided to run to the privy while I still could. Tiptoeing through the house, I eased outside, did my business, then dawdled on my way back. The air was heavy with the smell of pine and wood smoke. Train cars made a distant rattling in the direction of the sawmill, while overhead, the moon hung like the grin of the Cheshire Cat.

I breathed deeply of the pungent air, the tension of the past few days easing from my body and leaving me so exhausted I felt as if I trudged through wet sand. I wanted to sleep for a hundred years. No. A thousand.

Since Astra had fallen asleep next to my mother, I decided to go to my own bed. I was sure I'd hear if she cried. Not wanting to wake my father who slept in the parlor, I crept through the house and eased open the door to my room.

A sound alerted me. It was like nothing I'd ever heard before, causing the hairs at the back of my neck to raise. Instinctively, I grew still, my heart pounding so loudly in my ears I was sure the whole house could hear it. But the two figures in the middle of the room were completely unaware of me.

I don't know how long I stood there, my eyes adjusting to the dimness. Instinctively, I knew I should back away and close the door, but I couldn't move. I couldn't tear my gaze away from my father. His body was in profile etched in the glow of moonlight that poured into the room. He was standing at an odd angle, his feet braced slightly apart, his pants wadded around his ankles, his belt lying like a snake on the floor.

To this day, I wish that I'd followed my first instincts and returned to Mama's room. But I was too young to know that I was in very real danger. Instead, I was transfixed by the way my father's head was flung back in abandon, his eyes squeezed closed. And his hands...

His hands were tangled in Rebel Mae's hair, holding her on her knees in front of him. While she—

Too late, I stepped back. The floorboards beneath me creaked.

In an instant, the tableau was broken. Rebel Mae's eyes opened and she reared back as if burned.

Knowing it was only a matter of seconds before my father realized the source of her distress, I ran. I ran outside, into the night, plunging into the same woods that had frightened me so many years before.

By this time, I'd learned how to use the shadows to my advantage. I lunged beneath the branches of a huge pine tree just as I heard my father slam from the house and call out my name.

Shivering, I drew my knees tightly to my chest, trembling. Closing my eyes, I scrubbed the heels of my hands over my eyelids as if I could scour the scene from my memory.

My father. His head flung back. And Rebel Mae…

Try as I might, I couldn't wipe away the image. It lay in sharp relief as if it had been seared into my eyelids.

I sobbed, clapping my hands over my mouth.

But it was too late. He'd heard me. Pine needles and forest litter crunched beneath the soles of his boots as he made his way to my hiding place. Before I could even react, his hand shot out and he was yanking me from my prickly nest.

I cried bitterly all the way home—not knowing why I should feel so frightened or ashamed, yet sensing that something was wrong. Horribly, horribly wrong. And I was the person to blame.

For that, I would be punished far more seriously than I'd ever been before.

RueAnn

# Chapter Four

## Sweet Briar, U.S.A.

The *ka-chick* of a round being pumped into a shotgun split the night like a lightning bolt. Charlie rolled off the bed and onto his feet, his body tightly coiled and ready to spring.

But when two men stepped out of the darkness, armed and angry, he knew things would not be as simple as exchanging a few fisticuffs.

RueAnn screamed, dodging for the door. Before she could take a half-dozen steps, the younger man took the lid from a scarred wooden box and tossed the contents onto the ground at her feet.

It took several seconds for Charlie's addled brain to comprehend what he was seeing. Snakes. Angry snakes with tails that shook like maracas, and heads that wove back and forth as if they debated whether they should strike at RueAnn or Charlie first.

"Bloody hell! Have you lost your ruddy minds?"

Without thinking, Charlie snatched at the linens, throwing a heavy quilt over the reptiles. Then he grasped RueAnn and pulled her behind the shield of his body. "Who the hell do you think you are?"

The larger, hulking shape leveled the double-barrel shotgun at his chest. "I am her father."

Charlie supposed he should have known. Really, who else would have attacked them so savagely? But that didn't stop the utter disbelief, then the shame—and yes, a touch of fear that raced through him. *Bloody, bloody hell!* Wasn't it just his luck to be caught making love to the proverbial minister's daughter?

But how—

As if reading his mind, RueAnn's father drew a small business card from his pocket. "Your roommates were very helpful, RueAnn. After a little…persuasion…they offered up the address of this man's lawyer." His scathing gaze settled like a brand on Charlie. "He proved equally obliging."

Charlie inwardly railed against his own carelessness. He'd written the name of his hotel and the room number on the back of his solicitor's business card when he'd first arrived in Washington D.C. He'd never thought such an innocent act could lead to such dire consequences.

"Look, I—"

"Quiet!" RueAnn's father shouted at him. "She will answer to me."

Charlie became aware of the way RueAnn trembled violently behind him and suddenly, it all made sense—her reticence, her shyness, and yes, even her explosive hunger. She'd freely admitted that she needed to run away from this man. But Charlie had been so sure they were safe, that no one would think to look for them here.

Ice swept through his veins as the snakes writhed beneath the blanket mere inches away. But even that was nothing compared to the weapon aimed in his direction.

*Shit!*

Suddenly, he remembered the scars he'd briefly seen on RueAnn's back. The criss-crossing strokes. With a surety that surprised even himself, Charlie acknowledged the rage rising within him and he knew, then and there, that he would have to do everything he could to help RueAnn escape from this zealot. If he didn't…

Charlie felt an icy dread spread through him as he met the man's black gaze. His eyes were as dark as RueAnn's. Even darker. But there was a meanness to him that RueAnn would never have. A rabid fanaticism that cloaked him like an ominous cloud. This man would kill her if he was given a chance.

Drawing to full height, Charlie tucked her even more firmly

behind the wall of his body. "This is private property—*my* property. You need to vacate the premises immediately or I'll be calling the authorities."

RueAnn's father gave no indication of even having heard him.

"RueAnn Boggs, you have defiled yourself in front of God. This time, He will not save you. He will send his serpents to smite thee and to fill thee with the poison of thy iniquity!" He used the barrel of his rifle to point to the writhing shapes beneath the blanket. "Remove the blanket and pick up the serpent." When she didn't respond, he shouted, "Now!"

Charlie felt a spasm of disbelief when the woman behind him moved and actually bent. He grabbed her wrist, forcing her to stay where she stood.

"No, RueAnn. Ignore him."

"I am her father! She will answer to me!"

"And I'm to be her husband!" Charlie shouted in return, not knowing why he uttered the words, merely sensing it might the only argument that could save them both. "Show him the ring, RueAnn."

When she didn't move, he glanced at her over his shoulder. "Show him the engagement ring I gave to you this afternoon."

At long last, she understood. Holding out her left hand, she revealed the cheap metal ring she'd taken from the Cracker Jack box. Charlie could only hope that in the light of the fire it looked convincing.

"You're a liar," the man ground out through his teeth.

"We've been seeing each other since I came to the States." Dear Lord, let him weave a story with the ease that his mother had claimed came second nature to him as a child. "I have to return to England soon, but we decided not to wait any longer before being married. We were planning on a small ceremony with the Justice of the Peace tomorrow morning, but things got...a little out of hand in the meantime."

RueAnn's father pinned them both in a withering glare, before he turned his gaze on his daughter. "Is this true?"

RueAnn's chin tilted defiantly. "Yes."

"Weren't you taught the sacred commandments? Weren't you taught that fornication is as grievous a sin as murder?"

He suddenly shouldered his shotgun, sighting down the barrel. "You have betrayed God, your father, and your good family name! I should exact the Lord's revenge here and now!"

"The Lord's revenge?" RueAnn retorted bitterly. "Or yours?"

The words shivered in the cool night air, issuing a challenge that Charlie didn't understand, but that he was sure shouldn't have been uttered.

She eased from behind Charlie's shape, appearing especially small and vulnerable in the too-big nightgown. "I'm not the only one who's given in to temptation. If God can forgive others, why can't he forgive me?"

The room suddenly trembled with an explosive silence, and Charlie thought he saw a flicker of fear in the elder man's eyes.

"You've carried the stamp of the devil with you since the day you were born," he rasped in disgust. "You've been nothing but trouble!"

She didn't move, didn't flinch, but Charlie ached for her.

The man's gaze flicked to Charlie again and he sneered. "It's time to be done with you once and for all. You'll marry this man within the hour. Then you'll be his responsibility." He held up a finger, stabbing it into the air in front of her face. "Once you're married, you'll be dead to me. You will have no contact with your mother or your sisters ever again. You will be exorcized from our family. I will not have you spreading the disease of sin to others."

Her knees suddenly buckled and Charlie quickly wrapped his arms around her waist to support her. Obviously, now that their bluff had been called, she was sure that Charlie would leave her in the lurch.

Sadly, he realized that she'd read his character correctly. He was a love 'em and leave 'em kind of fellow. But as he stared down into eyes the color of rich loam and fertile fields, he couldn't do it. He'd been a cad for most of his life, chasing one scheme after another on the off chance that he might find something that would give him that sense of purpose that he craved. He'd even begun working for the British Secret Intelligence Service in an effort to help him settle down and make a man of himself. Yet, he'd still felt unsatisfied.

Until now.

If he couldn't do anything else of value, he could help this woman escape from an untenable situation.

"You'll still marry me, won't you, luv?" Charlie said.

RueAnn imperceptibly shook her head. It was clear she didn't want him to commit to such a drastic step merely because she was afraid of her father's wrath.

But this time, he wasn't thinking so much about future consequences. He was clutching at straws, doing something totally uncharacteristic. All because, for once, he wanted to be a hero in someone's eyes.

Not allowing RueAnn to voice her misgivings aloud, he stated for her father's benefit, "We know just where to go to find the Justice of the Peace, Mr. Boggs. If you and your... companion would like to follow us in your truck, you can be our witnesses."

* * *

RueAnn's marriage to Charles Emerson Tolliver was completed in little less than an hour. They drove back to the service station where that afternoon they'd drunk bottled colas and laughed at the owner's placard advertising his services as mechanic, barber, and Justice of the Peace.

At first, the Honorable Rupert Haddock had been irritated at being disturbed in the middle of the night. But a glimpse of the shotgun only partially concealed beneath Jacob Boggs's overcoat had clearly convinced him that it would be worth his while to perform the ceremony with haste, despite the numerous irregularities involved. He'd been flustered as he'd prompted RueAnn and Charlie to exchange their vows, pausing often to mop his bald dome with a voluminous bandana. Then, after accepting the fee and handing Charlie the properly signed documents, he'd slammed the door upon them all and thrown the deadbolt.

RueAnn stood shivering in the cool autumn air, her arms wrapped around her for warmth. She was exhausted beyond belief. Her head throbbed and she was sure that the faint odor of sex that clung to her body marked her as a woman of easy virtue. She wanted nothing more than to sleep and forget this night had ever happened.

Charlie took her elbow. "Get in the car, RueAnn."

"But—" She started, realizing that this marriage hadn't been a complete sham. She and Charlie might be intimate strangers, but the paper she'd signed had made their union real.

"Get in the car," he repeated. He squeezed her elbow reassuringly, but there was a thread of steel to his tone. "I want to have a word with your father."

"No, Charlie!" She tried to stop him but he very firmly led her to the borrowed sedan, opened the door, and settled her inside. Then he moved to the dark pair of shadows made by her father and brother.

Without warning, Charlie lunged, tearing the shotgun from her father's hands. He leveled the weapon at Jacob's chest, barking an order at her brother. Gideon hesitated, then reluctantly pulled a pistol from the waist of his pants. He dropped it into the dust and kicked it away.

Harsh words were exchanged on either side. Then Charlie gestured toward the truck with the barrel of his weapon. Reluctantly, the two men climbed inside and sped from the parking lot, gravel spewing in all directions, a blast of buckshot serving as a final punctuation mark before the air grew still and silent.

Then and only then did Charlie scoop up the pistol and return to the car, dumping both guns onto the back seat before climbing in himself.

He sat there for several long seconds, staring out of the window, his hands unconsciously curling into fists, releasing, then curling again.

"What did you say to them?" RueAnn finally whispered.

He turned suddenly, as if surprised to find her there. Then he blinked and offered curtly. "I made it clear that they weren't to bother you again."

He started the motor and drove back in the direction of his aunt's house. "We need to lock up, put out the water heater and collect our things."

She nodded.

He glanced at his watch, swearing softly. "I've only got a few hours before my train leaves. It's the last one that can get me to New York in time to take the boat to England."

"Then we'd better hurry."

His eyes filled with apology. "If there was any way I could stay longer, I would."

"You need to go."

"RueAnn, I—"

"Please don't say anything," she interrupted. Then more softly, "Please don't say anything more."

They closed up the house in silence, making sure that even the tiniest ember had been doused in the fireplace and the hot water heater. RueAnn quickly stripped the bed again, placing the soiled linens and the nightdress in the closet since there was nothing else she could do about them.

The return to Washington D.C. was completed in silence. Afraid of what Charlie might say to tarnish the memory of those stolen moments amid the roses, she leaned her head on the back of the seat and turned her face away from him, pretending to sleep while an ache clawed at her chest and unshed tears built up to a point that made her heart pound.

She didn't need her father's voice echoing in her head to remind her that she'd behaved totally out of character. She was usually so tongue-tied around men, but with Charlie...

She'd given him her body...

And her heart.

RueAnn squeezed her eyes shut, trying to deny that such a thing was possible. A person couldn't fall in love so quickly.

But she had. She loved him. Even though she might never see him again. And if she were given the events of the past few days to live over again, she wouldn't exchange a single moment of her time with Charlie. Her only regret was that they would be separated so soon. She longed to feel his arms around her, his body pressed close to her own.

Pressing her face against the cool glass, she pushed back her want and her grief. She only roused when Charlie pulled into a parking place near the train station. With each mile closer to Washington D.C., the weather had grown more sullen. Thunderclouds loomed overhead, lightning flashing in the distance. The first few drops landed with a splat on the window.

Charlie glanced at his watch again. "My train's due to leave in the next few minutes."

She nodded, avoiding his eyes. "What about the car?"

"Take it back to Glory Bee as soon as you can. Then gather your things and get a hotel room for the night. I don't want your father to know where to find you. Take the guns with you. You might need them. If not, sell them."

Fat raindrops exploded onto the windshield and the hood of the sedan. His fingers flexed and gripped the wheel as if he debated what to say next.

"RueAnn, I—"

"You'll miss your train," she interrupted quickly. Before he could say anything more, she opened her door and stepped outside, hurrying through the vaulted entrance.

Charlie followed more slowly, taking a suitcase and a hat from the trunk and placing the weapons in their place. RueAnn waited near the passageway that would lead them to the platforms, watching as he checked to see where to find his train. Then, he removed a set of documents from his bag and stuffed them into his jacket pocket, before arranging for a porter to take his luggage.

Finally, he was moving toward her.

Although she'd known him for only hours, his loose-limbed stride was as familiar to her as breathing. While his attention was distracted by the crowds, she hungrily took in the waves of his hair, the angular planes of his face. She wanted to imprint everything about him into her memory, every word he'd ever said, every caress, every kiss. But the seconds were rushing by so quickly, she could only absorb the images in stuttering frames, like an out of sync movie.

"Platform six," he said when he joined her.

His hand was broad and firm in the hollow of her back as he led her outside. The train lay panting and ready, most of the passengers having taken their places.

"I've only got a minute or two," Charlie began, then stopped, as if searching for a way to express the inexpressible.

Lightning flashed again. Thunder rumbled like the overladen luggage trolleys being pushed into the station. When the noise passed, it was RueAnn who spoke.

"I'm so sorry," she whispered, unable to meet Charlie's eyes. She gripped her pocketbook with both hands, numbly wishing she'd had a comb to neaten her hair. As it was, she felt bedraggled and plain.

"For what?"

He restlessly shifted his weight from foot to foot. Even in his rumpled suit, he looked the epitome of an English gentleman—polished shoes, cuffed trousers, and a carefully knotted tie. Where her hair had begun to frizz, he'd managed to comb his away from his face in a severe style that showed the path of the tines like furrows in a field. He held a hat in his hands and she longed to see him, just once, with the Fedora set at a jaunty angle.

RueAnn glanced up from her deathlike grip on her purse to his bright red tie then back again.

"I didn't mean to get you involved in my troubles."

He shrugged. "What's done is done. We'll figure out how to resolve this, one way or another."

She nodded, waiting for him to tell her where to proceed from here. For all her avowals of independence and freedom, she was discovering that she didn't have much experience in making her own decisions. For years, her father had done that for her. And now...

Now was she so willing to surrender her will to another man, albeit her husband for a day?

"All aboard!" the conductor yelled as he began his trip up the platform.

RueAnn panicked. What was she supposed to do? Pretend this marriage had never happened? Or wait for him to send for her, to make a go of their unorthodox union? Away from here.

Charlie tipped her head up with his finger. His eyes studied her with such intensity that she had to steel herself to keep from cringing. She was afraid of what he'd find if he looked too closely.

More than anything, she wished she knew his true feelings. Since he'd offered to marry her, he'd become so guarded and… careful. Did he resent her? Or did he feel a portion of the longing she experienced whenever he was near? He had stamped his possession on her body if not her mind and she longed to be in his arms again. Just one more time. To make the world go away.

She feared he must have read her thoughts because he cupped her cheek. When he spoke, his voice was husky. "I've got to go. I can't miss my connections or there'll be bloody hell to pay."

Was she right in thinking that his words held a tinge of regret?

"I know."

"If we had more time, we could sort out this damned mess."

She trembled. "I know."

"Last call!" the porter shouted.

Charlie leaned down and brushed her lips with his own, the merest of pressures. But with it came an echo of passion.

He felt it too. She knew he felt it, because he kissed her again, deeply, hungrily. Then, tearing free, he took a step toward the sleeper car. Paused.

Turning to face her, he reached into his jacket and withdrew his wallet. Behind him, the train shuddered and hissed.

"Look, I've got a few American dollars left." He glanced at the wheels as they jerked then began to inch forward.

He held out the money, but she childishly hid her hands behind her back. If he paid her, it would feel too much like…

He grasped her hand and opened her fist, pressing the

money there. "I want you to take it. Get a place of your own where your father can't find you. You can get my address from Glory Bee or my solicitor. Write and let me know where you've gone. Then we'll work out what to do next."

"No, I…"

The train was moving now, inching its way down the platform. Charlie bent to kiss her, hauling her body against his, soft curves to hard planes. Then he broke away, walking backward. "You're my wife now. It's my right to make a few demands, you know."

She bristled, and he must have noticed because he grinned to let her know he was teasing. It was a smile that involved his whole body, making him radiate with life and energy—as if the world was one big punch line. Then, without another word, he turned, running to snag one of the handrails and swinging himself aboard the moving cars.

RueAnn stood there, cold, shivering, trying to brand the memory of that smile into the very core of her brain until the red rear light disappeared into the pounding rain.

## London, England

Susan stood at the door to the garden while, around her, all hint of life was sucked from the air surrounding London. First to go were the backyard noises—the rasp of push mowers, children's laughter, boisterous voices. Next, the lumbering sounds of busses and the lighter squeaks and squeals of cars.

Until it seemed that the entire country held its breath.

Toward the front of the house, Susan heard her father fiddling with the dial on the wireless, Matthew's low admonishments, and Sara's subdued chatter.

Sara.

She'd never come to the Primrose Dance Hall two nights earlier. She'd spent the evening at Bernard Biddiwell's, helping to settle his mother down after the news from Poland had her nearly in hysterics. Sara had come home tired and cross, so much so that she hadn't even bothered to ask Susan how things had gone. Her only comment about their arrangement came the following day when Paul had left to spend the last few days of his holiday with his brother. After being given a passionate kiss at the gate, Sara had sidled up next to Susan to whisper, "Well *you* obviously had fun at the fancy dress."

Soon, even Sara's demands for details had faded beneath the rumors of war. Bernard Biddiwell had made it clear that if a declaration came, he would be joining the navy. Paul and Matthew had been discussing the merits of the RAF—*ad nauseum*, in Sara's opinion. In no time, Sara had grown morose and fractious as she wondered how many of her male friends would answer the call of duty.

So Susan had been left alone in her misery, stewing over the need to tell Paul the truth about her feelings for him, and fearing what his reaction might be if she did.

She'd played him like a fool.

But surely he would be able to see that her feelings for him were genuine.

At long last, the crackle of static eased to the familiar tones of the BBC. Susan knew she should join the family around the wireless—just as nearly every other person in Britain would be doing. But she couldn't bring herself to move. Not yet.

Closing her eye, she leaned her head back against the jamb, one foot in the house, the other on the stoop as she sought even a breath of air to ease her misery. A lump rose in her throat as, from the front parlor, she heard Chamberlain's familiar nasally tones.

> "…*I am speaking to you from the Cabinet Room at ten, Downing Street.*
>
> *This morning the British Ambassador in Berlin handed the German government a final note stating that unless we heard from them by eleven a.m. that they were prepared at once to withdraw their troops from Poland, a state of war would exist between us.*

*I have to tell you that no such undertaking has been received,
and that consequently this country is at war with Germany..."*

Sobs rose in her throat, thick and strong. Not just for her and for a relationship that would never be, but for the funny, brilliant, and charming men who would soon be taken from their midst, one by one, to face unspeakable horrors.

Chamberlain's voice receded, becoming otherworldly.

*"...Up to the very last it would have been quite possible to have arranged a peaceful and honorable settlement between Germany and Poland, but Hitler would not have it..."*

Susan bit her lip, refusing to cry, refusing to think of anything beyond this moment. With Chamberlain's words, the world had suddenly lurched sideways, and those things she had always assumed would be permanent—a safe home, the lives of her rollicking family, perhaps even marriage and a family of her own—had become more tenuous. She couldn't allow herself the luxury of wallowing in her own desires. She had to think of the greater good.

Which meant that even her fantasies of contacting Paul, of trying to explain what she'd done, could no longer be indulged. She was alone again, forced back into her role as the family touchstone. The sensible one. The practical one. And Susan could clearly see the path ahead of her. Her father would grow even more absentminded as the pressures of the factory intruded upon him. Her mother, bless her heart, would worry herself to distraction. Sara would become engrossed in her endless charity drives. Matthew, at twenty-three, would join the RAF, while Phillip, who was sixteen, would wait anxiously for two more birthdays to come so that he could be in the Expeditionary Forces. The younger children, Michael, who was ten, and Margaret who was barely five, would probably be sent away to the country or to live with Uncle Joseph in Canada.

God willing, being split apart for a time would be the worst that would happen to their family.

A tear slid down her cheek. Then another. Another. She

wasn't naïve enough to think that the war wouldn't bring hardship and loss. Standing there, rooted in the doorway, Susan sensed that she was poised in the tenuous "now." From this moment on, her life would be forever divided into "before" and "after."

Suddenly, she couldn't absorb the sights, the scents, the sounds of the last few moments of innocence fast enough. Even as she fought to memorize the dappled pattern of sunlight weaving through the foliage of her mother's flower garden, Chamberlain's final salvo was shot over the airwaves.

> "...Now may God bless you all. May He defend the right. It is the evil things that we shall be fighting against—brute force, bad faith, injustice, oppression, and persecution—and against them I am certain that the right will prevail."

Quickly swiping the moisture from her cheeks, Susan forced herself to turn her back on the garden and walk into the house where the frightening new slant of her life awaited.

Sweetheart,

I still remember the first time I went up in a plane. My grandparents lived in Cornwall then, and every summer, we would go to visit them during the Harvest Festival. Besides the annual showings of farm animals, vegetables, and flowers, there would be a carnival provided by the local Ladies' Aid Society.

Somehow, when I was twelve, the women in charge convinced Nathan Biggs, the famous World War I flying ace to be in attendance. In the afternoon, just after the Queen of the Harvest Ball was announced, he offered a thirty-minute air show.

I'd always been one of those lads who would hang around near the aerodromes, watching the pilots taking off and landing, but this was flying like I had never seen before—loops and barrel rolls and dives. He'd be a mere speck in the blue sky one minute, then he'd be diving and swooping over the crowd mere yards from the ground! I remember one particular maneuver where he seemed to go straight up, then hang suspended for a moment before cartwheeling and spinning all the way down until I was sure he would plummet into the grass. But at the last minute, he altered his course, zipping over my head like a mosquito.

When I discovered that he would be offering rides, a pound per person, I begged my parents to let me go. Naturally, after what they'd seen, they refused. I think they were under the impression that Nathan would continue his dangerous antics with his eager volunteers.

I was so desperate to fly that I began to cry, not quite the thing to do when one is twelve and in public. Still, my parents refused.

I can't remember ever being so disappointed. I was sure

LISA BINGHAM

that life would end there and then and the rest of my years would be spent pining bitterly over lost opportunities. But then, my grandmother—who had to be in her nineties at the time—opened up her reticule and withdrew two pound coins. One for me, and one for her.

My parents were aghast, but my grandmother—who was not the sort of person to be trifled with—took my hand and marched us up to the front of the queue. She was the first to take her ride, needing the assistance of several hearty males to even get her into her seat. I waited impatiently, hopping from foot to foot as the plane roared down the field, circled the fairgrounds three times, then landed.

I had rarely seen my grandmother with anything other than a stern expression on her face, and I'd never seen her rumpled. But when she was lifted out of the plane again, her hair was wild and her features had taken on a look of complete and utter joy and I knew that I was in for a treat.

Then, it was my turn. I was quickly strapped into place, and holding my breath, I squeezed my eyes shut as we went barreling down the pasture, hopping and bumping so fiercely over the gopher tracks, I feared we would never gain enough speed. Then, I felt curiously heavy, and opening my eyes, I saw the ground drop away. In an instant, I felt as weightless as a feather in the wind as we climbed higher and higher, looping around the festivities, once…twice…three times, before landing again in a series of gentle bounces.

My own face must have been a mirror of my grandmother's as my disapproving parents led us both away to the pig exhibition. But there was a moment when Nanna leaned down, whispering to me, "Now we know what it's like to be an angel, Paulie. When I die, I'm going to be an angel."

Nanna's thoughts had turned to the divine, but as I glanced over my shoulder to see the next ride being given, my goals were far more practical.

"I'm going to be a pilot," I swore to myself.

P.

# Chapter Five

London, England
August, 1940

Long shadows were beginning to fall by the time RueAnn gathered her luggage and made her way out of Victoria Station to the queue of taxis waiting at the curb.

Something had been taken from her. Stolen. And after being ignored for nearly a year, she intended to get it back.

She clenched her jaw as she made her way through the tide of passengers surging outside. The station teemed with people—men and women in uniform, plump housewives with packages, and harried businessman sporting battered briefcases. But she moved around them as if they were mere flotsam. After coming so far, waiting so long, she had no desire to waste another minute.

The air was heavy with heat and humidity, and inwardly, RueAnn felt as dark and oppressive as the weather. Charlie hadn't come to meet her train—not that she'd expected him. The plans for her journey had been made at the last minute and her telegram had been brief. She'd known all along that the likelihood of his getting leave from the Expeditionary Forces were slim at best—she wasn't even sure if he was still in England. He could have been shipped out since she'd last heard from him. Nevertheless, a part of her had hoped that this confrontation would be over as soon as possible.

"Where to, Miss?"

She handed the cabbie a card with the address, then the suitcase she'd bought in New York. The luggage had been a splurge she really couldn't afford. But knowing Charlie lived in London with his mother Edna, she hadn't wanted to appear like a pauper.

"Is that all, Miss?" the squat little man asked after stowing her things.

"Yes, thank you."

He held the rear door open and she slid inside, grateful for even the hard bench seat of the taxi.

She was dead tired from her journey, first by ship, then by rail. After an hour in line at customs and jostling through the late afternoon crowds trying to make their connections, her feet ached and her temples throbbed. More than anything, she wanted to slip into a hot bath, then between cool sheets, and sleep for a week.

But first, she wanted what belonged to her. Only then would she be able to decide how to handle Charlie.

*Her husband.*

No. She couldn't think about that now. She was tired of reliving the events leading up to their unconventional marriage. She was weary of wondering if Charlie had been stationed in England or beyond, if he would welcome her arrival or pretend that they'd never even met, let alone married.

Although she knew England was at war—and she'd followed the updates in newsreels and papers left behind at the diner where she'd found a job—she was still shocked by what she saw. Tape crisscrossed the windows of the passing shops and sand bags had been stacked up against foundations and doorways. Trenches and anti-aircraft guns scarred the public parks, and placards proclaimed the location of underground air raid shelters, while overhead, the lumbering shapes of barrage balloons hung like bloated whales. But most disturbing was the aura of efficient urgency that lay over the city like a layer of fine gray dust.

*Dear God, what had she done?* RueAnn asked herself for the hundredth time since leaving New York. But even as the question popped into her head, she already knew the answer. She'd received only sporadic letters from Charlie since that rainy morning when she'd said goodbye to him at the station. He'd let her know where to contact him, his unit, the address where he'd lived with his mother Edna. But other than that, he'd allowed her no other glimpses into his personal life.

"Here we are, Miss."

The cab slid to a stop at the curb. Squinting, RueAnn stared through the window, then couldn't entirely squelch her disappointment. In the year since she'd last seen Charlie, she'd imagined a thousand scenarios—from his living in a castle next to the king, to a manor house in the country. What she hadn't envisioned was something so...

Ordinary.

The structure in front of her was boxlike and tall, with brick on the bottom floor, stucco and timber above—as if the architect had made a weak attempt at a Tudor design. She supposed the steeply pitched roof might look more authentic if it were thatched, but clay tiles gleamed dully in the setting sun.

Perhaps the most remarkable feature was that the dwelling shared a communal wall with another house. The arrangement was unsettling, as if RueAnn were staring into a mirror hung askew since one half of the domicile had been painted with bright green trim, the other in white.

The cabbie retrieved her luggage, then opened her door. "Would you like me to carry your case?"

She shook her head. "No. Thank you. I'll do it."

Come what may, she intended to face the next few minutes on her own, whether it was Charlie who met her at the door or his mother, Edna Tolliver.

She handed the man her fare, knowing that she had very little left in her pocketbook after this final expense. She had truly burned her bridges behind her in coming to England. If worse came to worst, it would take some time before she would earn enough to return to the States.

So she waited, loath for the driver to witness the next few minutes. The taxi hiccupped, gears grinding, then jolted forward, its tires crunching in the loose gravel of the gutter before the black car veered around the corner like a beetle scurrying for shelter from the beating sun.

RueAnn took a compact from the inner pocket of her handbag. Before her departure, Glory Bee had visited from Washington D.C. She'd given her a few tips for her hair and makeup, but the sight of carefully tweezed brows and eyeliner still gave her a bit of a shock. RueAnn had touched up her powder and lipstick at the station before leaving, but she couldn't resist a final peek. She needed to look her best, regardless of who might answer the door.

After infinitesimally adjusting the tilt of her hat, RueAnn reinserted the bead-tipped hatpin. Taking a handkerchief from her sleeve, she dabbed at the perspiration on her brow, damning the way her best crepe dress was smudged and creased. But it couldn't be helped. She could only pray no one would see the damp patches forming under her breasts and arms.

Steeling herself for what was to come, she replaced the mirror, smoothed her palms over the wrinkles at her waist and lap, and picked up her valise.

As she moved forward, the fierce August sun simmered low on the horizon, heating the concrete so that it seared the soles of her feet through her shoes. The past few weeks had been unaccountably hot, she'd been told time and time again since debarking from the steamer. But heat was something she was used to bearing. Nothing was worse than standing over a griddle at the Fifth Street Diner in mid-July.

Juggling her case and her pocketbook, she negotiated her way through the narrow gate and down the walkway to the front door. Setting her bag on the ground, she vainly smoothed her skirt and dabbed again at her face. Then, after squaring her shoulders, she pushed the bell.

The door opened so suddenly that RueAnn took an involuntary step back. Scarlet streaks of sunset revealed a tall woman of about sixty. Iron gray hair had been pulled away from her face in a series of rigid Marcel waves before being pinned in a knot at her nape. Heavy powdering highlighted a fine map of wrinkles, while the rouge of her cheeks was too bright and too perfectly round to appear natural.

"Yes?"

Edna Tolliver—for this had to be Charlie's mother—was what RueAnn's ma would have described as a "handsome" woman. Grim and angular, she was a study in gray. Gray sensible shoes, a gray faille skirt, gray silk blouse with a crisp organdy collar, and severely tamed silver hair that hugged the curve of her scalp so rigidly her head appeared too small above the fullness of her girdled bosom.

"I wish to speak with Charles Tolliver."

"I'm afraid that isn't possible. Good day."

Mrs. Tolliver hurried to shut the door, but RueAnn had come too far to be rejected so summarily, so she pushed her foot into the space next to the jam.

"Please," RueAnn said firmly, the word emerging more as a command than a pleasantry.

"My son isn't here."

RueAnn inwardly withered as she met Edna Tolliver's drilling gaze. Lord help her and Charlie if this woman decided to meddle. The intractable glint in her eyes warned that she would prove to be a formidable opponent.

When it became clear that Edna would offer no further explanation, RueAnn said pointed, "Then I'll wait."

Mrs. Tolliver didn't move.

"I'll wait." RueAnn added again, frustration and nervousness and thwarted expectation all swirling together deep in her chest like a roiling thundercloud. Having no other outlet, her emotions zeroed in on the woman who presented the last obstacle to her journey's conclusion. "I'll wait. All evening. On the front stoop, if necessary. However, I cannot promise that I will wait quietly."

Edna Tolliver's mouth thinned, a flush blooming beneath her too-rosy cheeks. "I don't know who—"

"I'm Charlie's wife." RueAnn held up her hand, revealing the ring that Charlie had mailed along with a set of documents which had allowed her to enter the country with a minimum of fuss. She wondered if he'd bought the band second hand, since it was scratched and worn in spots. But the slight widening of her mother-in-law's eyes made it clear that Edna recognized the ring. A family piece, perhaps? If so, Edna couldn't possibly understand that the ring held less sentimental value to RueAnn than the cheap metal Cracker Jack prize suspended on a long chain around her neck.

Reluctantly, the older woman opened the door wide.

"Come in, then."

*Before someone sees you,* RueAnn could almost hear the woman add.

Once RueAnn had stepped inside, Edna frowned, her gaze raking over the younger woman's rumpled form from the brim of her straw hat to her uncomfortable open-toed shoes.

Feeling much like a horse at auction, RueAnn kept her chin at a defiant angle. RueAnn's mother would have recognized the look and scolded her for "having her dander up." But Edna Tolliver remained unfazed.

"So you're the girl."

*Girl.* The word was said with such disdain that RueAnn felt she'd been verbally slapped. The implied criticism merely added to the indignities she'd already suffered.

Tears stung the backs of her eyes, but she willed the weakness away. She wouldn't think about that now. Just as she wouldn't allow herself to remember the way she'd clung to her mother and sisters during that final secret farewell, all the while knowing that if her father discovered her presence in Defiance, there'd be hell to pay.

*But he had seen her. He'd found her saying goodbye to Astra—and for long moments, he'd stared at her, his eyes growing blue-black with flecks of green. Like the deep waters of the quarry, but cold, cold as a grave...*

"I suppose if you've nowhere else to go, you'll have to stay here until other arrangements can be made."

RueAnn inwardly sagged in relief. She wasn't sure what she would have done if Mrs. Tolliver had sent her away.

But Edna hadn't finished. "Mind you, I expect you to wipe your feet well on the mat and take off your shoes. I won't have you marring the finish on the floors."

"Yes, ma'am."

RueAnn quickly toed her shoes off, then seeing nowhere to

store them, she scooped them into her free hand, still clutching her suitcase with the other.

As she closed the door, Edna's displeasure rolled from her in tangible waves. The woman's starched figure made RueAnn even more conscious of her own limp dress. A run in her hose had begun to work its way toward her shoe, creeping down, down, prickling her skin like the progress of a phantom spider.

"Your telegram indicated that you wouldn't be here for another week."

So the woman *had* known RueAnn was about to arrive. Though the woman remained impassive, there was a glint of a bully in her eyes.

Just like her father's had been when RueAnn had brought him a report card bristling with A's. She'd been so proud of her efforts. That report card was proof that—even though she might not be a boy—she was clever. Valuable. But Jacob Boggs hadn't even bothered to look at it. He'd tossed it onto his workbench where it had fluttered like a wounded butterfly to the sawdust-covered floor, becoming trapped beneath the hobnail sole of his work boot.

"You could have sent word informing us of the change in plans," Edna stated the words pricked RueAnn's skin like bits of chipped ice.

"Yes, ma'am," RueAnn said, refusing to be baited. "But the weather held, allowing the steamer to make better time than expected."

The white lie slid from her tongue with only a faint taint of bitterness. In truth, RueAnn had changed her travel plans at the last minute in order to leave for England as soon as possible after her visit to Defiance.

The weight of her suitcase tugged at her arm and her flesh prickled at the remembered panic of her hasty retreat. There had been countless times she could have warned the Tollivers of her revised itinerary, but she'd been afraid. Afraid that if she'd sent word too early, Charlie might try to avoid her. Or worse, he'd prevent her from coming at all.

But that was between RueAnn and her husband.

Edna's lips pursed. "I'll show you to one of the rooms upstairs. You may wash there and change into something more…suitable. Dinner is at seven-thirty. I couldn't possibly hold the meal at this late notice."

"Yes, ma'am."

Feeling more like a newly hired maid than a daughter-in-law, RueAnn obediently trudged up a steep set of stairs. They passed a closed door, a second, a third, then took another narrower flight of stairs to a part of the house where the air was stuffy and thick, then up again to the garret portion of the home where a room had been carved out under the eaves.

"This will have to do for now," Edna said, throwing open the door to reveal an attic space with a narrow window, an iron bedstead with a rolled up mattress, and a corner sink with a single tap. There was no closet or wardrobe, just a small bureau and a trio of hooks bolted to the wall. Heavy blackout fabric had been tacked over the only window.

"I suppose you'll want a few minutes to pull yourself together." The way Edna's eyes raked over RueAnn from tip to toe, it was obvious that Edna expected miracles to be performed before the younger woman reappeared. "We will eat in twenty minutes. Do not be late."

The last thing on earth that RueAnn wanted from this woman were favors, but she blurted, "Excuse me, Mrs. Tolliver?"

The woman turned, her hand still on the doorknob.

"Can you tell me how I can get in touch with Charlie? I need to let him know that I've arrived safely."

She kept her tone level, even though it galled her that she was forced to ask her mother-in-law for the information.

For an instant, RueAnn thought she saw a brief flicker of something vulnerable crack the older woman's icy façade. But Edna quickly recovered.

"I would have thought they would have sent you notice."

"Notice?"

"Charles' unit was not one of those evacuated from Dunkirk. He's been listed as missing since June."

• • •

Susan Blunt wearily twisted a key in the front lock and let herself into the front vestibule just as the last feeble rays of sunshine began to dim and fail. Once the door had closed behind her, she set her pocketbook on the side table and removed the pin from her hat. As she gazed at her sorry reflection in the mirror, she didn't even bother to smooth her hair.

In one short year, times had changed—the world had changed. England was at war and most of the men her age had gone, so she no longer had the will or energy to fuss about her appearance. Nor did she have time to dwell on her loneliness now that her fledgling career as a stenographer was underway. Her work wasn't nearly as satisfying as she'd thought it would be. Instead, she was left feeling as if a part of her was missing.

No. Not now. Not tonight. She wouldn't wallow in her maudlin thoughts. She was exhausted, that was all. All she needed was a long cool bath. Once she'd scrubbed herself clean of the dirt and stickiness of the day, washed and combed her hair, she would feel right as rain again.

"Oh, you poor dear," her mother exclaimed as she burst into the hall wearing an apron over a faded cotton dress. "You must be famished."

"Mmm."

Indeed, Susan had passed "famished" hours earlier. In the fortnight since she'd obtained a position as private secretary to Mr. Meade at Meade Ironworks near the docks, she'd come to accept that the hours she'd been quoted at her interview were more a suggestion than actual fact. Soon after England had declared war, the Ironworks had been converted from a modest business that crafted artistic wrought iron gates and banister railings to a war plant that now welded submarine and aircraft parts.

"You need to start taking an extra sandwich with you in the morning."

"It would only dry out, Mum."

"Then at least take something from the garden."

"Too hot. The docks were positively seething today."

Millicent Blunt made a *tsk*ing noise. "Poor thing, I've saved a plate for you in the larder. Eat first, then you can lie down for a bit."

"I just want to take a nice cool bath."

"Sara's up there getting ready for one of her gentleman friends. Eat while you're waiting."

It wasn't the first time that Susan had been forced to wait for her turn in the loo while her twin sister primped and preened, and she supposed it wouldn't be the last. But tonight she felt a prickling of irritation. Sara had already had most of the day at her disposal to pretty herself.

With men enlisting or being called up, there were jobs aplenty for a woman who could keep a level head and work long hours. While Susan contributed to the war effort at the Ironworks, Sara had found a position as a clippie on the Green Line bus route. It was a job she enjoyed immensely since it allowed her to be "out and about" as Sara called it. She loved chatting with the passengers and offering suggestions for connections. But today she'd had the day off. So why was she still in the bathroom?

Sinking into one of the chairs at the gleaming kitchen table, Susan sighed when her mother placed the plate in front of her. A sliver of roast beef and a single potato lay next to a mountain of boiled vegetable tops.

"The garden is bursting at the seams with greens."

Which meant that each day, the meager portion of meat and butter allowed by the rationing system was generously augmented by whatever the Blunts could grow.

"*Dig for Victory!*" had become the command to anyone with a plot of land large enough for planting that spring. And Mrs. Blunt had watched with tears in her eyes as her husband had torn up most of the rose garden to sow a variety of seeds.

In June, they'd feasted on strawberries, radishes, and carrots. In July it had been baby cucumbers, peas, and snap beans. But the unaccustomed heat of the summer had stunted some of the plants, leaving the Blunts with tomatoes and peppers withering on the vine...and an abundance of greens—kale, dandelion, turnip tops, and spinach.

Susan loathed them all.

"Couldn't I just have bread and butter?"

Her mother offered her a plate with what was left of a loaf of bread wrapped in a dishtowel. "We've used the butter ration." Millicent said as she cut a thin slice. She lowered her voice conspiratorially. "But I managed to save you a bit of the jam I put up last summer. It's the last of it, I'm afraid."

After setting the pot next to Susan's plate, her mother disappeared from the kitchen again—probably to arrange the blackout curtains and check on the younger children. Michael and Margaret were sent to bed precisely at eight, regardless of the irregular hours of the rest of the family. Phillip, at sixteen, was permitted to stay up until ten.

Susan's stomach growled and she immediately forgot her pique over Sara's monopoly of the water closet. The dense bread and sweet jam brought her hunger rushing back and Susan quickly devoured the slice, then moved on to the beef, the potato, and yes, the greens. When she'd finished, she longed for a rich gooey dessert, but knew there was no sense in asking for pudding. Her mother had been saving sugar rations since the system was imposed that winter. Millicent was determined to have scones and cake available if Susan's older brother Matthew should ever be given leave from the RAF.

Susan felt a shiver of unease at the thought of her brother. The Germans had ended the "Phony War" with a vengeance weeks ago, ferociously targeting military bases in Southern England. She couldn't say for sure that Matthew had been stationed there, but she couldn't help worrying that he was in the thick of things.

"Sara's out of the bathroom, dear," her mother said, bustling back into the kitchen and collecting Susan's dishes. Susan felt a pang of guilt at the way her mother took the dirty plate to task. There was a time when the whole family had revolved around a rigid schedule of meals so that her mother could spend two hours in front of the wireless with her feet up, darning endless piles of socks, or knitting jumpers and woolen mufflers for the winter while she listened to her favorite programs.

Lately, she'd become a slave to the kitchen. No sooner had one person eaten, than another arrived demanding food. Millicent had grown incredibly thin. Her hair, which had once been a rich chocolaty brown, was streaked with gray.

"Mum, I'd be glad to help."

A ring from the front door signaled the arrival of Sara's companion.

"If you'd get that for me, there's a good girl."

Susan sighed. She didn't feel much like exchanging polite chit-chat with Bernard Biddiwell or any of the other men who came to call on Sara. Since becoming a clippie, Sara had begun to collect stray servicemen the way others might collect abandoned puppies. She brought them home for tea or agreed to meet them at the local dances. Susan had long since lost track of most of their names.

The blackout curtains made the parlor feel more like a cave than a sitting room. With the heat of the day still lingering in the trapped, airless room, Susan felt a momentary sense of claustrophobia.

Of all the restrictions the war had brought, the blackout had proven to be the most difficult for Susan. She hadn't yet adapted to the sense of being closed in, trapped. She missed the gleam of moonlight washing over her bed and the twinkle of stars like bits of chipped ice sparkling just outside the window. And the utter lack of nighttime breezes throughout the summer had been unbearable. Every possible chink of light that could escape had to be thwarted. To that end, Susan had helped the younger children cut paper squares from grocery bags and attach them to the panes of glass with rubber cement. Shutters and frames had been made to cover those windows which would be left uncovered during the day, and yards and yards of blackout fabric had been made into curtains. To ignore even the smallest infractions could result in a hefty fine…or worse yet, a bomb being dropped on your block.

In order to prevent any light from seeping around the front entrance, Mrs. Blunt had hung a curtain rod overhead.

Thick, lined woolen panels were pulled into place as soon as the shadows began to fall.

Extinguishing the hall light so that she could open the door, Susan slid the drapes aside. Then, after twisting the knob, she gestured for the shape outside to enter. Once the door was closed again, she slid the drapes back into place and flipped on the light.

A gasp lodged in her throat as light bathed the tall lean figure. Her stomach lurched, then flooded with heat.

*Paul Overdone.*

*Paul who'd kissed her in the darkness. Who'd held her body tightly. Caressing her. Filling her veins with fire.*

"Paul!" she whispered, taking an involuntary step forward. She held up a hand, to touch him, to assure herself that he was real and not a product of her overly active imagination.

But he was real. As he swept his cap from his head, tucking it beneath his arm, a brief puff of air swirled around her, redolent with the scents of Brylcreem and tobacco. Underneath it all was a faint wisp of cologne. Bay Rum.

He peered at her carefully, a quizzical gleam to his chocolate brown eyes. "Susan?" he asked hesitantly.

She nodded, then died a little when his eagerness faded and he drew himself up to a more formal stance. "Good evening, Susan. Is Sara at home?"

Susan opened her mouth, wanting to speak.

*Don't you know me? Don't you recognize me? Can't you sense that I'm the one who danced with you, kissed you?*

Disappointment surged through her with the strength of a tidal wave. Afraid that what might emerge would be inarticulate gibberish, she nodded. Turning her back to him, she busied herself with ensuring that the blackout curtains were firmly in place.

Paul. Here. Tonight.

Unable to delay any longer, she whirled to face him again. As much as it pained her to be so weak and needy, she had to assure herself that he was unhurt. She'd heard second-hand reports of Paul's exploits at Flight Training from Matthew's letters. Then the pair of them had been sent to France. Just before Dunkirk.

"You're well?" she asked, wondering if he heard the thread of torment she couldn't entirely conceal. She'd been beside herself in June when, after the British defeat in France, Matthew's letters had begun to grow more clipped and taciturn. Only once had he mentioned how hard it had been to lose so many of his friends. She'd prayed he hadn't meant Paul, but until this moment, she hadn't been entirely sure.

"As well as can be expected," Paul said.

Susan hungrily drank in the sight of him. His hair had been clipped even shorter than before. The brilliant blue of his uniform accented his tanned skin, and a pair of silver wings on his left breast gleamed in the light. But she could see no sign of injury.

"You're still with the RAF, I see."

"Yes. I've got a short leave before returning to my base."

"Somewhere close?" Could he hear the breathless quality to her voice.

"I'm not at liberty to say."

"O-of course, not," she said, flushing.

*Loose lips sink ships.*

Suddenly, she didn't know what to say. She didn't dare ask too much about his flying or his experiences in the war, but she couldn't blurt out that she'd missed him terribly either.

After all, as far as he knew, Paul had spoken to her less than a half-dozen times. He couldn't possibly know that Sara and Susan had traded places. Just for a night. For a few scant hours.

The most magical hours she could have ever imagined.

The silence twined around them, uncomfortable and fraught with hidden danger. More than anything, Susan wanted to rush toward him and see for herself that he was truly alive and in one piece, but she couldn't manage to think, let alone move. As if she stood in quicksand, she was slowly drowning in want and regret.

"Paul!"

Sara squealed in delight from the top of the stairs, then

raced down them to throw herself in Paul's arms. He held her tightly, his eyes squeezing closed as if he'd suddenly found a piece of heaven. Then he released her and stepped away to a more respectable distance.

"You look lovely!" He was so clearly delighted that Susan felt a tangible pain in her chest.

Sara blushed in delight and Susan had to concede that she did indeed look pretty tonight. She wore a pink organdy dress piped in white with one of her mother's few remaining rose blossoms tucked in her belt.

"And you're a sight for sore eyes." She reached on tiptoe to plant a kiss on his cheek, then bounced away again. "Would you like to come with us, Susan? We're just going for a drink at the Triple Crown."

Paul looked a little alarmed by Sara's impetuous invitation.

More than anything, Susan wanted to accept. But as much as she'd fantasized about having Paul turn to her, recognize her as the girl he'd kissed and held, she realized that real life was rarely that neat and tidy.

"Yes…Susan. Please come."

His grudging invitation was her deciding factor. "No. I've just arrived home from work. You two have fun."

Sara linked her arm through Paul's. "Next time you have to come with us. You could bring a fellow pilot for her, couldn't you?"

The last thing Susan wanted was for Paul to provide her with an escort since she was clearly too pitiful to come up with her own. Suddenly vexed, she plunged the hall back into darkness, flung the curtain aside, and opened the door. "Enjoy yourselves at the pub."

The two of them disappeared down the walk, Paul's palm firmly planted in the hollow of Sara's back. Susan remembered just how it felt to be touched like that—the warmth, the weight of his hand.

An involuntary sob rose in Susan's throat, but she refused to let it escape.

Susan had only herself to blame for this mess. She'd known

from the instant that Sara had proposed the idea that they shouldn't switch places. They were too old to play such childish games. Where once people might have been amused by the ruse, they would not take kindly to adults playing that sort of a prank.

Which was why she could never, ever, let on what she'd done, she vowed.

But as she closed the door, she couldn't keep from casting one last glance in Paul's direction—as if she could will him to turn around and see *her* not her sister.

"You're a coward," she whispered to herself.

"What's that, dear?" her mother asked as she came down the stairs.

"Nothing, Mum. Just muttering nonsense to myself."

Sweetheart,

In the RAF, waiting is the worst. From 4:30 on, we're dressed and ready...then it could be minutes or hours before we're summoned to action. A few of the fellows have grown so weary of the incessant delays that they've scrounged up deck chairs and discarded furniture. They've set it up next to the dispersal hut like a twisted version of a sitting room. We've even got a settee, a rickety table, and an ancient Victrola.

Madson, the beggar that he is, tends to rouse everyone early on by playing a scratched rendition of Tchaikovsky's 1812th Overture. Says that it gets the blood flowing.

As if any of us need it. From the moment we're dumped at the dispersal hut, every muscle is tensed. Your heart thuds slow and loud in your ears and your nerves are stretched so taut you'll see hands shake as the men pass around Woodbines and matches.

There's an attempt at normality—if there even is such a thing anymore. Blokes play cards or toss a ball. We've even been known to set up a cricket match from time to time. But most days the boys are too keyed up for anything more than sitting, eyes trained on the telephone or the planes.

The moment Bertie shouts from inside the hut, there's a mad scramble for the Spits. At times, it's another spate of waiting, or we might even be called back. But if the "Tally-Ho!" is given, it's an amazing sight as the aircraft roll across the field in tandem, lifting one at a time, awkwardly at first—because the Spit can handle like a pig on the ground. But once they've gained purchase, it's like gliding on silk as they climb up, up, up into formation.

Then all the waiting, the nerves, the tension is forgotten as you begin scouring the skies for the first sign of your prey, moving like the devil to get high as you can with the sun at your back.

P.

# Chapter Six

*Charles' unit was not one of those evacuated from France. He has been listed as missing since June...*

For the first time since her arrival, RueAnn welcomed her mother-in-law's chilly demeanor. As soon as she'd made her pronouncement, she marched from RueAnn's room, closing the door behind her.

Her footfalls made sharp, rapping sounds as she descended the stairs, each one like a hammer to RueAnn's already pounding head.

RueAnn felt as if she'd been encased in concrete, becoming thick, slow-witted as she was buried in the remnants of her shattered fantasies of England and Charlie. Her husband was deeply embroiled in the war. Missing.

No wonder Charlie hadn't responded to her letters. She'd written to him time and time again, demanding the return of her property—or at the very least, an explanation for his continual silence. Each missive had grown more forceful, more strident. When she'd received no response, another coal had been heaped on her blazing fury.

Then she'd begun to plead. Did he want an annulment, a divorce? As much as she'd feared the answers, she'd waited week after week for his reply, praying that he wouldn't cast her adrift. Not when she wanted to see him again. Just one more time.

Shame washed over her. She'd been so selfish, so shortsighted. She'd known that he might have been deployed. She'd even considered that it could take time for her letters to be redirected. But she'd never considered that he could be missing or dead.

He'd probably been in combat most of the time they'd

been apart.

What little energy RueAnn possessed bled from her limbs. She dropped heavily onto the bare box springs, abandoning her charade of poise and respectability. Ignoring the pinch of the bare metal coils, she drew her knees up to her chin and squeezed her eyes shut tight, tight, tight, against a tidal wave of panic.

She'd prepared herself for a dozen different situations: that Charlie was deployed; that he'd been refused leave; he was sick; he was injured. But she had never even considered the possibility that the situation could be worse. So much worse.

Missing.

Possibly dead.

She'd been so naïve.

A sob wormed its way up from her chest, but she fought to keep it unuttered, enduring the pain as it lodged in her throat like a swallowed wooden block.

She wouldn't cry.

She mustn't cry.

Not when Charlie's mother waited like an imperious, disappointed monarch. If Edna were to discern even a hint of redness to RueAnn's eyes, the older woman would pounce upon that weakness, RueAnn was sure.

Her fingers trembled as she covered her mouth in horror, gazing wild-eyed around the room as if the wood and mortar of this house were a living witness and could share its secrets with her.

But her only answer was silence. Charlie. Charlie was *missing*. She refused to think beyond that. He was *missing*, which meant that he would be back. One day. Until she had proof to the contrary, she would stay. Because she intended to talk to him, face to face, and demand an explanation for his betrayal. Only then would she know what to do next.

Nevertheless, she was still faced with one formidable obstacle to her goal. Edna Tolliver. Without Charlie's presence or the promise of his imminent return, there would be no reason for Edna Tolliver to temper her zeal. Judging by her blatant antagonism, she would do everything in her power to drive RueAnn away.

A glance at the ticking alarm clock next to the bed reminded RueAnn that her time was limited. Mrs. Tolliver had given her twenty minutes—and most of that time had already elapsed.

Uncurling from her near-fetal position, RueAnn forced herself to stand, her muscles and joints protesting like those of an old woman. The last thing she wanted at this moment was food. RueAnn would much rather have unrolled the mattress and fallen asleep atop it with only a blanket to cover her. But she needed to be civil. Perhaps, there was still time to create a more favorable impression with Edna.

Summoning what little strength still remained, RueAnn washed as best she could, donned a clean skirt, crisp blouse, and a comfortable pair of shoes. After combing and plaiting her hair, then pinning it around the crown of her head to control the wayward tresses, she made her way downstairs.

It wasn't hard to find her way back to the place where this strange odyssey had begun. The stairs bottomed out at a narrow foyer near the front door. Black and white floor tiles made RueAnn's weary eyes cross. But even the few scant minutes which had elapsed had brought change. Heavy draperies had been pulled over the windows and doors, leaving the rooms airless, the walls closing in upon her.

RueAnn stood gripping the newel post, the pads of her fingers absorbing the warm oak made satiny smooth by countless hands rubbing over the polished grain. She palmed the dark wood like a gypsy warming a crystal ball. If she closed her eyes, could she feel a remnant of energy left by Charlie's last touch?

Before she could investigate the notion, Edna swept out of the room to her left, emerging from a formal sitting area made even more stilted by weighty furniture covered in sensible, darkly patterned fabrics. A single lamp spilled a puddle of light onto the floor next to a huge, cabinet radio, its dial glowing like a Cyclops eye.

"There you are," Edna announced as if she'd been waiting for the better part of an hour rather than minutes. Her cool gaze raked down RueAnn's form and she sniffed but made no comment on her appearance. Instead, she said, "You'll find I keep an orderly, God-fearing home."

She peered at RueAnn sharply, waiting. When it became apparent that RueAnn would issue no argument, she continued.

"This is the sitting room," Edna explained, her mouth and jaw so tight, they could have been carved from marble. "I expect you to keep it tidy. No newspapers, no personal items." She pointed to the closed doors opposite. "Through here is the dining room. We eat breakfast at seven without exception. Evening meals vary according to my schedule with the WVS." At RueAnn's blank look, she supplied, "The Women's Voluntary Service." She then gestured to another doorway at the end of the hall. "The kitchen is through there."

"Yes, ma'am."

Edna sailed past RueAnn toward the dining room, sweeping open the pocket doors as if she were unveiling the private quarters of royalty. She made her way to the head of the table, indicating that RueAnn should take the seat to her left.

No sooner had RueAnn sunk into the chair than the door connecting to the kitchen swung open and a plump, middle-aged woman dressed in a black uniform and crisp white apron emerged. She set a tureen of soup in the middle of the table.

"Louise Thompson, I'd like you to meet..." Edna glanced at RueAnn, waiting for her to supply her name.

"RueAnn Boggs." RueAnn cursed herself when she realized she'd forgotten to give her married name. "Tolliver," she added more firmly.

"Louise helps with the housekeeping and the cooking."

"I'm very pleased to meet you, Louise."

The woman smiled—the first genuine, welcoming gesture that RueAnn had received. "And you, Miss. Master Charlie is a lucky fellow to have married someone so pretty."

Edna gave the woman a crisp, "Thank you, Louise. That will be all for now."

In an instant, Louise disappeared into the kitchen—and RueAnn immediately wished the woman hadn't been dismissed so quickly. There'd been a friendly twinkle to Louise's eyes that had bolstered RueAnn's spirits. But like a ray of sunshine obscured by clouds, that hint of warmth was gone, leaving RueAnn to wither in Edna Tolliver's blatant disapproval.

"Once she's finished serving, I'll instruct Louise to make up your bed and unpack your things."

"No!" The word emerged like a gunshot, short and sharp, and RueAnn cleared her throat and said more calmly, "I don't wish to impose. I'm more than capable of doing it myself."

Edna's gaze was pointed, but she didn't bother to press the issue. "As you wish."

The rest of the dinner was an uncomfortable affair, fraught with long, tense silences. It soon became clear that Edna might have begrudgingly offered RueAnn the use of her home, but she was not about to make idle chit-chat. So after complimenting Edna on her home, trying to converse about the weather, and remarking on the smartness of the older woman's attire, RueAnn stopped trying. If her mother-in-law wished to be impolite and inhospitable, that was her business. RueAnn was far too weary and disheartened to make an effort to change the woman's mind.

So she forced herself to eat, forced herself to listen to an hour's worth of radio—a program filled with dire reports of German air raids and the RAF's daring retaliation. With each grating tick of the mantle clock, each flicker of light from the radio's glowing Cyclops eye, she felt her nerves draw so tight, she feared that they would shatter like blown sugar.

Finally, knowing she could not continue to mask her distress, RueAnn stood and excused herself on the pretense of needing to recover from her journey.

Edna gave no indication of having heard her. She listened raptly to the mellifluous tones of a reporter interviewing pilots preparing for battle "somewhere in England."

As soon as she'd surmounted the first set of stairs, she all but ran up the other flights until she could dodge into the room she'd been assigned and slam the door. Leaning her back against the painted panels, she flung back her head, taking huge gulps of air.

She would not cry.

She would not cry.

Her fingers curled into her palms, her body shook with the effort to maintain control. Bit by bit, she managed to push the worst of her desperation aside.

A sudden knock on the other side of the door caused her to jump.

"Miss RueAnn?"

It was Louise.

Quickly running her hands over her hair, her cheeks, she ignored the thrashing, irregular cadence of her heart and opened the door just a crack.

"Yes?"

Louise smiled at her, her cheeks bunching like plump apples.

"I've brought you a few things to make you more comfortable," she whispered.

Trembling, RueAnn opened the door.

"I brought you some flowers from the garden," Louise said. The warmth of her tone and the lilt of her British intonation slid over RueAnn's frayed nerves like a mantle of silk.

She bustled into the room and set a squat glass vase on the dresser. Above the hobnail lip fluttered a bouquet of pink roses—some in tight little buds, others unfurled to release their heady scent.

RueAnn stared at the flowers, overcome with memories of Charlie. His touch. His kisses. The warmth of his body over hers.

"We don't have many blooms this year, more's the pity," Louise continued, her voice coming from miles away. "Most of the bushes were dug up for the veg garden, but I managed to find enough to brighten your room."

With some difficulty, RueAnn focused on Louise, on the way the woman's bright smile dimmed as she surveyed the garret. "Ooo, it's stuffy up here, isn't it?" She clucked to herself, setting a pile of fresh towels, sheets, and a blanket on the rickety chair. "I don't know why Mrs. Tolliver didn't move you into Master Charlie's room."

As soon as the words were uttered, she flushed, clearly embarrassed about the implied criticism toward her employer.

She hurried to the bed, unrolling the mattress, then grasped a set of crisp white sheets.

When RueAnn would have helped her, she waved her away. "I'll have things set to rights in a jiffy, never you fear. Sit. Sit."

Louise's motherly care threatened RueAnn's tenuous hold on her emotions more than anything that had occurred throughout the tumultuous day.

"I'm sorry to say the window is sealed shut with layers of paint. But I'll have my mister take a look at it tomorrow and see what he can do. Then you could crack it open to catch the breezes at night, provided the light is out.

"That would be lovely."

"This was the maid's quarters years ago, but no one has used it in ages. The rooms below us have been closed up for some time, so I suppose Mrs. Tolliver felt this would be the easiest solution for now." With a flick of her wrists, Louise snapped the sheet free of its folds and settled it onto the bed, then proceeded to tuck in the edges with the efficiency of a career soldier.

"Master Charlie is a lucky man to have found such a pretty girl—and an American, at that." She smoothed on the top sheet, then draped a blanket over that. "Tomorrow, I'll bring in your coverlet. But it's such a warm evening, the blanket will do, I think."

"Yes, I'm sure it will be fine."

Tucking a pillow beneath her chin, Louise wrestled an embroidered pillowcase over its plump shape. As she worked, the crisp scent of sun-dried linens twined around the muskier perfume of roses.

Once she'd plumped the pillow and set it in place, Louise turned. "I've brought towels and face cloths for you, dear," she said, gesturing to the pile of linens still waiting on the chair. "If you need more, there's a closet in the loo downstairs piled high with bathroom supplies and linens." She sighed. "Soap's rather dear, more's the pity, but I managed to find you a small cake to keep up here." She pointed to RueAnn's single piece of luggage. "Would you like me to help you put things away?"

RueAnn unconsciously moved in front of her suitcase. "No. That's not necessary. I'm so tired, I think I'll just find my nightgown, wash my face, and call it a night."

"Of course, dear." Louise paused at the door, her eyes so gentle. Like a mother's. Like RueAnn's mother's had been, oh, so long ago. Before things had gone so horribly, horribly wrong. "Sweet dreams."

The door closed behind her with only the faintest of clicks.

The sobs came then, thick and strong, wrenching free from a black, black place so deep within her that she shoved her fist against her teeth as the eruption of emotion threatened to consume her from within.

Whirling, she rushed to the suitcase, flipping open the latches. Digging deep, deep, deep, she ripped at the lining and pulled up the cardboard cleverly disguising a false bottom. Removing the bulky shape wrapped in layers of velvet scraps, she held it against her chest for a moment, surveying the empty room. Finally, she hurried to the bureau, sliding open the bottom drawer and peering underneath.

Just as she'd hoped, there was a hollow cavity formed where the bottom of the drawer didn't quite meet the underside of the dresser.

Gently, she settled the package into the scant space and slid the drawer back into place. Then, quickly, in case she should change her mind and run back in the direction of the railway station, she unpacked her things and tucked them into the remaining drawers.

After a cursory splash of water on her face, she stripped down to her slip, too tired to even don her nightgown.

But she couldn't sleep. Not yet.

If Charlie had been gone all these months, then perhaps, somewhere in this house, he'd hidden her letters.

Moving to the door, she pressed her cheek against the cool, painted panels, listening for the slightest sound. Around her the house gradually settled with stray squeaks and pops. RueAnn heard Edna climb the stairs, the other woman's shoes making sharp taps on the treads before disappearing into the bedroom somewhere two floors below RueAnn's. Louise had said that the entire floor below the attic was unused. On the level below that, there were three rooms. Nearest the stairs was Edna's quarters. In the middle was a bathroom.

Which meant the room facing the street must be Charlie's.

RueAnn waited until the house had grown completely dark and quiet. Stealthily, she crept down the staircase, treading as close as she could to the wall so that the boards wouldn't creak. Then she moved to the door which had remained closed throughout the day.

Feeling much like a thief, she twisted the cut glass knob ever so slowly until the latch clicked in release. After noting the blackout curtains were in place, she switched on the light, and then quickly shut the door behind her.

The weak glow emitted from the overhead fixture streamed into the dark corners, dappling the floor and the gleaming furniture. Unlike her own room, this one clearly waited for an occupant. The high tester bed was covered with crisp sheets, a thick blanket, and an intricate matelassé bedspread. A matching double wardrobe fashioned of carved mahogany had an inset mirror that reflected a washstand and a dresser as well as a clothes tree and a bookcase filled with trophies, pennants, and books.

Despite efforts to keep it neat and polished, the room belonged to a full-blooded male who left a wave of untidiness in his wake.

She needed to search—drawers, wardrobe, cupboards. But even though she was frantic to find what she'd come for, her body trembled with such weariness, she could no longer stand. Sinking onto the edge of the bed, she gripped the covers, needing something to ground her in this reality.

She was married.

She was Mrs. Charles Tolliver.

And he was missing somewhere in a war she didn't entirely understand.

Only then did the tears come, crowding hot and heavy and streaming down her cheeks. Drawing her knees up, she clutched a pillow against her face to stifle the sound of her sobs.

She'd made a mistake in coming here. A horrible mistake. But Charlie had stolen her secrets. Her very soul. What else could she have done?

\* \* \*

A *tap, tap…tap, tap, tap* woke Susan from a fretful sleep. Frowning, she gave up all pretense of slumber and squinted into the darkness.

Since blackout restrictions had been imposed, London had become a more formidable place once the sun went down. She was so used to the street lamps that caused an ever-present glow to hover over the city—especially in the winter, or just after a rain.

But London had grown dismal and bleak once the lights were extinguished. So much so that Susan wasn't the only person loath to leave home at night. Where once there had been a constant symphony of lumbering busses, cars, foot traffic, and distant trains, now she listened for footfalls. The heavy lumbering tread of Mr. Wamsley, the local ARP who trolled the streets looking for chinks in the blackout. He would pace to the end of the block, then pause, gazing upward in case German paratroopers had managed to escape his eagle eye and fell like silent, deadly snowflakes. Then there were the quick steps of women returning late from their war work. Sometimes, they giggled and whispered along the way, more as a way to dispel their uneasiness than through actual light-heartedness. After twelve hour shifts, they were tired, nervous, hungry, and eager to be off their feet. Then, more often than not, in the early hours, Susan would hear the uneven *thu-thump* of young Kyle Rampnell-Hoskins who'd lost a leg in Norway. They said after being pinned for more than a day in the wreckage of a bombed hotel, he couldn't sleep, couldn't abide being closed in a house. Long before dawn arrived, he would gather his crutches and begin his nocturnal exploring. Sara said he kept a pistol with him in his coat pocket, but Susan didn't know if such suppositions were mere gossip.

*Tap. Tap, tap…*

What on earth?

Dragging her robe over her arms, Susan hurried to the window and drew back the blackout curtains just as a pebble hit the glass.

Down below, she saw a dark shape, but the moon had already set, so there was no way to distinguish who it might be.

Another pebble hit the glass and she quickly raised the sash.

"Who's there?" she whispered harshly.

"Good. I've finally managed to rouse you."

A rush of sensation thrilled her like a too-fast elevator. Instantly, she recognized the voice wafting up to her from the darkness.

"Paul?"

"I need to talk to you."

"But—"

"Please. I've got to be back to the airfield by four-thirty this morning or there'll be hell to pay. God knows when I'll get another leave."

She could tell by the infinitesimally paler wash of darkness that he was looking up at her.

"Come down. Just for a few minutes. Things were so… awkward between us earlier, that I spoke to you about silly, superficial things. But now that I've screwed up my courage, I'd like to tell you what I really came here to say."

Try as she might, Susan couldn't make out his features— which meant he couldn't see her either, right?

Good Lord, she hoped not.

"Just a minute. I'll be down."

She ducked back inside. For a moment, she considered waking Sara and sending her downstairs. But a rebellious streak she hadn't even known she possessed caused her to rush to the dressing table instead. Squinting in the direction of the mirror, she quickly ran a comb through her hair and pinched her cheeks.

Moving as quietly as she could, she abandoned her robe and nightgown and dragged on the first dress she could find. Then, after slipping her feet into a pair of Sara's open-toed shoes, she tiptoed from the room.

She didn't allow herself to think of Sara asleep on the bed—or even the future consequences of her actions. Paul was outside. Within hours, he would be back at the airfield. So many men had already been killed in the past weeks. So many pilots. For months now, she hadn't known if he were alive or dead. This moment was hers—*hers*.

She made hardly any sound as she all but flew down the front stairs—all the while refusing to remember the way Sara had launched herself at Paul only hours before. Pausing only long enough to release the latches, she slipped outside.

The heat of the day had eased, although it was still unseasonably warm for so early in the morning. All of London huddled beneath a blanket of uncertainty and foreboding.

When would the Germans bomb London in earnest?

When would the invasion of troops begin?

But she refused to think of that either. As an airman, Paul had been in the thick of things for weeks. She couldn't allow herself to think of what awaited him at dawn.

Paul.

She sensed, rather than saw him. Turning, she reached for him in the darkness, feeling first the wool of his jacket, then the strength of the man beneath.

Momentum sent her into his arms and once there, it was the most natural thing in the world to wrap her arms around his neck and hold him close.

He sagged against her, his breath leaving in a rush.

"I couldn't leave without seeing you one more time."

She became suddenly conscious of the way she'd literally thrown herself into his arms. But when she would have stepped back, he held her tightly.

"The boys will be here soon to give me a lift."

"The boys?"

"Some pilots from my squadron." He laughed bitterly. "Three weeks ago, there were nearly thirty of us. Now there are three. That's why we were given leave in the thick of things. They finally brought in some new pilots to…fill in the gaps."

He glanced up and down the street. "I've only got five or ten minutes until Collin and Joseph arrive."

"No!" The word was a puff of air, but he must have heard her because his grip tightened.

"You were so…distant earlier. I was afraid you were peeved that I rang you up with so little notice."

"No. No!"

"I was hoping…perhaps…if you wouldn't mind…"

He drew back and she could just make out his face in the darkness.

"If I were to write…"

"I'll write to you. Every day," she said without letting him finish.

He chuckled softly. "I've been writing for weeks, did you know?"

"What?"

"But I never mailed them. We've known each other for such a short time. I didn't want to presume—"

She stopped him with a kiss—a quick peck on his cheek that with a twist of his head became a full-on embrace.

It was what she had dreamed of for months. The touch of him, the taste of him…It was all she wanted and more, so much more.

She pressed herself against him, offering him her lips even as his arms swept around her and he kissed her fully, deeply, crushing her to him. Just as before, a rush of sensation swept through Susan's body, thrilling her. Terrifying her.

A horn tooted from the curb and she could have wept. Not now. Not yet!

But Paul was stepping away. One hand taking hers, holding it, holding, until they were forced to separate. The other men in the car whooped and called, but she hardly heard them.

"I'll write," she promised.

"Send me a picture."

"Yes."

He lifted a hand in final farewell just as one of his fellow pilots opened the rear door and pulled Paul in.

Immediately, Paul rolled down the window, poking his head out to call, "Until my next leave, Sara!"

And she froze, her hand lifted in a wave.

How could she have allowed herself to be in this situation, this moment? How could she have forgotten that he didn't want *her*, he wanted Sara?

Just as every other male, he'd been drawn to Sara, to her vitality, her spontaneity, her giving nature.

And what about Sara? Sara had trusted her enough to ask Susan to take her place for a few hours on that night nearly a year earlier. She would be hurt to discover that Susan now had designs on a man she herself was interested in. Then again, he'd said Sara had been distant. Did that mean he'd sensed a difference between the sisters?

Groaning, Susan sank onto the step and rested her head in her hands. She was wrong to have met with him again. So wrong. And she'd always prided herself on being trustworthy. She followed the rules. She *always* followed the rules.

Even when following the rules hurt.

Sweetheart,

I think that we all believed ourselves to be invincible. Until Dunkirk.

We'd grown used to our routine—waiting at the dispersal hut for the call. They were days of boredom, interspersed with brief spurts of absolute terror. But we had convinced ourselves that we would hold off the Germans and eventually push them back where they belonged.

Until suddenly, the German forces seemed to be everywhere—tanks, infantry, and especially in the air. Looking at it now, I can see that we didn't have a chance. The Germans had brand new equipment with the latest advances, while we had a rudimentary force, some of them using equipment from the Great War.

We were scrambled immediately, and the day soon became a blur. I had less than ten hours in a Spitfire up to that point, and suddenly I was supposed to down Stukas and Messerschmitts being manned by pilots who'd already been in battle.

Not many people know this, but a Spit only has a few seconds of firepower. You have to ease up behind your target and shoot him in quick bursts so you don't use up all your ammo at once. Then, as soon as your magazine is empty, you're completely vulnerable, so you have to fly like a bat out of blazes to the aerodrome to be rearmed.

We tried our damnedest to get a handle on things, but it soon became apparent that our forces were being overrun and everyone was told to retreat toward Dunkirk.

I can still see the streams of men and machines, desperately trying to retreat from the advancing German army. We tried to provide as much cover as possible, but we were suffering our own losses, especially as the defensive lines began to shrink toward the sea. Machinery had to be abandoned when they ran out of fuel. I heard they were dumping dirt into the gas tanks to disable trucks and tanks and ambulances that couldn't keep up with the retreat. And all the while, we were wondering what the blighters were supposed to do once they reached the Channel. Swim for it? Meanwhile, the German Luftwaffe was strafing the boys as they tried to get away, shooting them like fish in a barrel.

I've since heard some of the squibs saying the RAF didn't do enough when the flotilla of little ships arrived to help in the evacuation, and that's total nonsense. They couldn't see us on the shore because we were inland. We were all that was keeping the Germans at bay long enough to get anybody at all out of France. I suppose most of us have got a chip on our shoulder about that.

We won't get caught napping again.

P.

# Chapter Seven

Rouen, France

Charles Tolliver woke to pain. Blinding white-hot pain that seared through his midsection like a knife.

One moment, he existed in a hazy world of hurt. In the next, the gauziness was stripped away, leaving him alert, trembling, sickened by the sudden bolt of adrenalin that hit his system like a sucker punch.

Charlie fought against the force that stole the strength from his limbs. Before he could make any headway, a hand slapped over his mouth and a voice hissed in his ear.

"Shhh!"

The sharp command was so low that Charlie could have thought he'd imagined it. But the urgency of that simple syllable sliced through his consciousness, centering his panic into the *thump, thump, thump* of his heart thrumming in his ears.

"Patrols."

Reality rushed over Charlie's head, swamping him, threatening to drown him in memories of blood and chaos and the noise of gunfire when they'd nearly been captured by a railway patrol for not having the proper papers. Then the secretive hush of their attempts to flee.

Rex, Alec, and himself.

No. Not Alec. Alec had drowned when they'd attempted to cross the river just outside of Rouen.

"Lie still, mate." The voice was Rex's. Low. Gravelly from too many years with too many cigarettes. Cigarettes which had been finished days ago, leaving Rex snappish, out of sorts...

And mean enough to mow down a brigade of Germans single-handedly if he were given the ammunition and half a chance.

Blinking against the blackness, Charlie eased away from Rex's grip, signaling that he'd heard and understood the warning. His muscles trembled, already spent with that small spurt of alertness. Bit by bit, he sank into the ground, into the soft, soft, ground…

It was then that Charlie became aware of the smell. The stench was unmistakable, overwhelming.

Shit. He was literally mired in shit, his body sunk several inches into the muddy, gooey mess.

"Oh, God!" Charlie whispered hoarsely, gorge rising in his throat as he bucked against the hands that held him.

Above him, the craggy face of Rex Carmichael swam into view. How long had they known one another now? Days? Months?

Forever?

Time had become as much the enemy as the Nazis, Charlie realized. Their mission had been simple then. England had barely declared war when the British Expeditionary Forces had been sent to protect the Maginot Line in France. Meanwhile, knowing that it was only a matter of time before the Germans threw their full weight against their vulnerable neighbors, Charlie, Alec and Rex were assigned the task of disguising themselves as Swiss businessmen and moving deeper into Nazi-occupied Europe. According to the information gathered from Jean-Claude Foulard and other sources, they had deduced that a secret propulsion facility was being erected near the border in a little town called Hausman. Charlie and his men were to gather as much information as possible and return to the front lines before the whole continent became a battlefield.

But they'd been too late. The factory site had been bombed. Abandoned. Worse yet, they'd just arrived in southern Germany when the Nazis had begun to gobble up the Low Countries. Rather than a quick trip in and out of The Fatherland, they'd been evading Germans and attempting to reach a possible pick up point ever since.

Charlie grappled with Rex in his efforts to rise, but his friend pushed him deeper into the muck.

"Shh! I didn't have a huge selection of hiding places. This pigsty was the only real cover I could find. Figured the stink alone would keep the Germans away."

The sound of footsteps grew louder. The guttural, sharp-edged murmurs were definitely German.

Rex held a finger to his lips and reached for his sidearm, locking the hammer in place with a perceptible click.

Charlie swallowed against a gag reflex that threatened to overpower him. The searing pain in his gut, his shoulder, and his thigh began to throb in tempo with his pounding heart. Vaguely he wondered what would get him first—enemy soldiers, or the filth.

With eyes squeezed tight against the pain, he took gulps of air through his mouth until the intense, stabbing waves of nausea had passed. Then he peered through the slats of the sty to the woolen darkness beyond.

A slice of a moon spilled its glow to the ground, the light too weak to let him examine the state of his injuries, but too bright to allow real cover. Against the fuzzy shapes of the trees and outbuildings, the green-gray wool of the Germans' uniforms moved through the darkness like patches of smoke. Silvery light gleamed off their helmets, the shiny buttons of their uniforms, the highly polished boots above muddy soles.

Rex rolled noiselessly in the muck, his pistol centering on the gap in the wall. He bent low to whisper in Charlie's ear, "If they come this way, I'll shoot; you run." But the cockeyed grin he slanted Charlie's way made it clear that if they were discovered, neither of them would be running anywhere soon.

Reality slipped, faded, then rammed into sharp focus again as Charlie panted in the blackness. He blamed himself for getting shot escaping the patrols at the railway station. Bloody, bloody hell! If he'd dodged a second earlier, taken cover a split-second sooner...

Instead, he lay with a bullet lodged in his shoulder and

LISA BINGHAM

another shot through-and-through just above his hip. At first,
the adrenaline had been enough to help him keep running,
but now...

Now he vacillated from cold to hot, alert to barely conscious.

The shivering was taking its toll on him, exhausting him
beyond anything he'd ever felt before. A warm, enveloping
blackness beckoned to him, sucking him deeper into a rabbit
hole of sensation so that he felt as if he were spinning, spinning,
and the spinning was making him sick to his stomach, making
his head throb, making his extremities numb...so numb...so...

"Charlie? Charlie!"

Charlie's eyes rolled in his head. With some effort, he
managed to locate and focus on Rex's face.

It appeared lighter this time, a grayish tinge fuzzing the
edges of Rex's figure so that he could have been formed of
frayed watercolor paper. In that grayness, Charlie could see the
purplish welt over his friend's eye and the caked blackness of
dried blood seeping down from his hairline.

"You're...filthy."

Rex grimaced. "Bugger off, y' bloomin' idiot. We both are."

Charlie's gaze dipped to his chest and he shrank back.
Good Lord, he was covered in grime that smelled too much like
a barnyard and worse. The sickly-sweet odor of infection, the
coppery tang of blood.

Where...

Pigs. There'd been something about pigs.

And butternut toffee. No. Not toffee.

Coffee.

Coffee-colored eyes.

"Charlie. Charlie!"

Rex shook his shoulders, causing Charlie to cry out as a
fiery bolt of lightning shot through his shoulder and stabbed
him again somewhere low by his hip.

Rex lifted his head to look through the bower of trees that
hid them.

Trees.

They'd been somewhere else...was it last night? Last week?

Rex leaned close again, "Charlie, you've got to listen to me. I can't...I..." He swallowed hard. "You're sick, mate. I've tried my best to clean you off and patch you up, but..." He cleared his throat when it emerged tight and high. "But you've got to know my half-assed efforts aren't worth shit."

Shit. He'd been lying in shit.

Charlie's eyes started to slip back in his head and Rex slapped his cheeks. "Charlie! Stay with me, old boy, okay?"

Rex waited his eyes narrowed, his gaze so pointed, so commanding, that Charlie was sucked out of the blackness that threatened to consume him.

Focus. *Focus.*

Using more effort than he would have thought possible, Charlie tipped his head in the barest semblance of a nod. Even that small movement caused his stomach to lurch.

Hungry. So hungry.

He swiped his tongue over lips that were painfully cracked and swollen.

"Water," he croaked. It shocked him when the word emerged as an unintelligible croak.

Rex moved away and the multi-colored patches of color from the leaves and the gray light beyond bled together like the muddied palette of an artist. Then the dappled patterns dipped. Swayed.

Charlie's eyes flickered and he took short, quick breaths to keep himself from passing out again. But such efforts were growing harder and harder. He was trembling again, not from cold, but from an unbearable weariness that radiated through his body.

Using what little strength he had left, he reached for his breast pocket, assuring himself that the letters were still there.

RueAnn's letters to another man. A mysterious "J." A correspondence so frank and beautiful that they made his chest ache with regret.

He'd treated her badly, he knew that now. He'd done the minimum he could do to help her, not knowing...not realizing...

Dear God, would he ever see her again? Would he ever

have the chance to tell her he was sorry? Sorry for taking something so personal…so painfully honest? He didn't know what was worse, to admit he'd taken the letters…or to confess he'd read the secrets printed inside. Painfully frank, heart-wrenching entries that had the power to flay the layers of thick-skinned guardedness from his own soul and leave him weak and trembling and ineffectual against her obvious need.

He'd treated her badly.

So badly…

"Charlie!"

He could hear Rex calling to him from far, far away. But it was too late. He was falling, falling, falling into the deep, dark hole of unconsciousness and he welcomed it.

Anything to block out his regret and self-recrimination.

## London, England

A piercing whine woke RueAnn by degrees. Lifting her head, she realized she'd fallen asleep on Charlie's bed, wrapped in his dressing gown. A dressing gown that still smelled like him. Squinting at his alarm clock, she discovered that the darkness around her was misleading. It was the blackout curtains which gave the illusion that it was closer to midnight than first light.

Groaning, she closed her eyes again. She'd slept like the dead, a heavy, thick slumber that was filled with disturbing dreams of roiling shapes, her father, and a pistol that had been fired at her husband at point blank range. Vaguely, she remembered trying to stem the flow of blood with her outstretched hands while a puddle of crimson threatened to consume them both. And all the while, there'd been a whining scream that grew and grew in intensity, subsided, then grew again until…

Blinking, she froze. The sound in her head had not disappeared upon waking.

*Dear God. An air raid siren.*

Scrambling to her feet, she threw open the door to Charlie's bedroom just as another door yanked wide further down the hall.

RueAnn didn't bother with social niceties. "What are we supposed to do?"

Edna stiffened, clearly upset that RueAnn had emerged from Charlie's room. To her credit, she didn't openly chastise RueAnn, but tore a frilly boudoir cap off her head and attempted to smooth her hair into place, despite its pins. Although she'd gone to bed in an extravagant lacy nightdress, she'd covered it with a utilitarian woolen robe belted at her waist and jammed her feet into practical, low-heeled oxfords. In her arms, she clutched her handbag and a book.

"Are we supposed to head for the public shelters?" RueAnn asked.

Edna sniffed in disapproval, taking a pair of pince-nez spectacles from her pocket and pinning them to her robe. "As if the public shelters are any safer than the streets. Little more than hastily constructed brick boxes used by vagrants and riff-raff." She tipped her chin haughtily. "The sirens are simply a nuisance meant to keep us disconcerted and uncomfortable for a few hours. You're free to return to your *own* room," she said pointedly, "or join me in the space under the staircase."

With that, she brushed past RueAnn and made her way downstairs.

Although a part of her bristled at the woman's rudeness, another portion noticed that Edna moved stiffly, imperceptibly favoring her right leg.

Since Edna had appeared prepared for any eventuality, RueAnn rushed up to her room to retrieve a robe, a blanket, and her shoes, then thundered downstairs.

Edna clearly wanted to say something about the noise and RueAnn's unladylike charge, but she snapped her jaw shut and wrenched open a door which had been cut to the shape of sloping treads. Twisting a switch, she turned on the single bulb that hung overhead.

Inside, RueAnn could see that a narrow cot had been set up along the wall. A crate, serving as a nightstand, held a stack of candles and a box of matches.

"You may set up your things on the floor here," Edna said as she settled on the creaking cot and opened her book.

"But what if—"

"The Germans won't be coming this morning," Edna said firmly—so firmly, that RueAnn felt the woman didn't entirely believe what she said. She clipped the spectacles to the bridge of her nose. "The gallant boys in the RAF will see to them."

She then began to read with such pointed concentration that RueAnn feared interrupting her again.

Settling onto the floor, she wished she had something of her own to pass the time. Peering beneath her lashes, she tried see the title of Edna's book in the dim light.

*A History of the English Language.*

In an instant, RueAnn knew she wouldn't be asking to borrow the tome in Edna's lap. Good Lord, as if the scream of the siren weren't enough to send RueAnn 'round the bend, the sheer boredom of the subject would do her in completely.

Sighing, RueAnn wadded her blanket into a semblance of a pillow. By lying on her side, she could just fit into the space beside Edna's cot.

Tucking her hands beneath her cheek, she tried to think of something—anything—to keep her mind occupied with trivial things. But try as she might, she strained for the slightest noise beyond the siren—shouts, screams, the approach of German bombers.

Under normal circumstances, she would use the early morning hours to make a mental list of tasks that needed to be completed by dark. But she was at a loss as to what duties the day might hold. She meant to share in the household upkeep until she could find a job somewhere in the city. But until then…

Until then, she was forced to drag air into her lungs, in and out, in and out, while the walls of the closet closed in on her and the confined area became hot from the overhead bulb. Like bursting fireworks, she saw snatches of her childhood flash before her eyes—the dank cellar, the smokehouse, the closet in her father's church. How many times had she been locked in those tiny airless spaces as a means of punishment? Not just for hours, but sometimes days.

Suddenly, she burst to her feet, swamped by the need to escape, to feel cold, cool air touching her cheeks.

Edna looked up from her book as if RueAnn had suddenly taken leave of her senses. "What on earth?"

Instead of returning to her nest of blankets, RueAnn took an involuntarily step backward. "I-I've never tolerated small spaces very well."

She swung the door open and took a giant step backward, dragging huge gulps of air into her lungs.

Edna's expression grew grim. "There's little sense in taking refuge if you're going to stand there with the door open. If a bomb *were* to fall in the neighborhood, we could be injured by flying glass. Or worse."

But RueAnn couldn't do it. She simply couldn't get back into the shadowy cupboard.

Without another word, she stepped out of the way and closed the door behind her. Needing fresh air so badly her lungs burned, she hurried through the hall, pushing past the swinging door into the tidy kitchen beyond. A frantic glance around the unfamiliar room revealed two doors on the far wall. One held mullion panes carefully blacked out with paint and crisscrossed with tape.

Divining that this must be an exit, she dodged outside into...

Nothing. Beyond the door, the sun was beginning its climb and the air was warm on her skin. There was a faint droning, as if bees had come to the garden in search of pollen. And the sky...

She squinted uncomprehendingly. The sky overhead was the crisp, robin's egg blue found only in early morning. It hung over her head like a mirror, yet there were odd, streaking scratches to its surface that wound in upon themselves, as if the mirror were losing its silver.

"It's amazing, isn't it?"

RueAnn started at the voice. Twisting her head, she saw a young woman of about twenty smiling at her from the other side of a closely cropped hedge. She held a cigarette loosely between her fingers. Belatedly, RueAnn realized that besides sharing a common wall, the two houses also shared a yard dissected by a section of privet.

"What?"

The woman pointed to the vapor marks with her free hand. "It's not often you see a dogfight. Usually there are too many clouds."

Looking upward again, RueAnn realized that the white streaks were being made by a pair of planes high above them. The distant drone she'd taken for bees were actually aircraft.

"Dear God," she whispered.

The woman squinted at her, then smiled. "You must be Charlie's girl."

RueAnn couldn't account for the thrill that raced through her veins. This woman not only knew Charlie, but she'd heard him talking about RueAnn. For some odd reason, that fact brought a jolt of confirmation. She truly belonged to him and someone else knew it.

"Yes." RueAnn reached her hand over the hedge. "I'm RueAnn."

The woman grinned. "Sara. Sara Blunt." She took a deep drag on her cigarette, blowing the smoke over her head as she eyed RueAnn with interest. "American?"

RueAnn nodded.

"Good Lord, whatever made you come here?"

"My husband. Charlie. I...needed to see him."

Sara's eyes widened in patent astonishment.

"You and Charlie... *married*?" Her shock was so heartfelt that RueAnn's newfound confidence waned. Charlie had introduced her as his "girl" evidently, not his wife.

"That should teach me to listen more carefully to fence line gossip," Sara proclaimed. "I'd heard rumors he was serious about someone, but no one mentioned he'd actually married."

RueAnn would have laughed if the ramifications weren't so tragic. Clearly, Charlie hadn't told anyone of their marriage—other than his mother, that was.

"Susan! Come here!"

Sara gestured to a figure beyond RueAnn's line of sight. RueAnn watched in utter astonishment as Sara was joined by her carbon copy. No, not quite an exact replica. Where Sara was adorned with the latest movie-star hair and make-up, this woman was more simply dressed.

"RueAnn Tolliver, this is my sister Susan. Susan, this is Charlie's *wife*."

Susan's jaw dropped as she shook RueAnn's hand. "Charlie's married?"

"It gets even better. She's *American*." Sara drew out the word as if RueAnn's nationality were unheard of.

But then the two girls looked at one another and grinned.

It was Sara who leaned close to whisper, "And his mother hasn't died of apoplexy yet?"

"Sara!" Susan remonstrated.

Sara had the grace to look ashamed, but her remorse lasted seconds before she dissolved into giggles. RueAnn couldn't help but join in.

"You can't have been here long," Sara said when she could speak again, "or we'd have seen you already."

"I arrived yesterday."

Sara's artfully shaped brows rose. "You mean to tell me you weren't already in the country? That you left the safety of the States for a war? And Charlie didn't stop you?"

The twins regarded RueAnn with open curiosity.

"When did you and Charlie marry?" Sara asked bluntly.

"Sara!"

"There's no sense beating around the bush, Susan. One way or another, we're bound to find out. Why not get the information from RueAnn rather than the neighbors?"

RueAnn laughed. She found Sara's honest exuberance refreshing—especially after the veiled hostility of Edna Tolliver.

"Last September."

Sara's eyes widened, her cigarette hovering forgotten halfway to her mouth. "A *year*? You've been married to Charlie for a whole *year*?"

"Just about." Too late, RueAnn wondered if Sara might have

been romantically involved with Charlie at one point in time. RueAnn couldn't blame him if he had. The girl was absolutely lovely with snapping blue eyes and an infectious enthusiasm.

"And you've only just come to England?" Susan asked, clearly mystified by the delay.

Again, RueAnn nodded.

"Then you'll be living next door, alone, with Mrs. Tolliver until Charlie comes home," Sara prompted.

"Yes. I suppose so." Was that so terrible? To have sought shelter with a mother-in-law she didn't know?

Sara grinned and shook her head. "Then dearie, we'd better be showing you the gap in the hedge. You'll be needing it sometime soon. You can escape to our side of the fence for a cup of tea and sympathy."

"Sara, I swear!" Susan chided, clearly shocked by her rudeness.

"Really, Susan," her twin offered with a roll of her eyes. "You've got to admit that Mrs. Tolliver can be an absolute a gorgon at times."

Susan regarded her twin with something akin to horror, her gaze skittering toward the open door leading into the Tolliver abode. "You shouldn't say such things!" she whispered. "Mrs. Tolliver is her *mother-in-law!*"

Sara made a face. "She's a woman to be respected and admired, but good Lord, can you imagine living with her day in and day out? Charlie would be the first to admit she can be positively difficult."

At the mention of her husband's name, RueAnn's fingers began to worry the frayed edge of the pocket on her husband's robe. With studied casualness, she asked, "So Charlie spent time at your house?"

Sara's grin was as clear and guileless as the morning sun. "Sweetie, who do you think *made* the gap in the hedge?"

A swooping hum filled the air.

"There's the all-clear," Sara said, reaching across the neatly trimmed privet. "I've got runs on the Green Line nearly back to back for the next couple of days, but would you like to have

tea with us at the end of week? Say, Sunday, five o'clock?"
She turned to her sister. "Shall we go to Grimshaw's or have
something here?"

Susan smiled. "Let's have it here. Mum would enjoy the
company and I'm sure she'd love to meet Charlie's wife."

RueAnn was a little disconcerted by the impulsive invitation.
In the Boggs household, strangers were regarded with suspicion
and had to earn the right to be invited into one's inner circle.

Nevertheless, her mother had drummed in the importance
of manners. "Should I bring something?"

Sara grimaced. "Good Lord, no. Just yourself. I think it's a
bit early for you to be nicking something from Edna's larder."
She giggled. "Although it might be fun to see what happens if
you did."


Rouen, France


This time, it was the cool kiss of water being poured over his
feverish skin that drew Charlie from a dark, dark place made of
fantastical nightmares of roiling snakes, roses with enormous
fangs for thorns, and pig shit. He was mired in pig shit, covered
in pig shit…

Rex offered him a crooked grimace of a smile. "Welcome
back, old boy."

Somewhere, Rex had found an old dented pail which he'd
filled nearly to the rim with water. He'd ripped a strip of fabric
from the hem of his shirt and was using it to bathe Charlie's face.

"…Hot…" Charlie said after clearing his throat.

Rex nodded, understanding his mental shorthand. "You've
got a raging fever."

He soaked the fabric in water again, then folded it into a
loose square and laid it over his brow.

Charlie focused on that point, on the coolness against his
skin as it warred with the fever.

Rex abruptly spoke. "I've got an idea. Not a great idea. But it's the best I can come up with." The last word emerged more like a croak and Rex covered it quickly with a bitter laugh. "You always said I had the judgment of an out-of-control goat—and I swear this isn't much better but…"

"Shoot…me…" Charlie whispered.

The words were nearly inaudible, but they seared into the silence like a hot knife.

Rex reared back as if he'd been struck. "No! I'm not…I didn't mean…"

"Shoot. Me. Don't leave me…to the…Nazis."

Rex's scowl grew fierce. "Bloody hell! I didn't haul your soddin' ass all this way just to—" He clamped his mouth shut, a muscle at his jaw clenching furiously before he consciously relaxed his expression and said, "If I shot you, it'd be a waste of lead. You're going to get better. To shoot you now would deprive His Majesty of one of his finest agents."

"Bullshit," Charlie growled.

"You'll be getting better. I promise. 'Cause I've got a plan, see?" He bent closer as if they might be overheard. "I've been thinking about it all afternoon."

Afternoon.

When had it become morning, let alone afternoon? Charlie only remembered the night. The pigsty. The patrols.

Or had there been a patch of day somewhere in between?

"Listen, mate, I've got a hare-brained scheme that might, just might, work."

Charlie's gut twisted as cramps clutched his innards. He could feel the heat and pressure of infection as it ate away at him.

"Shoot…me…"

A solitary bead of moisture began to track from the corner of his eye down to his temple.

"Shut up and listen!" Rex hissed. He pointed to a spot beyond Charlie's head. "Just up that road is an old estate the Germans have converted into a hospital. There was some trouble at a bridge near there earlier today—an explosion, gunfire."

Charlie shook his head, clearly not understanding.

"I'm thinking that if we could steal a kraut uniform, we

could dump you somewhere close by, see?"

Charlie blinked at him in confusion.

"Don't you get it? If they think you're a German, they'll patch you up, fill you full of *Wienerschnitzel* and *schnapps*, and send you to some cushy camp to recuperate. By the time they figure out you're not one of them, you'll be strong enough to run for it."

Again, Charlie shook his head.

Sadness darkened Rex's eyes to the color of crushed leaves. "Come on, old boy. Think about it. As long as you kept your mouth shut and your eyes closed, you could buy yourself some time. At best you could escape. At worst…a prison camp where you wait out the war."

They both knew that wasn't the worst that could happen. To be caught wearing an enemy uniform could mean a firing squad. But Rex wasn't about to consider the unthinkable, let alone utter it out loud.

"Will you do it, mate?"

Charlie's eyes closed. Despite dodging enemy patrols, eluding capture, being wounded, it was the first time he had truly faced his own mortality. He had no illusions. His body couldn't go on much longer as it was. He would be lucky to live through the night.

"Charlie," Rex whispered, clearly fearing that Charlie had lapsed into unconsciousness.

But Charlie opened his eyes again. Through parched, cracked lips, he whispered, "Do it."

Sweetheart,

I have an unaccustomed afternoon off. Not enough time to come to London, but long enough to sit and feel sorry for myself. With a few more hours to my disposal, I could have caught a train and made a hurried visit. But I'm stuck here—even though I'm not allowed to tell you where that might be.

The other fellows headed to the pub for a pint. But after a few minutes of their antics with the chippies, I found I couldn't stay. Not when I miss you so much that my body aches. And my heart.

I hesitate to burden you but...

I watched a friend die. Milt and I grew up on the same block. As luck would have it, we joined the RAF at about the same time and were assigned to the same training session. Then, a few months back, he was transferred to my squadron.

It was good to see someone from home. When I got into trouble in the air yesterday, I couldn't believe my luck when he swooped in from behind, downing a Gerry that was on my tail. I'd hardly had a chance to celebrate before the air was thick with them. They were coming in from all sides, closing in on us like locusts. I immediately started to climb, hoping that if I could maneuver into the clouds, I could shake them.

And then, just like that, the sky was clear again.

That is, it was clear except for a thin plume of smoke. As I swung down, I knew immediately it was one of ours and moved in closer. Since I was out of ammo, I figured I could help a fellow pilot limp back to base.

But as I drew near, I could see it was Milt. His Spit had been severely damaged at the tail and left wing, and it was clear that his landing would be iffy at best. So I pulled in close, motioning for him to ditch even as I shouted to him over the headset.

It was then I read the fear in his expression. The canopy sometimes has a tendency to stick, and in order for a person to escape, one has to fling back the canopy, roll the plane, and literally fall out.

Milt was trying to handle the stick even as he pulled at the canopy again and again, but nothing was happening and he was losing altitude fast. Worse yet, I could see the panic setting in.

Hoping to calm him down, I told him to proceed to the airfield and make an emergency belly landing. But he didn't answer, so I was afraid his com system had been damaged. I tried to use hand signals, but I don't think he saw me. I don't think he saw anything but the jammed handle and his dwindling altitude.

Then, without warning, the small plume of smoke flared into open flames and I knew he didn't have much time. I was shouting at him to land in a field up ahead when suddenly, he began banging on the canopy with both hands, trying to break the windscreen. His face was filled with such terror, his mouth open in a silent scream. Then a ball of fire engulfed the cockpit and his plane dipped nose-first and he slammed into the ground.

I've seen men die before. Too many to count. And I know the numbers are against me. There aren't many of us original blokes left anymore. I suppose if I have to go, I'll know I've given it my all. When it's all said and done, it's not going to be my time in the air that I'll regret. I've worked with a jolly good lot, right down to the last. If I had it to do all over again, I'd still volunteer. I've seen enough of what the Gerrys have done to France to know I'll do anything to keep that from happening over here.

No, the only regrets I'll have will be from the things I'll miss—a home, a career, a family. It's funny how so many brushes with death can hone one's wishes down to the most important few.

And principal to them all, is you. I want to hold you. I want to love you. I want to drown myself in the scent of you. If I were to be given one last moment in time, it would be to fall asleep in your arms and wake to you again in the morning. I long for your company so completely that there are times when I wonder if I can gather another breath without seeing you just once more.

If I sent for you—if somehow I were to receive more than a few hours leave—would you meet me? I know I'm being presumptuous. I should court you properly with flowers and long afternoon walks. But such idyllic hours have become luxuries that few of us have. I'll understand if you won't come, honestly, I will. And I promise that even if we were only to meet for tea and I could hold your hand beneath the table, it would be enough. I would never want to pressure you into an uncomfortable situation.

But I'm growing weary of the blood and gore, the noise and confusion. If I could have a few hours of peace, with you, I could go on a little longer.

That being said, perhaps I should discourage you from coming at all. As I watched Milt fight so desperately, I knew what he was thinking. He wasn't fighting for God and Country in that instant. He was thinking of his new wife and a baby on the way. He would have done anything to be with them. Anything at all.

So maybe I should save you the pain of such an end and wait until this hellish war is over. I can't help thinking that my own number could be up at any moment.

Just please...Dear God...

Don't let me burn.

P.

# Chapter Eight

## London, England

If RueAnn had wondered how she would spend her days until she received word of Charlie's welfare, she quickly found her answer. The moment the all-clear sounded, Edna emerged from her cubby under the stairs as if she were a cork shot from a bottle of shaken soda.

RueAnn was just stepping back into the kitchen when Edna pushed through the swinging door.

"Has Louise arrived yet?"

Bemused, RueAnn shook her head.

"Well, don't stand there dawdling, we have a mountain of work and only a few hours to complete it." She frowned, glaring at the pale blue sky. "And that's only if the Germans manage to stay away for the day."

It was clear from her scathing tone that she didn't believe the dreaded Hun would cooperate.

"Since Louise has probably been detained, I'll need you to pitch in and help."

"Yes, ma'am."

Edna made an abrupt about-face and marched toward the staircase. "Can you dust?"

*Could she dust?* What kind of question was that? Did RueAnn look like a pampered socialite? Or an imbecile?

Although a peppery retort leapt to the tip of her tongue, RueAnn hurried to catch up, offering, "Yes, ma'am," instead.

"Good. The WVS is meeting here tomorrow and this house needs to gleam, positively *gleam!* Marjorie Wilkes-

Hamilton hosted the last meeting and I won't be outdone by her. I simply won't!"

Feeling much like a stand-in performer who hadn't yet learned her lines, RueAnn said again, "Yes, ma'am."

"After the dusting, we'll need to polish the silver. I think I'll use the Sunday set, not my best. We'll use the Royal Doulton teacups and snack plates. I'm sure I've got enough. They'll all need to be washed and dried and set out for tomorrow. Can you cook?"

Edna plunged up the staircase with such vigor that RueAnn was forced to keep up.

"Enough to scare hungry from the door."

At that, Edna suddenly stopped and glared at RueAnn over her shoulder, nearly causing RueAnn to crash into her. Too late, RueAnn realized that her reply had a bit too much West Virginia vernacular for Edna to comprehend.

"I can cook the basics," she clarified.

"Louise will be here soon enough. She'll probably ask you to help in the garden or run to the grocers. We'll be needing Vim soon enough."

*Vim?*

RueAnn was saved from a reply as Edna continued her march to the top of the stairs.

"We'll continue this discussion in the kitchen in ten minutes," Edna said as she strode into her bedroom and shut the door behind her with flourish.

Leaving RueAnn staring at the painted panels with her mouth agape. What nerve! Edna was determined to slot her in the role of a newly-acquired scullery and treated her with about as much courtesy. RueAnn should leave the woman to her own devices.

But even as she considered rebelling and returning to the States, RueAnn wilted in defeat. She couldn't—wouldn't—leave the country until she knew what had happened to Charlie. And as much as she might want to lash out at the woman for her rudeness, RueAnn couldn't afford to lose her lodgings. She'd come here to confront Charlie about the letters he'd taken from her and she wouldn't leave until she'd talked to him face to face.

So, even though the words galled her, she clicked her heels together, snapped her hand to her forehead in a smart salute and muttered under her breath, "Yes, general!" Then, sighing, she went up to her garret room to change.

*  *  *

For the remainder of the day, RueAnn found herself thrown into wartime voluntary work much like a beginning swimmer being tossed off the end of a pier. For hours, she and Louise followed Edna's bidding—cleaning, polishing, and dusting. Soon, the already immaculate house gleamed with a fresh coat of polish and bee's wax. What few flowers remained in the garden were cut and carefully arranged.

When Edna was satisfied with the result, her attentions settled on the menu. She and Louise poured over cookbooks and clippings from newspapers and magazines. Although the refreshments had been planned weeks ago, after RueAnn had gone with the women to the shops a few blocks over, shortages at the grocer's had forced a few changes. Adding the restrictions caused by rationing further complicated matters.

Soon RueAnn's head was swimming with an overload of information about wartime rules and regulations as well as the bewildering layout of the London streets. The heat from the day filled the kitchen, causing her dress to cling to her skin. Needing a breath of air, she stepped outside, surreptitiously peering over the hedge, hoping for a glimpse of the twins she'd met earlier. There were children playing in the yard next door, but she saw no hint of the older sisters.

Spying a hoe and a pail, she gathered the tools and made her way to the garden that butted up against the back fence.

Back home in Defiance, they'd always had a large garden. For as long as RueAnn could remember, it had been her job to weed the long rows and haul buckets of water to nourish the fragile plants. She still remembered filling the metal bucket up at the pump, then dragging it to the far end of the property, the handle biting painfully into her palms, the rough lip scratching her shins and catching on the hem of her dress, water splashing against her legs with each bouncing step until the bucket was nearly half empty by the time she reached the tomatoes, peppers, onions, and potatoes. By mid-summer, the bottoms of her feet would be calloused and immune to the sharp bits of rock and debris that littered her path. She would have squelched her instinctive recoil to the bugs and spiders and worms. And she would have found a measure of peace.

Away from the house.

Away from her father.

Now, years later, she was still searching for peace in the middle of the garden, digging her hands into the crumbling earth to wrench out the voracious weeds. Bending to her task, she ignored the sun that turned her skin an uncomfortable pink. The work helped to focus her thoughts and hone in on her most pressing needs.

As much as she'd proved useful today, she had no illusions that Edna would find her indispensable. Nor did she want to become the newest addition to Edna's "staff." No. If she was going to stay in England she needed to find the means to support herself. That meant employment, no matter how humble. But being a foreigner might prove a bit of a stumbling block. She doubted that any of the war work would be open to her.

"Miss RueAnn?"

Louise's soft voice interrupted her furious weeding.

Looking up, she met the woman's hesitant smile. "It's time for tea, dear."

"Tea?"

Louise folded her hands over her ample stomach. "Come along, dearie. You look in need of a bite to eat and something to drink. Then you can tell me what has you glaring so fiercely at the tomato vines."

RueAnn peered around her. "Mrs. Tolliver—"

"Has gone to see the vicar, so it's just you and me, luv. Come along. Master Charlie would skin me alive if I didn't take care of you. And you look as if you need a proper sounding board. Master Charlie couldn't keep his secrets from me and neither should you."

Smiling, RueAnn stood, brushing the dirt from her knees. Suddenly, England wasn't quite as lonely as she'd thought it had been.

For the next hour, she and Louise talked and laughed over cups of tea and tomato sandwiches. She confided in Louise about her need for employment, and Louise sagely agreed in the wisdom of such an idea. By the time Edna returned, RueAnn was feeling rejuvenated and better able to face the challenges that still remained. Nevertheless, when the air raid sirens sounded soon after dark, she still couldn't bring herself to sleep in the cramped space under the stairs, so she made up a bed for herself under the kitchen table instead.

*Where are you, Charlie?* She thought as her weariness overtook her and the faint scent of roses wafted in from the garden. *And where the hell did you put my letters?*

* * *

Susan sighed, shifting her weight from one foot to the other, then glanced surreptitiously at her watch. She'd been waiting in line at the chemist's for nearly a half hour in order to collect a prescription for her mother. But the chemist, much like any other shop in the city, was suffering from a shortage of supplies and help, which meant an inevitable delay in being served.

Tapping her toe, she debated whether she should leave and try again another time. Mr. Meade had given her an hour to run her errands and grab something to eat, but Susan didn't want to take any longer than necessary. Requisitions were pouring into the factory faster than they could finish them, and it had fallen to Susan to fill out the proper paperwork and keep the work orders neat and tidy. If she spent too long away from the office, Mr. Meade had a tendency to dump important invoices willy-nilly on her desk to be sorted out later.

"Susan?"

She glanced up from her watch and smiled as she recognized

Dr. Plymsome, their family physician.

"Dr. Plymsome! How are you?"

The Plymsomes had been close family friends for ages. When Susan had been a child, the doctor and his family lived in a house at the end of the block. But a few years ago, the doctor had moved into a newer, larger building which had allowed his clinic to be below stairs and the family living quarters to be above. With an invalid wife, the arrangement had proven more satisfactory to the aging doctor and his family.

"As well as can be expected."

"And your wife?"

"She's gone to live with a friend in Scotland for the time being. The cooler weather up north has proved most agreeable to her health."

"I'm so pleased to hear it."

"And your own dear mother?" the doctor asked.

Susan paused before answering honestly. "She looks tired. Pale. I worry that she's overworking herself."

The doctor made a *tsking* sound with his tongue. "I thought I was quite clear with her about spending part of her day lying down. Has she had any more pains?"

"Pains?" Susan echoed blankly.

"Any shortness of breath? Swelling of the ankles? I warned her that if she didn't begin to follow my instructions, her heart problems would compound."

"Heart problems?" A lump of dread gathered in the pit of Susan's stomach. "My mother has heart problems?"

Dr. Plymsome's eyes grew sad and infinitely weary. "She didn't tell your family, did she?"

Susan shook her head, then glanced down at the sheaf of papers she held. "Then these medicines…"

Plymsome breathed deeply. "Will help to some extent, but she really must slow down. These pains she's having are simply a symptom of a more serious underlying condition. I've given her a strict diet to follow as well as a regimen of rest." He squeezed her hand. "I certainly didn't mean to blurt the news to you myself. But perhaps, now that you know the truth, you can urge your mother to use more caution in her activities. Will you do that for me?"

Susan nodded, still stunned. Her mother had always been so invincible, so…immortal. Yet, in Susan's hands was written proof that such was not the case.

Dr. Plymsome squeezed her hand yet again. "You have my number. Call if you need me."

"Yes, sir. Thank you. For everything."

"Not at all."

The doctor settled his hat on his head and made his way out the door, leaving Susan numb.

Her mother was ill. Needed rest.

Why hadn't Mummy said anything? Why had she kept her health such a secret? Had she refused to tell anyone? Even Susan's father?

Susan immediately pushed that thought aside. Surely her mother wasn't keeping the knowledge from her father. Susan had never known them to keep secrets from one another. Yet, Susan couldn't imagine her father willingly allowing Millicent Blunt to continue on with all of her duties if the doctor had explicitly ordered her to rest.

That night, as soon as the factory was closed to all but a skeleton crew who would clean the building, replenish supplies, and ready the plant for the next day's work, Susan gathered her things and rushed out into the gathering gloom. She wasn't sure yet how to approach her mother, but Susan knew she had to say something—if only to remind her of Dr. Plymsome's orders.

But as she let herself into the house, it was to a foreign peace. There were no thundering footfalls from the younger children, no clamor for tea, no racing up and down the staircase. Instead, she peeked into the parlor to find her mother sitting in the over-stuffed armchair which had been her favorite perch for listening to the radio for as long as Susan could remember.

"Mother?"

Millicent had been resting with her cheek in her hand. In her lap lay a torn envelope and several folded sheets.

At Susan's call, Millicent started and made to rise. "Goodness me! Look at the time!"

When she would have stood, Susan pushed her down and sat on the ottoman at her feet.

"Are you all right?" Susan asked softly, noting the pallor that clung to her mother's cheeks as well as the hollow set to her eyes. In the past, Susan had attributed her mother's gauntness to Matthew's absence, but now that she knew the truth, she could see that her worry was only part of the problem.

"I'm fine, dear," her mother said with forced brightness. "Sara and Bernard Biddiwell breezed through here about a half hour ago and told Phillip, Michael, and Margaret that they would take them to Grimshaw's for tea if they'd hurry through their chores—which they immediately did, Lord bless them. The house was so suddenly quiet once they left that I decided to put my feet up for a few minutes. Your father's working late again tonight. The children haven't been gone for long. I'm sure you could join them if you'd like."

Susan shook her head. "Are you sure you're feeling well?"

"Of course, dear. What's got into you?"

"It's only that…" Susan reached into her pocketbook and withdrew the sack she'd stowed there. "I brought your medicines from the chemist." She hesitated before continuing. "I saw Dr. Plymsome while I was there."

Millicent stared at her daughter for several long moments before grumbling, "I'll bet the meddling old fool spoke out of turn."

Susan smiled. "It wasn't really his fault. He thought I already knew about your…heart troubles."

"Troubles," Millicent grumbled. "There's not a thing wrong with me that having Matthew home and a full larder for the rest of my children couldn't cure."

"Be that as it may, Dr. Plymsome is concerned that you're not following his instructions."

Millicent's cheeks flamed. "I'll have him know I've been eating his horrid diet and doing calisthenics just as he ordered."

"He's also concerned that you're over-exerting yourself."

"I can't be playing lady of leisure when I've got a house full of children needing food and clean clothing."

"You need your rest. Susan and I can help with the children until you're feeling stronger."

"Nonsense."

"Mother, please," Susan urged.

Millicent became positively rigid in her chair. Folding the papers that had been spread out in her lap, she jammed them into the envelope and said, "I don't know why everyone thinks they have a better idea about what I should or should not be doing. Dr. Plymsome thinks I should spend my days in a chaise lounge. Your father wants me to take all of you to the country. Even your Uncle Joe orders me about, telling me to gather up the wee ones and come live with him in Canada until the war's over."

She jumped to her feet, jamming the envelope into the pocket of her apron.

"Frankly, I think the lot of you should mind your own p's and q's and leave my affairs well enough alone!"

Millicent stormed from the room, and Susan sighed. Blast it all. She rubbed her face with her palms and made her way back into the hall where she unpinned her hat and looped her pocketbook over a brass hook on the hall tree. Turning, she rifled through the pile of mail left on the table. She'd sent for a new crochet pattern. With more women going to work, snoods had been making a roaring comeback and Susan had thought that they would make excellent gifts for Sara, her mother, and...

Her fingers suddenly stilled. There in the stack of bills and correspondence were three...no, *five* letters with Paul's firm hand scrawling out her sister's name and address.

*I've been writing for weeks, did you know...But I never mailed them. We've known each other for such a short time. I didn't want to presume...*

Of their own accord, her fingers reached out and snatched up the envelopes—even as she felt her cheeks flame. Shoving them into the pocket of her dress, she stood panting, wondering at her own brazen dishonesty. Yet, even as her conscience shouted at her to put the letters back—*Now!* Before she was discovered!—her fingers tightened around the envelopes in her pocket so fiercely that she could hear the paper crackle.

All at once, the door burst open and the younger Blunts came tumbling in.

"Susan!" Margaret called, rushing forward to wrap her arms around Susan's knees. "We had tea at Grimshaw's!"

"So I heard." Susan wriggled free from Margaret's grip enough to kneel and pull her close for a hug.

Of all the Blunts, little Margaret was the pet, and there was no denying it. Barely five, with brilliant blue eyes and ginger curls, she was so earnest, so angelic, so easily brought to a state of wonder that there was no way she could ever be lost amongst the shuffle of the other children.

Margaret leaned close to whisper. "I brought Wuzzy to Grimshaw's and no one knewed it." She pointed to a bulge in her pinny where she'd stuffed her toy rabbit.

Susan tried not to laugh. There wasn't a member of the family who wouldn't have known that Wuzzy had accompanied Margaret to tea. But since Margaret was trying so hard to be "grown up" and relinquish the toy which had been her constant companion for most of her babyhood, no one would have dared to say anything.

"I'm so glad you kept him hidden. I don't think the staff at Grimshaw's allow animals on the premises."

"He was very quiet."

"All the best bunnies are, and Wuzzy is definitely cream of the crop."

Margaret bobbed her head in emphatic agreement.

"Who has studies to do?" Susan said, standing.

Phillip and Michael reluctantly raised their hands. "Off you go to the kitchen then, and get out your books."

She took Margaret's hand. "And you, young lady, must help me with the blackout. Then it's time for a hot bath, a story, and bed."

"Will you read *Mary Poppins Comes Back*?" Margaret asked excitedly.

"Only if your nails and ears are exceptionally clean."

Margaret squealed, taking the stairs as quickly as her little legs could carry her, the blackout clearly forgotten in her haste to continue the further adventures of her favorite character.

"Is Mum home?" Sara asked as Susan followed more slowly. "I need to see if I can borrow a pair of her gloves. Bernard is taking me dancing tonight."

"Yes, I believe she's in the kitchen." Fuming about Susan's interference, no doubt. No matter. Susan would have a word with her father later, then see how best to proceed.

"Any mail for me?"

Susan nearly stumbled on one of the risers. If not for a quick grasp of the railing, she probably would have landed face first.

"I'm not sure. The pile's on the table there."

Then, before Sara could comment on the sudden heat flooding into Susan's cheeks, she scurried up the stairs. All the while, she berated herself for being a liar, a thief and a coward— even as the envelopes burned at her hip, their warmth flooding into her in anticipation of what they might say.

* * *

And so began her daily ritual of deceit. In a show of dedication, Susan worked through her usual lunch hour at the ironworks, typing forms and letters which had been left on her desk after the morning's sessions of dictation and departmental meetings. By three-thirty or four, Mr. Meade would come tutting into the outer office insisting she take time for a "cuppa." Feigning surprise at the lateness of the hour, she would gather her things and walk sedately from the building—moving nonchalantly to the end of the block.

But as soon as she was out of sight of the office, she would dash pell-mell to the Tube where she would catch the first train home.

More often than not, she would arrive mere minutes before the postman. After snagging an apple or a handful of carrots, she would sift through the letters and take any she found from Paul. Then, heart pounding, she would race back to the Tube station again, arriving breathless at her desk mere minutes under her allotted break time.

On those days when there were no letters, guilt and shame would burn within her. Nevertheless, by the following afternoon, she would begin her late afternoon pilgrimage all over again, stuffing the next envelope into the inner pocket of her purse to join those she had already collected. Soon, she knew she would either have to find the courage to deliver them to her sister unopened and confess her sins, or betray that final bond of trust and read them herself.

Until then, the letters smoldered in her consciousness. Every waking moment, every thought, every action was colored by their presence. At times, she felt as if by resisting their overwhelming temptation, she was doing penance, enduring the ache of curiosity. With each day that passed, she felt more powerful in her ability to delay gratification, yet infinitely weaker since she knew that it was only a matter of time before she would surrender to their siren's call.

## Rouen, France

Charlie woke to pain, a burning, ever-present pain that enveloped him like a blanket of nails. Panting, he moved carefully, studying his surroundings through half-slit eyes.

Rex had pulled him into a thicket of bushes and covered him even further with broken branches and leaves.

Charlie lay still, waiting, listening. But there was nothing. He didn't know if Rex was nearby sleeping or had gone to scout the area. Except for the distant sounds of chickens, the idle barking of a dog, and the faint clang of a tram bell, Charlie heard nothing, certainly nothing to signal that the Germans were within spitting distance.

Squeezing his eyes shut against a fresh jab of pain, he reached into his pocket, touching the packet of letters yet again.

RueAnn.

It had been a year since he'd seen her. A year since he'd stroked her hair, touched her cheek, gazed into eyes as deep and dark as midnight.

He'd wronged her, used her for his own selfish purposes in order to evade the dark-haired man who'd been following him in Washington D.C. And yet…

In the scant hours they'd spent together at Sweet Briar, he'd grown to care for her, so quickly, so completely, that he hadn't been able to believe in his feelings himself. He'd instinctively felt the need to protect her and mark her as his own. But upon leaving the States, he'd begun to believe that day, those emotions, were nothing short of an aberration.

So he'd left her to fend for herself when she'd needed him most. Worst of all, he'd violated her trust and her privacy.

Because he'd taken her letters. Letters so blatantly vulnerable that she must cringe at the very thought of their being in another person's possession.

Worse yet, he'd read them.

Re-read them.

Memorized them.

And with each reading, he'd become more desperate to see her again. If only to say he was sorry.

The trembling began, a feverish chill that wracked through his body, sapping him of what little strength he had left.

But he had to hold on. He had to find the strength to return to RueAnn and make things right.

## London, England

"Louise, we'll have tea at five."

"Yes, Mum."

RueAnn didn't even bother to look up from her weeding. As much as it clearly vexed Mrs. Tolliver—who didn't feel it was proper for Charlie's wife to be "grubbing about in the dirt"— RueAnn had at least found a way to offer some small measure of help in the household chores.

Truth be told, she enjoyed the few hours spent outside each day. The yard was peaceful and she had always been good with plants. Moreover, it gave her a respite from Edna's hypercritical gaze. At least tomorrow, she could look forward to tea at the Blunt's home. Edna, it seemed, would be too busy to attend.

Thank the Lord for small favors.

Pulling the basket closer, she filled it with the weedy bits she'd pulled from the loamy earth. On her way into the house, she would drop them into the bin she'd devised. With luck, by next spring, she'd have rich compost she could fold into the dirt to make the seeds flourish.

*Next spring.*

She wasn't sure if she could envision a time so far away. Where once she had thought she was finally free to plot her own future, she now discovered that there were things beyond her control that made even tomorrow too far away to count on with any real certainty.

After glaring at her from the kitchen doorway for several long minutes, Edna disappeared into the house again.

RueAnn sighed. The past few days had been filled with a flurry of cleaning. The WVS had met once already this week, but another meeting was scheduled for tomorrow. Lord help anyone who brought a speck of dirt into the house on her shoes.

"Mrs. Tolliver?" Louise called from the door. Then more softly, "Miss RueAnn?"

RueAnn looked up to find Louise beckoning to her. Flushing, she realized the "Mrs. Tolliver" Louise had been referring to, was RueAnn.

Tucking the gardening tools into the basket, she stood, brushing the dirt and grass from her knees. Of everyone she'd met here in England, Louise and the Blunt sisters from next door had treated her with the most kindness.

"Sorry," she said with a laugh. "I'm afraid I'll always think 'Mrs. Tolliver' is Charlie's mother."

"It won't be long before Charlie returns and then perhaps then the two of you can have a home of your own."

*If Charlie returned.*

RueAnn wasn't sure what she would do if the war dragged on without any word of his condition. She supposed she would stay as long as she could, but if she received word of his death, she doubted she'd be welcome to stay with Mrs. Tolliver. The woman's antipathy toward her grew with each hour that passed.

"I managed to collect a few things from the garden."

Louise beamed. "Wonderful! I'll wash them up for later." She pulled a slip of paper from her pocket. "I wondered if I could impose on you to pop down to the local shops to pick up some things."

"Of course."

"Are you sure you can find your way? You've only been there once, and I'm sure your mind was spinning a mile a minute."

"I'm pretty sure I can remember."

"Wonderful!"

As she took the proffered list, RueAnn barely managed to keep the eagerness from her tone.

"And dearie," Louise bent close to whisper, "there's a little tea shop just a few doors down from the grocer's. There was a sign in the window this morning advertising for a position on the wait staff. If you're still looking for employment…"

"Yes…yes!" RueAnn laughed, impulsively kissing Louise on the cheek. "Thank you, Louise!"

Rushing into the house, she quickly washed and changed into the same crepe frock she'd worn her first day in England. How many days had it been now? Four? No, five. The dress was nice without being fussy and should prove suitable for an interview. She combed her hair until it gleamed and drew it away from her face into a crocheted snood, then topped it with her hat. Grasping her purse and a pair of gloves, she hurried down the stairs again.

Louise was at the door. "Here's the ration books and the market money. I've clipped a little note inside for Mr. Greeley. All you'll have to do is hand him the books."

"I can do that." RueAnn tucked them safely away in her pocketbook.

"Then good luck to you, dearie," Louise whispered as she opened the door for her.

"Thank you, Louise."

Although RueAnn had trailed behind Edna and Louise on her second morning in England, this was the first time she'd had a chance to go on her own. Under other circumstances, she would have dawdled and explored, but with only a few hours until tea, she didn't dare do anything which might delay her return to the house.

The sun was hot on her shoulders as she quickly navigated two blocks south and three blocks east. There, close together, was the grocer's, a butcher shop, a tailor, a toyshop, and Grimshaw's Tea House.

RueAnn's heart pounded in her chest as she quickened her pace. Silently, she prayed that the job hadn't already been filled. To be able to work so close to the house would be convenient and allow her to save on bus or Tube fare.

As soon as she saw the neatly printed placard in the window, RueAnn felt a tug of relief. Slowing her pace, she glanced in the windows she passed, checking to make sure she still appeared neat and tidy. Then, pressing a hand to her thumping heart, she stepped inside.

The shadowed interior of the little shop was cool and welcoming. A floor of tiny gray and white tiles gave the narrow property a feeling of spaciousness that it didn't possess. Delicate wire tables and chairs—like one would see in an American soda shop—were draped with matching linens and hurricane lamps.

A portly woman with pin curls hurried forward with a menu. "Just one?" she asked breathlessly.

"A-actually, I've come about the job," RueAnn stammered, suddenly nervous.

"Oh! Oh, my." The woman studied her stem to stern. "Have you ever served tables before?"

"Yes, ma'am. I worked for nearly a year as a waitress in New York before coming to England."

"Did you now," the woman murmured. "What kinds of duties did you have?"

"I helped prepare the tables before the diner opened, stocked salt and pepper shakers, cleaned and bussed tables, as well as serving food. A few times I stood in for the short order cook, but that was rare."

The woman blinked at her for a moment and RueAnn wondered how many American terms she'd used. Did they have diners in England? Short order cooks?

"Can you brew a proper pot of tea?"

"I think so. If not, I'm a fast learner."

A crash from the direction of the kitchen caused the woman to wince.

Sensing she was about to lose the woman's interest, RueAnn hurried to explain. "Please. I've come all the way from America to be with my husband, only to discover that he's been declared missing somewhere in Europe. I won't leave until I know for sure if he's...he's...*when* he's coming home. So I need a job. I'm a hard worker and a quick study and I'm willing to work a week without pay to prove that I'd be a help to you, if you'd like."

The woman's expression eased into one of sadness. "No need, Mrs...."

"Tolliver. RueAnn Tolliver."

"I'm Mrs. Buxton. Be here tomorrow at seven please. You'll need a dark dress, but I'll supply the apron. Come in through the back entrance at the alley. I'll go over my rules and the menu with you in the morning."

"Thank you, Mrs. Buxton."

Another jangle of dropped crockery had the woman turning on her heel and hurrying toward the kitchen in the rear.

"Remove the sign, please, on your way out, Mrs. Tolliver!" she called.

"Yes, ma'am."

Elated, RueAnn snatched the sign from the window, folding it in half, then in half again. As she stepped outside, the bell over the door chimed in congratulations.

A job. She had a job!

She was just stepping up onto the sidewalk when a low whine spooled into the summer air, growing higher and louder, building up to a shrill squeal before dropping again.

In the few days that she'd been in England, RueAnn had grown intimately aware of the warning system. Most nights and intermittently during the day the siren would go off. In the past weeks, air bases throughout southern England had been hard hit and the radio had been filled with dire reports of casualties. But Edna insisted that the RAF were rallying and the Germans were being given "what for." In late August, when a German plane had managed to pierce the lines and drop a bomb on London, the gallant boys in blue had retaliated with an answering raid on Berlin—something Hitler had sworn would never occur.

As the siren ramped up again, RueAnn stopped, suddenly indecisive. Should she seek shelter or hurry home?

There weren't many people on the road. A few folk scurried indoors, but most of the passersby were intent on completing their own business. It was daytime. It was hot. The last thing most Londoners wanted was an hour or two hunkered down in one of the shelters for another false alarm.

Unconsciously, RueAnn turned and began walking toward the Tolliver residence. But she'd only gone half a block when a prickling began at the base of her neck and she felt suddenly uneasy. As if she'd stumbled upon a hive in the woods and had caught the first angry grumbling of the disturbed bees.

*Bees.*

She was not imagining the sound.

Stopping, she looked up, shielding her eyes with her hands as the sun was suddenly cast in shadow. As she looked up above the tumbled-block shapes of the buildings, past the tiled roofs and chimneypots, she saw a dark line of birds staining the skyline.

No. Not birds.

Planes.

Hundreds and hundreds of planes.

The swath of black grew larger and larger, completely blotting out the sky above. Huge bombers flanked with darting fighters.

Instinctively sensing this was not a show of force by the

RAF, RueAnn turned and began to run—even as the now familiar Spitfires converged on the wave and began to give chase.

Her last thought as the bombs began to fall was that London had finally become a target.

Sweetheart,

I don't know when or if I'll have another chance to write. The wave of Gerry bombers this time is worse than I've ever seen. It could be a precursor to an invasion, so it's essential that we're up in the air as much as possible. As it is, I've already logged more than twelve hours flying time today. I've been given about twenty minutes for my plane to be rearmed, then I'll be at it again. The crew chief has promised to see that this gets mailed.

We've been hit hard. Can't tell you where. My squadron is decimated—so much so, that I'm the "Old Man" of the bunch. Some of these blokes haven't even been in a Spit before they're posted. Others are used to the Hurricane.

I can't remember ever being this tired. Tired of everything. The adrenaline that used to give me strength has long since given out and I'm doing my job through sheer repetition, which is dangerous. Above all else, a pilot should be fresh when he gets behind the controls, but there's no one to spell us off. The only thing that gives me any sort of peace is the thought that you're out there, believing in me and I have to do my part to keep you safe.

Have you written? Please tell me you have. Mail is sporadic, so I may find a letter from you on my bunk when I return. Send the picture you promised. I'll tape it over my controls for luck. I need the luck.

I'm being called, so I don't have time for more. Just know that I would do anything to hold you one more time.

P.

# Chapter Nine

Susan arched her back and removed the last letter from the typewriter, adding it to the others that Mr. Meade had dictated to her earlier that morning. Tapping the edges of the pages together, she carried them into the main office, leaving them in the center of Mr. Meade's blotter.

She'd only been working at the Ironworks for a short time, but already, she knew more about arc welding, pig iron, and submarine rivets than she ever would have thought possible.

Glancing at her watch, she wondered what had delayed her employer. Punctual to a fault, Mr. Meade's every movement could be predicted to the second—which meant that there must be a problem on the factory floor.

Susan gnawed at her inner lip in frustration. She'd hoped to rush home for another "late lunch" and a check of the mail, but there probably wouldn't be time now.

Crossing to the window, she sighed when the distant whine of an air raid warning sliced through the muted din of hammers on metal, hissing welders, and sanders. Company policy demanded that machines be stopped, the work floor be cleared, and all assembly line employees evacuated to the basement storage area as soon as the warning sounded. As a member of the office staff, Susan was not required to join them. Several times in the past week, she'd ignored the air raid warnings in favor of completing her work. She'd always imagined that if the Germans were to appear, she would have plenty of time to rush downstairs.

"Are you coming with us, Miss Blunt?"

She glanced up to see William Cross, the projects manager, standing in the doorway.

"In a moment, Mr. Cross. I need to lock up the ledgers first."

He nodded and disappeared in the direction of the stairs.

Susan supposed there was no getting around it now. She'd have to go down. She reached for the keys kept in Mr. Meade's top drawer.

"Miss Blunt?"

This time, it was Ed Naft, Mr. Meade's errand boy, who called to her from the hall.

"Mr. Meade has requested that you—"

A giant hand slammed into her from behind, throwing her to the ground amid heat and noise, broken glass and masonry. Her jaw hit the floor with such force that fireworks exploded behind her eyes, then she was thrust into darkness and a strange, muted world where time crawled and everything around her moved with macabre slowness.

Clawing at the dirt and debris beneath her palms, she fought to move an elbow beneath her, propping herself up. But when she attempted to push herself to her knees, she realized that pieces of Mr. Meade's ruined desk pinned her in place.

Bit by bit, she dragged one leg forward until she could push on the desk and free herself. Pieces of broken glass and brick dug into her shins, scraping, slicing, but she finally managed to scramble free. Panting, she staggered to her feet, even as the floor shuddered beneath her.

Lunging toward the door, she gasped when she saw Ed slumped against the wall.

"Ed. Edward!" She could hardly hear herself over the roaring that reverberated in her ears. Kneeling beside him, she sobbed when she lifted his head, then recoiled again, scrambling backward when the bones of his face moved beneath her fingers like bits of crushed chalk. His eyes were open. Glassy. Blood oozed from his nose and ears.

Pressing her hand to her lips to hold back her gorge, Susan lurched into the hallway, making her way to the iron stairs that led to the factory floor. Renewed shudders nearly knocked her from the treads and she realized in horror that the bombs were falling faster. The air around her was growing hot and difficult to breathe, laden with smoke and dust.

Once at the bottom, she turned to run toward the evacuation shelter, only to confront a collapsed wall blocking her way. She had no way of knowing if the others had made it to safety or if they were now entombed by the rubble.

*The Tube.*

She headed for the back door, but found countless obstacles in her way. Heavy workbenches had been tossed aside like children's toys. The lockers lining the far wall were crumpled like old cans, doors peeling free and hanging crazily by their hinges.

A gaping hole lay where the exit had once been and she clambered over the rubble, emerging into the very epitome of hell.

Flames leapt from crippled buildings on either side of the street. A hot unnatural wind blew down the canyons of the dockside businesses, whipping at her skirt and robbing her lungs of air.

Turning, she panted, trying to make sense of a world where she was marooned, left to battle the unfamiliar elements. And even though this portion of the city was as familiar to her as her own back garden, she found herself lost in a landscape that had suddenly been stripped of markers she'd relied on since she was a child and her father—

*Daddy.*

Sobbing, she turned. She had to find her father. She had to—

Just as she would have darted into the heat of the firestorm, a hand grabbed her elbow, dragging her back. She fought against the man's grip, but he held tight.

"No, Miss. Get t' the shelter."

Although she didn't know the man, she recognized the uniform of the ARP.

"The docks are on fire!" he shouted, leaning close so that she could hear. "Ye've got t' get t' safety!"

"But my father—"

"Ye'll do him more good being safe than trying t' find him in a bloody air raid!"

As much as she wanted to argue, his fingers clutched her so tightly, she feared that he would drag her bodily toward the Tube, so she allowed herself to be propelled toward the next block where the ARP warden all but pushed her toward a stone staircase nearly obscured with sandbags.

Numb, trembling, she filed into position behind others who were looking for refuge from the confusion above. Down, down, they moved like numb sheep, descending escalators robbed of power and frozen in position, following an unknown leader until they found themselves crammed into a space far too small to hold them all. The air was dank and damp, rife with the stink of sweat and urine and fear.

Bracing her back against the tiled walls, Susan positioned herself as close to the wooden escalator as possible. Images popped in her mind like flashbulbs. Edward's crumpled form. The docks ablaze.

Her lower lip began to tremble and she turned away. Since the shelter was crowded predominantly with men, she didn't want them thinking she was a hysterical female about to come unglued. But when she thought of what lay just at the top of the stairs and the fact that her father could be out there…

The sobs came, whether or not she willed them away.

* * *

As the streets around her dissolved into chaos, an overwhelming, inexplicable need to return home swamped RueAnn like tidal wave. It didn't matter that Charlie's house had not proven to be a "home" yet. Nor did it matter that the inhabitants of Exington Street were all but strangers to her. She needed to get back, to make sure that Edna and Louise had found shelter. Hiding under the stairs would do them no good if a bomb dropped on the house.

But the streets were suddenly crowded—mothers with prams, businessmen, shoppers with packages, men and women in uniform. RueAnn soon found herself swept away with a current of humanity pressing forward toward the entrance to the Underground. Unable to resist the flow, RueAnn eventually gave in to the swell, riding the wave down the stalled escalators, down to the subway platform below. Once there, she stood trembling, listening to the distant *thud, thud, thud* of bombs.

Shivering at the sudden chill found underground, RueAnn listened intently to the eerie symphony. As soon as there was a pause in the barrage, she would hurry home to ensure everyone was safe.

Agonizing minutes ticked by. A quarter hour. A half. And still the cacophony above continued. Shock gave way to frustration, then anger at the Germans. Then despair. This was no flyover, no random bombing. This was a calculated raid that went on and on and on.

When it became apparent that there would be no quick respite, RueAnn sank to the floor with the others. Wait. She would have to wait.

But even as she leaned her head back against the tile and willed her heart to ease its thumping, her mind continued its racing.

Was this what Charlie had been enduring for months? This noise, fear, frustration…

Regret?

So many regrets.

Shuddering, she realized that this wasn't what she had planned for herself all those years she'd plotted an escape from her father. She'd been determined to make something of herself, to prove that she was valuable. Worthy of consideration. Yet, she'd done nothing of the kind. Instead, she shivered in a dark hole like a cowering rabbit, still as much beneath her father's shadow as she'd ever been. Worse yet, she'd compounded her problems by marrying a stranger.

Did he ever think about her? Did Charlie ever wonder what could have happened between them if the war hadn't intervened? Were his dreams plagued with memories he would rather forget? Bittersweet dreams where his arms were around her, his lips…

Without warning, a siren split the gloom.

*The all-clear.*

RueAnn's head jerked up. Glancing at her watch, she stared in disbelief at the dial. She'd been down here for hours.

Scrambling to her feet, she hurried up the stairs, flight after flight, pushing past those as eager as she to escape the close confines of the Underground.

Bursting out onto the street, she paused, breathing deeply of muggy air laden heavily with smoke. But as her eyes focused on her surroundings, she grew still.

Not long ago, this had been a beautiful city lane with neatly painted shops and spotless sidewalks. Now much of the block had been razed. RueAnn stumbled forward, picking her way through the debris littering the street—bits of brick, broken glass, torn curtains.

A tiny shoe.

Disoriented, RueAnn searched for familiar landmarks and found none, until, pausing at the corner, she saw a dustbin. And there, scorched and covered with ash, was the "help wanted" poster she'd thrown away moments before the air raid had begun. Turning in a wide circle, RueAnn eyed her surroundings, finally focusing on the wreckage of Grimshaw's Tea House. Despair and defeat pressed in upon her as she realized she wouldn't need to return to the restaurant early the next morning.

Briefly, she wondered what had happened to the harried proprietor, Mrs. Buxton, and the nattily dressed customers who had been sipping tea. Had they made it to safety? Or had they gambled on hunkering beneath the tables, unaware of the utter devastation to come.

Whirling away from the sight, RueAnn began running in the opposite direction. She had to get home. Now.

What had been a ten-minute walk earlier in the day took twice as long on the return, but as she rounded the corner, she was relieved to see that the houses on this block were relatively untouched. A few roof tiles had fallen, and some of the homes sported broken windows, but the buildings were still standing.

Rushing to the Tolliver's, she let herself in, startling Edna who'd been sweeping up dust from the floor.

Although the older woman didn't speak a word in greeting, the tense line of her body eased.

"Louise?" RueAnn whispered.

"She went home to check on her family."

Edna's voice trembled and she pressed her lips tightly together, so RueAnn didn't press. Instead, she took the dustbin from Edna's hand and bent to hold it steady so that the older woman could sweep the damage away.

* * *

As soon as the all-clear sounded, Susan emerged into an alien world of flames and smoke. The docks were ablaze, factories and offices destroyed. The fire brigade was already at work, pumping water from the river. Hoses snaked over the ground. Sparks and spray mingled in the air with bits of ash.

Coughing, Susan covered her mouth with her hand and squinted against the acrid smells that stung her nose and caused her eyes to water.

Slowly, she picked her way back to the Ironworks. Her father's workplace would be two blocks to the east, butted up against the river. He would be all right. She knew he would be all right. The factory where he worked had a bomb shelter. He would be all right.

But it was difficult to continue her litany when the destruction of the docks was so overwhelming. Roads and walkways had been obliterated. A false twilight had fallen, obscuring visibility for more than a few yards.

Rounding the corner, Susan froze in horror. Amid the rubble in front of her, dozens of naked bodies littered the road, their skin gleaming dully in the shifting light of flames and sunlight. Recoiling, she turned to run, then paused when she realized that she wasn't looking at real human flesh, but the broken forms of display mannequins that had tumbled from a nearby warehouse.

Nervous laughter bubbled from her throat, but she pressed it back with her fist, her heart still pounding in her chest. At least now, she had her bearings. The mannequins had come from the collapsed Peterson Tailoring and Supply Company, which was only a few yards away from her destination.

Picking her way forward, she ignored the limbless plaster torsos, mangled unpainted faces, twisted support stands, until she reached the alley beyond.

It wasn't far now. Only a few scant feet. A few…

She stopped, seeing the gaping crater ahead of her, the tumbled wreckage of the building, the seeping water from the docks already forming oily, black puddles. And this time, the bodies she saw were real.

The German bombs must have scored a direct hit on the factory and its shelter.

Sensation drained from her body like grains of sand. Her extremities prickled as she picked her way through the ruins. She knew a few of the men she found—Mr. Grover who fed her peppermint drops whenever she dropped by to see her father, Peter Wilkinson, a boy Matthew's age who used to come to their house when Matthew was on the cricket team. Elton Fullery. The foreman.

An icy shudder caused her to stumble. Bile rose in her throat.

She should go, get out of this place. She didn't want to see any more. Her father had probably gone in search of her— he might be halfway home by now. He would be angry that she'd come here, that she'd subjected herself to such sights, that she'd—

Without warning, her gaze caught on a bloody hand emerging from the rubble. Even as she refused to believe what she saw, a trembling began in the soles of her feet, radiating up, up, up, until she could no longer stand.

It was only a hand.

A hand.

But she knew it as well as she knew her own. The slender fingers, the knuckles enlarged now with arthritis, the calluses upon the palm. How many times had that hand stroked her hair or patted her cheek, the rough skin slightly scratchy, but familiar? Oh, so familiar.

Gingerly, she began to shift the rocks and brick, the splintered beams, the dust. Until she exposed an arm...a shoulder...then the sweet profile of her father's face.

Kneeling beside him, she pressed her cheek to his, seeking reassurance—a hint of warmth, the scant caress of his breath.

But there was nothing but cold stillness.

* * *

The air raid sirens began their low, escalating scream long before RueAnn and Edna could finish their cleaning. For the most part, the house had escaped the bombing raid relatively unscathed. A few patches of cracked plaster, a shattered window, and, of all things, a boot which had been thrown into the tomato plants. Even so, the barrage had shaken the house to its very foundation, letting loose decades of dust and debris hidden within its pores.

As they'd bent over their task, RueAnn had comforted herself with the thought that the Germans couldn't do much more to them. Not for a day or two.

But she'd been incredibly naïve in that regard. The Germans were launching a second wave and she and Edna had only a few minutes to get to safety.

This time, there was no inner vacillating as to whether or not to take shelter. RueAnn had already seen a portion of the German might and the inefficiency of a table or closet to defend against a direct hit. And she had no desire to subject herself to any more than necessary.

RueAnn and Edna had been working upstairs, scrubbing the floors and woodwork with cloths dampened with Vim. But as the siren crescendoed, they both ran to the window overlooking the front yard.

"We've got to go to one of the Public Shelters," RueAnn insisted.

This time, she received no argument from Edna. "The Underground station is only a few blocks away."

RueAnn frowned. Edna was pale, her gray eyes overly large, the rouge of her cheeks garish.

"Edna?"

Edna shook her head, collecting herself. "W-we'll need blankets a-and pillows…since I don't expect the Hun will finish…will finish…anytime soon," Edna said.

The day's events must have taken a toll because the vitriol Edna usually used when speaking about the Germans fell flat.

The older woman turned, her movements unsteady. "I'll collect those items if you'll…if you'll run down to the kitchen… and gather the emergency basket I've…assembled and put in the larder."

Nodding, RueAnn raced pell-mell down the stairs. She gathered the basket, what was left of a loaf of bread from the counter, and a pair of apples from the bowl on the table. Then, heart pounding, she snatched a knife from the drawer and slid it in between the items tucked under the dishcloth. There wasn't time to go to her room for anything more. But if German bombs were to be followed by German paratroopers, she wanted some form of protection, however small it might be.

Racing back to the staircase, she waited impatiently, sure that she heard the low drone of planes beneath the whine of the siren.

"Edna? Edna, we've got to hurry!"

The drone was growing more recognizable now, the hum of the fighter escorts, the grumble of the bombers.

"Edna!"

When there was still no response, RueAnn set the basket on the bottom tread and hurried upstairs. Was Edna having trouble carrying everything?

But as soon as she reached the top, RueAnn saw the crumpled shape of her mother-in-law.

"Edna?"

Rushing toward her, RueAnn carefully rolled the woman to her back, wondering if she'd tripped on the rug and dazed herself.

But as soon as she looked at her mother-in-law, she knew what had happened. The left side of Edna's face was unnaturally slack, her mouth drooping as if pulled by an invisible string. A small rivulet of saliva rolled down her chin. Her nostrils flared as she fought to breathe. Her eyes were wild and filled with fear.

As hateful as Edna had been to her since she'd arrived, RueAnn felt nothing but pity. And shock. The speed with which Charlie's mother had been leveled from imperious matriarch to invalid was incomprehensible.

Framing Edna's face in her hands, RueAnn tried to calm her, fearing that her sobbing inhalations could only exasperate her condition.

"Edna. Edna, I think you've had a stroke."

Edna's eyes teared, her breathing still spasmodic.

From somewhere in the distance, the distant *thump* of bombs heralded the arrival of the Germans.

Although Edna needed medical attention, there was an even more pressing need for shelter. But there was no way that she could carry Edna and to attempt to drag her down the staircase…

Racing back downstairs, RueAnn grabbed the emergency basket and the first aid kit that Edna kept bolted to the rear of the larder wall. Although there was probably nothing inside that could help Edna's condition, at least she would have a few rudimentary supplies.

As she rushed toward Edna again, tears welled over the woman's lashes and ran down her temples into her hairline. Too late, RueAnn realized that Edna must have thought she'd been abandoned.

Unintelligible sounds emerged from Edna's throat, but RueAnn patted her cheek, shushing her as if she were a child.

"Shh. I'm not leaving you. I promise. I just wanted to get the emergency basket."

The noise grew louder, the rumble of the engines overhead causing the window panes to rattle.

"Edna, I need to move you somewhere a little safer, do you think that would be okay?"

Again, an incomprehensible garbled noise gurgled from her throat.

"I'll be careful. I promise."

Vainly searching the hall and then the bedrooms, RueAnn

finally saw a rudimentary means of protection.

Returning to Edna's side, RueAnn tried to offer her a bright smile. "I'm going to move you back into your bedroom, okay? The tester bed is high enough that we can take shelter underneath it. Do you think I could move you that far?"

Slipping her hands under Edna's arms, she dragged her inch by agonizing inch, trying to move slowly, gently. Finally, panting, she left Edna next to the bed. Stripping away a pillow and a blanket, she tucked Edna into a warm cocoon. Then she tugged at the bedpost, head, foot, head, foot again, until Edna's shape disappeared beneath the bedstead. Leaving the basket nearby, RueAnn wriggled beneath the bed as well, taking Edna's good hand in her own.

"There!" she said with forced brightness. "Right as rain! We'll just wait out the air raid, then we can get you to the hospital straightaway."

But as she met Edna's gaze, she knew the older woman wasn't fooled. The raid could continue on for hours, and even then, there would be no quick medical attention. Not when thousands of Londoners were caught in the midst of such terror.

RueAnn squeezed Edna's hand. "You rest. I'll be here. I'll take care of you."

Edna's eyes finally closed, her sobs quieting. Her body was suddenly so still, so lax, that RueAnn feared she'd died. But the faint rise and fall of her chest testified that she'd merely slipped into unconsciousness.

Only then did RueAnn allow her own sobs to surface.

"What do I do now?" she whispered into the din of a besieged city. "What do I do now?"

## Rouen, France

Charlie felt someone touch his cheek, and for a moment he smelled roses. Roses that sifted down on him like snow.

"Charlie."

Rex cupped Charlie's cheek to help him maintain his focus. "Hey, old boy. Stay with me now."

Charlie tried to swallow, then gave up all effort to speak, nodding.

"I managed to finish the job when you passed out. You're looking like a regular kraut, if I do say so myself."

Charlie patted his side, then slid his fingers over rough wool.

"I changed everything down to your skivvies."

Charlie nodded.

"The trousers were a little big, but not so bad." Rex grinned. "At least you smell a little better."

They both knew that was a lie. He stank of sweat, pig shit, and the sweet-sour odor of infection. Idly, he wondered how much longer it would take for the putrefaction to kill him from the inside out. A day? Two?

He focused on his friend, knowing that it was long since time for them to part.

"Go...now."

Rex shook his head. "Nah. I'll wait a few hours until it's a bit darker. The Resistance blew up Gestapo headquarters last night. The krauts have been rounding up suspects in the area all day long." He hesitated before adding, "I had trouble carrying you. Every time I haul you up, you bleed all over me. You owe me a new shirt when we get home."

Charlie nodded.

"We're still about four kilometers from the hospital, but I don't dare take you any closer with all the patrols combing the area. There's a tram stop near here. Once the moon sets, I'll drag you to the road and—"

Charlie gripped his wrist with more power than either of them would have thought possible.

"Now. Go...home."

"There's plenty of time, Charlie boy."

Charlie's head rocked in the crushed grass.

"No more...time." He dug his fingers into Rex's wrist. "Now."

Rex opened his mouth, then shut it again. "Charlie, I

need…" he swallowed hard. "I need to take the letters with me."

At first Charlie didn't understand. The only letters were those he'd taken from RueAnn. He'd carried them for weeks now—originally bringing them along to keep his mother from discovering them more than anything. But once he'd begun to read them…

They'd become his talisman.

For the first time since their flight from Germany, since being pursued, shot and thrown in dung heap, be felt alone. Alone and defeated.

He opened his mouth to protest. He was a dead man anyway. What did it matter if he were discovered with letters written in English?

But then he realized that if the Germans found them, they would never believe he was alone. It wouldn't take long for them to realize he was one of the men stopped at the railway station and they'd pursued three men with forged papers. Three. The moment any of them was caught, the search for the others would be intensified. Alex was beyond helping. But if Charlie remained unidentified for a few hours, a day, two, Rex would have a better chance of surviving.

His hands shook as he handed the packet to Rex. "If…*when*… you get back to England…mail them back to RueAnn. Don't… don't tell her…I…read them. Took them…by accident…"

A muscle worked fiercely in Rex's jaw, then he nodded abruptly.

Taking the packet from Charlie's hand, he was sliding them inside his shirt when he stopped. Moving quickly, he untied the dirty pink ribbon that held them together, looped it around Charlie's wrist, knotting it tightly.

"Tell everyone it's a trophy from a *fraulein* in a beer hall that you nailed during an air raid."

Charlie nodded, involuntarily laughing, then groaning when the pain sliced through his abdomen.

"See you…soon…"

The muscle in Rex's jaw worked double time.

"Don't forget…return…letters."

"You know I'll remember."

Charlie hissed, closing his eyes against a fresh stab of pain. "Go…"

Charlie purposely relaxed his body, pretending to lose consciousness again. He waited out the silence, rich with the mournful tune of crickets and frogs. He remained still, breathing slowly and shallowly as Rex touched his arm. Then he steeled himself as Rex gathered his things and moved stealthily into the shadows.

Fear rose within him like bile. Charlie grew chilled and numb, his body beginning to shake uncontrollably. Rolling onto his side, he pulled himself into a fetal ball, hugging the unfamiliar greatcoat around him. Then, needing something other than the pain, his fear, and his hopelessness to keep him company, he rubbed the frayed ends of the ribbon between his fingers until his body floated and he could have sworn he caught a hint of roses…

The clang of the tram bell woke him with a start. Heart pounding, Charlie wondered how long he'd been gone this time.

Moments?

Days?

As his eyes sought the darkness, he saw a shape creeping through the shadows clinging to the trees along the road.

Rex. He'd recognize his hulking shape anywhere.

Another clang caused him to flinch. The tram. They hadn't accounted for the tram in their timing.

Straining forward, he saw Rex step deeper into the shadows, drawing himself so tightly against the rough bark that he could have been a part of the trunk.

The tram rumbled to a stop at the far end of the lane. Three people disembarked. An elderly couple who turned away from Rex's hiding place and a young woman with a purse who began walking in Rex's direction. If she continued on her course, she would walk directly past him.

A gust of wind tore at her skirts and she gripped her scarf more securely around her face, her head down, plodding.

Blackness crowded in on his vision and Charlie took gulping

breaths to drive it back. Nearby, someone was cooking cabbage and the odor faintly clung to the breeze, making his stomach growl in protest.

The tram rumbled away, and at the last minute, Rex burst from his hiding place, running, using the sound of the squeaky metal car to mask his footfalls. As he brushed past the woman, she inhaled sharply, side-stepping into the trees.

Too late, Charlie heard the distant murmur of voices. A shout.

"Halt!"

Without warning, gunshots peppered the evening stillness. Rex stumbled, twisting as the bullets slapped into his body, arms extending, windmilling, papers flying from his fingers to be caught by the wind and blown into the bushes near Charlie's hiding place.

Shrinking deeper into the shelter of the leaves, Charlie waited, his pulse pounding in his throat as the Germans ran toward Rex who lay prone in an ever-expanding pool of blood.

Charlie ground his jaws together. There was no doubt Rex was dead. The barrage of machine gun fire had left gaping holes in his chest.

Bile rose in his throat as one of the Germans bent over Rex's body, then kicked him in the head. Talking low among themselves, they joked about the accuracy of their marksmanship. A soldier turned, whistled, and Charlie shivered uncontrollably as he heard the rumble of a truck. Making himself as small as possible, he panted softly as the men waited for the canvas-covered truck to ease forward. Then, scooping up the corpse at their feet, they threw it into the back and clambered in behind it. Gears ground sharply, the truck shuddered and whined, then lumbered heavily down the lane toward the center of town.

Charlie waited, his pulse thrashing in his throat, the world tipping crazily as he fought to stay alert. He counted to one hundred, then counted to one hundred again.

A rustling noise alerted him, and too late, he remembered the woman who'd stepped off the tram. She was moving from the shadows of the trees on the opposite side of the street.

She appeared to be as shaken as Charlie, moving slowly, testing the now-quiet street timidly as if a soldier might loom from the shadows. As she crept forward, her foot fell on one of the scattered letters, causing it to crinkle. Curious, she bent low, retrieving an envelope. She paused for a beat. Two. Then removed the letter from inside, skimming the contents.

Looking over her shoulder lest she was being watched, she began to gather the scattered envelopes, following them like bread crumbs in the darkness. She was so intent upon her task that she didn't see Charlie sprawled in the dirt until she stumbled into him.

Gasping, she shrank against the trunk of a nearby tree, trying to make herself as invisible as possible.

Her shape tipped crazily as he was swamped with a wave of dizziness. He closed his eyes to keep from retching, a moan slipping unbidden from his throat. He was cold...so cold...yet so, so hot...

Someone touched his shoulder, yanking him out of a dark pool that spun around and around, dragging him down to a place that was frightening and oh, so alone.

He tried to open his eyes, tried to remember. Had someone been speaking to him?

"Rex?"

Too late, he realized he'd muttered the word aloud.

His eyes searched for purchase before settling on the face of a woman bending low over him.

"RueAnn?" he whispered, hope flickering.

The woman instinctively reared backward. Losing her footing, she fell into the soft weeds. In doing so, her hand fell on Charlie's boot.

He saw the realization spread over her features at the same moment that reality returned. Too late, he realized the error. His boots weren't German-issued. They were brown leather and thick-soled. Scuffed and scarred.

Time spooled into an eternity of heartbeats. Painful thrums that reminded him of the ache radiating through his body.

Moving slowly, she crawled toward him, mindful that if he

was dressed as a soldier, he could be armed as well. Since he lay on his side, she carefully rolled him onto his back.

A fresh bolt of agony shot through him like sizzling lightning, causing his head to arch back and his eyes to squeeze closed.

The woman waited until his panting eased. *"Wie heißt du?"*

He saw her lips move, heard the sounds, but he was slipping away into the blackness again. He squinted as the woman's face seemed to shift into more familiar planes.

"RueAnn?"

Why didn't she help him? Was she angry because he'd taken her letters?

"You're hurt." This time, she spoke in English.

He offered a bitter laugh that became a moan.

"I'm sorry. So sorry," she said as she began unbuttoning the coat, spreading it wide. Despite everything she'd already seen on the road, she recoiled.

Charlie's moan became a sob.

*Don't leave me. Don't leave me here alone.*

He couldn't be sure if he'd spoken the words aloud. The woman quickly rebuttoned the coat, saying, "We've got to get you out of here."

He grasped her wrist, his grip surprisingly strong. "My wife…"

"RueAnn?"

His brow furrowed in confusion.

"The letters are yours, aren't they? Is she your wife?"

He couldn't speak. He tried to grip her wrist, but his hand kept slipping.

"Never mind," she said. "Right now, we need to get you away from the road before the patrols return." She hesitated before asking. "The other man? The one who was running? Was he with you?"

He couldn't control the sob that burst from his throat.

Her eyes softened then, and she slid an arm through his. "Do you think you could walk? I will help you, but we've got to get away from here as quickly as possible. The soldiers will come back as soon as they realize that it is not a Resistance member

INTO THE STORM

that they've killed, but a Brit."

He nodded, knowing that it was a danger to trust this woman—to trust anyone. But also knowing that if he didn't trust her, he would be a dead man.

The journey seemed to take an eternity, even though they traveled less than a few blocks. His legs were trembling so badly, he felt sure he would collapse when finally, she turned down a narrow path and made her way to the back of a small house—a mere shack made of rough boards and peeling paint.

As Charlie braced himself against the outer wall, she fumbled with her key, opening the door and swinging it wide.

"We need to hide you, yes? The Germans might begin a house-by-house search if they think an enemy soldier was in the area."

He nodded, too exhausted to speak.

She gazed around the narrow kitchen and living area. Even to his own eyes, there were no real hiding places.

"Sit."

He all but fell into a chair as she crossed to the middle of the kitchen and pushed a sturdy kitchen table to one side. Throwing back the rag rug underneath, she exposed a trap door.

"You will need to go down into the cellar. It is the only way to keep you out of sight."

She threw back the door, then gathered a lantern and bedding from a nearby cupboard. After touching a match to the wick, she hurried down a narrow set of stairs.

A few moments later, she returned.

"I've made a pallet for you on the floor. It is not the best hiding place, but it will do for now."

Charlie wasn't sure he could stand, let alone navigate the stairs, but he knew he had no choice. Above all else, he could not put this woman in any more danger.

As soon as he reached the blankets in the far corner, he collapsed.

"I am going to heat some water for you. I will clean you up as best as I can. I-I work in a hospital, but I have no medicine."

Charlie was panting against the pain that began to surge

175

over him in waves.

"I will warn you. I have only turpentine to clean the wound."

*Dear God.*

"I'll work quickly. I promise."

He kept his eyes squeezed tightly shut. As she gently drew back his clothing, exposing his wounds, the blackness edged closer.

And this time, knowing that he was hidden from the Germans, he allowed the blackness to swamp him and pull him into the depths.

Sweetheart,

I'm tired. So tired. But there's nothing to do but tuck my head down and carry on. At least, tonight I've been promised some sleep.

Still no letter. Is something wrong? Are you safe? Dear God, I don't know what I'd do if I didn't know you were out there, waiting for me.

I ache for you each and every day—not just physically. I'm not that much of a cad. I would be content simply to hold your hand and hear the melody of your voice in my ear. Sometimes I dream of you at night—sweet, sweet dreams. But I wake to a nightmare.

I entered the RAF thinking it would be flags and glory. Since then, I've learned that war is noise and chaos and destruction. I've lost more friends than I can count. Others have been badly injured, burned.

As of yet, I am unharmed for the most part. Bullets strafed my canopy and I got banged up a bit—a black eye, cuts and scrapes, but nothing too serious. At least I'm being given twelve hours off to rest and recuperate.

Still no letter. Have you changed your mind? Found someone else? If so, I'll understand. Just write something so that I know you're safe.

And send a picture. For luck.

P.

# Chapter Ten

## London, England

Mere minutes after the air raid siren sounded, the new barrage began—this time made all the more terrifying without being hundreds of feet underground. The bombs fell distantly at first, then began to crawl nearer and nearer, until RueAnn wasn't sure if the Germans aimed with any efficiency, or if they flew inland until they found a likely spot, then dropped their deadly payload across the city.

It had been years since she'd prayed, years since she'd thought of God in any light at all other than through her father's interpretation. God, according to Jacob Boggs, was a vengeful being intent on destruction of anyone who might not follow his edicts to the letter.

But religion hadn't always been so fearsome in the Boggs' household. There had been a time, when Rue Ann was very little, when her mother had knelt with her each night, helping her to recite her evening prayers. During those times, her mother had spoken to God as if he truly were an absent, benevolent father.

It was to this God that RueAnn began to pray as the cacophony of noise assaulted her ears and the distant fires began to paint the walls with an eerie rosy glow.

At one point, Edna's eyes flickered open, glazed with confusion. Not sure how much she remembered of her situation, RueAnn stroked her cheek and shushed her as if she were a small child until her lashes fluttered shut again and she slept.

It was then that RueAnn began to weep—for herself, for Charlie, and yes, even for Edna who had been less than kind, but who now lay at the mercy of the "dreaded Hun" as she called them, with only a tester bed to protect her.

A pounding began. Closer, different somehow. It took several minutes for RueAnn to realize that it didn't come from the bombs or fires but...

Knocking?

As if on cue, she heard the tinny ring of the doorbell.

For a moment, she feared the Germans had begun the invasion in earnest, but then she realized that if paratroopers were storming London, they wouldn't ring the bell.

Scrambling from her hiding place, she hurried down the stairs, two at a time, and flung open the door.

The fellow standing on the stoop was as surprised to see her as she was to see him. But he quickly gathered himself together asking, "Excuse me, Miss. Could I possibly use your phone?"

Of all the words she had expected him to utter, these would never have occurred to her.

"Pardon?"

"Your phone. I need to call in and report."

RueAnn stared at him, her mouth agape, sure that this was an elaborate prank.

"Ma'am. Your phone."

She swept her hand wide even as outside the destruction continued. As the din of battle rang in her ears, the dour-faced gentleman strode to the phone, shouted instructions into the hand piece, then set it back in place.

He touched a finger to his metal helmet. "I may need to use it again, if it's not too much of a bother."

*Bother?* Having to wait in the ration line was a bother, cleaning up the sifting dust was a bother.

"If you don't mind my saying so, Miss, you should get to shelter while you still can. It doesn't look like this barrage is about to let up any time soon."

"I-I can't. My...my mother-in-law. I think she's had a stroke." She touched the man's arm, tugging him toward the staircase. "Could you help me? Please?"

The man looked toward the door, clearly torn, but he

allowed himself to be drawn upstairs.

"I put her under there," she said, pointing to the blankets she'd draped over the edge in case of flying glass.

The man dropped to his knees, then shimmied his upper body beneath the bed enough to examine Edna. When he rolled out again, his expression was grave.

"I think you're right."

"Can you call for help?"

He shook his head. "Even if I did, it's unlikely anything but fire services would be dispatched until the all clear. It's hell itself out there."

The noises from outside grew louder. The house shimmied and shook, threatening to be pulled apart at the very seams.

"There's a cubby under the stairs."

"You need a proper shelter," he said reluctantly.

"Please. I can't take her all the way to the Tube, but I can't leave her here alone."

The man finally relented. "I'll carry her downstairs until we can get her some help, at least. Then I've got to get back to my post."

Pushing and prodding, they managed to move the tester bed away. Then, after wrapping Edna in a blanket, he hefted her into his arms, staggering.

Gathering as many pillows as she could carry, RueAnn hurried down the stairs. At the last minute, she avoided the small space under the stairs. Headroom would be at a premium, as would a spot for RueAnn to care for Edna. So she made a beeline for the sturdy farmhouse-style table in the kitchen. She arranged a nest of pillows, then stood back as the stranger set Edna down. He panted, braced himself on one knee for a moment, then struggled to his feet.

"Once…I can find someone…an ambulance or something…I'll send them your way."

"Thank you." She walked with him to the door. "And feel free to use the phone whenever you'd like," she added, the words sounding ludicrous amid the din of the bombardment.

As the man hurried outside, RueAnn wondered if Edna

would chide her for allowing a stranger off the street to track up her floor.

But then, with a start, she realized that Edna could not offer her objections.

Staggering, she hurried to the kitchen, but just as she pushed through the door, the shudder of a nearby explosion threw RueAnn to her knees. Instinctively, she threw her arms over her head, squeezing her eyes shut as the ground trembled. Beside her, Edna cried out and RueAnn forced herself to scramble toward the woman.

Her mother-in-law's eyes were wide with panic.

"Shh, shh," RueAnn soothed. "You're safe now. A fellow—a soldier—helped me carry you downstairs."

An inarticulate noise emerged from Edna's throat. The right side of her face sagged like a candle left too long in the sun. Pitiful. Hideous.

Edna's left arm scrabbled across her body, reaching toward RueAnn, but when RueAnn tried to grasp Edna's hand, she batted it away, her agitation growing.

Then, suddenly, she squeezed her eyes closed, sobbing. Within moments, the unmistakable odor of urine filled the room.

Edna, her humiliation complete, turned her head away, her chest still convulsing with strangled sobs.

Stunned into silence, RueAnn scrambled for something to say, then realized that there was nothing she could offer to restore the older woman's dignity, so she reached out, squeezing her hand. Then, amid the scream of aircraft and the syncopated thunder of explosions, she made her way upstairs in search of fresh clothing for her mother-in-law.

Rifling through the woman's bureau, she found a clean housecoat that buttoned up the front. Unsure what to do for undergarments, she abandoned the idea altogether. There was no way that Edna could make her way to the loo, so she grabbed a stack of towels instead.

So intent was she on her errand, that when the window at the end of the hall suddenly shattered, she screamed, whirling, and dropping to the floor. She lay there for long moments, the sound of battle increased tenfold.

Standing, shouting obscenities at Germans, she feared that the bombing was only a precursor to the horrors that were to follow. She'd seen the newsreels of the Nazis invading Europe—tanks racing through open fields, marching soldiers, urban combat.

Dropping Edna's belongings near the top of the stairs, she rushed up to her own room. The door slammed against wall as she hurried to the bureau. Wrenching the bottom drawer free, she threw it on the floor, then reached inside to retrieve the velvet-wrapped parcel. Tearing the scraps of fabric away, she cradled the heavy revolver in her hands, the blue-black metal at once reassuring and abhorrent.

Slowly, she rose to her feet, the gun pulling heavily on her arm until she let it fall at her side, her thumb automatically stroking the hammer, her finger curled around the trigger.

Calmer, more determined, she took a deep breath and turned toward the stairs, knowing that this gun had killed before. If need be, it could do so again.

* * *

Susan huddled in the darkness of the public shelter, her knees drawn up and her arms wrapped around her legs. She couldn't stop shaking. Not because of the cold, but because of the noise. A frightful noise that brought everything back with a rush—the explosion at the Ironworks…the heat and wind of the burning docks…her father's hand in the rubble…

Tears gathered behind her eyes and her shoulders shook with silent sobs as she tried to shrink further into the shadows. She mustn't worry her mother. Millicent Blunt had been devastated when she'd heard the news. Susan had watched as her mother seemed to deflate before her very eyes, becoming somehow older and infinitely more weary in the space of a heartbeat. Yet, she'd refused to cry, refused to shed a tear in front of the younger children. She'd merely drawn them all close, whispering that they would all continue to do their best. For Daddy's sake.

Suddenly a hand touched her shoulder and Susan started, her head rearing up. But it was only Sara. Sara, who understood her in a way that no other person ever could.

Sinking onto the ground beside her, Sara wrapped them both in a blanket, then drew Susan's head down onto her shoulder.

"Shh," she whispered, her own eyes bruised and hurt. "I know...I know..."

Then, in a way that only close sisters can, she wrapped her arms around Susan's shoulders and rocked her from side to side as if she were a child in need of soothing. And in those long moments, as they huddled together as they used to do in the nursery when a fierce storm woke them from their beds, Sara was the stronger twin. Susan's rock. Her foundation in the buffeting winds.

Alone, they were lost,

But together, they would find a way to survive even this.


## Rouen, France


He was hot, so hot. His body radiated warmth with the same ferocity of desert sand seething under the midday sun. But just when he felt he could bear it no longer, a coolness touched his brow. His cheeks. Then a dribble of moisture entered his parched mouth.

Yes...*yes*...

"Shh..."

The sound melted out of the darkness. A hand touched his forehead when he tried to lift himself toward the saving drops of water.

"Lie still...lie still..."

His eyes flickered—and for a moment, he panicked when the darkness enveloped him. Then, he began to pick out shades of gray that slowly resolved themselves into shapes.

A face.

Above him, a woman smiled.

Squinting, he thought, just for a moment that he knew her. Coffee-colored eyes. Dark, dark hair.

"RueAnn?" The word tasted sweet on his tongue. Familiar. Grounding him when he thought he might float away.

But then, blinking, the face shifted again, settling into the unfamiliar planes of a delicately boned stranger with red gold hair.

Her eyes were gentle. But they were gray. Even in the shadows, he could see they were gray.

"No," she soothed.

She placed a wet cloth against his face again, and he sighed as the dampness drew some of the heat from his body. Then, settling it on his forehead, she whispered, "Would you care for more to drink?"

His nod was jerky, his body recalcitrant in obeying his commands.

Sliding a hand under his head, she set a cup to his lips.

"Slowly now. I spent a great deal of time stitching you up. I don't want you coughing and spoiling my handiwork."

He drank greedily. Thirsty. So thirsty.

But after only a few swallows, she removed the cup.

"We'll take things slowly, yes? A little at a time."

Charlie closed his eyes, panting, damning the way that so small an exertion had taxed him beyond measure. Pain radiated through his body. A searing, omnipresent pain.

But different somehow.

For a moment, his stomach lurched. The water that he'd so greedily consumed threatened to come right back up.

The cloth was replaced with a cool one, giving him something to focus on other than the nausea, until soon, his gut spasmed. Then relaxed.

"Sleep," the woman whispered. A velvet command.

His mind slipped and skidded, following fantastical threads of thought like a rabbit darting into the underbrush, running this way and that. And it was only as the last shreds of consciousness flitted away that a tiny, coherent part of him realized that the woman who bent over him spoke English.

## London, England

RueAnn woke with a start.

Silence. Blessed, blessed silence.

Twisting from her nest of blankets next to Edna, she quickly felt the woman's cheek, then shuddered in relief when she found it warm to the touch.

She'd survived the night.

They'd *both* survived the night.

Lying on her back, RueAnn flung an arm over her eyes. She was tired, so tired. She didn't know how long she'd cowered under the table as the world raged beyond their doors. Where the barrage had first filled her with an unmistakable fear, sucking her ability to move or even think, she'd become so absorbed with caring for Edna that her terror had soon been swamped by anger at the Germans, at her circumstances, at Charlie for his betrayal.

But then, as the hours and the air raid continued unabated, her emotions had consumed themselves and her energy had drained away, leaving her filled with a black despair. It was clear that the Germans meant to either bomb them into submission or oblivion. And there was nothing, *nothing*, that RueAnn could do to stop it.

Crawling from beneath the table, RueAnn pushed herself to her feet and staggered to the back door. As she stepped outside, a whine of the all-clear filled the late morning air.

Today, the air was thick with storm clouds.

No.

Not clouds.

Smoke.

Smoke that roiled and turned in upon itself, tainting the breeze with its acrid stench. And where she'd thought she'd been greeted with silence, her senses began to awaken, bit by bit, until she realized that she was surrounded with noises of a different kind—the clamor of bells, shouts, the low roar of distant fires.

Breathing deeply, RueAnn closed her eyes, squeezing them

tighter, tighter still, then opening them again, praying that she was in the midst of a nightmare from which she could awaken. But just as she feared, when her gaze latched onto a wounded barrage balloon that sagged and twisted in the breeze, bumping carelessly into chimneys and knocking roof tiles free as it continued its death throes, she realized this was her reality now.

Turning back to the house, RueAnn hurried to the telephone in the front hall. Lifting the receiver, she prayed that she could somehow rouse some help for her mother-in-law.

But the line was dead.

She dodged back into the kitchen, assuring herself that Edna was still sleeping. Then she ran to the front door. She needed to find a policeman or a member of the fire brigade—someone, *anyone*—who could tell her where she could get a doctor.

Blindly, she ran down to the end of the walk and through the gate just as straggling group of people began to trudge from the entrance of the nearest shelter, their arms heaped with pillows and bedclothes.

RueAnn shuddered in relief when she recognized two blonde sisters in the midst of the first group. She ran toward them, stumbling on stray bits of masonry that had been thrown into the lane. She'd gone scarcely half a block, before she saw Susan touch her sister's arm and point in RueAnn's direction.

"Please!" RueAnn gasped as she approached. "Please, I need help."

Alarmed, Susan handed an armload of blankets to a tall boy at her side. "What's wrong?"

"Edna. She's had a stroke."

Sara handed her own load of bedclothes to the young children at her side, a little girl with red curls and a skinny, knob-kneed boy of about ten.

A thin, graying woman of about fifty asked, "Have you tried calling—"

"The phone isn't working."

Before RueAnn could say another word, the woman took charge. "Margaret, Michael, take our things back to the house. I want you to fold them neatly and stack them by the front door in case we need them again. Then hurry into the kitchen, slice the bread as thin as you can, and make everyone some sandwiches. Can you do that, my darlings?"

They nodded, wide-eyed.

"Run along, then."

"Really, mother. Sandwiches?" Sara asked.

"It will keep them busy." Mrs. Blunt turned to the gangly teenager. "Phillip, run and fetch Dr. Plymsome. If he can't come right away, make sure he understands the urgency of the situation. Make him promise to be here as soon as he can."

"Yes, Mum."

He handed his own armful of blankets back to Sara.

"Hurry, dear. Hurry!"

As he ran in the opposite direction, Mrs. Blunt took RueAnn's hand. "Come along, RueAnn. Let's see what we can do in the meantime."

◦ ◦ ◦

In the end, there was little more that the women could do to help Edna than RueAnn had already done. Although Edna would have been more comfortable upon a bed, they feared that another air raid might leave her vulnerable again. So with the twins' help, they carried the mattress from RueAnn's cot downstairs to the kitchen and set it on the floor. Millicent Blunt sent Susan scurrying back to their own house, where she unearthed a rubber sheet from the depths of a closet in the nursery. After dressing the mattress with clean linens, the rubber sheet, then a layer of towels, they carefully lifted Edna onto the makeshift bed and covered her with a blanket.

"There, there, now, my dearie. You rest. We've got things well in hand. The doctor has been summoned, and soon you'll be right as rain. You'll see!"

A tear trickled from the corner of Edna's eye, wriggling its way down her cheek and Millicent clucked at her, tucking the blankets tightly under her chin.

"Have you got any meat rations left?" Millicent asked

RueAnn as Edna's lashes fluttered, and the ferocious grip of her good hand eased around the edge of the covers.

"N-no."

"How about vegetables from the garden? We'll make some broth for her. She'll need something nourishing to keep her strength up once she wakes again."

"I'll get it, Mum," Susan said.

Millicent made a shooing motion in RueAnn's direction. "Go with her, dear. Sara and I can see to sweeping up the dirt and plaster."

The back door burst open and Phillip stumbled in, out of breath. "Dr. Plymsome…will be here as…soon as he can. But there's a queue of walking wounded outside his surgery nearly a half-block long. It could be some…time."

He pressed a hand to his side.

"Very well." Millicent nodded. "It's not the first time in history we women have been left to care for one of our own without the help of a doctor, and I don't suppose it will be the last." She offered RueAnn an encouraging wink. "We'll simply muddle through on our own until that meddling old fool can see fit to make an appearance."

* * *

Two days. It took two days before Dr. Plymsome was able to examine Edna Tolliver. But RueAnn could not fault the man. The Germans had left very little time for any of them to carry out normal business. Instead, the raids came hard and fast upon one another, over and over again, until day bled into night, night into day, relieved only by those intermittent hours of calm when London's beleaguered citizens were able to stagger from the shelters and go about their business.

Even RueAnn was able to settle into a routine of sorts. When Louise was able to make her way through the damaged streets to work, RueAnn would make a round of the shops, standing in endless lines, carefully hoarding her ration coupons for that special something that might help Edna regain her strength—a marrow bone for broth, a precious bit of sugar, a pot of jam traded with a neighbor for the week's ration of butter, and a basket of onions.

But weaving through her attempts to help her mother-in-law was a grinding weariness from too little sleep, worry, and anger.

She wasn't the only person stumbling through her days bleary-eyed and exhausted. When she made her way into town, RueAnn recognized that same expression on her fellow Londoners as well as a steely chord of determination. If Chancellor Hitler meant to pound them into submission, he was not succeeding, because as soon as the all-clear sounded again, the streets would grow crowded with shoppers and businessmen. The parks would bristle with mothers pushing prams and old folks sunning themselves.

Life would go on.

When Dr. Plymsome emerged from the kitchen into the sunshine of the back yard, RueAnn turned.

If she'd thought her weariness was profound, the doctor's must be even more so. Deep lines etched the grooves on either side of his mouth and his skin hosted a gray pallor. RueAnn couldn't imagine the demands placed on him since the raids had begun over London. There were few doctors left in the city. Most had been absorbed into the military.

Nevertheless, he managed to offer her a warm smile.

"You've taken very good care of her, RueAnn."

"I've had help," she replied.

"So I see." He tugged the stethoscope from his neck and tucked it into his bag. "As feared, Edna has had a stroke, but the worst of it appears to have passed. I won't sugarcoat things—" his eyes twinkled "—I couldn't afford the rations even if I wanted to."

She smiled at the weak attempt of humor.

"For now, give her lots of fluids, broths, sweet tea when you can manage it. Some of the loss she's suffered is profound—speech, mobility—all of it primarily on her right side. I can't give you a long-term prognosis, just yet. These things are tricky. By rights, she should be in a hospital, but with bed space at a premium and supplies scarce…" He shrugged, sighing. "She's probably in better hands here than in an understaffed clinic."

He patted her arm reassuringly. "I'll return in a few days. In the meantime, I've left some medicines on the kitchen counter as well as a list of instructions. If you have any problems—or her condition takes a turn for the worse—don't hesitate to send Phillip with a message."

"Thank you."

"No, dear. Thank you. It's a remarkable thing you're doing, keeping home and hearth going in Edna's time of need. Not many women would have stayed by a new mother-in-law's side during such trying times."

He patted her hand again, moving to say goodbye to the Blunts, leaving RueAnn rooted with guilt.

If only he knew. If Charlie had met her at the train. Or if RueAnn had followed through with her plans to search Charlie's room that first night. If she'd managed to find the letters he'd stolen from her…

She might not have stayed long enough to see bombs fall on London, let alone come to the aid of Edna Tolliver.

• • •

"Millicent. Susan."

Dr. Plymsome offered them both a warm smile.

"I have other patients waiting, but I believe I can safely say that I'm leaving Edna in good hands."

Millicent tipped her chin in RueAnn's direction. "She's a good girl, that one. She has a level head on her shoulders. I think, if the Germans will cooperate, we can manage."

"And you, Millicent. How are you feeling?"

She offered him the same disapproval that she shot Michael on those occasions when she'd caught him with his hand in the biscuit tin.

"You've been talking out of turn," she accused the older man. "Thanks to you, my entire family thinks that I should be wrapped in cotton wool."

He chuckled. "In my defense, I thought that you would have communicated your condition to your children."

"I have no... *condition* that's worth worrying about. As you may have noticed, there is a war on—a situation has resulted in a few more stresses in my life, which—"

"How about if we check the extent of these...stresses?" the doctor interrupted smoothly.

"I beg your pardon?"

"Since I am already here, I'd like to check you over. Briefly. To see the extent of your...willingness to cooperate with my instructions."

Her cheeks flamed. "I don't think it's necessary to—"

"Perhaps. Perhaps not. But I'm not leaving until I've had a listen to your heart and checked your blood pressure."

"But—"

"I'm a busy man, Millicent. Far too busy to argue." He waved in the direction of the Blunt household.

"I don't think—"

"Millicent, my dear, dear friend. I know you want to keep a brave front with your children nearby. But your son told me that your husband was one of those killed in the first wave. I just want to assure myself that the shock hasn't been too much for you."

Millicent's face suddenly crumpled, her body sagging as if someone had cut the strings to a marionette. Wrapping his arm around her waist, Dr. Plymsome led her through the gap in the hedge.

For long moments Susan battled with her own emotions. The loss of their father had been devastating, leaving their family like a rudderless ship floundering in unfriendly seas. And with so many dead, dying, the funeral homes had been overwhelmed. Without service or ceremony, it was so easy to believe that her father wasn't really gone. That he could burst through the door and demand his supper.

Rushing through the gap in the privet, she waited until Dr. Plymsome emerged.

"Will you walk with me?" he asked without preamble.

She fell into step as he strode back in the direction of his clinic.

"Do you have the means to evacuate the city?"

The question was so unexpected, she stumbled traversing a crack in the sidewalk.

"I-I…My uncle extended an invitation for the little ones to live with him in Canada."

He nodded, then stopped, heaving a tired sigh. "With so little time at my disposal, I must be blunt, Susan." His eyes were sad. "Your mother is unwell and the medicines are not having the anticipated effect. Moreover, after the past few days, I fear we're in this war for the long haul."

He glanced up at the barrage balloons wallowing in a cloudless sky as if he expected to see the shadow of bombers at any moment. "Whether the air raids continue or, God forbid, an invasion occurs, the stresses involved will be overwhelming. And your mother will not survive them. The medicines she takes will soon be in short supply. If, as you say, you have the opportunity to get her to safety, I would do so immediately."

He held up a hand when Susan would have argued. "I have no illusions that your mother will go willingly. She's a stubborn woman. Always has been." He squeezed her arm, his smile sad. "If you can accept the advice of a meddling old fool, avoid telling her that we've had this little chat. Find a compelling reason for your mother to leave of her own volition. Something that will involve the wee ones, if need be. But please, get her to go."

Even as Dr. Plymsome finished speaking, the low growl of the warning siren began, winding tighter and tighter until it reached its high-pitch scream.

With one last squeeze of her arm, the doctor hurried away while around her, shopkeepers and mothers, children and businessmen began shuffling wearily toward the nearest shelter.

Turning resolutely toward home, Susan damned the Germans yet again. They'd murdered her father.

And now, they were bent on killing her mother as well.

Sweetheart,

I miss you. I miss you so much that sometimes I don't know how I can go another minute without seeing you. I still haven't received any letters and after hearing about the raids on London, I can understand why.

I want you to know that I love you. Don't be upset with me for making such a bold statement when we really don't know each other very well. But in the last few weeks, I feel like I've lived a thousand lifetimes. I've learned that there may never be another chance to say what one feels, so say it now.

I love you. I love the way you made me feel when I was with you. I love the hope you give me when I think I can't go on.

You are so beautiful. Your eyes, your lips. The way you tip your head to the side when you are considering something I've said. Dancing with you was like dancing with an angel.

Don't give up, sweetheart. I know things are tough for you right now. I know that you must be frightened. If I could be there, I would. I would take you in my arms and hold you until the world melted away and there were only the two of us.

Please write as soon as you can so that I know you're well and safe.

And send me a picture.

For luck.

P.

# Chapter Eleven

As the raids continued with unrelenting force day after day, night after night, Susan stumbled through the hours, moving with a single goal: to get her mother, Michael, and Margaret to safety.

It took time to make the arrangements—telegrams to Uncle Joe, wrangling with ticket offices. And through it all, she balanced the preparations with the grim details surrounding her father's funeral.

But as the Blunts huddled around his open grave, the reality of his death became so unbearable, Susan feared that her mother would fade completely into her grief and disappear. So Susan stepped up the timetable for departure, calling in favors from her father's cronies, friends, fellow church members, until she managed to finagle three tickets on board a ship called the *S.S. City of Benares* which had already been slated to evacuate hundreds of children and their volunteer chaperones to Canada.

At first, it had been Susan's plan to send Phillip to Canada as well. She'd been sure that her mother would consider him too young to stay behind. But since there were only three tickets and it had been imperative that Millicent make the trip, Susan and Sara had convinced their mother that Phillip would be fine with them. He could continue his schooling during the day and get a job during the afternoons. Then, by next summer, their finances would probably be sorted out enough that the rest of the Blunt children could follow.

As they waited at Victoria Station, it seemed all of London was determined to leave the city before the Germans arrived again. Although it was only a little after seven in the morning, the platform was packed with women, children, and the elderly intent on somewhere—anywhere—safer than Hitler's prime target.

Susan wrapped her arms around her body, watching the little clumps of families saying their goodbyes. Despite the heat, most of the youngsters wore jackets, hats, and sturdy shoes and gripped the single suitcase they were allowed to bring. Tags with their names and destinations printed on them had been pinned to their chests as if they were bizarre parcels about to be mailed. Stern, middle aged women with clipboards made their way from group to group, ticking off new arrivals and encouraging parents to say their goodbyes and leave.

Only days ago, Millicent Blunt had abruptly changed her mind about splitting up the family, and Susan had worried that she wouldn't be able to convince her mother to make the trip to Canada for any reason whatsoever. But when a downed German Dornier had crashed into an apartment house less than four blocks from their home, killing four children, Susan had seen the first chink in her mother's armor.

"Mum, are you sure you wouldn't like to find something to eat? There's still time before they'll begin boarding the train. You're looking a little peaked."

Millicent pasted a brilliant smile on her lips, but the forced nature of the grimace made her pallor all the more pronounced.

"Don't fuss. I'm just a little tired. Once I'm on board, the sea air will do me good. I'll have nothing to do for days but sit and stare at the waves. I'll be such a lady of leisure, your Uncle Joe won't even recognize me." She took Susan's hands, squeezing them. "I should take you and Sara with us. It's not fair that you'll be left behind."

"You know you can't do that, Mum." Not only did she and Sara have responsibilities at work, but unspoken and large as an elephant between them was the issue of money. Until Walter Blunt's pensions and insurances could be sorted out, it would take everything Sara, Susan, and Phillip could scrape together to keep the household afloat.

"I should stay," Millicent insisted suddenly, standing as if she meant to march from the railway station.

Sara quickly tugged her back onto the bench. "No, Mum.

We've been through all this. It's imperative that we get the younger children to safety. You wouldn't want them to make the trip alone."

"And Uncle Joe is counting on your help once you get to Prince Edward Island."

Millicent's eyes filled with tears. "I don't know what I would do without you girls."

Susan fiercely fought the moisture that gathered in her own eyes. There was a tug at her skirts and she looked down at Margaret.

"Don't cry, Susan," her little sister whispered. "I know you'll be lonely, but I left you a present. I put Wuzzy on your bed so he can kiss you goodnight instead of me doing it."

The statement nearly brought Susan to her knees. Her little sister was sacrificing her most prized possession to comfort *her*.

Kneeling, Susan pulled her close for a tight hug. "Thank you, Magpie. That was so kind of you. But I think, after a week or two, that I'll pop Wuzzy in the post. You'll need him too, I think."

Margaret sagged against Susan in relief. "Do you promise?"

"I promise."

* * *

Days and nights blended together for RueAnn. Her world shrunk to the kitchen, her mother-in-law's health, and the nest of blankets and pillows beneath the table.

Hour after hour, day, night, the raids continued, intermittent with brief periods of calm when the beleaguered inhabitants would crawl from their hidey-holes and pray that this time the quiet would last for more than a few hours.

For RueAnn, the raids were all the more terrifying since she was essentially trapped at her mother-in-law's side. Edna remained weak, frightened, and often confused, a fractious child trapped in a defective aging body.

Knowing that lying on the floor beneath the table would do Edna no good in the long run, she enlisted the help of the Blunt sisters and their brother Phillip to move a good portion of the dining room furniture to the attic and replace it with the narrow cot from the garret room. The windows were boarded up to prevent flying glass. RueAnn brought down the bedside table from Edna's quarters as well as a few personal items in an effort to make the space more cheery, then moved her own belongings into Charlie's room.

Seeking any diversion possible during the bombardments, RueAnn pushed and tugged the cabinet radio from the parlor into the corner of Edna's new room so that they could listen to music, news, and RueAnn's favorite program, Edward R. Murrow's *London at Night*. Searching the house, RueAnn had collected a stack of books, foregoing Edna's history tomes for lighter novels such as her own favorite, *Jane Eyre*. She sang, played Benny Goodman on the Victrola, danced, anything to draw Edna's mind away from the gloom of war.

But even as Edna grew a little calmer, RueAnn felt her desperation mount. Parts of London might have been leveled and many of the streets were impassible save for a swathe down the road where the bulldozers had come through to push away the rubble, but the mail arrived like clockwork. The gas bill had arrived yesterday morning, and she had no illusions that others would soon follow. Even without the household expenses to consider, the lines at the grocer's were growing longer and prices rose as shortages increased. RueAnn had no money of her own to draw from and no way of knowing how Edna had paid for such things as electricity and gas. At the moment, they were living off tins from the larder and the garden—which meant that RueAnn needed to find work. Immediately. But even that solution led to more obstacles. Who would care for Edna while she was out of the house?

One afternoon, the space between raids stretched to hours—*hours*—and RueAnn escaped the stuffiness of the house to sit on the front stoop where the sun could melt into her skin and ease away the stress that pulled the muscles of her face and shoulders into painful knots. As she watched, a lorry lumbered down the street and drew to a halt at the curb.

Pushing herself to her feet, she saw a burly driver emerge. Referring to a clipboard, he glanced at the numbers bolted above the door, then strode toward her.

"Mrs. Tolliver?"

"Yes."

The name *Thomas* had been embroidered over the man's left pocket and a peaked hat shielded his eyes.

"I've got a delivery." He extended the clipboard. "Sign here."

RueAnn quickly scrawled her name.

"Where would you like me to unload the Anderson?"

RueAnn shrugged, at a loss as to what an "Anderson" might be. But since it would be too difficult to explain that the delivery was meant for the elder Mrs. Tolliver, she waved a hand toward the house. "I-I don't know. The front parlor, I suppose."

The man blinked, clearly taken aback. "You're joking, right?"

To her relief, RueAnn heard Louise approach from behind.

"What is it?" she asked, wiping her hands with a towel.

"He says he's delivering an…Anderson?"

Louise's face broke into a wide smile. "Wonderful! Take it to the back garden, please." She pointed to the side of the house. "The gate is just through there."

The man touched the bill of his hat. "Thank you, Mum," he said with evident relief, casting a pitying glance at RueAnn before turning on his heel and walking briskly to the truck waiting at the curb.

As he shouted directions to his helper, RueAnn asked Louise, "What exactly is an…Anderson?"

Louise's eyes sparkled in delight. "Our own personal bomb shelter."

RueAnn's eyes widened. "Really?"

"Really. Edna ordered it months ago. Thank heavens it's come at last."

The sight of the delivery truck gathered the attention of the twins from next door as well as their brother Phillip.

"New furniture?" Sara asked.

"No, an Anderson shelter."

Like children following an organ grinder, they traipsed into the back garden to watch the deliverymen unload sheets of corrugated metal and boxes of hardware. Then, after handing them a bulky envelope, he tugged at the brim of his cap and he and his assistant disappeared.

As RueAnn ripped open the envelope, Louise and the Blunts gathered around her to peer over her shoulder as she rifled through the pages of instructions and schematic drawings.

"Oh, dear," Susan sighed.

RueAnn's gaze skipped from the pieces of metal lying on the grass to the papers she held in her hands. "How on earth are we supposed to put the thing together?"

Even Louise's enthusiasm grew dim. But she tucked the dishcloth into the pocket of her apron and began rolling up the sleeves to her dress. "I suppose it's much like eating an elephant."

RueAnn's brows rose questioningly.

"One bite at a time." Louise disappeared into the kitchen for a moment, then returned with her hands full—a dressmaker's tape measure, a spool of string, and a handful of broken lathe strips which they used to brace plants in the garden.

"First things first. We've got to decide exactly where to put the Anderson, then measure the proper dimensions and mark it on the grass.

Plotting out the location for the shelter proved to be the easiest portion of their task. When they discovered that the building would have to be sunk into the ground, they realized that the shelter would involve a good deal more work than they had originally anticipated.

With only two shovels between the pair of families, work moved slowly. Phillip, of course, was equal to the task. But since the ground was wet and thick with clay, their progress slowed considerably.

Soon, their enthusiasm dimmed and their faces grew flushed, streaked with sweat and grime. Leaning wearily against a crate, they greedily drank tea and wolfed down sandwiches Louise had prepared for their lunch.

"At this rate we'll be lucky if we finish the thing before the war's over," Sara said morosely. In the hours they'd been working, they'd managed to carve out a respectable square, and haul away the sod, but the instructions stated that the shelter should ideally be placed four feet below the surface. They'd barely managed to dig down six inches.

"I could get some of my mates to come 'round sometime," Phillip said from where he'd sprawled on his back in the grass. "But right now, they're busy with the Home Guard."

"The Home Guard!" Susan exclaimed. "There isn't a one of them old enough to be in the Home Guard."

Phillip cut his sister a quelling glance. "They aren't so particular about a person's age now that bombs are dropping on London. I've been thinking of joining up myself."

Sara grimaced. "You'll do no such thing. A right lot of good any of them will do if the Germans do invade. A bunch of old men and boys armed with broomstick handles and billy-clubs won't have much effect against rifles and tanks."

"You'd be surprised what the Home Guard has got up its sleeve should they need it."

"I'm not discounting them completely. They're well intended. But what we really need are a couple of platoons of..." Sara stopped in mid-sentence. "What time is it?"

RueAnn glanced at her watch. "Nearly six."

With a squeal, Sara jumped to her feet. "I've got a scathing idea!"

She rushed to the garden hose where she quickly washed her hands and face, then smoothed her hair.

"Hurry! Lipstick. Does anyone have lipstick!"

Startled, Louise drew a small tube from the pocket of her apron.

"Fabulous!" Sara used the reflection of the windows in the back door to apply the make-up, then handed it back to Louise. "I'll be back in a few minutes."

"Where are you going?" Susan demanded.

"Just to the bus stop. There's a new group of Royal Engineers training in the city and a half dozen of them are billeted down the block. They usually meet at the Duck and Dandy Pub about this time. If I can intercept them..."

She hurried toward the garden gate, unfastening the top two buttons to her blouse as she went.

"What on earth?" RueAnn breathed as Sara disappeared in a whirlwind.

"There's no sense even asking," Susan said as she stood and wearily picked up the shovel again. "Sara's brain works in its own convoluted fashion and there's no telling what scheme she's devised. But I long ago learned that if she announces she has a 'scathing idea,' it's best to stay out of her way."

The words were said with such a depth of feeling that RueAnn's brows rose questioningly. But Susan flicked a glance at her brother and imperceptibly shook her head.

"Let's just say, that as children, such a pronouncement usually led to trouble."

They didn't have long to wait the outcome of Sara's most recent scheme, because, within minutes, she returned, a half dozen off-duty soldiers trailing behind her. She'd already explained their predicament and outlined the proposed shelter. Before RueAnn quite knew what had happened, the boisterous men had stripped down to their shirtsleeves, rounded up more shovels and tools from the neighbors, and were hard at work building the bomb shelter in the back garden.

Suddenly displaced, RueAnn and the other women moved to the kitchen where they gathered together their meager foodstuffs for refreshments. As she made her way among the men, offering them tea and fresh vegetable sandwiches, the men passed around the hat, but she refused to take their money after all they were doing for her.

But as they returned to their tasks, she was struck with her own "scathing" idea.

London was teeming with military personnel and families displaced by the air raids, while she and Edna rattled around in a house too big for them both.

As if her thoughts were a grass fire doused with fresh fuel, the idea began to grow in size and intensity. She could move her own bed into the dining room with Edna. That would free up the maid's room in the attic, Charlie's room and Edna's—

and who knew what lay behind the locked doors of the upper rooms? Space would be at a premium, but with a little planning, it could work. The garden was large enough for now, and come spring she could plant more. They would even have the Anderson, which could only improve her chances of finding boarders, couldn't it?

For the first time in days, RueAnn began to feel a faint glimmer of hope. So much so, that when the air raid siren began and the Blunts and the engineers disappeared for the public shelters, RueAnn sat on the floor beside Edna's cot. Hunched over a piece of cardboard she used a pen and ink set she'd found in Charlie's room to carefully print a placard for the window.

*Rooms To Let.*

. . .

"You're sure you want to take lodgers?" Susan asked, leaning her hips against the counter.

"It's the only real answer I've got. If I provide room and board, I can stay home with Edna and still meet the challenge of paying the bills."

"How many rooms do you have?"

"There's two on the floor above us," RueAnn said. "Charlie's could take two small beds if a couple of people wanted to share it. Edna's is a little larger, with the tester bed."

"And the floor above that? You should have three rooms there if the house is identical to our own."

"There are three doors, but they're locked. I haven't been able to find a key anywhere."

Susan's eyes suddenly twinkled. "Ahh. In that respect, I can help you."

She withdrew a hairpin from the braids she'd looped around the crown of her head. "Let's go look."

They tramped up the stairs together until they reached the floor just below RueAnn's original garret room. Grinning, Susan deftly slid the hairpin into the keyhole and twisted. In mere seconds, the lock clicked.

"Good gracious. How'd you learn to do that?"

Susan laughed. "I have five siblings." Twisting the knob, she swung the door wide. "Voilà!"

They both stepped into what must have once been a nursery. A disassembled cot leaned against the far wall and carefully labeled boxes containing clothing and Christmas decorations had been stacked around the edges.

"This will make a nice room," Susan said thoughtfully. "It shouldn't be too hard to scrounge up a bed and mattress. We might even have one tucked under the rafters next door."

They moved to the next room where Susan again employed her unique talent for picking locks. This room was smaller, little more than a closet, really.

"I suppose you could squeeze a cot and a dresser in here, but not much more," Susan said. "But you'd still be able to rent it out provided your guests are allowed to use the sitting room downstairs."

They moved to the last room. This time, the latch proved to be more recalcitrant than the others. It took several more minutes before Susan managed to unlock it.

As the door swung wide, the girls were suddenly speechless. The bedroom was pristine. No dust, no cobwebs, no chaos. Frilly white Pricilla curtains hung at the windows, delicate birds-eye maple furniture was graced with ruffled pillows, while a flounced canopy bed dominated the room. Everything was pink and white—from the scatter rugs to the wallpaper. A baby doll lay in the place of honor next to the pillows while a huge antique dollhouse waited just below the window.

"Charlie has a sister?" RueAnn breathed.

"No, I…" Susan shook her head. "Charlie and his mother have lived next to us for as long as I can remember. I always assumed he was an only child."

RueAnn moved to the bureau to the single framed photo. She recognized a younger Edna, her hair piled onto the top of her head with an elaborate upsweep. In her arms sat a little girl with a head full of curls held back by a large bow. There was a brightness to her eyes, a ready smile on her lips. And there… down in the lower corner, beneath the glass, was a lock of blonde hair held together with a faded pink ribbon. Scrawled faintly in pencil was the name Francine.

"Edna had a daughter," RueAnn said, her thumb stroking the line of the little girl's cheek. Then she looked around the room which had been so lovingly maintained all these years later. The fact that it awaited the arrival of a little girl who would obviously never return bespoke a tenderness and longing in Edna that RueAnn never would have imagined.

Susan peered at the image over RueAnn's shoulder. "Edna was always so protective of Charlie when he was little. I remember that her constant hovering used to drive him mad. She would tell him when to wear his overshoes, how to fasten his scarf, what to eat, when to breathe." She turned to study the room yet again.

So cautious that when an unknown woman from America stole her son and married him after a mere day's acquaintance, Edna must have been on her guard even more.

Setting the frame back on the bureau, RueAnn followed Susan into the hall, closing the door behind her.

"Will you rent out that bedroom?" Susan asked, her voice hushed.

RueAnn shook her head. "I don't know." She stared at the closed panels. "I wish I knew what had happened."

But even as the words crossed her lips, she wasn't sure if they were true. To know Edna's secrets felt too much like a betrayal of her privacy.

Just as Charlie had betrayed hers.

Again, her stomach gnawed at her, but this time the anger she'd felt since realizing Charlie had taken her letters was duller. So much had happened since she'd first arrived in England. The self-righteous indignation had eased to an ever-present ache. And she realized now, that as much as she'd feared Charlie might read her letters and thereby be given a glimpse into her hungry soul, what had hurt her most had been the fact that, having read them, he hadn't bothered to contact her. Her pain had not even been worthy of a response.

*Unless he hadn't read them.*

But he must have read them. She'd searched his room. They weren't there. The only evidence of her presence in his life had been the Cracker Jack compass he'd placed in a box of cufflinks. The closest thing she'd found to an envelope had been stranger still, one holding a list of names and sheaves of legal documents—most of them written in French. The papers had been hidden, taped to the back of his bureau mirror. She wouldn't have found them at all if her comb hadn't fallen behind the dresser and she'd been forced to move the piece of furniture to retrieve it.

So he must have taken her letters with him.

Or thrown them away.

*No. He wouldn't have done that. He couldn't.*

Because the only thing worse than Charlie's having read them, would be his having read them and thrown them away with utter disregard.

## Rouen, France

Charlie woke to utter stillness. Lifting a hand to his shoulder, he hissed when he touched a thick bandage.

A noise alerted him, and he tipped his head just as a woman with coppery braids coiled at her nape made her way down a narrow staircase from a trap door overhead. She carried a tray which she set on an overturned crate next to his bed, then settled onto the packed earthen floor. Seeing the way he probed gingerly at the bandages, she said, "It is healing nicely."

"I don't remember…"

"Good. Because it took some time to get the bullet out of your shoulder."

He grimaced, grateful that he'd passed out.

"I've brought you some broth."

Charlie eased into a sitting position, bracing his back against the rough wall. As he did so, he became acutely aware of the fact that he was naked beneath the sheets. Self-conscious, he pulled the sheet more tightly against his waist.

She must have sensed the gist of his thoughts because she said, "Your clothes were beyond repair, I fear." She gestured to a neat pile on a nearby chair. "I managed to find you new ones. With luck, they'll fit."

"Where did you get them?"

"I stole them," she said matter-of-factly. Lifting a bowl and spoon, she scooped up a portion of soup and held it in front of his mouth. "Eat."

Charlie automatically obeyed, his stomach growling. The broth was simple, rich with vegetables and herbs. He honestly couldn't remember anything tasting so good.

"How long…"

"You've been with me nearly two weeks now."

He took another swallow of soup, his brow furrowing as he tried to remember.

"Where…"

"I found you along the side of the road."

"Rex?"

Her dark eyes grew sad. "The man who was running?"

He nodded.

"The Germans killed him. He made the mistake of stumbling into the same area where they'd had skirmishes with the Resistance earlier in the day. I believe he was mistaken for one of them."

Charlie closed his eyes, suddenly remembering—the darting shape, the sound of gunfire, the laughter as the Germans threw Rex's body into a truck.

The soup heaved in his stomach before he was finally able to swallow against the nausea.

The woman waited patiently until he looked at her again. Then she resumed feeding him.

"Why—" He couldn't utter more than single syllables. His voice emerged like the squeak of a rusty hinge.

She studied him, gauging his character with that long,

piercing look.

"When I found you, there was something…not quite right about your uniform." She needlessly stirred the soup. "When you began to mutter in English, I knew you were British."

Charlie leaned his head back against the wall, trying to remember more details from that night, what he'd said to betray himself.

"What…did I say?"

This time, it was her turn to look away. "You called out a name. RueAnn."

He swore softly under his breath.

"In my experience, the dying call out one of two names. Either that of their mothers…or their sweethearts."

She waited until he finally satisfied her curiosity. "My wife."

"Ahh. It is as I suspected." She held out the spoon to him again. "You have been parted for a long time?"

Charlie wondered what she would say if he told her the truth. That he'd married his wife after a single day of knowing her, that the ceremony had been attended by her father and his shotgun…

And that Charlie had all but abandoned her.

"More than a year," he said gruffly.

She nodded, her eyes brimming with a wealth of understanding, but when she didn't explain herself, he didn't press.

"You miss her?" she asked softly, staring down into the bowl of broth.

"Yes."

"Then it is fortunate that you were not found by the Germans," she said with sudden brightness. But her cheerfulness was forced around the aching chord of loneliness he saw in her own eyes. Instantly, he sensed that he wasn't the only one to have been parted from loved ones by the war.

When she would have scooped another bit of soup into his mouth, he shook his head, turning away.

"You are making great progress," she said as she set the tray on a nearby table. "At first, I feared the infection, but things have begun to heal."

He moved gingerly, testing the soreness at his hip.

"When you are feeling a little stronger, you might want to come upstairs when I am home. As long as you make no noises that might arouse my neighbor's suspicions. While I am at work, you will need to stay down here. It will be safer."

Charlie sobered when he realized he might have endangered the woman's job as well. "How have you managed—"

"The first week you were too far gone to make any noises, so I was able to make my shifts. For the last two days, I've feigned illness, but I need to get back to my duties as soon as possible."

He shook his head, humbled by the lengths she'd gone to in order to keep him safe. A stranger. "Why would you...do this for me?"

She considered her answer for several long minutes, her gaze so fierce, so penetrating, he feared she could plumb his very soul. Then she said simply, "How could I not?"

Standing, she took the napkin and the tray. "Your revolver is under that sack of potatoes in the corner. It is still loaded, so take care when you move it."

As much as Charlie willed himself to jump from the bed, don his clothes and leave this place, he couldn't move. Exhaustion pulled at him, making his body feel heavy as lead.

"You will rest now," she said in the doorway. "I have to go to work. Keep quiet, keep still. Then tonight, when I return, I will bring you more food. Until then, it is imperative that no one discover you are here."

"Wait!"

She turned, startled.

"Your name. What do I call you?"

She hesitated for several beat of silence, then said, "They call me Elizabeth."

Before he could comment on the strange phrasing of her reply, she closed the door.

## London, England

A noise from the back garden had Susan rushing toward the window, but as she pulled aside the curtain, it was to discover that the sound was nothing more than a loose roof tile which had fallen to the ground.

She needed Phillip to get the ladder from the garden shed and check the rest of tiles. But Phillip was the primary reason why she spent her time pacing from window to window. As if things weren't bad enough at the Blunt household, her sixteen-year-old brother had not returned home for nearly two days and she was worried sick.

She was going to skin him alive when he came home! It didn't matter that he'd pinned a note to the memo board saying he would be participating in Home Guard training for the weekend and not to worry.

*Worry?* Susan had passed mere worry after the first evening. Since then, her emotions had simmered and boiled until now she fairly fulminated with fury and panic and dread.

Less than a week had passed since she'd been put in charge of the Blunt household and things were quickly disintegrating from bad to worse. Sara had received word that her job at the Green Line would be "suspended until further notice" due to the bombardment, bills were beginning to arrive in the morning post, and Susan's hours with the Ironworks had become intermittent while the factory was being relocated and new staff hired to replace so many of the men who'd had been injured or killed in that first fateful raid. But Susan couldn't contend with any of these concerns until she'd assured herself that Phillip was safe.

A fresh wave of anger washed over her. Phillip wasn't even old enough to join the Home Guard. Why hadn't someone sent him summarily home?

The tinny ring of the front doorbell had her rushing the length of the house. It must be Phillip. He was always forgetting his key.

Flinging the door wide, she opened her mouth to chastise

her brother for his selfishness. But the world abruptly froze in its frame like a jammed motion picture projector. The blue of the sky, the crisp shapes of the leaves on the trees, the faint scents of smoke and marigolds burned themselves into her memory along with the tall, gangly figure of a telegraph delivery messenger.

Susan's heart stalled in her chest before slowly wallowing back into motion, pumping sluggishly, moving blood to her numbed extremities with such excruciating slowness, she feared she would never be able to move. The girl's mouth formed words. Words that Susan couldn't process. Then the woman's hand extended as she held out a flimsy envelope.

From somewhere at the corner of her vision, Susan saw a shape move toward her. A woman's figure, slipping through the gap in the privet hedge. She floated like an apparition, climbing the steps, taking the proffered letter before slipping an arm around Susan's waist, taking her weight when Susan would have crumpled to the ground.

Then, as the messenger backed away, her expression sad, so sad, as if she'd seen such sights too many times before and had been tainted with the bleakness of the news she delivered, she turned and made her way back to the street to continue her grim errands.

"Let's go inside, Susan."

Susan heard the words. Heard them, but couldn't bring herself to obey them.

But it seemed her body could move without conscious commands, because the arm at her waist was holding her, helping her, moving her back into the sitting room, drawing her down upon the settee.

Beside her, RueAnn waited, the envelope held loosely, like a wounded bird in her palm.

"Read it," Susan whispered through lips that were numb.

Beside her, RueAnn grew infinitely still. Her arm still wound tightly around Susan's waist, the warmth of her body warring against the chill that had settled into Susan's bones. Then, slowly, ever so slowly, she moved away enough to take the envelope in both hands and slit it open, unfolding it to reveal the cryptic message within.

Susan tried to focus on the typed lines, but her vision became jumbled, swimming with sudden tears. From a distance of a thousand miles and a thousand years, she heard RueAnn slowly pronounce,

"We regret to inform you that the *S.S. City of Benares* was torpedoed September 17, 1940 at 2205 hours. Millicent Blunt, age 50, and Michael Blunt, age 10, are confirmed among the casualties. Margaret Blunt, age 5, is missing and presumed dead."

A chill settled so deeply into her bones, Susan felt as if she were suspended in a block of ice. At some point, she must have taken the telegram, must have insisted she wanted to be alone. Because RueAnn melted away. Sun became shadow.

When Phillip charged into the house blithely calling, "Hullo, Susan!" she must have responded, must have hidden the telegram away in the pocket of her dress. Later, the air raid sirens began. But for the first time Susan didn't care if she hurried to safety. Woodenly, she made her way to the staircase, climbing up, up, like an old woman, until she reached her room. There, she sank onto the bed and stared at the dusky shadows painting their way across the rug. Until finally, a finger of darkness reached the bedpost, seeming to point at the spot where she'd looped her pocketbook.

Her hand trembled as she reached out to unhook the strap. Releasing the catch, she reached into the inner pocket, now bulging with Paul's letters.

In her mind's eye, she could see him clearly—the dark lock of hair flopped onto his forehead, brown, brown eyes like melted chocolate, the cleft of his chin that begged for the touch of her finger.

Sitting up, she crushed the envelopes to her chest, squeezing her eyes shut, trying to breathe around the lump of pain lodged in her chest. Then, unable to bear the ache another moment, she ripped open the first letter, holding the delicate sheaves of paper up to the light. And when she began to read, it wasn't the words that slipped through her brain, but the deep bass of his voice.

*Sweetheart…*

My Dear Wife,

I don't know if I will ever see you again. Nor do I know when or if these letters will ever be delivered. For now, I fold them up and place them in my pocket next to yours. Some might think me foolish to even hope to one day mail them when I am caught behind enemy lines, but I need to write to you. I need to believe that someday they will be placed in your hands, and you will know how I have been longing for you since that long ago morning when I said goodbye to you in the rain.

I owe you an apology. I'm sure I've hurt you deeply, and I have absolutely no excuse for my behavior.

I took your letters. I took them and I read them. It began innocently enough. When you dropped your purse that day at the theater, you neglected to pick them up, so I stuffed them in my pocket, then forgot about them. I could have returned them to you later that day—or even at the railway station. But I must admit, by that time, I was so enamored with you that I kept them.

Maybe, I thought that by reading them I would know you better. But I never could have anticipated how much you would reveal. And it shames me to admit, that in reading your innermost secrets, I have learned more about your thoughts and dreams than I could have divined in a lifetime. All through deceit.

I realize now that I was a total cad. I thought only of myself. Even in marrying you, I was being selfish. After holding you, loving you, I wanted to be a hero in your eyes.

I never should have left you standing there in the rain. I should have stayed with you until things could be sorted out between us. But, like a coward, I returned to England and tried to forget you. Yes, I went through the motions. I sent travel papers and my grandmother's ring. There was so much more I could have done, but I extended the bare minimum in emotion and time, because I was hoping that you would refuse my offers and continue on without me.

But now, that is my greatest fear, that you will abandon me. I know that the letters were private—written to a man whom I pray isn't my rival. But it was through your writing that I grew to love you more than I would have ever thought possible. Everything I do is in the hopes of returning to you, of begging your forgiveness, and praying that you will allow me to start fresh.

I want to court you, RueAnn Boggs Tulliver. I want to prove that I'm a man worthy of your love. I want to live with you by my side for years and years to come with our children and our grandchildren.

If it weren't for this war, this bloody war, I would be there now. I can only pray that you will wait for me. Because no matter what happens, I am yours forever.

Charlie

# Chapter Twelve

Rouen, France

The noises came again. The scraping of footfalls on the stoop, the jiggling of the doorknob.

Charlie braced himself against the wall, pressing himself into the shadows. His thumb drew back the hammer of his revolver and his finger curled around the trigger.

Three times that day, someone had approached the front door, knocked, jiggled the door handle, then left. At first, Charlie had been able to ignore the noises, lying quietly in the dark, his heart pounding so loudly he could scarcely breathe. By the third time, he was on edge, determined not to be caught like a rabbit in a cage.

Retrieving his revolver from beneath the potato sack, he'd made his way up the stairs to the kitchen, step by agonizing step. Then, he'd collapsed on a chair, grateful that Elizabeth had seen fit to draw all the blinds because he didn't think he could have managed the task himself.

When he'd heard footfalls again, he'd stood, flattening himself against the wall.

This time there was no knock, no gentle probing. Instead, the lock grated. Metal against metal. Then the door eased open mere inches at a time. He stood still, his heart thrashing against his ribs as a shape slid inside and closed the door again.

For several long seconds, the shape stood still in the darkness. As if sensing his presence, he felt, rather than saw a face turn toward him. Although there was very little light, he recognized enough of the familiar contours to lower the revolver and step forward.

"There's no one here but me," he said lowly.

Elizabeth's breath escaped in a rush. "*Merde.* I thought I told you to stay in bed," she said as she made her way to the table. The rasp of a match brought a flare of light which she touched to the wick of a lantern. Then, blowing out the flame, she began to unpack vegetables from her market sack.

"Someone knocked on the door earlier. It startled me." He was leaning heavily against the wall, panting. "I didn't know if the same person had returned."

Elizabeth frowned, then offered, "It was probably *Madame* Deneuve. She often comes over to borrow something. She's a widow, nearly ninety, and starved for company. I've had to dodge her over the past few days."

Charlie's lips twitched. "Then I shall do my best to dodge her as well."

"Once you're safely stowed in the cellar, I'll invite her over for coffee." She grimaced. "Or what passes for coffee these days. It will help to allay her suspicions, if she has any."

She turned to prod at the embers in the stove, adding a few precious lumps of coal. Charlie feared the added light would reveal the way his legs trembled with the effort to keep him upright. Now that the threat had passed, his revolver hung next to his thigh, feeling unbelievably heavy.

"Get back to bed before you fall down, *mon ami.*"

He shook his head and limped toward the table instead. Slowly, gingerly, he lowered himself into one of the chairs and set the pistol on the polished wood.

"Where have you been?" he asked.

"Work."

She took a pan from the stove and filled it halfway with water from an old fashioned pump. Then, using a stiff brush, she scrubbed the meager collection of potatoes from the counter as well as the carrots and turnips she'd collected from the market.

"You're late."

She shrugged. "I stopped by the market. The selection was rather poor today. Mostly root vegetables. But I've got a precious onion left from my last trip into town and a tiny bit of chicken, so the two of us won't starve at least."

Elizabeth began to calmly chop the vegetables and then scoop them into a pot. Lifting her head, she pointed to her bag with the knife she'd taken from a drawer. "There's bread in the rucksack there. You can get yourself a piece. "

He shook his head, watching as she attacked her chore with stubborn zeal.

"I'll wait."

"It will be a few hours before the soup is ready."

"I'll wait," he repeated.

She worked in silence for several long minutes.

"Where do you work?" he asked after her jitters seemed to have eased.

Elizabeth clearly debated telling him the truth, she finally said, "I found a position as a charwoman at a German troop hospital."

"Ahh." He considered that information for a moment. "That explains how you knew my…disguise wasn't quite complete."

"One of my duties is to disrobe soldiers before surgery. I knew immediately that there was something wrong. Your shoes were brown, more a civilian style than military issue. A German's boots are black."

He shook his head. "Such a small detail."

"But one that would have given you away eventually, *n'est-ce pas?*"

His thumb tapped idly against wood grown velvety from years of scrubbing. "It probably wouldn't have mattered if you hadn't found me and brought me here. I was all but dead even then."

She paused, met his gaze, then looked away. "*Oui.* I believe you are right."

"So, why would you help me?"

She scooped the vegetables into the pot and set it on the stove. Carefully, she added salt, pepper, a careful ration of dried spices. Then, when she could avoid the question no longer, she took the seat across from him.

"You asked my name," she said, avoiding an immediate answer. "May I ask yours?"

"Charles. But most people call me Charlie."

"Well...*Charlie*...I have my own reasons for hating the Germans." She traced a knot in the wood with her fingernail. "I was in Warsaw when the war began. My...fiancé...managed to get us out of the city, away from the German onslaught. He met up with an old friend who was a pilot. But there was only one seat in the plane—an old bi-plane from the Great War—and therefore only room enough for one person to squeeze in with the pilot." She shrugged. "So I was taken away, while Aleksy was left behind."

Her eyes grew sad. "Unfortunately, things did not go as planned. Rather than making my way to safety, I once again found myself behind German lines. So I...hide in plain sight, you might say. Right beneath the Germans' noses."

"Until I made your position more vulnerable than ever."

"*C'est ça.*"

He took a deep, shuddering breath. "I'll leave as soon as I'm able."

"*D'accord.* But not just yet. I have not gone to so much trouble only to have it wasted, *mon ami.*"

She stood again, making herself busy and he took that as a sign that she wasn't comfortable saying anything more. He didn't press. He knew that he'd endangered her with his presence—more than he would probably ever know. So he sat in silence, watching her bustle around the room, gathering ingredients that soon became a dough that she kneaded with fierce determination. Then, taking out a rolling pin, she made a flat piece that she cut into strips and dumped into the broth.

Dumplings. She was making dumplings.

Charlie's stomach rumbled noisily in response, but it was the domestic simplicity of the scene that lulled him, offering a peace to his spirit that he hadn't known he craved.

By the time the soup was ready and they'd eaten, Charlie's shoulder and hip had begun to ache again with untold fury. Without needing to be told, Elizabeth came to his side, wrapped his arm around her shoulder, and helped him stand.

"I don't think it would be wise to try the steep steps to the cellar. Use the bed for tonight. Then, tomorrow, I will help you go back downstairs."

Charlie would have argued if he could have summoned the energy. She'd done enough for him, more than he could ever repay. He didn't wish to put her out any more than necessary.

But as he stumbled forward, he knew he'd already taxed his newfound strength too much. Pain radiated from his wounds with such ferocity, he feared he would collapse before he could even make it to the little closet-like area that served as a bedroom.

He sank onto the sheets, allowing her to lift his legs up and cover him with the blankets.

"Sleep now," she whispered, patting his shoulder.

Before she could move away, he grasped her wrist.

"Thank you."

His eyelids were heavy and he succumbed to their weight. He felt, rather than heard her as she slipped out of his grasp and stepped from the room.

More than anything, he wanted to disappear into a haze of sleep, but the pain thrummed so potently through his veins that he moved restlessly, trying to find a more comfortable position.

When the door opened again, he quickly shut his lashes. The last thing he wanted was for Elizabeth to worry about him now. She'd had a long day, made longer by caring for him.

She approached the bed—probably to check on whether or not he was sleeping. Instead, she opened his fist, pressing a sheaf of papers into his palm. Then, she slipped noiselessly from the room.

As soon as the door closed behind her, he glanced down, not recognizing the import of what he held until his gaze slid to the handwriting. Handwriting that was more familiar to him than his own.

Emotion and exhaustion and pain all rumbled together, welling up inside him with an equal measure of regret and shame.

Sobs rose thick and strong in his chest, rough unmanly sobs that threatened to rip him asunder. But he could not stop them, could not tamp them down.

He could only pray that someday soon he would have the opportunity to make amends.

## London, England

As the tragic news of the torpedoing of the *S.S. City of Benares* and the rescue of its few survivors trickled in, Susan felt as if she were a rubber band being pulled, pulled, pulled, in several directions until she feared she would snap.

Somehow, in all of the confusion and grief, Susan had more than just her work demanding her attention. She'd also unwittingly become the "mother" of the home. Sara sank into a deep depression. When she wasn't training for her new position with the Women's Transport Corp, she spent most of her time curled up in bed, staring at the wallpaper as if it held the secrets of the ages. Phillip, on the other hand, had clearly taken leave of his senses. The moment he returned from school, he began drilling and marching with the rest of the Home Guard, sporting a broomstick on his shoulder as if it were a rifle and bayonet— all the while asserting that soon, *soon*, he would receive proper armaments and a woolen uniform.

So it remained to Susan to keep a level head, see to it that food was kept in the larder and coal in the scuttle. She couldn't let on that she'd lost her mind as well, reading and rereading Paul's letters until they etched themselves onto her consciousness and she need only close her eyes to see the looping, spidery script. Worse yet, she'd begun to write back, explaining the tragedies which had befallen her family and the challenges she now faced. She didn't allow herself to think of the gravity of her deceit—not just to Paul, but to her sister. Instead, she signed her letters with an "S", then resolutely refused to think of the consequences. And to further seal her punishment, she forwarded the picture her father had taken of the two of them the night of the fancy dress party.

Quickening her step, Susan glanced at her watch. If she hurried, she would have time to make herself a bite to eat before going back to work. Thankfully, the Meade Ironworks had been able to find a new location for their plant—one that was actually closer to home. It meant that she could still make her daily trips to intercept Paul's letters, but give her ample time to check on things as well.

Running the last few steps, she reached for her keys, but when she touched the latch, she discovered the door wasn't locked. Frowning, she let herself in, her heart pounding, wondering if Sara had come home unexpectedly. Her stomach flip-flopped. What if she'd discovered one of Paul's letters?

But as the door swung wide, Susan found the mail on the runner where it had fallen from the slot. Seeing at a glance that there was nothing from Paul, Susan tiptoed forward.

Noises were coming from the kitchen, low murmured voices. An odd smell hung in the air.

Looking around her for a weapon, Susan grasped an umbrella from the stand. Holding it firmly in both hands like a cricket bat, she crept toward the kitchen. Rations were tight and lines were long. Had someone broken into the house to raid the larder?

A floorboard creaked beneath her feet and the noises in the kitchen suddenly hushed. She heard whispers. Low whispers. Moving swiftly now, she burst through the kitchen door, the umbrella raised high above her head like a club.

The click of a revolver being primed reached her ears at the same time the door slammed against the opposite wall and two male figures gaped at her wild-eyed, one of them sighting down the barrel of a gun.

Susan screamed. Phillip squeaked. His companion, a boy about the same age, whirled and dodged out the back door, thundering through the garden to disappear over the back wall into the yard of their rear neighbor.

Phillip quickly dropped the revolver, his hands shaking so badly he could scarcely unarm it.

"Good Lord, Phillip! You could have shot me!" Susan

shouted, her heart pounding a rough tattoo somewhere in the vicinity of her neck before plummeting to the tips of her toes. Then, her eyes widened as she took in the sight on the kitchen table.

Bottles of all shapes, sizes, and hues had been lined up on newspapers. Most of them were filled with a noxious liquid, then tamped with corks while a half dozen still waited their turn. Empty square cans and jugs littered the floor. Susan caught only a few of the labels: kerosene, turpentine, wood alcohol…

Her jaw dropped. "Are you trying to blow this house to kingdom come?"

Phillip's expression became mulish as he tucked the pistol into his waistband.

"You're being overly dramatic."

"Overly dramatic," she repeated, her voice rising. "You leveled a pistol at me!"

"I wouldn't have shot you. I only have one bullet."

"It only takes one!"

"Well, I wouldn't have wasted it on *you*," he said, his voice dripping with scorn. "I merely meant to scare you."

Her knees were trembling so violently she sank onto a chair. "In that respect, you succeeded." She waved an arm to the mess on the table. "What's all this?"

"Never you mind. It's Home Guard business."

She gaped at him, the contents of the table, then back at her brother again. He stood with his arms folded tightly, daring her to make a comment.

"What sort of…*business*?" she asked, the last word lingering scathingly on her tongue.

"Protection."

"Protection?" Try as she might, she couldn't manage more than to repeat his outrageous statements.

"From tanks."

"Tanks."

"German tanks," he added when it became clear she was too dull-witted to fathom his meaning. "The invasion is bound to happen soon enough and the Home Guard plans to meet the

Germans with a fight. I'm doing my bit."

"By making…"

"Petrol bombs."

Susan jumped to her feet. "No. No, no, *no!*" She jabbed her finger in the direction of the table. "You get rid of this…this… *mess*. Then you clean yourself up and march yourself over to whomever is in charge and tell them you're underage and you *will not* be participating in this…in this fool's enterprise!"

Phillip stiffened. "No."

For several seconds, Susan was so stunned, she couldn't speak. When she finally managed to find her tongue, she whispered, "What did you say?"

"I said 'no'!" he repeated more forcefully. "I will not clean up this '*mess*,' as you call it, until I'm good and ready. Then, when I'm done, I'm going to store them under the floor in the tool shed with all of the others I've made."

"Others?" She was back to parroting him, but she couldn't help herself. "Have you lost your mind?"

"No! No I haven't lost my mind! I've lost my father and my mother and my baby brother—and little Margaret too! And it's their fault!" he exclaimed, flinging an arm toward the window.

Susan was torn. More than anything, she wanted to keep him safe. Her family was shrinking and she didn't think she could survive another loss.

But she couldn't stop him from doing his part, no matter how much she might object or how much his involvement would add to her worry.

Standing, she drew her brother close, holding him tightly as he wept, his heart seeming to break. He clutched at her with both hands, crying with frustration and grief—and yes, from the weight of keeping his activities a secret from her.

Finally, when his emotions had spent themselves and he stood trembling in her arms, she handed him a handkerchief.

"Wait here," she said, her own voice husky from unshed tears.

Moving into the hall, she called the Ironworks, explaining to Mr. Meade that she was needed at home for a minor emergency.

Dear, sweet Mr. Meade didn't ask any questions. He simply stated, "Of course, Miss Blunt. We'll muddle through without you, never you fear."

Taking the pin from her hat, Susan returned to the kitchen. Putting her hat and her pocketbook on the counter, she took one of her mother's aprons from the hook on the door and slipped it over her head before tying the strings tightly around her waist.

"Now. What exactly needs to be done?"

* * *

"So what did you do then?" RueAnn asked after Susan had related her encounter with Phillip's Home Guard preparations.

"What do you think I did? I put on Mum's apron and helped him build the blasted bombs.

RueAnn snickered, trying to imagine pragmatic, no-nonsense Susan huddled over Molotov cocktails spread out over her kitchen table.

"Where did you put them all?"

They were working in the Tolliver's garden, picking what ripened vegetables they could find to feed the Royal Engineers. As promised, the men had come back to RueAnn's home time and time again to work on the Anderson—and they were nearly finished. Each visit, they brought a few items to augment a meal—cheese, a bit of bread, vegetables, and sometimes a precious tin of fruit.

"They're hidden beneath the floorboards of the toolshed for now, but I've made Phillip promise that they'll be moved by the end of the week."

RueAnn grinned. "I don't know whether I should feel safer since there's an armory nearby or more terrified that the whole block could go up in flames."

Susan rolled her eyes. "If we take a direct hit, we'll go up fast enough."

RueAnn offered a careless shrug. "If we take a direct hit, it won't really matter." She still found it difficult to believe that in only a few weeks of arriving in England, she'd not only become inured to the constant bombardment, but that she'd begun to joke about it.

"It wouldn't matter if we did have a bomb drop nearby. You'd be just fine in that Anderson," Susan said, dropping radishes into a basket and pointing to where four Royal Engineers packed sod on top of the shelter they'd built. They'd since learned from Sara that the men were part of a new unit that specialized in disarming the unexploded bombs that littered London after each raid. The job was dangerous to the extreme. Yet, for some reason, the men found an outlet for their stresses by puttering in her back garden—although RueAnn thought the fact that a home-cooked meal and the presence of the unmarried Blunt twins might have something to do with it.

Whatever the reason, the Anderson they'd built was a sight to behold. Long ago, RueAnn had realized that engineers had a different mindset from most folk, because they'd worried over drainage and water tables and tensile strength—and so many other things that escaped her completely. All she knew for sure was that her shelter was the wonder of the neighborhood. Moreover, she had two lodgers already, Captains Carr and Rigdon, two soldiers from the UXB unit, who would share the larger upper room of the house. A Mr. Peabody, who had seen the placard during his daily commute, was coming to look at the second room at the end of the week.

Rather than disturb Charlie and Edna's quarters for the moment, RueAnn had decided to test the arrangement for a month or two, before looking for more lodgers. In the meantime, she'd also begun taking in laundry for the men in the UXB unit and Louise had passed cards around to friends and neighbors announcing that RueAnn was available to take in sewing and mending as well.

Not for the first time, RueAnn discovered that her upbringing, however difficult it might have been, had equipped her with a set of skills that allowed her to scrape by for the time being.

"Have you heard anything from Matthew?" RueAnn asked

as they gathered up their tools and headed toward the house.

"No. And I'm really concerned. He's always been good about writing." She bit her lip. "I've been sending him a letter every week, but I still haven't told him about Mum and the wee ones. I figured that if he was out there somewhere, hurt, or exhausted, the last thing I should do is worry him more."

RueAnn squeezed her hand. "Give it time."

Time. If only time could be the cure-all. RueAnn kept telling herself that soon things would right themselves, the bombardments would stop, Edna would recover, Charlie would return. But she wasn't sure if she believed such platitudes any more.

Time, she'd learned, wasn't always on her side.

• • •

The Anderson Shelter was finally finished, and feeling the need for a ceremony to christen it as their second home, RueAnn had invited the Blunts and the men of the Royal Engineers to a special celebration.

Slipping through the hedge with her brother and sister, Susan was pleased to see that Edna was also in attendance. The older woman grew a little stronger each day—enough so that she could sit for a few minutes in the ancient mobile chair that the men of UXB had liberated from who knew where.

Standing just a little apart from the group, Susan's gaze drifted again. She watched as her sister approached the Royal Engineers with an ease that she would never possess. Not for the first time, she felt a pang of envy.

Why had God seen fit to make them so different? Why was Sara able to move around the yard like the Queen Mum while Susan stood rooted to the outskirts of the party like an interloper?

Sadly, she realized that she'd only felt completely comfortable in the presence of one male. Paul Overdone. Her sister's beau.

Well, one of her beaux. Sara had a plethora of male friends—Bernard Bidiwell and most of the UXB engineers.

A twinge of shame came swift on the heels of that thought. Sara wasn't promiscuous, merely friendly. The men around her knew she saw them all as a herd of adopted big brothers. But that didn't stop them from trying to change her mind.

RueAnn approached with a wide grin.

"You look so serious."

Susan shook her head, forcing a smile. "Merely woolgathering."

RueAnn nodded, turning to survey the group from Susan's vantage point. Her head dipped in the direction of Susan's twin.

"Is Sara feeling all right?" she asked, handing Susan a mug of tea.

"What do you mean?" Susan asked, folding her fingers around the warmth of the cup.

"She looks pale."

Susan watched as her twin took a handkerchief from her belt and patted at her lips and brow. She took two quick breaths, before pasting a quick smile on her face. And for the first time, Susan had to admit that Sara's carefree expression looked forced.

The ever-present weight of responsibility that Susan wore like a leaden cloak grew heavier still. She had to admit that Sara had been preoccupied lately. Her work schedule had become so erratic, that Susan rarely knew when to expect her sister—which was odd in and of itself. Surely the WTC would be more structured than that.

Even the Germans were keeping to a schedule. The RAF had begun to take such a toll on the German aircraft that, more and more, their raids were shifting to the evening hours. But as if to compensate for the lack of daylight raids, the ordinance they used became more deadly. Or perhaps, they'd simply improved their aim.

These fresh new worries combined with those that already plagued her—Susan's uncertainty about Matthew, Phillip's madcap involvement with the Home Guard, and that unspeakable fear that came each time the sirens sounded and they all trudged to the public shelter, wondering what new horrors would befall London before morning.

If it weren't for Paul's letters, Susan didn't know how she would survive. She watched for them each day. Then, in the dark of the night, as bombs exploded around London and she hunkered in the dank, sweaty confines of the concrete bunker, more often than not, she ripped them open and devoured them, reading them again and again like an addict with a measure of opium.

She could trace the path of his thoughts with each missive—the chatty letters before his leave in London, his concern when she hadn't responded as she'd promised, and then, as if a hidden dam had been broken, the notes after she'd finally written to him in return. At that point, Paul's letters changed, blossoming with sudden ardor.

Love letters.

The man had begun to write her love letters.

"Susan, is something wrong?"

Susan shook her head, damning the way that tears threatened to fall.

"No, I'm...I'm just tired."

RueAnn nodded sympathetically. "What I wouldn't give for a night, a single night of uninterrupted sleep." She took Susan's hand. "Now that the Anderson is finished, you won't be going to the public shelters anymore." Her eyes grew kind, knowing. "I appreciate all your help these past few weeks, and now it's time for me to extend a bit of my own. The gap in the hedge goes both ways, you know. Edna ordered the largest shelter possible. I see no reason why our families shouldn't share it."

"No, really, I—"

"I won't accept 'no' for an answer," RueAnn said firmly before moving back toward the kitchen for more tea.

* * *

It didn't take long before the Anderson was put to use. Less than an hour after their party broke up and the Engineers began making their way toward the pubs for the evening, the shrill call of the air raid siren split the evening air.

This time, instead of trying to hunker down in Edna's bedroom, RueAnn and Susan lifted the woman into her mobile chair and pushed her out into the back garden, easily navigating the ramps the engineers had built for them, and rolling her into the shelter and from there transferring her onto one of the lower built-in bunks.

For the first time since Edna's stroke, RueAnn saw her settle into her pillow with something akin to relief rather than abject fear. And miraculously, long before the bombers actually arrived, she drifted into a heavy sleep.

"I think she feels safer out here," RueAnn murmured as she lit the lantern she'd brought with them, keeping the flame low—as much to save the precious fuel as to prevent any light from escaping the canvas flap that served as a door.

"She must have been terrified," Susan agreed. "It's frightening enough to sit through the noise and turmoil… but to be completely incapacitated and unable to run away if something were to happen…"

RueAnn looked down at her hands as the distant rumble of bombers soon competed with the staccato *ack-ack-ack* of the anti-aircraft guns.

"She never really liked me, you know," RueAnn admitted with great reluctance. "Not at first."

"I know."

Susan's reply was so stunning in its bluntness—especially from a woman so concerned about ensuring that everyone around her was comfortable, that RueAnn's chin dropped. Then, simultaneously, the two women burst into giggles.

The air began to whistle. The ground shook beneath them.

At the last minute, Sara scrambled into the shelter, Phillip hard on her heels.

"What took the two of you so long?" RueAnn asked, still grinning.

Phillip grimaced. "The Germans know the minute I step into the bathtub." He shook his head and droplets of water scattered over the shelter.

"Phillip!" Sara said, lifting her hands in defense, then

pressing a hand to her mouth. "Oh, God."

She suddenly burst from the shelter. Even with the din of the bombardment, they were able to hear her plainly enough as she wretched into the bushes. Several minutes later, she staggered back inside.

"If I were placed in front of a German at this moment, I would tear him apart with my bare hands," Sara rasped.

"Are you ill?"

Sara shivered. "I don't know. Mrs. Biddiwell had a cold last time I saw Bernard, but this feels more like the flu."

"Get into bed," RueAnn said, gesturing to the nest of blankets and pillows above Edna's spot. The other bunks had not yet received the same treatment.

"No, really I couldn't," Sara demurred.

"Go on, now. Up you go."

"But this is your first night in the shelter. I couldn't possibly…"

RueAnn hitched her chin toward the bunk. "Not another word. Get up there and go to bed."

Sara's eyes sparkled with tears. "Thank you. I will."

The moment she'd huddled beneath the blankets, RueAnn bent toward the basket of supplies that she'd stowed in the corner. "Well now, I think the rest of us should entertain ourselves, at least for a few hours."

"What do you suggest?" Susan said, still eyeing her sister in concern.

"I think it's time to introduce the two of you to an American tradition. A forbidden art, in my family, but one which, much to my father's horror, I learned to perform with amazing thoroughness."

She'd succeeded in capturing both Susan's and Phillip's full attention.

"What on earth?" Phillip said with a grin.

With a flourish, she produced a pack of cards.

"Poker!"

* * *

RueAnn's first boarders moved in early the next morning. The all-clear had barely sounded before Richard Carr and Gerald Rigdon thundered up the stairs, stowed their kit, then disappeared again, saying they had a pair of bombs in Piccadilly awaiting their attention.

Close to noon, just as RueAnn had helped Edna to wash and comb her hair, then dress in a fresh gown and bed jacket, the doorbell rang.

Leaving Edna in her chair by the large picture window facing the street, RueAnn made her way to the door.

"Yes?" she asked, swinging it wide.

A middle-aged gentleman waited on the stoop. He scooped the hat from a shock of curly hair and offered her a bob of his head.

"Mr. Peabody?"

He nodded. "Yes, I have an appointment to see a room."

"Of course. Come in, please."

She closed the door behind him.

"I'm Mrs. Tolliver. RueAnn Tolliver. I spoke with you on the phone." She gestured toward Edna in the mobile chair. "This is my mother-in-law, the elder Mrs. Tolliver."

Mr. Peabody clutched his hat to his chest and offered another courtly bow in Edna's direction.

"If you'll come this way, I'll show you the room."

RueAnn led the way up the first flight of stairs. "The bathing facilities are through the center door, there. A towel and face cloth will be provided with the other linens in your room. Your toiletries will be your responsibility. Because we have other lodgers, we ask that you keep your bathroom visits as short as possible." She pointed to the doors which remained tightly shut. "The other two rooms on this floor are, as yet, still used by the family."

He nodded, clearly embarrassed by her frank talk in regards to the loo.

"Your room will be this way."

RueAnn led him up the next flight of stairs, ushering him into the bedroom next to the old nursery which was being used by the two Royal Engineers. Susan had helped her move Edna's tester bed into the ground floor room the older woman used. Then, they'd brought the smaller cot up here. The sheets were crisp and drawn tautly around the mattress. A pillow had been fluffed and placed invitingly at the head, and a patterned woolen blanket had been freshly laundered and folded at the foot. Against the opposite wall was a narrow highboy borrowed from the Blunt household. The arrangement left very little walking space, but ample storage.

"Your rent is expected weekly, in advance. If you're willing to provide us with your ration card, we will supply a hot breakfast and evening meal. Should you require your laundry done as well, it will only be a few shillings more."

She stepped to the window overlooking the back garden. "As you can see, we have an Anderson but we share it with the neighbors next door. In addition, my mother-in-law is an invalid, as I'm sure you noticed, and she requires special care. However, there is a public shelter at the end of the block as well as a cabinet under the stairs that you may use if you wish."

As the man glanced out the window, RueAnn prayed that her demands for reimbursement weren't too steep or that he wouldn't be put off by being asked to reserve the shelter for family use only.

The Royal Engineers hadn't quibbled over her terms—indeed, they'd insisted that she reserve the Anderson primarily for the women's use. They'd spent enough time at the house already so she supposed they already knew what to expect in regards to meals. Plus, she feared the close proximity to several pubs and the beautiful twins next door had proved an immediate plus in their estimation.

"Do you have any questions, Mr. Peabody?"

He shook his head. "If I could have a moment alone to consider the arrangement," he said slowly.

"Of course, of course!" she quickly stepped from the room. "I'll meet you downstairs whenever you're ready."

* * *

RueAnn busied herself with dusting the parlor until Mr. Peabody finally appeared. He stood hesitantly in the hallway until she approached.

"I believe that the arrangement should prove very agreeable, Mrs. Tolliver."

RueAnn smiled in delight. "Wonderful!"

"If it wouldn't be too much trouble, my work requires that I type reports each evening. It will cause some noise which could be a concern."

"Nonsense. You'll find we interact like a family, Mr. Peabody. We're a very tolerant bunch."

"I'll also accept the offer of the meals and the...er... laundry services." His cheeks flamed. "Would it be too much of an imposition to move in this evening?"

"Not at all. We serve dinner at seven. If you'd like to bring your things before then, we'll introduce you to everyone, air raids permitting."

He offered the slightest of smiles. "I would enjoy that. Good day to you, Mrs. Tolliver."

"RueAnn, please," she said as she ushered him toward the door. "It will save confusion."

"Very well, Miss RueAnn." He nodded in Edna's direction. "Good day to you as well, Mrs. Tolliver."

To RueAnn's delight, Edna dipped her head in acknowledgement.

As she closed the door on him, RueAnn said, "I think he'll prove a good fit, don't you Edna?"

A noise escaped from the older woman's lips. RueAnn wasn't sure, but she thought that Edna was offering her approval.

My Dear Wife,

I'm not very good with words. I've never been able to express my feelings. For years, I've done my best to remain aloof and unaffected by emotion as much as possible, but it wasn't always that way.

Most of the people who know me, think that I'm an only child, but that isn't the case. I had a baby sister once. Francine.

I loved my baby sister so much. We were close in age, only two years apart. And since my father was killed in the Great War, there were only the three of us: my mother, my sister, and me.

My earliest memory of Francine was the way she would slip out of bed and hurry down the stairs to my room whenever there was a storm. We would huddle under the covers together, and I would tell her outlandish stories until she forgot about the thunder and lightning and fell asleep.

We were inseparable.

Until Francine got sick.

I know now, as an adult, that Francine had diabetes. But when we were little, I didn't understand what had happened. I only knew that I had lost my playmate and a sickly, fractious girl had taken her place. Moreover, my mother seemed to change overnight. She became so vigilant, so critical of the slightest things. I mustn't bump Francine. I mustn't let her get too tired. More confusing still was that suddenly, food had become taboo. Francine couldn't share my lollipops or take a bite of my sandwich. Burned starkly into my mind is the image of Francine, sneaking beneath the table and stealing a piece of bread from my plate. She would shove it into her mouth, chewing furiously as my mother caught her around the shoulders and held her down, trying to remove the bread before she could swallow.

The disease ravaged my sister's body. She became weak, her fingers and toes turning dark purple. One night, when there was a storm, I knew she wouldn't have the strength to come down to my bedroom, so I went up to hers. I burrowed beneath all the girlish ruffles and held her close, whispering her favorite stories until we both fell asleep.

The next morning, I was the only one who awakened.

After that, I was broken somehow. I couldn't, wouldn't allow myself to love anyone. I swore to myself that nothing was worth that ache, that loneliness. That loss.

Nothing at all.

Until I met you.

Charlie

# Chapter Thirteen

"Phillip?"

It was more than a week after Mr. Peabody had joined the household when RueAnn let herself in through the Blunt's back door. She'd received a call from Susan only a few minutes earlier. Susan hadn't been able to break away from work and Sara had been invited to spend the day with Bernard Biddlwell and his mother. Since Phillip was starting a new job helping to unload freight for a war supply warehouse that afternoon, Susan had asked RueAnn to drop by and check to make sure he left in plenty of time, had his hair combed, his face washed, and had donned the freshly laundered clothing she'd laid out for him.

Amused at Susan's motherly tone, RueAnn had assured her that she would check on Phillip immediately. In truth, after so many shared evenings in the Anderson, she was as concerned about Phillip's putting his best foot forward for his employer as Susan. She knew how much the added income would mean to the Blunts and Phillip had a tendency to focus on fun rather than performance.

But as Phillip thundered down the stairs and into the kitchen, RueAnn realized that neither she nor Susan had any cause to worry. He was dressed to the nines in his freshly pressed clothing. His hair had been combed neatly into place, the tines of his comb still leaving pinstripe-like furrows in his recently trimmed hair.

"Your sister couldn't make it home, so she rang up and asked me to see if there was anything you needed."

He shook his head, clearly nervous. "How do I look?"

"Splendid."

He stood indecisively for a moment.

"Do you have bus fare?" she asked.

"Yes."

"A bit of extra change for emergencies?"

He patted his pocket. "Susan gave it to me before she left this morning."

"You've eaten something, haven't you? It will be a long day."

"Yes. A bit."

RueAnn suspected that he'd probably been too nervous to eat very much.

"I made you a lunch," she said handing him the sandwiches and vegetable slices she'd carefully arranged in a shoebox. The offering had used up the last of their bread supply, but she wasn't about to send him off without something to eat. She'd have time this afternoon to wait in line at the grocer's for flour and perhaps a precious egg or two. With the extra ration cards from her boarders, she would be able to gather foodstuffs a little more efficiently.

"Thanks, RueAnn."

"Is there anything else you need?"

"I-I don't think so."

She patted his arm. "Then impress them with your amazing skills."

He rolled his eyes. "I'm doing little more than hauling bags off delivery lorries and stowing them in the warehouse."

"Ah, yes. But you'll be the best man they've ever hired for that job."

He grinned.

"Off you go, then. You don't want to be late for your first day."

"Thanks."

He took a couple of quick steps, stopped, then turned and impulsively hurried back to plant a quick kiss on her cheek.

Then he was hurrying toward the front door.

For several long minutes, RueAnn stood staring at that spot, feeling a strange sense of loss, like a housewife who had just sent her child off to school for the first time, and the thought gave her pause.

Is this what it would feel like to be a mother? This sense of joy at his accomplishment mixed with worry—and yes, a nervousness that probably equaled Phillip's?

As she began to close the door, she saw a figure on a bicycle stop in front of the house and carefully set the kickstand. An icy chill began at the tips of RueAnn's fingertips, spreading up, up, as the young woman checked the numbers on the adjoining houses. Then, settling on the Blunt's path, she pushed her way through the garden gate. Nearing the stoop, she dug into the leather pouch slung over her shoulder and removed a small clipboard and an envelope.

"Is this the Blunt residence?"

RueAnn could only nod, her mouth had grown so dry

"Sign please."

She automatically signed the roster, then reached for the telegram, her stomach lurching, her body numb.

"Good day, Miss," the woman said, her eyes sad. Then she hurried back to her bicycle and rode away as if the hounds of hell were at her heels.

RueAnn stood for long moments, staring down at the crumpled envelope.

How much more could this family take? They'd lost their parents, siblings…would God demand yet one more?

The state of the plants was forgotten as RueAnn closed the door, ensuring the lock had snapped into place. Then she made her way through the gap in the hedge—one that grew a little wider with each passing day. Stepping into her own home, she gathered her hat and pocketbook, then went to the kitchen.

"Louise, could you see to Edna for a little while? I need to…find Susan."

The woman turned from the sink, curious at RueAnn's sudden departure. But when her gaze fell on the little envelope that RueAnn still clutched in lifeless fingers, she pressed a fist to her lips.

"Oh, my dear Lord, no," she whispered.

Turning, RueAnn made her way into Edna's room where the older woman was propped up on a mound of pillows so that she could see out the window.

"Edna, I'm stepping out for a few minutes, but Louise will be here with you. I've got to find Susan."

Edna's gaze slid to the envelope as well. An inarticulate sound burbled from her throat and tears welled in her eyes.

"Yes, it appears the Blunts have suffered another blow," RueAnn said, the words made husky by the tightness of her throat. "I'll hurry back as quickly as I can."

. . .

Susan arched her back, dragging the invoices from the typewriter, quickly separating the copies. Her carbon paper was getting fainter by the day, leaving some portions of the duplicates difficult to read. But with shortages, she had to make each waxy sheet stretch as far as she could.

"You look in need of a cup of tea, Miss Blunt," Mr. Meade said as he strode from the factory floor back into the suite of offices.

"Perhaps in a minute."

"Make sure that you do. We've got a late night ahead of us, sorry to say, and you'll be needing to keep your strength up."

"Yes, sir."

He disappeared into his office, shutting the door behind him.

Susan had meant to type one more invoice, but with weariness threatening to overtake her, she pushed back her chair and stood, rolling her cricked neck.

Mr. Meade was right. They had a long night ahead of them, and she'd never make it at this rate. A fortifying beverage was just what she needed.

A small table with a hot plate, kettle, and tea supplies had been placed beneath the window overlooking the machine floor. Filling the pot with fresh water from the cooler, she set it to boil while she readied the leaves.

Idly, she looked out, watching the flash of the welders and the mini-firework display of sparks as the men huddled over their tasks.

After the bombing of their factory near the docks, so many familiar faces were missing. Bit by bit, Mr. Meade had hired new workers, but with so few men available to fill the specialized requirements, the orders kept backing up. She'd heard rumors that Mr. Meade would go another week. Then, if he couldn't find enough skilled workmen, he would open up the positions to women—even train them himself, if necessary.

The door to the street opened, allowing a beam of light to spill across a floor scattered with metal shavings and bits of ash. Idly, Susan watched until the visitor stepped into view.

RueAnn?

Susan smiled. RueAnn must have sensed her near panic over the phone and had come to reassure her that Phillip had gone on his way without a hitch. Reaching for another mug, Susan began gathering supplies for a second cup of tea. Her hand froze in the air. RueAnn looked so serious as she took the stairs to the office. So somber.

Bit by bit, Susan felt an ominous tingling begin in her extremities. Something was wrong. Terribly, terribly wrong.

The door opened, letting in a blast of noise from the shop. She saw RueAnn's lips move, felt her hand on her arm, drawing her toward the small settee opposite her desk. She must have sat, because she watched as RueAnn reached into her purse, withdrawing a flimsy envelope.

Swallowing, she managed to push the words, "Open it" from her lips.

After tearing the flap and removing the telegram, RueAnn held it out to Susan. The paper crackled as Susan held it too tightly in nerveless fingers. She read it once, uncomprehending, then briefly squeezed her eyes shut and began again. But her mind stuttered like the needle of a phonograph skipping over a scratch in a record.

...Matthew Blunt...believed dead...

The paper fell from her bloodless fingers, fluttering like a wounded bird onto the floor.

Then RueAnn was there to hold her, to keep her from collapsing as the sobs came, threatening to tear her asunder.

## Rouen, France

With each day that passed, Charlie felt himself growing stronger and more impatient to be on the move. The longer he stayed with Elizabeth, the more dangerous it became for both of them, and after everything she'd done for him, he didn't want to repay her kindness with carelessness.

So, unbeknownst to Elizabeth, when she left for work in the morning, he dressed in his peasant clothing and slipped out of the house to explore the surrounding area.

He was careful to keep to crowds where he could blend in, hunching his shoulders and walking with a pronounced limp—one that was not entirely feigned— as he began to put more and more weight on his injured hip. He feared that as a man of military age, he would attract too much attention, but people doggedly went about their business, heads down, eyes averted, lest they catch the eyes of the soldiers who prowled the sidewalks.

Within the first few jaunts, he had located several avenues of escape should he need them. One led into the woods, another to a nearby river, another led straight into the heart of the city where a twisted series of avenues might allow him to evade pursuit.

But what he was most intent upon, was retracing the path that Rex had taken after Charlie had been injured. Somehow, he needed to find his way back to the spot where they'd camped the night before entering the city and making that fateful visit to the railway station.

So each day he went a little farther, explored a little more, trying to rely on the snatches of memory he had of that long-ago night.

At first, he was sure his search was fruitless. But then he found the spot where Rex had been killed. The stains of his blood still dark in the packed earth. From there, he began to circle, finding the bushes where they'd hidden part of a day, then a series of farms with corrals and pigstys, one of which was probably where Rex had hidden him in the mud.

It was growing dark by the time he returned to Elizabeth's house. He'd been out too long. The patrols were growing more numerous. But he'd pushed himself a little farther, until, finally, he'd been able to recognize the landmarks he'd tried so hard to memorize.

Another few days. Maybe a week. Then it would be time to go.

A truck suddenly screeched to a halt a few feet away. Even before it had completely stopped, several soldiers jumped from the back and ran toward him.

Charlie reacted instinctively, flattening himself against the wall, already prepared to make his capture as difficult as possible. But the men ran past him to the door of an apartment house.

Knowing he had to get away—now! Charlie backed toward one of the alleys, even as the soldiers dragged a pair of men from the building, forcing them into the truck. Ignoring the pain in his hip, he pushed himself harder and faster, weaving in and out of the alleyways, sticking to the shadows as much as he could.

By the time he reached the outskirts of town and could see Elizabeth's house in the distance, he was winded and hobbling. Bloody hell, just let him get the last few yards undetected.

Once he was across the street from the ramshackle shack, he waited, knowing that he'd been gone too long. Getting inside undetected would be more difficult as the tram disgorged the last of its passengers before curfew.

Leaning against the trunk of a tree, he remained in the shadows, damning himself for stupidly thinking that he was well enough to go so far. Dragging air into his lungs, he waited and waited, praying that darkness would come, that the street would grow quiet before his muscles completely cramped up or he collapsed where he stood.

Nearly an hour later, he saw his first opportunity, and knowing that he couldn't afford to hesitate much longer, he hurried across the street to the bushes and trees that bordered the property, ignoring the front door and skirting around to the back. Then, after a quick glance around him, he grasped the latch and let himself in, swiftly shutting the door behind him.

There was no mistaking the click of a pistol hammer being eased into position. A light flared.

Charlie blinked, then focused on Elizabeth who pinned him down with his own revolver.

"Shit!" he gasped, then sagged against the door.

As if sensing he'd reached his goal, his muscles suddenly gave way and he collapsed, sliding down the length of the door, his legs splaying out in front of him.

"*Merde,* Charlie! What have you been doing?"

He couldn't speak. He shook his head from side to side, his eyes closing beneath the pounding thrum of his hip and shoulder.

"Are you trying to kill yourself?" she demanded with a harsh whisper. Rushing to his side, she hooked his arm around her shoulders.

"No," he gasped. "I can't…give me a minute…"

"Now. Now before you aren't able to stand at all."

He groaned, planting his feet against the floor, pushing, pushing, until he managed to struggle to his feet.

"Into the bedroom."

"No. Cellar."

She looked as if she were about to argue, then obviously thought better about it because she helped him to the hinged panels, bent for a moment, and flung the door open.

"Careful," she warned as they took the steep, narrow steps.

Charlie tried to lean as much as possible against the wall rather than on Elizabeth's slender frame. Half-walking, half-stumbling to the pallet on the floor, he collapsed, panting.

"I need to see if you've re-injured yourself," she said, reaching for the buttons of his shirt, but he pushed her hand away. "No…just tired…went too far."

"*Mon dieu!* What were you doing out there!"

"I—"

"You didn't just endanger your own welfare, you endangered mine!"

"Eli—"

"Do you think that I would do all this—" she waved her arms wildly "—shelter you, tend you, feed you, simply to have you waste all my efforts in a moment of thoughtlessness?"

"I—"

"What if someone had seen you? What if my *neighbors* had seen you? The Germans are offering rewards for escaped soldiers."

"You're right. I know you're right. And I'm sorry. I had no business endangering you or drawing you into my own private battles."

Her chin tilted proudly. "You are not the only one battling the Germans, *mon ami.*"

## London, England

When the all-clear sounded, a thin strip of pink was just tingeing the horizon. RueAnn slipped through the canvas flap, chaffing her arms against the morning chill.

After September and October had been so warm, RueAnn had begun to believe that autumn would never arrive in England. But the past few nights had heralded a bite to the air—and a new concern. Once winter came, they would need a better door on the Anderson as well as a means to heat the shelter.

She was so intent on her thoughts that she nearly didn't see the figure sitting hunched at the kitchen table.

"Richard?"

She hardly recognized her new boarder, Richard Carr. Blood and grime covered his face and hands; his clothes were torn and sooty, revealing more lacerations beneath.

He stared at her blankly, clearly in shock.

"Richard, what happened?"

He shook his head numbly. "Bomb...exploded." He held up his hands, not recognizing them as they trembled violently. "I'd gone back to the lorry for a spanner...when the whole thing went up."

"And the rest of your men didn't take you to the hospital?" she asked in disbelief as she hurriedly gathered a basin and went to the sink for water. But when she twisted the spigot, nothing happened.

"My crew…were working on the bomb."

RueAnn whirled to look at Richard in horror, then, seeing the pallor beneath the filth, she hurried to the stove where a teakettle should—yes! It was half-filled.

Since the coals in the stove still smoldered, the water was only slightly warm, but it would do for now. Grasping a clean dishcloth, she hurried back to the table and began to dab at Richard's face.

"What about Mr. Rigdon? Gerald."

Richard shook his head. "Don't know. He was at a different site."

A part of her sagged in relief.

"Do I need to take you somewhere, notify someone?"

Richard's brow creased. "I-I…don't know."

RueAnn paused, cupping his face in her hands and gently lifting it so he looked at her. "Richard? Richard, I think you're suffering from shock. Richard!"

He blinked at her uncomprehendingly.

For a moment, she was at a loss of what to do. But then, as an icy calm washed over her, she closed her eyes and drew upon the information she'd gleaned from the first-aid spotlights that regularly aired on the radio. Wrapping Richard's arm around her shoulder, she said, "Come with me. We've got to get you lying down."

He rose unsteadily to his feet.

Knowing she could never navigate the stairs, she led him into the parlor and helped Richard to lie down on the couch. Rushing to Edna's room, she gathered all the linens she could find. Then she returned, stacking pillows and folded blankets beneath his feet, until she'd propped them as high as she could. Working quickly, she untied the laces on his boots and tugged them off. After layering him more blankets from upstairs, she hurried back to the Anderson and slipped inside. Creeping to the bunk where Susan slept, she softly shook her shoulder.

Susan awoke with a start.

"Richard Carr has been injured and I need your help."

Between the pair of them, they managed to remove his tattered clothing down to his underwear. Then, while Susan began to sponge his face and arms clean, RueAnn went in search of water.

Unsure where or how far she would have to go, RueAnn paused at the front gate, two metal pails held securely in each hand. Seeing more smoke toward the south and east, toward the Thames, she headed in the opposite direction.

It never ceased to amaze her how London came alive as soon as the all-clear sounded. Since air losses had forced the Germans to change their tactics and focus primarily on nightly bombing raids, the inhabitants of the city had quickly adapted to their dual lives. Nights were spent trying to sleep in the crowded shelters. But the days...

The days were precious nuggets of normalcy.

Even as weary mothers began to shepherd their sleepy children toward home, the work force began to appear—businessmen in suits, office girls in their smart dresses and heels, and the myriad branches of military. Bus stops and Tube entrances were soon crowded, neat queues forming without a word.

RueAnn joined the tide flowing in the opposite direction, housewives and youngsters with pails seeking water for washing and cooking.

* * *

Richard Carr was sleeping peacefully on the couch. The color had returned to his face and his skin had lost its waxy sheen.

"He looks better than before," RueAnn whispered.

Susan nodded. "I gave him some sweet tea." She grimaced. "I used the last of your sugar. Sorry."

RueAnn waved away the apology. "It doesn't matter."

"Gerald came by. He was truly relieved to find Richard

alive and well. He'll get in touch with Richard's superiors and let them know he wasn't…in the middle of the blast. He's gone out again. Evidently, the Germans are purposely setting some of the timers to explode long after the bomb has landed and the UXB boys are flooded with calls. He'll try to check on Richard later in the day."

RueAnn nodded.

Susan adjusted the blanket around Richard's shoulders, then sighed. "I've got to get to work."

"Of course. Thank you."

Susan was nearly to the door when RueAnn called out. "Do you need a pot or a frying pan?"

"A what?"

RueAnn grinned when Susan looked at her as if she'd lost her mind. "According to tattle at the line of women waiting for water, Mr. Marbury, the grocer off Tottenham, found some cookware when he cleaned out his storeroom."

"Found?" Susan said, one brow arching.

"Quite miraculously, yes. I thought I'd go get us a new pot in the morning. Do you want one as well?"

Susan's smile was broad. "What for? Lately, we've been eating here more than at home." She laughed. "I'm thinking of breaking through one of the walls so I won't have to brave the bad weather between our two gardens once the snow begins to fly."

• • •

The following morning, RueAnn wasn't the only woman to begin the day long before the all-clear sounded. When she arrived at Marbury's shop, a line had already formed at the door and was snaking around the corner. Hurrying into position, RueAnn patted her purse to make sure her ration cards and pocket money were still safe.

"It's a bit nippy out, isn't it?" the woman ahead of her remarked, clutching her knitted sweater tightly against her throat.

No, not a sweater, RueAnn corrected herself. They called

them jumpers here in England, a fact which had caused her a bit of confusion when she'd first arrived.

"Are you here for a pot, dearie?"

"Yes. Mine is so badly dented, it tends to roll from the burner."

"I'm hoping for one of the frying pans, myself," she said, sniffing. The cold had turned the tip of her nose a bright pink. "I've heard some say that it's unpatriotic the way Mr. Marbury's selling the cookware rather than donating it to the metal drive or the Spitfire fund." She stamped her feet. "But I says it's equally unpatriotic to send the men folk off hungry every morning without a proper breakfast in their stomachs. I surrendered most of my cookery at the beginning of the war and I'm livin' to regret a bit of it now. How about you?"

"I-I wasn't here when war broke out. But judging by the supply at hand, I'd wager my mother-in-law did the same."

"Where you from? Canada?"

RueAnn shook her head. "America."

"America!" Her eyes widened. "What in heaven's name are you doing here?"

"I came to be with my husband."

"He's here? In London?"

"No. He's…he's missing in action."

The woman clucked sympathetically. Ahead of them, the sign in the window suddenly flipped to "open" and the crowd surged forward a few feet in anticipation. As soon as the door opened, a dozen women crowded inside. A few minutes later, an excited murmur rose as the first group of women emerged again, triumphantly holding their cast iron skillets.

"Your husband should have kept you with your own people, nice and safe," the woman said after a moment. Mr. Marbury must have been hurrying to distribute his booty before the authorities caught wind of it because the line was moving quite quickly now.

People? RueAnn felt a moment of confusion. She had no people. There were her sisters, but her father had poisoned them against her.

Startled, she realized that, however it had happened, these had become her "people." Her family. Fellow Londoners, the women of her neighborhood, the Blunts. Edna.

The realization brought an incomprehensible wonder along with a bittersweet sadness.

This remarkable sharing of their lives and their resources had brought her closer to these folk than she'd ever been with anyone else, including her own kin. Yet, she also worried that this same sense of…community could be stripped away as quickly as it had come. If Charlie were to return, if he demanded that they divorce and lead separate lives…

She would be alone again.

Without warning, the fierce roar of a plane overhead sent the women pushing into the shop and flattening themselves against the wall, shielding themselves as much as possible. Bullets smacked the streets and bits of cobblestone peppered them like nails. Then, within a heartbeat, the German Messerschmitt climbed up, up, as a Spitfire roared in pursuit, its guns firing from behind.

Suddenly, a blossom of black appeared at the base of the Messerschmitt's wing, then a lick of flame which dissolved into an explosion. The canopy opened, a figure emerging as the plane broke in two, the wing plummeting one way while the rest of the wreckage cart-wheeled into a building somewhere blocks away. The crash was deafening—a screech of metal and broken glass. Within moments, a puff of smoke began to rise up above the rooftops, while high above, a parachute opened and the pilot floated silently down, down, like a dandelion seed seeking purchase.

At the last minute, the wind changed direction, sending him back in the direction of the women waiting outside Mr. Marbury's shop.

A murmur rippled through the group, becoming louder, more frenzied.

"He's going to land there, right over there!"

For a moment, the neat queue was forgotten as those who had purchased their pans mingled with those who had not yet entered the shop. Then, the soldier landed, hard, upon the cobbled street, his parachute becoming tangled around a nearby lamppost. When he tried to rise, the women suddenly surged forward, wielding the only weapons they had at hand, their newly purchased skillets, pocketbooks, and shopping baskets. Before RueAnn could even summon the wits to move, the crowd overwhelmed the German and began pelting him with blows.

The shrill squeal of a whistle heralded the arrival of a pair of policemen. But the women would not stop. This pilot had become a symbol of their fear, and they continued to beat him until he sagged onto the street.

Only then did the shriek of the whistle penetrate. The group began to dissolve as one by one, the women backed away, some running, some panting, gathering breath for another attack.

"Is he…"

RueAnn strained to hear the policemen, watching as one of them bent to lay a hand on the German's chest.

"…just barely." He stood, waving the women away with his hands. "Go on, now! Go on!"

RueAnn trembled as she watched the last of the ladies disperse—some of them sobbing, others righting their hats and returning to their spots in line as if they'd merely stepped aside to retrieve something.

Forcing herself to turn away from the limp German and the women who stood placidly in line, their clothing spattered with blood, she fought to keep a cold panic from seizing her.

Who would have thought that such proper, mild-mannered English gentlewomen could have formed so quickly into a bloodthirsty mob? But then, as she was resolutely pushed forward into the shop, RueAnn thought: Who could blame them? It was a wonder that the women of London didn't stream into the streets each night to overpower the gun operators in an attempt to shoot down the bombers themselves.

Woodenly, RueAnn collected her pot, a small bag of sugar, and four ounces of ham sliced so thin it was transparent. She surrendered her coupons, paid her precious coins, and hurried back outside, craving the cold chill air, praying it would help to blow away the images of what she'd just witnessed.

Nevertheless, she purposely took a longer route, skirting the spot where the German flyer had lain. After what she'd already seen, she didn't want to add the image of the man's blood soaking into the granite cobblestones like so much grease and oil from passing cars.

My Beloved Wife,

I've spent a good deal of my time alone during the last few weeks. I'm not complaining. On the contrary. The woman who is hiding me is doing so at great risk to herself. It would mean death or imprisonment for her if I'm found, and my fate wouldn't be much better. Yet, somehow, she has agreed to help me. Each day, she heads off to work daily in the morning, not returning until late in the evening when she shares her meager rations and we talk. The rest of my time is spent in her root cellar, doing everything I can to remain as quiet as possible.

I won't worry you over-much with the details, but I've been wounded. I must confess that for a time, I thought I was a "goner." But, thanks to my new friend, I've survived and grow stronger every day.

I've done a lot of sleeping. All the rest has helped me to heal quickly, but I'm growing quite tired of the dark and the silence. Kerosene is much too precious for me to even think of wasting it on myself, and the blinds and blackout have to be kept in place night and day. So my only recourse is to prop open the trap door near midday. If I sit on the steps near the top, I can see well enough to write you a letter on the pieces of paper that my helper managed to find for me. I only have a few pages at my disposal, so I've rationed them. But if I write small and use narrow margins, I should have enough room to convey my thoughts.

As far as my situation goes, I don't dare be too specific. It would be dangerous if these notes were discovered and I'd given too many details of my reasons for being here or the woman who has come to my aid. But that doesn't mean that I can't tell you what I've discovered in these past lonely weeks.

A person learns a lot about himself when he's on his own for such long periods of time. I've spent a lot of time thinking about the things I've done. I've got regrets—far too many to count.

But I don't regret a single second of my time with you. I think that I can honestly say that the day I married you was a turning point in my life. It was at that moment, just after we'd exchanged our vows, that I'd realized I wanted to be different. You gazed up at me with such trust that I wanted to become the man you thought I was. I hope I get that chance. I hope that, one day soon, we'll be reunited. I want to look deep into your eyes again, and be warmed by your goodness. Your hope.

I will return to you, my love, my wife. Don't forget me.

Don't give up on me.

Charlie

# Chapter Fourteen

Susan stepped into the bathroom, her arms filled with her towel and her ever-shrinking supply of toiletries. It wouldn't be long before they would be completely out of soap again. She had only a dusting of powder left and a few drops of watered down shampoo. But right now, she didn't care. She wanted to soak in a hot bath until the first air raids sounded—hopefully hours from now. After the water supply had been cut for two days, she was longing for a proper wash.

She was reaching for the spigots, when her eyes fell on a dark black line circling the tub only a few inches from the bottom. Grimacing, she reached out to touch it, only to discover that it wasn't a dirty ring as she'd first supposed, but...

*Paint?*

"Phillip!" she bellowed at the top of her lungs. "Get in here this instant!"

Her brother staggered into the bathroom. "What? I was trying to get a nap before we go to RueAnn's."

She stabbed an accusing finger toward the tub.

"What on earth have you done?"

He glanced at the line. "Voluntary water conservation measures." He turned and staggered back in the direction of his bedroom. "'Course, with the way they send someone 'round to read the meter, it's probably not all that voluntary. Instructions came in a special morning post. Do not fill the tub past that line."

Susan glanced from her brother to the raggedy line permanently tattooed onto the surface of the tub.

How in heaven's name was she supposed to clean herself in that scant amount of water, let alone wash her hair?

"Out. Out!" Sara staggered into the loo, flinging open the

lid to the commode. Before she could even kneel on the ground, she emptied the contents of her stomach into the porcelain bowl, then huddled, retching.

Dropping her belongings on the edge of the tub, Susan quickly wet a facecloth with water and handed it to her sister, then reached around her to flush.

"You've got to see a doctor," Susan insisted as Sara twisted to lean her back against the wall. Eyes closed, she panted softly, indecisive as to whether the nausea had completely passed. "If you won't do it for yourself, then think of Phillip or Edna. You don't want to be passing this bug around."

Her sister laughed bitterly. "Trust me. This isn't something I'll be passing around any time soon." Her humor turned hysterical. "It'll be about five and a half months before I pass it around, to be exact."

Susan shook her head in confusion. "You're not making any sense."

Sara drew her knees up against her chest and regarded her twin through half-slit lashes.

"I'm pregnant, Susan."

Susan's mouth formed a wide "O". Then, sinking down on her knees in front of her sister, she said, "But, how? I-I don't understand how—"

"It happened the usual way," Sara said bitterly, throwing the cloth in the sink.

Susan thought of the letters hidden beneath her mattress. Sweet, sweet love-letters that she had stolen from her sister.

"Who? I mean, does…Paul…know?"

Sara eyed her in confusion. "Paul. Paul Overdone? Why on earth would I tell Paul anything?"

"I just assumed…I mean…You went with him…"

"To the pub," Sara said, enunciating each word. "Good Lord, I haven't even thought of the man in months."

"Then, who's…"

"You needn't pussy-foot around the issue, Susan. I'm not going to spontaneously combust if you allude to sexual intercourse."

"Sara!"

"Don't be such a prude." Her chin wobbled. "You can't be a prude, because…because I need you. I need your help."

Susan reached out, clutching Sara's hand. "What about the father?"

The tears came then, spilling over Sara's lashes and streaking her cheeks along with the tinge of smeared mascara.

"Bernard can't help me."

"Bernard? Bernard Biddiwell?"

Susan couldn't have been more shocked. Yes, she'd been well aware that Sara and Bernard spent a great deal of time together, but…

But Sara was beautiful and effervescent and fun. Men followed her like baby ducklings, and yet, she'd chosen to be with…Bernard Biddiwell?

"Don't look at me like that," Sara sobbed, the tears coming harder and faster. "I've known Bernard for…for forever."

"Yes, I know but…"

"But nothing! He's kind and sweet and…and…"

And short and balding. A complete homebody. He was nearly thirty and still tied to his mother's apron strings if Sara was to be believed.

"I've known him forever," Sara said. "When I'm around him, I feel…beautiful."

The comment stunned Susan. Her sister had always been so vibrant and comfortable around men that Susan would have never suspected that Sara had ever doubted her attractiveness.

"I-I know what you're thinking…th-that I could have had my pick of any of the men I used to drag home for Mummy to feed. But around them, I always felt as if I had to…act the part. But with Bernard…I can be…me…"

Huge sobs tore from her chest. Susan held her close, patting her back, trying to calm her.

"Where is Bernard now?"

If he had rejected Sara in her current condition, Susan would have the man tarred and feathered. She remembered in the past how her mother—her lady-like, mild-mannered, genteel mother—could suddenly appear ten feet tall and as fierce as a bear if one of her children had been wronged. And suddenly, Susan knew just how Millicent Blunt had felt.

But her sister began crying even harder, her tears soaking through Susan's blouse.

"He's been given his naval appointment on a destroyer. He sails a week from Friday next!"

And suddenly Susan understood her sister's tempestuous emotions. She was alone, pregnant, and about to be labeled "one of those girls" by the neighborhood gossips. Worse yet, her sweetheart was being sent into active duty, perhaps never to return.

Like Charlie.

And Paul.

"Can you get word to him?" Susan asked after the storm of weeping subsided.

Sara blinked up at her, tears sparkling on her lashes, her face smeared with mascara, her cheeks blotchy with emotion. Susan had never seen her sister looking such a mess...and yet, at the same time, so beautiful.

"I'm wondering—and mind you, I don't know anything about what would be involved in such matters—but I'm wondering, if perhaps, we could arrange a wedding." She hastened to explain, "Not just because you're pregnant, but because..." she used her palms to wipe the streaks of black from Sara's cheeks. "Because you're in love with Bernard—as I'm sure he is with you—and the two of you deserve to celebrate your happiness."

For the first time in weeks, Susan saw a bit of hope sparkle in her sister's eyes.

"Do you think we could?"

"I don't know. I really don't. I don't know if there's enough time to get the proper papers, arrange for a vicar..." As Sara's joy faltered, she promised, "But I'd wager that if it can be done—you, me, RueAnn—we can make it happen."

* * *

When it became apparent that the possible legal formalities could be set into motion and Bernard would be able to get leave, the women were immediately thrown into high gear.

The wedding would take place in the Tolliver home, since Edna's front parlor was more suitable for formal occasions. RueAnn and Louise launched themselves into the preparations, polishing the woodwork, scrubbing floors, beating rugs within an inch of their lives.

Even Edna, who was managing to do a little more on her own each day, rolled her chair next to the kitchen table and spread out the silver, diligently rubbing each utensil to a gleaming finish.

But the most difficult challenge they faced was the matter of refreshments.

Susan dug into the larder, discovering a long-lost pot of her mother's strawberry jam. Then, with a mental apology to Matthew—whom she refused to believe was dead without positive identification of his remains—she confiscated the meager sugar rations that her mother had been saving for more than a year and added the supplies to the pile taking shape on RueAnn's counter.

As soon as the neighborhood fence-line telegraph got wind of the nuptials, they were soon inundated with offers of fruit, spare vegetables from the garden, and a precious stick of butter.

Bringing a war ration cookbook to the Anderson, they pored over recipes with limited amounts of fats and sugars, finally deciding on a selection of small tarts, scones, and miniature savory pies. It meant that they would be eating nothing but vegetables from the garden until the end of the month, but a meeting amongst the boarders had been proven unanimous in splurging for the occasion.

Since it had become illegal for bakeries to ice a cake, they decided to make their own. Although they had barely enough sugar for the cake itself, they reserved a small amount so that they could drizzle a glaze over the top.

When the menu had been decided, they turned their attention to the bride herself. There were a few marigolds and chrysanthemums left in the front garden, enough for a bouquet—and the colors would be beautiful against Sara's skin.

When they began worrying about a dress, Edna became clearly agitated, pointing to the ceiling. After several minutes of fruitlessly trying to guess what she wanted, RueAnn finally hit on a process of reciting the alphabet, slowly, clearly. When she hit upon the proper letter, Edna would slap her hand on the arm of her chair.

"Dress? You have an idea for a dress?"

Edna shook her head and they began again.

"A…t…t…i…Attic! There's a dress in the attic?"

Edna's hand slapped against the arm of the chair and her head nodded emphatically.

"Do you want me to go look?"

Edna nodded again.

Pushing herself to her feet, RueAnn took a flashlight from the drawer and hurried up the staircase, past the "family floor" as it had been dubbed, past Mr. Peabody and the rat-a-tat typing, past the garret room where she'd been ushered her first night in London. A few feet farther, there was a smaller door that led into the attic space.

Other than right beneath the steep pitch of the roof, there was very little headroom and RueAnn was forced to stoop. Clearly, Edna was not a collector of things, because other than the furniture they'd brought up after moving Edna downstairs, the space was all but empty except for a few trunks piled in the corner.

Kneeling in front of them, she opened the first chest, uncovering a treasure trove of Christmas decorations—from delicate glass globes to tinsel, and intricately carved nutcrackers. Moving on to the next trunk, she smiled, realizing that this must be Charlie's. There were loving cups from various sports and school activities, yo-yo's and wind-up toys, a bundle of comic books, and a stuffed monkey, its fur nearly rubbed away.

The next trunk was more promising. Here, she found coats and scarves, mittens, and rubber galoshes. But nothing that even resembled a dress. Perhaps Edna was confused. There were still times when her frustration and emotions overwhelmed her.

There was only one other place to look. A suitcase that looked much too small to contain anything approximating a wedding dress.

But when she lifted the lid to expose a nest of tissue paper, her heart began to beat just a little faster. Pulling the protective layers aside, she exposed a beautiful silk, high-waisted gown with rows of tucks and lace interspersed with dozens and dozens of tiny mother-of-pearl buttons.

Lifting it high, RueAnn gasped as the delicate ivory silk flowed from her fingers like water. Beneath the gown, still swathed in tissue, she also found a veil edged in Chantilly lace as fine as a spider's web, a pair of satin dancing slippers, ivory silk stockings, and pale blue garters made from silk satin ribbon.

Looking at the beautiful garments, RueAnn tried to imagine a young Edna, one who had anxiously prepared to be a bride, carefully choosing silk and lace and ribbon. Had she been in love with Charlie's father? The house was rife with evidence of Charlie having been here as well as a little girl named Francine.

So what had happened to Charlie's father? Had he died? Or had Edna been abandoned? Either might explain the aura of bitter pride that had clung to her on that evening when RueAnn had first arrived.

Closing the attic door behind her, RueAnn hurried down the stairs, the silken ensemble cradled in her arms. The moment she walked through the door, Edna's mouth lifted in a crooked smile.

A sound that sounded very much like a slurred, "Yesh, yesh," burst from her lips.

RueAnn carefully laid the dress across Edna's lap. "Are you sure you want to loan it to Sara?"

"Gish."

"Give? You want to give it to Sara." She took Edna's good hand. "You can't mean that. This dress must hold happy memories for you."

Edna nodded, then said again, "Gish Shara."

"You're certain?"

Edna pushed the dress toward her, then made a cutting motion like scissors with her good hand.

Impulsively leaning forward, RueAnn placed a kiss on Edna's cheek. "You are a special lady, do you know that?"

Edna made a sound of scorn.

But there was no denying the glint of pleasure in her eyes.

. . .

Sara was married in Edna's front parlor with twenty-three guests in attendance—all close family and friends of the Blunts and the Biddiwells.

She looked beautiful in her borrowed dress, Susan decided. She'd been so touched by Edna's kind gesture that she'd refused to make any changes to the gown other than to baste the hem a little higher. Rather than a veil, she'd worn her hair up, with a coronet of marigolds tucked into the curls and her mother's best pearls around her neck.

*Something old, something new, something borrowed, something blue, and a sixpence in your shoe.*

The afternoon was magical, reminding Susan of those carefree days before the war—good food, rollicking music from the gramophone, laughter, and dancing.

Philip had manned his father's Kodak, snapping photos, capturing the bride and groom's first kiss as man and wife and the cutting of the cake.

The only thing conspicuously missing from the celebration, were the faces Susan most longed to see—Millicent and Walter Blunt, Matthew, Michael, and Margaret.

Susan and RueAnn had cleaned and decorated the Blunt house with flowers and vases of autumn leaves. For two days, it would be the "bridal cottage" until Bernard went to sea. Then Sara would go with Mrs. Biddiwell to Scotland where they would live in a cottage owned by Bernard's relatives until the tide of the war turned.

"I pray that they will have many more days to come," RueAnn murmured.

Susan hadn't told RueAnn about the baby. Not yet. There would be time enough for that. Just as they had for the wedding, she was sure that they would rally around Sara.

It was what women did in time of war or hardship.

"What about you, Susan? Will yours be the next wedding? Is there someone special in your life?"

Susan thought of Paul, of the beautiful letters she'd collected and hidden in the overnight bag she'd stowed in Edna's original bedroom where she would be sleeping for the length of her stay.

Her first thought when Sara had proclaimed her love for Bernard was that Susan was free to tell Paul the truth. She would no longer sign her letters with a simple "S". Rather, she would use her full name.

But almost immediately on the heels of such a thought, she was faced with the impossibility of it all. She had lied to the man. She had played him for a fool and he would not take kindly to her deceit. And with RAF casualties mounting as they fought to keep Germany at bay, she couldn't afford to clutter his mind with such nonsense anyway. She would continue to write, slowly weaning herself away from the correspondence until natural attrition doomed their relationship rather than conscious thought.

"No. There's no one," Susan said, realizing that RueAnn still waited for her answer.

"Give it time," RueAnn said, but they both knew it was a hollow promise. Men were already scarce and Susan felt as if she were drowning in responsibilities and regret. Since Sara had promised Bernard that she would live with his mother once he deployed, it remained to Susan to keep the home fires burning. With Sara unable to work, Susan was now the primary provider, the mother, the disciplinarian, even if it were only for her younger brother. She had nothing to offer any man who might take an interest in her other than a ready-made family and a stack of bills that she worked doggedly to pay each month.

Feeling suddenly older than her years, she pasted what she hoped was a happy smile on her face. But inside she felt hollow.

As she looked up, her gaze suddenly caught Edna's. And for a moment, she felt as if the woman could read her very soul. There was a wealth of sadness in the older woman's gaze, as well as a potent empathy.

Lifting the glass she held in her good hand, Edna offered a silent toast to Susan. And Susan, feeling more toward Edna than she ever would have thought possible, returned the gesture.

Rouen, France

Cursing softly under his breath, Charlie slipped through the shadows, easing up to the back door. Knowing that she might well blast a hole in him if he entered unannounced, he scratched on the door before easing it open enough to slip through.

"*Merde!*"

Just as he'd thought, she held his revolver trained on him. And though her hands shook slightly, there was no mistaking the accuracy of her aim.

"I was just taking a walk."

"Why can't you get it through your thick skull that it isn't safe—for either of us—if you're out roaming around!"

Charlie knew that she was right. He was well enough to travel—had been for days. The time had come to make his goodbyes. The fear stamped on her face convinced him. Elizabeth had enough to contend with in her life without adding the complications arising from a wounded enemy soldier, so he said with quiet dignity, "I'll be gone as soon as it's dark."

She stamped her feet. "Stop it! Stop being so reasonable… so…so *noble!*"

As quickly as her emotions had stormed and raged, they dissipated, like the calm after a violent cloud burst.

Lifting her chin, she said, "I need your word that you will stay here. Inside."

"I can't do that."

She eyed him with patent disbelief. "Why? Why can't you

err on the side of caution until I can find a way to get you back to England?"

He was quiet for long moments, watching her, weighing his options very carefully before saying, "You've always assumed that I was a wounded flyer."

She shrugged. "So you're infantry."

"No."

He limped to the table, settling himself into a chair and motioning for Elizabeth to do the same.

"Just before the Germans marched into France, I was sent to Austria to investigate a suspected weapons facility. Something experimental. But by the time my men and I were able to infiltrate into the area, the Germans had begun their march toward the sea. We found that the plant had been hit in an air raid. The facility was abandoned. So we began digging around, asking questions. The only piece of information we were able to uncover was that the family of one of the men in charge had suddenly packed up and moved to a spot just a few miles out of Rouen. So we made our way back, knowing we had very little time before the Germans would have the area clamped down so hard we wouldn't be able to arrange for a pick up."

She blinked at him. Growing still. "What are you? Resistance?"

He shook his head. "British SIS. The Secret Intelligence Service."

She regarded him blankly, then her eyes widened. "You're a spy?"

He grimaced. "Not a very good one, it would seem. My men and I buried supplies just outside of town, then headed to the railway station, hoping to gather information. What we didn't know was that the identity papers and travel documents had changed only a week earlier. We realized our mistake when a German patrol tried to arrest us."

"Which was how you were injured," she murmured.

"Yes."

"You said the facility was...experimental."

"Yes."

"So you still remember the names of the men involved."

"Some of them."

She collapsed into the chair opposite his. Absently, she traced a knot in the wood. "Today I was...approached."

It took several beats of silence before Charlie understood the import of her words. When he did, he searched her features carefully.

"Resistance?"

"Yes, thank God."

"What do they want?"

"Information." She licked her lips. "A man named Hauptman is in charge of inspecting all transports into the area. I've been asked to get into his office and alert my contact if certain names appear on the manifests." Her gaze held his as she said, "They are the names of top-level scientists the Resistance believes might have been captured by the Germans."

Charlie's breath hitched. Could his failed mission be revived? "Do you have this list?"

She shook her head. "They made me memorize it."

"Tell me."

She licked her lips, her mouth suddenly dry. "Heinrich Dieter."

He shook his head.

"Ernst Ruger."

Again, he shook his head.

"Wilhelm Geisler...Karol Von Treigenheim..."

"No."

"Erich Meissen...Georg Schultz."

"Yes," Charlie breathed.

"Claus—"

"Richter," Charlie finished for her.

Elizabeth abruptly stood, moving to the stove to begin a pot of tea.

"So that's why you've been wandering around? Trying to get out of the city and find...what? The secret weapons facility?"

"Not exactly."

"Then what, *mon ami*?"

He considered the consequences of his words, then said, "As I said, before Rex and I were nearly apprehended by the Germans, we buried...supplies...just out of Rouen. I've been trying to retrace our steps so that I could find the spot where they were stowed."

"What kinds of supplies?"

His gaze became piercing. "Ammunition, maps, a camera, and a radio."

She considered her words carefully before saying, "Could you tell me how to get to this place?"

"No, Elizabeth. This doesn't involve you."

She spread her arms wide. "But it does, don't you see? At least a few of the men you've been looking for are on the list the Resistance wants me to find. I can help you. I can help you retrieve your things and then, I don't know...Maybe we could combine forces and information...with my contact."

"I'll go with you," Charlie insisted.

"Without identification papers? *Non.* You'd be caught within a block. Especially since you're a strong healthy man of military age."

Charlie was silent for so long, she finally prompted, "Can you draw me a map?"

Sighing, he said, "I'll need paper and something to write with."

* * *

Elizabeth waited until Sunday, when she wouldn't be missed from work. One of her neighbors, Mr. Grimaldi, owned a bicycle, and she traded him a week's worth of butter rations for the use of the dilapidated vehicle, telling him she needed to visit a friend.

The weather was cold, so she'd dressed warmly—a thick sweater, tweed skirt, woolen stockings, and a knitted cap. In the rucksack on her back she'd packed a light wool jacket, gloves, and a scarf.

"You don't have to do this," Charlie insisted one last time.

"I could try going out at night."

She shook her head. There were bright spots of color on her cheeks and her eyes burned with determination in a way he'd never seen before.

"It's better this way." Then, hesitating only a moment, she lifted on tiptoe and kissed him on the cheek. "I'll be back as soon as I can. Don't worry."

Then she was gone, disappearing into the early morning gleam of sunlight on frost, leaving Charlie feeling more alone than ever before—and absolutely helpless. He returned to the cellar where any noise he made would be shielded and began pacing the room like a caged tiger, wishing there was something—anything—he could do to make time go faster. He tried to sleep, plan out the course of his career after the war. He re-read RueAnn's letters and wrote more of his own to her and to his mother. Then, as the house grew cold and dark, he made his way upstairs where he could listen for the slightest hint of her return.

Finally, when he thought he would be unable to bear another minute, he thought he heard footfalls in the back yard, the *clunk-thud* of firewood being gathered from the back stoop.

Shrinking behind the door to Elizabeth's bedroom, he held his thumb ready on the trigger.

The lock clicked and the door swung wide, then slammed closed. Then Elizabeth flattened herself against the wall. After breathing heavily for a minute, she hurried to the stove, opening a small door and placing the wood on the banked fire.

Charlie stepped into the kitchen. "Are you all right?"

She nodded, poking at the ashes until a flame began to catch hold of the larger sticks. Then she held her hands out toward the heat. "*Oui.* I had to run back from Mr. Grimaldi's because curfew is past and I didn't want to be seen." She shivered. "It's freezing in here. You should have stayed under the covers, *mon ami.*"

Charlie shrugged. He'd been too worried about her to even notice the chill, but now that she'd mentioned it, his body was wracked with shivers.

Latching the stove again, she turned and set her rucksack on the table.

"Did you find it?" Charlie murmured, his stomach churning with nerves.

"Yes." Her wide grin could have lit the room on its own. "I didn't have time to examine it, though. I had to take a circuitous way there and back to make sure I wasn't being followed. It took a lot longer than I'd planned. I wasn't sure I'd located the right place, but then I found the first landmark—the lightning-blasted tree. I did what you told me to do...meandered through the area, slowly making my way to the hiding place on the hill. I ate my lunch there, carefully digging beneath the gnarled roots until—*voilà!*—I felt the package"

As she spoke, Charlie took a bulky package wrapped in oilcloth from her bag. Blowing on her hands, Elizabeth reached to light the lamp, then sat on the chair, watching.

Charlie unwrapped the layers of oilcloth, carefully laying out his booty—a metal container of ammunition, folded maps printed on silk, and a tiny metal camera.

"What's this?" she asked, pointing to the miscellaneous pieces left over.

"The radio."

Her eyes widened. "A radio?"

Charlie quickly snapped the parts together. "Cross your fingers," he said, connecting the battery which had been cushioned in another smaller metal box wrapped with more oilcloth.

Within seconds, they were rewarded with a crackle of static.

Charlie laughed out loud, unhooking it again. For the first time since being wounded, he felt in control of his fate and the sensation was more heady than any drug. Finally, he had supplies, and even more important, he had information.

Quickly, he dismantled the radio again. Taking a dishcloth, he began to wipe away any moisture that might be lingering on the equipment.

"What are you doing? Aren't you going to contact your superiors?"

He shook his head. "The battery has been buried for months. I have no idea if it will last several hours or only a few minutes. As soon as I have something to report, I'll send them a message."

"So what do we do now?"

Charlie debated silently with himself before saying, "We get you into Hauptman's office so that you can look for the names of any scientists coming into the area. Then we contact the Resistance and pool our resources."

My Beloved Wife,

Last night, I dreamed of you. The dream was so startlingly real that even now I can't shake the image from my mind. You were standing in the rose garden behind my aunt's old house—the one where we first made love. In my dream, you were wearing a pale blue dress and the light was low and at your back. Your hair was down, the wind playing with the curls, tossing them against your cheeks. I was some distance away, closer to the house.

The moment I saw you, I moved toward you, needing to be closer, to touch you, hold you. But you turned away from me, calling to someone I could not see. For a moment, I felt a flood of uncertainty, fearing you were rejecting me. But then, a tiny figure bounded into view—a little girl that you swung into your arms before walking to meet me.

The scene was so vivid, so real. I could taste the tang of the salt air, smell the sweet perfume of roses. The grass rustled beneath my feet as I reached out to you, to the child in your arms. And then it all vanished like a puff of smoke and I woke to a sense of loss that was so all-encompassing that I could scarcely breathe.

Please, please don't give up on me. Don't let another man steal your heart.

Charlie

# Chapter Fifteen

## London, England

The house was quiet when Susan returned from work, dejected from the news she'd received. Last night's air raid had damaged the factory and it wouldn't be until after Christmas that The Meade Ironworks would be up and running again. That meant that Susan had been given a "Winter Holiday"—which was Mr. Meade's delicate way of saying she would be out of work and without a paycheck for the next few weeks.

Shivering, she hung her coat on the hall tree. It looked forlorn there. Where once, she would have been forced to juggle for space with her father's overcoat, her mother's fur collars, and the children's sweaters and jackets, now the hooks were empty. That meant Phillip must be about his Home Guard duties since his shift at the warehouse would be finished by now. Either that, or he was spending the evening with friends.

Sighing, she gathered the pile of mail still scattered under the slot and hurried to the kitchen where a scant amount of heat would radiate from the stove, at least. Quickly, she fired up the coals and set a kettle on to boil.

Gathering a mug and the tin of tea leaves, she decided she would probably make her way through the hedge and spend the evening with RueAnn. Occasionally, there were nights when the air raid sirens remained silent and it wasn't necessary to pile into the Anderson, but the bustling atmosphere next door had become more of a home than this empty shell of a house. Now that she'd been given time off, she supposed she should give the whole place a stiff cleaning, but she didn't even want to think about it.

Sitting at the table, she kept an ear cocked toward the kettle and shuffled through the mail. Thankfully, her father's pension and insurance payments had begun to trickle in, so they wouldn't starve. But it would still be a balancing act of bills until she could get back to work. She sorted them into piles, looking for something from Paul. She hadn't heard from him in nearly a week and she'd begun to worry that…

An envelope with an unfamiliar feminine flourish caught her eye. It was simply addressed to Miss S. Blunt.

A cold prickling began at the base of her spine, spreading through her limbs until even her hands began to tremble. Turning the envelope over, Susan slit it with her nail and withdrew the single sheet of paper.

> I am writing to you on behalf of Lt. Paul Overdone at the bequest of his fellow pilots. On December 1, 1940, Lt. Overdone was badly injured…

An anguished sob burst from her throat. The paper fell from her nerveless fingers.

No. Not Paul. Please, not Paul.

Forcing herself to pick up the letter again, she tried to continue, but her brain was suddenly incapable of assimilating the words.

> …bombing raid…fire…ditched into the Channel…badly burned…hospital…

She fought to breathe, black spots swirling in front of her eyes.

> …If you could see fit to visit at Nocton Hall…raise his spirits…

Susan jumped to her feet and hurried upstairs. Taking a suitcase from the hall closet, she filled it with underwear, a few changes of clothing, then her toiletries. She knew she was probably forgetting something, something important, but it wasn't as if she were going to the moon. There would be shops in Lincolnshire if she needed something badly enough.

Rushing down the stairs again, she slid her arms into her coat and pinned her hat to her head. Then, scrawling a quick note to Phillip, she prayed that he wouldn't think she'd gone to Bedlam by taking a hasty trip to see a wounded flyer.

Carefully locking up the house, she hurried through the gap in the hedge.

To her relief, when she burst into the kitchen, RueAnn was there alone, stirring a pot of soup that bubbled redolently from the stove.

"There you are. I was just about to send Richard over to fetch…you…" RueAnn's gaze fell on the suitcase and a pallor leeched into her skin. "Is something wrong with Sara?"

Susan shook her head, trying to wave away her concern. "No, I…I…"

She suddenly burst into tears.

RueAnn took the suitcase from her nerveless fingers and ushered her toward the chair.

"What's happened?"

"A-A friend of mine…Paul…he's been…wounded…"

And then, unbidden, the whole story—from switching places with her sister, to stealing his letters, to discovering he'd been hurt—spilled from her lips in a jumbled mess.

Her confession was like a purging, filled with self-recrimination and stolen joy, and having suddenly unburdened herself, she shuddered, feeling empty and at a loss.

RueAnn stood. And for a moment, Susan feared that she was so shocked at Susan's conduct that the other women meant to leave the room. Rather, she moved to the larder and withdrew a piece of cheese wrapped in a cloth.

"You'll need something to eat on the train," she said as she began to slice dense bread and slivers of cheese. "Do you have time for a bowl of soup before you go?"

"Didn't you hear what I said? I took my sister's place. I stole her letters. All this time, I've been pretending to be her. I can't go to Paul. I don't have the right to even talk to him after the way I've deceived him."

"Did I ever tell you how Charlie and I came to be married?"

"No."

RueAnn leaned back against the counter, her fingers curling around the edge in a white-knuckle grip.

"I'd known Charlie hardly any time at all before we…" she struggled for words "…became incredibly intimate." She lifted a shoulder in a self-deprecating shrug. "It was wrong. We didn't even know each other." Her eyes focused on some long ago scene. "And yet, when he touched me…I felt…safe."

The kitchen pulsed with long moments of silence.

"Then my father burst into the room where we were staying, threatening me. Charlie." She bit her lip. "Charlie married me to protect me."

She crossed to sit in the chair next to Susan's. "I both loved and hated Charlie for doing that because, within hours, he was gone again."

Susan couldn't prevent the way her brows rose in surprise.

"That's right. I knew Charlie for less than a day."

"And yet, you came here when you heard he was missing."

RueAnn shook her head. "I found that out when I arrived."

"Then…why? Why would you come to England, knowing that we were at war?"

RueAnn's laugh was bitter. "If you only knew how many times I'd been asked that very question." She sobered, taking Susan's hand.

"I came, because—inadvertently or by design—Charlie took a packet of letters I'd written. In them, I'd poured out every secret, every sordid, selfish, horrible detail of my existence onto paper. There were things there that I had written for no one's eyes but my own. I burned with shame and betrayal. This man—a man I'd known only a few hours—didn't just know my body. If he'd read the letters—and I was sure he had—he knew my soul. I couldn't live with that. I couldn't bear to think that he was delving into the festering wounds of my childhood as if he were carelessly enjoying a Penny Dreadful and never once had he even acknowledged doing so.

"So I came to retrieve the letters and perhaps obtain a

divorce. Then I would return to the States."

Susan regarded her friend in shock.

"What I didn't count on was a war, constant bombardments, and…falling in love."

"With Charlie?"

RueAnn's gaze was sad. "I still don't know Charlie. I was so sure that what I felt for him that long ago day was a form of love. But he's as much a stranger to me now as he was then."

"Then…what?"

"I've fallen in love with this," RueAnn said, waving her arm at the room around her. "I've fallen in love with this home, my new family of sorts. I've fallen in love with the person I've become. You see, I'm in the midst of a war, but I'm not frightened anymore. Because I have a place here and people who need me.

"But I'm still terrified of one thing: that moment when Charlie returns, fully aware of my secrets. How will it change things between us?" She leaned close to whisper huskily, "The only thing that could be more terrifying…is if he doesn't return at all."

She squeezed Susan's hand. "Go to Paul. No matter what happens. Because the only thing worse than facing him…is if you don't and you're never given that opportunity again."

The warmth of RueAnn's hand sank into Susan's chilled flesh for a moment longer. Then she stood and finished wrapping up the sandwich she'd made.

"I'll take care of Phillip and the house. Don't worry about anything here."

Susan stood, calmer now, more resolved. RueAnn was right. She had to see Paul. She had to take this mess to its conclusion, no matter what that conclusion might be.

"I'll call as soon as I've seen Paul and know how long I'll be in Lincolnshire."

RueAnn smiled. "We'll be here."

* * *

As RueAnn placed the last of the supper dishes into the hot water she'd poured into the sink, she rolled her shoulders to ease their ache.

So much had happened as autumn had given way to winter. Edna was beginning to show marked progress. Her speech grew more distinct and she even managed to stand on her own and take a few steps with the aid of a cane and a supporting arm.

With the return of a portion of her independence, her mood improved as well. She soon became the hub of the household, seeing that the boarders were comfortable and well-fed. Each weekend, she spent hours poring over her recipe books. With the help of Mr. Peabody's typewriter, which he loaned to her every Sunday, she planned out the menus and shopping lists, including a few alternate selections should shortages put a crimp in her plans. When RueAnn cooked, she would watch her progress, tapping the counter with her cane if RueAnn forgot an ingredient or Edna felt the dish needed extra spices.

RueAnn doted on Edna as she would her own mother, and in doing so, she realized that this act of nurturing was a part of her nature that had been missing since she'd run away from Defiance and everything it represented. She had sworn then that she would have nothing to do with marriage or children or caring for a house. She'd already done her "mothering." She'd all but raised her younger siblings, and look where that had got her. Except for Astra, they believed her the demon child as much as her father.

But in coming to England, in confronting her own hasty marriage, RueAnn had inadvertently thrust herself back into the very role she'd sworn she would never play again: that of running a household. But here, where each day felt like a lifetime away from her existence in Defiance, she grew more confident. And in doing so, she admitted that she needed to be needed.

"Such thoughts will only get you wrinkles."

RueAnn started when the deep voice came from behind her. Whirling toward the sound, she almost expected to see Charlie, but it was Richard Carr who leaned casually in the doorway.

"Still worried about Louise?" he asked softly.

Unwilling to explain the thrust of her thoughts, she nodded. It had been nearly a week now since the older woman had come to work. RueAnn had sent Phillip to her home to see if she'd fallen ill, but he'd returned ashen, saying the block had been leveled. RueAnn didn't want to think the worst. She wanted to believe Louise had gone to visit her sister in Surrey, or was lying in a hospital somewhere. But knowing Louise's dedication to the family, she feared, like so many others, that Louise had become a casualty.

"D-did you need something?" she asked, her voice tight, her gaze skittering away from Richard's like drops of water on a hot stove.

He shook his head. Where Charlie was fair and sandy-haired, Richard was dark—dark hair, dark eyes, his skin ruddy from work in the cold and wind.

"I came to ask you if you'd come with me to the New Year's Dance at the Officer's Club."

Of all the things she might have expected him to say, this would have been the last. She gaped at him, dishwater dripping onto the floor.

"I-I'm married, Mr. Carr. You know that."

"It's just a dance." He straightened, coming toward her. "I don't know anyone else, really. And it's one of those parties I'm expected to attend." He waved an idle hand to the kitchen. "Besides, if anyone deserves an evening of fun, it's you."

She turned back to her task, rinsed the last of the cups, then reached for a towel. "I don't think it would be a good idea. Perhaps Susan will be back by then."

"But I don't want to take Susan." There was a note to his voice, like a ribbon of chocolate that was at once tempting and forbidden. "I want to thank you for everything you've done for me."

"Mr. Carr—"

"Richard."

"Mr. Carr, I don't think—"

He touched her shoulders, turning her. She didn't realize how close he'd come. She could feel the heat of his body seeping into her own. And, sweet heaven above, she wanted to bask in that warmth. Just as she'd discovered she needed to nurture and belong to something akin to a family, she felt herself weakening under the thought of companionship. More than anything, she wanted to feel like a woman again, however briefly. She longed for the simple clasp of a man's hand around her own, his arm around her waist.

Perhaps her father had been right. He'd accused her of being a carnal creature determined to stray from God's commands. Jacob Boggs would not have been surprised that she would toy with her vows to another man, that she would be tempted by a single night of fun when her husband was missing, perhaps imprisoned, wounded, or worse.

"Will you come with me?" Richard asked, one of his fingers skimming her cheek.

She closed her eyes, trying to ignore the sensations that single point of contact awakened.

"Please?"

She shouldn't go. It would be wrong, so wrong.

But even as her conscience begged her to reconsider, she nodded.

"Good." The finger strayed, touching her bottom lip. "The dance is at seven, so I'll collect you at the bottom of the staircase at six-thirty."

Then, he backed from the room, his smile filled with triumph and satisfaction.

As soon as he'd disappeared, she gripped the counter. Regrets swirled around her. She should run after him and tell him she'd changed her mind. It was the right thing to do.

But her feet were rooted to the floor and an echo of her father's voice reverberated in her head. She could picture him so clearly, standing in front of her, a box of writhing snakes held out toward her.

*Mark my words, the devil has you in his grip and you will not escape damnation. You will spend your days living in the fires of hell.*

Lifting her eyes to the smoke-smudged London skyline, her mouth twisted into a rueful grimace. She'd already lived through the fires of hell night after night, day after day.

So what did it matter if the devil marked her as his own?

## Lincolnshire, England

Susan's train arrived in Nocton long after dark. Since the specialized burn hospital was located several miles into the country, she found an inn and booked a room, surrendering her ration card so that two meals would be included during her stay. After arranging for the bellboy to take her suitcase upstairs, she followed the gaunt proprietress into the pub.

"Would you be wantin' a corner where it's quieter?"

"Yes, please."

The woman ushered her to a shadowy spot away from the bar and a knot of RAF airman playing darts and drinking pints. One of the men sported an arm in a sling while another struggled to play with his hands and part of his face swathed in bandages.

"Are you here for Founder's Day?"

Susan shook her head, accepting the one page menu. "No. I'm visiting someone. In a hospital nearby."

"You must mean Nocton Hall."

"Yes. That's the one."

"Family? A sweetheart?"

Susan hesitated before saying, "A sweetheart."

The woman clucked sympathetically. "Never you worry, dearie. They do good work with our boys, they do." She motioned to the group playing darts. "Those lads are from the hospital. We get quite a few of them in here." She gestured to the menu. "I'll give you a minute to look things over, then I'll come get your order. Would you like a drink in the meantime?"

Susan hesitated, then asked, "Have you any ginger beer?"

"I believe we might have a bottle. Let me check."

Susan forced herself to glance at the menu as the woman wove her way through the tables. There weren't many choices, but it had been a long time since she'd eaten the sandwich RueAnn had given her, so all of the dishes looked good.

"Here you are!" The woman set a large glass of bubbly liquid on the table. "Have you decided what you'd like?"

"Shepherd's Pie."

"Lovely. I'll be right out with it. In the meantime, if you need something, ask for Mary."

She'd taken a few steps when Susan stopped her.

"Excuse me, can you tell me how far it is to the hospital?"

The woman considered her answer for a moment, then said vaguely, "It's a bit of a walk, I'm afraid." Her face suddenly brightened. "If you could hold off until mid-morning, the laundry next door makes a delivery to the hospital. The woman in charge is a friend of mine, and I'm sure she'd be happy to give you a lift in exchange for the company."

"I don't want to impose—"

"No imposition. I'll ring her up and see what she says."

"Thank you."

As she moved away, Susan took a sip of ginger beer. In an instant, she was swamped by memories of the fancy dress party, Paul's arm around her waist as they danced, the passion of his kisses.

Her gaze slipped to the men playing darts. They were loud and boisterous, egging one another on, but there was no denying that their wounds caused them a great deal of pain. It was etched in the lines around their eyes, the hitch to their steps, the fumbling movements of their hands.

Would Paul be equally scarred or worse? She'd heard the stories, the way spilling fuel from a wounded aircraft would pour over the plane, igniting, so that when the canopy opened, a river of fire swept over the pilot. The hands and face were most vulnerable. And if the pilot ditched in the Channel, the cold saltwater could be excruciating until help came.

"Here you are, dearie," Mary said, setting a steaming crockery bowl in front of her. "Sally next door says you can drop by the laundry just before noon. Eat hearty so's you can get a good night's rest."

Susan nodded. But after her most recent train of thought, she wasn't sure if she could eat it at all.

*  *  *

Just as she'd feared, Susan spent a sleepless night at The Two Horsemen. She alternated between yearning for morning to come so that she could rush to Paul's side and praying for more time so that she could decide what to do.

When dawn broke, her panic grew even more palpable. Paul must be gravely injured if she'd been contacted by a nurse to come lift his spirits. So what did that mean? Was he weak? Dying? Was it wise for her to see him at all? Should she have arranged for Sara to come instead?

No, she thought in horror. She'd written things in her letters to Paul, things so personal and intimate that she couldn't bear to have Sara read Paul's replies. No, having Sara take her place would have been so complicated, so embarrassing…

So incredibly easy?

Feeling much like a thief plotting his grandest heist, she prepared herself carefully. Rather than simply combing her hair and holding it back with hairpins, she arranged her hair into Victory Curls—huge barrel rolls on either side of her face, and an artful chignon at the back.

She'd originally planned on wearing her most serviceable serge suit, but she opted instead for a muted floral dress with a frilly organdy collar and cuffs. She carefully applied her make-up, more heavily than she had ever been accustomed to wearing. Finally, cringing at her vanity, she applied leg makeup—and twisting and turning in front of the mirror, drew a "seam" up the back of her calf.

Then, with her energy suddenly drained, she collapsed onto the edge of the bed.

What was she doing? Was she seriously considering visiting Paul with more deceit in mind? She'd put everyone in this position by allowing herself to be talked into taking Sara's place once before. Was she thinking of carrying out the same charade, this time of her own volition?

But as she squared her shoulders and retrieved her pocketbook, she told herself that there was no other option. Paul thought that he'd gone to the fancy dress party with Sara. He believed that he'd been writing to Sara. To suddenly visit him as someone else with far too much knowledge of their correspondence could be distressing to a man who might be gravely injured.

\* \* \*

The ride to Nocton in the rickety delivery van was made without a hitch. As Susan made her way to the front door, she huddled deeper in her coat. If she hadn't been contacted and told Paul was injured, that it was important for her to visit, she would have lost her courage long before reaching the worn stone steps. But as she ascended the same treads which had probably hosted the cream of aristocracy, she felt small and as false as a two-headed shilling.

She'd been wrong to come to him as Sara. She could have explained things. She could have told him that Sara couldn't come.

But even as the thought appeared, she dismissed it. A fine how-do-you-do that would have been, to meet an injured man and inform him that he hadn't been important enough to warrant a visit from the woman he most wanted to see.

A woman dressed in a WVS uniform had planted herself behind a small table. Amid the pajama-clad patients and uniformed doctors and nurses, she looked incongruous behind the delicate marble-topped sofa table—one which had probably been moved from a sitting room somewhere.

"Yes. May I help you?"

"I-I've come to see Paul Overdone. A nurse sent me word that he was here."

The woman didn't appear particularly interested in Susan's explanation. She referred to a small box, much like a recipe holder, bristling with index cards. Rifling through the contents, she finally found what she wanted, pulled it nearly completely out in order to peruse the information typed in faded ink, then put it back in its proper position.

Barely glancing at Susan, she pointed toward the massive marble staircase that wound in stages to a spot high above.

"Two floors up. Ward Six. You'll stay to your right, about halfway down the corridor. He's in treatment right now, but should be returning to the ward shortly. If you'll look at the ends of the cots, you'll see the patients' names printed there."

"Thank you."

Gripping the strap of her pocketbook with both hands, Susan wound her way up, up, up, until she reached the appropriate floor. The climb gave her a spark of hope. Unless there was a lift hidden somewhere within the bowels of the building, Paul must have been well enough to navigate the stairs, hadn't he?

It was quieter up here, making her feel even more like an interloper. She unconsciously tiptoed down the hall—past the first door which opened into a ward of about a dozen cots crammed tightly together. Patients sat on their beds smoking, playing cards, and writing letters. Although they all sported bandages, she was relieved to see that their injuries seemed minor—cuts and scrapes, bandaged hands, patches of inflamed skin.

The second door held another ward nearly identical to the first, as did the next. But the fourth ward was quieter. As she glanced in, Susan was shocked to a standstill. This ward held men who were clearly more ill. It was smaller than the others, holding only four beds, but the men lay with hands swathed completely in thick white bandages that couldn't completely disguise the fact that they'd lost several digits. Their faces were also wound with strips of white, leaving mere slits for their eyes and noses.

A patient cried out suddenly, then began to moan piteously, the sound lifting the hackles on her neck. Hurrying past, Susan bit her lip.

Dear God, why had she come here? What had she thought to find? A happy ending? There could be no happy ending to the deceit she'd propagated.

But as much as she wanted to turn and run from the manor, she couldn't force her body to obey. She was almost there. She would say her hellos to Paul, be bright and cheerful and raise his spirits, then she would be on her way back to London with the evening train. After a few weeks, she would find a way to end the correspondence between them.

Moving quickly now, she passed a door that was ajar. A small card tacked to the wall read "Saline Baths."

Unbidden, she glanced inside, then grew rooted in place. Paul?

She almost didn't recognize him. Almost. He had been stripped completely bare save for his shorts, disclosing his body and more. Burned flesh, some if it so deep and raw it exposed the musculature beneath, covered his hands, extending up past his elbows and down the full length of his legs. More burned flesh nearly obscured one side of his face, while the rest of his body was covered with welts and lacerations. His body was a brilliant pallet of bruises, especially around his knees and his midsection. And his face…his face was swollen. Distorted. But she recognized him nonetheless. Not from the whole, but from the parts—dark, dark hair, the jut of his shoulder, the slenderness of his hips, long lean legs.

As she watched, four men each grasped a corner of the sheet on which he lay and lifted him over a porcelain tub—one of many in the room. Gradually, they lowered him into the water, ignoring the screams that burst from his throat and the flailing of his body. When he lay completely under the water except for his head and a small portion of his neck, the four men knelt to hold him there when he continued to buck and cry.

"It looks cruel," a voice said from behind her.

Susan started, whirling around to see a young blond woman in a nurse's uniform moving toward her. She gently inserted herself between Susan and the baths, reaching behind her to close the door. Even so, the screams continued unabated.

"One of our doctors discovered that the chaps being pulled out of the salt water in the Channel healed much quicker than those who didn't go in the Drink. So he's begun an experimental treatment with warm saline baths. It's proving to be quite successful."

At what cost? Susan wondered. Paul's cries were so heartbreaking, she feared she would be torn apart from the mere sound of them.

"May I help you?" the nurse asked with a bright smile, but it was clear from the way it stayed in place far too long that she resented the fact that Susan had been privy to one of her charge's misery.

"I'm Su…Sara Blunt. I received a letter…" She blinked against the damning sting of tears. "I'm here to see Paul," she whispered hoarsely, weakly lifting a hand toward the room where his screams had subsided into heart-rending sobs.

"Oh, dear." The woman's too-perfect smile faded as soon as it had appeared. She pondered the situation for a moment, then said, "Come with me. He'll be soaking for a while yet."

She led the way down the corridor, but having already seen the man she'd come for, Susan didn't bother to peer into the other rooms.

The nurse ushered her into a tiny area at the end of the hall—a space little bigger than a closet. A rickety bridge table surrounded by four mismatched chairs had been crammed inside as well as a supply cabinet, a hot plate, and a battered teapot with a stack of white mugs.

"How 'bout a cuppa?" the woman asked. She didn't wait for Susan's response, merely turned and poured tea into two mugs.

"Sorry, we've got no sugar or lemon. But I could probably find a little milk."

"No. This is fine." Susan sank into one of the chairs, wrapping her fingers around the hot mug.

"I'm sorry you had to see him like that."

Susan could hardly hear her over the roaring of her ears. She kept seeing Paul's mangled body and hearing his screams of pain.

"He will get well, you know, provided we can stave off any infection. The baths help with that."

"Will he be in a lot of pain?"

The woman nodded. "It's unavoidable. Think of burning your finger on a hot pan and magnify that by a hundred." She took a sip of her tea. "I'm the one who wrote you." She stared down into the rippled surface of her tea. "A few of your letters were found in his pocket. His mates said you wrote faithfully to him."

Susan nodded.

"A man needs a reason to fight when he's in this much pain." She glanced up then. "I've seen lads only half as bad as him who fade away because they think things are over for them—either that they'll be scarred, or incapacitated, or will never be allowed to fly again."

"Will Paul...fly?"

The woman shook her head "It's doubtful. Once an airman is injured that badly, he rarely gets a chance to return to a Spit unless it's as an instructor."

"And will he be...incapacitated?"

The nurse regarded her again, before saying, "That remains to be seen." She leaned forward, resting her arms on the table as if too weary to even sit up straight. "No one will blame you if you don't stay." Her head tipped toward the hall. "You've seen what you're up against, and no one will think badly about you if it's just...too much."

Susan suddenly realized that she was being given the opportunity to leave, now, before Paul ever knew that she'd come.

"Some of the girls who come to visit—wives and sweethearts—find that they just can't stomach the change in their loved ones. It would have been far better if they hadn't come at all than to leave after offering a little bit of hope."

It was a challenge and a warning. Would Susan prove to be one of those women? Or would she have the courage to stay?

"I've come a long way to see him," Susan finally said. "And I have no plans for returning anytime soon."

Glancing at the watch pinned to her uniform, the woman said, "Well, then. He should be back in the ward by now. Let's take you to him."

The nurse led Susan back down the hall to Ward Six.

"He'll be very tired after his treatment. Don't worry if he's sleeping and doesn't immediately wake up to greet you."

"C-Can I touch him?" Susan asked.

The woman hesitated. "He's badly burned and in a great deal of pain…" She relented, saying, "You may touch him anywhere without a bandage. Lightly, mind you. He's got a lot of scrapes and bruises."

Susan nodded to show she understood, but she couldn't speak as she was led into the ward. It was one of the larger rooms. There were a dozen hospital cots crammed tightly together, only half of them presently occupied.

Susan was taken to a bed near the window. The nurse pointed to a rickety chair nearby, then stepped away.

Susan was immediately conscious of curious eyes following her as she pulled the folding bridge chair closer to the bed and sat. But she soon forgot them as she drank in the sight of Paul.

Just as the nurse had warned her, he appeared to be asleep. The raw burns she'd witnessed had been swathed in fresh white bandages, so much so, that if she hadn't seen him without them, she probably wouldn't have recognized him.

Unsure what she should do now that she was here, she set her pocketbook on the table next to his bed. Then, needing some point of contact, she gently laid her hand on his chest.

The rise and fall, rise and fall was comforting. As was the faint bump of his heart.

Dear God, he'd nearly died—could still die.

Tears filled her eyes. She longed to draw even closer to him, to burrow up next to him and rest her ear against that same spot and listen to the steady rhythm of life that thrummed within him. But she had to content herself with that single point of contact. She didn't want to do anything that would bring him any extra pain. He'd already been through so much.

Though she swiped them away, the tears began to fall silently down her cheeks. Damn. Now wasn't the time to cry. Not with all of the mascara she'd applied.

Paul's eyes flickered. Opened.

Susan offered him a watery smile, swiping the last of the moisture away.

"Paul?"

At his name, he reared back, a sound of distress bubbling from his throat.

"Paul, it's me."

He shook his head, his hands scrambling as he batted her away.

"Get…out."

"Paul, it's—"

"Out! I don't…want you…here."

Shock rushed through her system so quickly that Susan felt as if she'd turned to a solid block of ice.

"Out! Get out!" He scrambled against the bedclothes as if he were a trapped animal suddenly cornered in his enemy's lair. "Don't…come…back!"

The nurse rushed into the room, followed by a pair of orderlies. While the men rushed to Paul's side, the woman pulled Susan into the corridor.

Susan's limbs trembled so fiercely, she could hardly stand. She tried to make her way around the sister, but the woman held her firmly in the hall.

"I'm so sorry," the nurse said. "Sometimes this happens."

Susan wrapped her arms around her waist, sobbing. But where only minutes ago she couldn't control the tears, now they locked painfully in her chest, robbing her of breath.

"What…*Why?*" she choked out.

The nurse's eyes grew sympathetic.

Susan struggled to find her equilibrium. Above all, she didn't want to make a scene. Nor did she want this woman or anyone else to become witness to her pain.

He didn't want her.

*He* didn't want *her.*

"I think it would probably be best to…give it some time before you visited again."

Susan wasn't fooled by the woman's diplomatic suggestion. The nurse clearly thought she should board the next train and head for home.

Nevertheless, Susan nodded, backing toward the staircase. But just as the woman was about to re-enter the ward, she hurriedly asked. "My sister...could she try visiting tomorrow?"

The woman hesitated, then reluctantly nodded. "Visiting hours are from eleven to three."

Susan thanked her, then scrambled down the marble staircase and out into the cold. Taking deep breaths, she hurried down the lane, away from the curious stares and good-natured catcalls from some of the patients. Once she reached the main road, she turned resolutely toward town.

Tomorrow, she would be back.

This time as herself.

Charlie,

You've read my letters, I suppose. I've come to terms with that. I can't imagine that you've had them all this time and haven't read them. I'm not sure what your reaction will be after hearing the kind of family you've married into. I think about that over and over and pray that you'll judge me by my own character, and not by my father's.

Nevertheless, I find myself drawn to pen and paper once again. I refuse to believe that you're dead and the thought that you're out there where I can't reach you haunts me. So once again, I've begun to write my letters, but this time, rather than writing down my hopes and fears to Jesus, I'll write directly to you. One day, I know you'll read them. Until then, at least I'll know that I've completely purged my soul.

What you've read so far is grim. But I haven't told you everything. There were things that happened that I couldn't bring myself to set down on paper until now. I thought I could tuck them away so deeply that they would never again see the light of day.

But after everything I've seen, I've become keenly aware of the fragility of life. And like so many others, I find myself needing to make a more permanent mark on the world—or at least to make sure that if something happens, I've left no loose ends behind. So I may as well finish the sordid tale so that you understand that the time I spent with you was not a casual affair.

Just as I told you the day you left, I have never been prone to rushing into relationships. In fact, I'd sworn to myself that I would never allow a man a place in my life. Not ever. Not after what I'd endured at the hands of Jacob Boggs.

After I caught my father with Rebel Mae Patroni, he punished me. Not just that night. No. He seemed determined to break my spirit, if not my body, and I would never have another peaceful moment in his presence. Where once, his gaze had caused my skin to prickle with unease, now I felt as if I were a rabbit being stalked. Every move I made had to be plotted carefully because I could not be alone with him. Not without a cold fist of fear gripping my chest.

At the time, I didn't understand the subtle change in power that had taken place. It wasn't until later, that I realized my father was afraid. He feared I would reveal his true nature, like lifting a rock in the forest to expose a nest of maggots beneath.

But before I could fathom what I had seen, what my father had done—the depth of his betrayal to my mother—my father changed. Where once his physical strength, his power over his family, and his work at the sawmill had been the axis of his existence, he now turned to God.

I didn't know then that he intended to bury his ugliness beneath a veneer of righteousness. I only knew that suddenly the days became longer in order to include prayers—morning and night, at meals, at special events, or whenever the mood took him. We were flayed with my father's interpretation of the scriptures, commanding us to be meek. Obedient. Subservient to the will of our patriarch.

And through it all, my father seemed to cling to one single commandment: "be fruitful and multiply the earth."

Despite her fragile health, my mother was destined to be pregnant or nursing, so we had a succession of young girls who came to help with the housework. None of them lasted long. Invariably, within a few months, their clothes would begin to grow tight around the middle and soon after, they would disappear. Not just from our house, but from Defiance altogether.

And still I watched, waited. Knowing instinctively that no matter what sorts of muffled noises I heard late in the night, I should not leave my room.

My mother, worn out with childbirth and a deep sadness that could not be alleviated, sank into a fervent, mindless devotion to anything that might ease her inner torment. Her room became cluttered with pictures of Catholic Saints, tacky dime-store picture postcards, and clippings of film stars—most predominantly, Shirley Temple. She began taking "medicinal sips" of alcohol and laudanum-laced cough medicine.

And as her mind slipped away into this hazy netherworld, she seemed to grow resentful of me. Perhaps she knew that I'd been the one to uncover my father's sordid secrets. Or perhaps, she found it the only way to handle the crushing humiliation she must have felt to have her own worst torments privy to her children.

I only know that at times when I would least expect it, I would turn to find her gaze on me, laced with such bitterness that I would be forced to look away. Then, my mother would return to her fervent supplications to St. Jude, Curly Top and the Golden Gate Bridge, until it became apparent that religion had become an escape for reality to my mother and a vengeful threat for those whom my father believed committed evil of any kind.

And he was forever finding fault with me.

RueAnn

# Chapter Sixteen

Saint Sebastian, France

Charlie crouched low behind an outcropping of rocks, blowing on his hands to warm them as Elizabeth and her companion slid into position beside him.

"You're sure this is the place?" Elizabeth's Resistance contact asked, his voice a murmur. Charlie had been told to refer to him by his code name Olivier.

Elizabeth nodded. "The papers in Hauptman's office listed the old abbey as the final transport point for the men on your list."

"And what is your theory?" the man asked Charlie.

Charlie met his gaze, taking in the pale silver color of his eyes, the hair which had long since turned gray. But he sensed that Olivier wasn't nearly as old as he let on. Probably early fifties, short, compact, with the sagging jowls of a bulldog. With his rough peasant clothing and gnarled hands, he was so ordinary, so unremarkable, that he could easily remain unnoticed in a crowd.

"The men on your list are believed to be part of a secret propulsion project."

"Meaning?"

"Rockets. In essence, a bomb that can fly itself."

Olivier looked skeptical, but didn't comment. Unbuckling his rucksack, he removed a pair of binoculars and studied the area below. "It looks quiet."

"It's early yet," Elizabeth said, looking up at a sky still pink at the edges. Thick gray clouds hung low on the hills. A skiff of snow had fallen during the night, making the ground hard and crisp—each blade sheathed in a sweater of ice.

"I don't see any movement. Usually, the Germans display their guards quite openly."

"May I?" Charlie held out his hand for the binoculars. Lifting them to his eyes, he adjusted the focus. Just as Olivier had said, the old abbey looked abandoned. The outer walls were crumbling, the windows were dark—some of them cracked and broken. And with the weather as cold as it had been this past week...

Cold.

*Ice.*

Charlie adjusted the slant of the binoculars, then hissed, his lips curling into a satisfied smile.

"Look at the grass."

He handed the binoculars back to Olivier knowing what he would see. As the first rays of sunlight slanted over the frozen sod, it illuminated a path of footsteps in the frost, prints that crossed over and over themselves as if a single person had made a circular route around the perimeter.

"Ahh," Olivier breathed in satisfaction. "It would seem that it isn't the abbey they are using but..." He grinned like a cat having just snapped up the canary. "Over there. The outbuildings further to the west."

Charlie retrieved the binoculars and looked where he'd been told. The old stone buildings at the edge of the forest were all but obscured by the trees, but there was no disguising that the walls around this section of the old monastery had been reinforced with razor wire. He could just make out a transport truck carefully shrouded in camouflage netting—and he would hazard a guess that it wasn't the only one.

"What were those buildings used for originally?"

He gave Olivier the field glasses and the other man quickly stashed them back into his rucksack. When he met Charlie's gaze again, there was a gleam of satisfaction in his silver eyes.

"The monks were famous for their wines—elderberry, blackberry, currant. If I remember correctly, those outbuildings were their workshops..." his grin widened "...while underneath, there were a series of buried tunnels where they stored their bottles."

For the first time since becoming trapped in Rouen, Charlie felt a small kernel of satisfaction unfurling in his breast.

"The perfect place to conduct secret research," Elizabeth murmured.

"*D'accord.* It's doubtful the Allies would have spotted it from the air, and even if they did, the tunnels would be protected during a bomb blast."

"So what do we do?" Elizabeth asked.

"Make a quick sketch of what you see."

She nodded, taking a stub of a pencil from her own rucksack and quickly drawing what she could see on a scrap of paper from an old composition notebook. Then she shoved everything back in her bag.

When she was finished, Olivier nodded toward the road. "We head back to Rouen—" he gestured toward Charlie—" before this one attracts too much attention. The papers I gave him will not pass inspection if he's approached and knows no French. I'll send some men to watch the Abbey. We need to know more before we can proceed: when deliveries are made, guards refreshed, supplies delivered. Then and only then can we add more details to your map and begin to plan."

"Plan?" Charlie asked. "You have something in mind?"

"*Absolument.* It won't be easy, but I think that we would do well to blow the Germans to kingdom come before they can advance too far in their research, *n'est-ce pas?*" He squinted down at the valley below. Then he looked at Charlie. "Do you think your friends in London could donate some materials toward that end?"

Charlie thought of the crystal radio set that had been dismantled and hidden under a floorboard in Elizabeth's house. He grinned. "Once I make contact, they should be able to drop supplies within forty-eight hours."

"Then we'd best hurry before Hauptman realizes his office has been breached."

Charlie nodded, regarding the innocent looking ruins of

the monastery. They were all playing a dangerous game of cat and mouse—Charlie, Olivier, Hauptman, and Elizabeth.

It only remained to be seen who would emerge the cat...

And who would be the mouse.

## Lincolnshire, England

On her second day in Nocton, Susan left the Two Horseman in plenty of time to walk to the hospital. The chill breeze and long trek would give her time to compose herself and collect her thoughts—because her emotions had been running high since her first encounter with Paul. She'd alternated between crying inconsolably from the sheer hurt of being sent away, to castigating herself for her foolishness. This charade had continued far too long. Somehow, she had to find a way to end it. But first, she had to see if, by coming as herself, Paul might allow her to stay a little longer.

As she made her way down the lane to the hospital, she felt as if a flock of swallows fluttered in the pit of her stomach. She was more nervous today than she had ever been. Not just because of Paul's abrupt send-off the day before, but because today there was no artifice to hide behind. She had come as herself—her hair simply combed, a favorite crepe dress, and serviceable shoes.

As she made her way up the worn steps, she noted that, this time, she garnered very little attention. She could have been another villager coming about her business rather than someone's sweetheart.

A clock from somewhere in the main sitting room began its tinny chimes as she stepped up to the ornate table in the front hall. The same woman guarded her recipe box of information as if she were a leprechaun hoarding a pot of gold.

"Paul Overdone, please."

She supposed she could have gone straight up to his ward, but after yesterday, Susan didn't want to inadvertently stumble in upon Paul if he was in the middle of his treatment.

The woman rifled through her index cards. "It's his rest time in the sunroom." She pointed to a corridor near the stairs. "Take that hallway there, turn left at the far end, third door on your right."

"Thank you."

Susan's heels rapped against the black and white tiles as she made her way through the foyer. As she followed the woman's directions deeper into the building, she noted that the furnishings on the main floor were nicer than upstairs, the paint work a little smarter. Perhaps the previous owners had run out of money and had simply kept up the façade of grandeur in the rooms that would be visited most.

As she turned down the last jog, light spilled into the hall several yards away, and she suspected she had found the sunroom without even needing to count the doorways. She hesitated, feeling an uncontrollable urge to pull the compact from her pocketbook and check her appearance, even though she knew she would find the same face that always stared back at her. And yet…for the first time, such thoughts didn't disappoint her.

Her steps were slow, measured, as she made her way to the sunroom. At the threshold, her gaze took in the faceted jewel of a room that bowed out into the garden in panels of glass. There were potted plants and trees—some of them gasping for a little attention—interspersed with a myriad assortment of chairs brought in from other areas of the house. Men in hospital pajamas and various uniforms hunkered around card tables, a puzzle, a dart board, or simply sat basking in the winter sun made warmer by the walls of glass and a dogged set of radiators.

She scanned the assortment of men, no longer startled by the seriousness of their apparent injuries and bandages. This time, she saw faces as she searched for one that was familiar to her.

And then she saw him.

Paul sat in a wheel chair a little apart from the others. He was staring out at the cold December day, but she sensed he didn't really see his surroundings. Instead, his gaze was hard. Unblinking.

She moved toward him, resisting the urge to smooth a hand over her hair. There was a metal bench opposite where he sat and she paused just as she reached it. Nevertheless, he didn't look up.

The room was incredibly warm, so she shrugged out of her coat, laying it over the arm of the bench and placing her purse beside it. Then she sat down, right in Paul's line of sight.

He blinked, focused on her, then looked away.

"How are you?" she asked softly.

There were several beats of silence, then, "Did Sara tell you to come here?"

Susan shook her head. "No. I came of my own volition. As soon as I heard you were hurt."

"You shouldn't be here."

"Why not? A friend of mine is in the hospital. Where else should I be?"

"Home with your mother."

Susan paused only a moment. "My mother is dead. She, Matthew, and Margaret were killed when the *S.S. City of Benares* was torpedoed. My father was killed during the Germans' first raid over London. My brother Matthew is believed missing or possibly dead." She met his look head-on. "So you see, keeping in touch with a friend is very important to me."

Paul held her gaze for long moments, before finally breaking the contact. "I'm sorry to hear about your family." The words were low. Ashamed.

He lapsed into silence and Susan didn't press for conversation. For the moment, she was content to be here, content at not having been sent away.

"Did your sister tell you how beastly I was to her?"

She wasn't sure how to respond, so she said instead, "Does it matter?"

For the first time, she saw a glint of humor. "That you talked to her? Or that I was beastly?"

"Either."

He shook his head. "No. I don't suppose it does."

"Why?"

"Because I don't want her coming back."

Susan swallowed, whispering, "Why?"

His gaze returned to a spot somewhere outside. "Because I don't want her to see me this way."

"Alive?"

His mouth twisted. "Disfigured."

She glanced down at her lap, her fingers twisting together. "Do you think that matters to her?"

"Yes."

"Why?"

"Because your sister is...beautiful."

*Where she, Susan, obviously was not.*

"I don't think you're being entirely fair," she said, unable to help herself.

"Life, as you may have noticed, is never fair."

"No. I suppose not."

He grimaced, realizing that he wasn't the only one to have suffered the vagaries of fate.

"Tell her I'm fine. Tell her...I've survived. But tell her I don't ever want to see her again." He closed his eyes, hissing in pain.

Susan waited until the spasm had passed.

When he opened his lashes again, he looked surprised that she was still there.

"You can go now."

"As you wish."

She stood, collecting her coat and pocketbook. "Is there anything you would like me to bring tomorrow?"

Paul shook his head. "You've done your duty. Go back to London."

"You've never been a duty, Paul," she said. Before she could stop herself, she reached out a hand, touching the top of his head, ruffling his hair, reveling in the way the dark strands flowed through her fingers like silk. Bending, she pressed a light kiss to his bandaged forehead.

"Fine then, if you have no requests, I'll begin by bringing

you something to read."

Then, before he could say anything to the contrary, she walked away, her fingers still echoing with the caress of his hair.

## London, England

With Christmas swiftly approaching, RueAnn began to make plans. Despite the restrictions and shortages, she wanted to host a celebration for her little "family." So drawing Edna aside one night, she confessed her intentions.

Edna immediately brightened, turning to her recipe books to decide on the dishes for their feast. If they were careful with the ration coupons, they should be able to come up with something special

Having delegated the responsibility of the meal, RueAnn turned her mind to the gifts. Although most of their funds were spent on keeping the house running, with a little creativity, she was sure that she and Edna could offer a small present to each of their friends and boarders.

For Susan and Sara, she planned on crocheting lacy edgings onto delicate silk handkerchiefs which could be draped over belts or used to adorn the pockets of their Sunday dresses.

Tonight, the raids were closer, the noise more fierce. The Anderson was nearly empty, for once. The sirens had gone off before the engineers had returned, and RueAnn prayed they were safe. Mr. Peabody was out of town on business and Susan was still in Lincolnshire. Phillip had gone to stay with a friend in the Tube. So there was only Edna to keep her company, and she'd fallen asleep.

Slapping her arms to keep warm, RueAnn added another lump of coal to the little potbellied stove that the engineers had vented to the outside about the same time they'd made a more permanent door. But even with the space completely enclosed, the night was bitter and the wind buffeted the corrugated tin.

RueAnn paused to check her stitches on the handkerchief

she was making, then swore softly under her breath. She'd missed a few chains nearly an inch back—probably when the reverberation of a bomb had caused her to flinch. Now she would have to unravel nearly a half-hour's progress.

"Bother," she murmured to herself, pulling on the cord. Since she'd wanted the lace to be particularly fine, she'd been using a spool of silk thread she'd unearthed in the bottom of Edna's sewing basket. If there was any left over after her project she would add some lace to Edna's—

A sudden wave of heat and noise threw RueAnn from her chair onto the floor. Her crocheting materials flung from her hands as she was pushed down onto the cold earth by an explosion of such magnitude that her ears popped and the air was driven from her body. For seconds, hours, she fought to remain conscious, all sound becoming muted, her gasps for air rasping in her ears until finally, she was able to breathe again—hot, hot air with the stink of fuel and gunpowder and melting rubber.

She was trembling so badly that she had to drag herself to her knees, the icy, hard earth biting into her skin beneath her nightdress and robe. Gripping the rails of the wooden bunk, she managed to brace herself so that she could check on Edna.

"Are you all right?"

Edna nodded, wide-eyed and pale, the blankets dragged up to her chin, her silken boudoir cap askew on her head.

"You're sure?"

"Yesh…yesh…"

Pushing herself to her feet, RueAnn stumbled to the door, pushing, pushing, then pushing again until she finally managed to scrape it open far enough to peer outside.

Adrenaline surged through her system, her heart jolted, pounding from the vicinity of her throat as she feared that the yard had scored a direct hit—and at first it seemed so. The garden was awash with a blazing light that shimmered and jumped. But as she staggered out into the snow, she realized that the blast had occurred further down the block. Huge flames enveloped the house on the corner. Beyond that was the black hole of a crater which had swallowed the mangled metal remains of a bus. Debris had been thrown in all directions—masonry, bits of timber, and the minutiae of life, books, clothing, torn curtains, and rubber tires.

And all of it, all of it was on fire.

A mountain of splintered beams had fallen near the spot where the hedge butted up against the communal wall, and RueAnn watched in horror as the flames began spreading from the beams to the hedge, licking against the barren foliage. Sputtering, popping, the conflagration leaped to life with the fresh fuel.

Dodging back into the Anderson, RueAnn panted, "Give me your blanket. Quickly! The house is in danger of catching fire!"

Edna pushed the woolen covering toward her and scrambled from the bunk, grasping her cane.

Running toward the hedge, RueAnn began batting at the blaze, praying that she could stop it before it reached the house. If the wood siding or decorative trim caught fire, she would never be able to put the flames out.

Panicking, she renewed her efforts, damning the ineffectuality of her efforts, wishing that she had more help. Why were she and Edna alone tonight of all nights?

"Rue…Ann!"

She turned to find Edna staggering toward her, a dented pail of water hanging from her good hand.

"Wesh blaksh!"

Throwing the blanket over an unaffected portion of the privet, she threw the water over it, wetting the wool, then handing the pail back to Edna.

"More!"

As Edna limped back toward the house, RueAnn began slapping at the conflagration with renewed fervor. The blanket was heavier now and more awkward to use. But she was rewarded with a hiss.

Just when she feared she would not be able to lift the blanket another time, Edna returned with a fresh pail of water. Grasping the handle, RueAnn threw the contents onto the burning hedge, handing it to Edna again, then renewed her efforts with the blanket.

Again and again they went through the same process—while all around them, the night became a cacophony of noise—the rumble of bombers overhead, the whistling of bombs, the reverberating explosions. And then, the clang of fire trucks.

Filled with renewed energy, RueAnn was finally able to push the flames at bay, back onto the pile of burning timbers, while all around her, the clanging noises became deafening. Shouts. And finally, the hiss of water as hoses were directed onto the shooting flames.

Panting, her lungs screaming in pain from cold and smoke, RueAnn dropped the blanket, leaning forward to brace herself on her knees as she fought for breath. The muscles of her arms and shoulders burned in pain and a cramp settled beneath her ribs. But finally, finally, she was able to calm herself enough to turn saying, "We did it, Edna! We…"

The words died in her throat as she saw the crumpled shape lying near the back door.

"Edna!"

Slipping in the mud and ice, RueAnn ran toward her mother-in-law's frail form. Stark shades of red and gold from the remaining fires flickered over the older woman's features. But even the garish colors couldn't disguise the gray pallor to her skin and the dark bruises that had settled in under her eyes. Her arms were bent, as if the muscles had tightened, until they looked like the wings of an injured bird. But it was her eyes that caught and held RueAnn's attention.

There was such fear there that RueAnn could not bear it. Lifting the older woman, she scooted beneath Edna, resting her mother-in-law's silvery head on her lap.

"I'm here, Edna. I'm here."

The panic eased as Edna met RueAnn's gaze. Tears gathered at her lashes. A garbled noise bubbled from her throat.

"Shh," RueAnn said, stroking her cheek. "Don't talk. I'll get you help. I'll…"

Edna shook her head, her good hand clawing at RueAnn's

clothing until she bent closer.

"Char...lie..."

RueAnn wanted to push Edna's concerns aside. She wanted to reassure her that she would see Charlie again, that this was just another setback in the road to Edna's recovery. But looking down, she could see what little color remained in her cheeks was seeping away, leaving her skin waxy and lax.

"Don't worry, Edna," she whispered, knowing that if there was nothing else she could do for Edna, she could ease these last few moments. "I'll take care of Charlie. I love him, you know."

Edna nodded, her grip still strong. "Love...you..."

RueAnn tried to smile, even as her chest began to ache with unshed tears.

"Yes, I suppose he loves me too."

Edna shook her head, suddenly desperate. "No...no..." she gulped air into her lungs. "Love...you..."

RueAnn frowned uncomprehendingly.

Edna swallowed, her breathing becoming more labored. "I...love...you...dear...daughter..."

Then, before RueAnn could truly comprehend what was happening, Edna's hold grew slack and she became still.

And in that instant, as the fire raged around them and the cacophony of battle began to crescendo, RueAnn felt the life drain from Edna's form. Peacefully. So peacefully. Leaving only the shell of her body behind.


## Lincolnshire, England


Susan stamped her feet as she let herself into Nocton Hall, then swept the wool scarf from her hair and draped it around the collar of her coat.

The weather had been mild enough for walking when she'd left the Two Horseman, but a wind had begun to blow, warning of a storm to follow. There would be more snow in the forecast for tonight, she would wager.

"Hello, Mildred," she said to the volunteer perched behind the marble topped table with its recipe box full of records.

"Good morning, Miss Blunt. Lt. Overdone is in the library. He told me to have you meet him there."

"Thank you," Susan said as she altered her course.

In the dozen or so times she'd visited, Susan had learned the names of most of the staff, and they'd grown accustomed to her visits. Susan arrived punctually when visiting hours began, and didn't leave until the precise second they were over. If Paul happened to be in treatment or asleep, she visited the men in the recreation room. She would help them write letters or push their wheelchairs around the grounds or the halls to give them a change of scenery.

Paul's improvement had been slow but measureable in the two weeks since she'd arrived, but he was still prone to frustration and bouts of anger. More than anything, he wanted to be back with his comrades, back in his Spit. But with his legs and hands still weak from burns only now beginning the painful healing process, it was difficult to know whether or not such a thing would ever become possible.

Susan had seen firsthand how tenuous progress could be among the burned pilots. The greatest fear was infection. A patient who appeared right enough one day, may be facing amputation the next if gangrene set in.

But Paul couldn't accept "wait and see" as any form of prognostication. And Susan had seen him grow more despondent and short-tempered with each day that passed.

Susan had tried her best to divert him—bringing books and magazines, playing cards and board games. But nothing had helped. So she was hoping to cheer him up with the news that they would be showing a motion picture in the dining hall on Saturday. Laurel and Hardy. Just the ticket for recovering servicemen.

Stepping into the library, she scanned the long, narrow room, automatically unbuttoning her coat. Here in the East Wing, the radiators pumped out enough heat for Lucifer himself, while on the opposite end of the manor, the rooms could become quite nippy.

Finally locating Paul at the far end, she moved toward him, not calling out yet. These first few moments before he realized she had arrived allowed her a chance to study him freely without worrying how he might react. It was the only time he was completely unguarded and honest in regards to his condition. In the few seconds it took to walk up behind him, she was able to see from the tense set of his shoulders that he was in pain but not quite as restless as yesterday.

Touching him lightly on the shoulders, she bent to brush a quick kiss to the top of his head, then rounded his chair to sit on the settee opposite.

"How are you this morning?" she asked, tugging her gloves from her fingers.

Paul didn't immediately answer. When she glanced up, he was staring out the window. A muscle pulsed at the base of his jaw.

"Is something wrong?"

She placed her gloves in her lap and set her purse on the cushion beside her.

He didn't answer her immediately. When he finally spoke, he said flatly, "I want you to go home."

Susan frowned. "Aren't you feeling well today? Have you told the doctor you need something for the p—"

"I want you to go home to London, not the Inn."

He looked at her then, his eyes lifeless and dull.

"But—"

"I want you to go home to London and I don't ever want to see you again."

Her stomach plummeted as if she'd been dropped off a precipice into a freezing pool.

"Wha—"

He reached into the pocket of his robe and withdrew a card, throwing it onto her lap.

Her fingers were trembling so terribly, she fumbled in trying to open it. Finally, she managed to spread it wide, the looping handwriting inside jumping out at her.

*Just heard about your difficulties from Phillip. Bernard and I wish you a speedy recovery and all our best wishes for your future.*
Sara Blunt-Biddiwell

A giant hand gripped her chest, making it impossible to breathe.

"What kind of game have you been playing, Susan?" he asked, his voice hard.

"I don't—"

"Don't lie to me! The handwriting," he said, pointing to the card. "It doesn't match the script on the letters I've been receiving—passionate, loving letters from a woman whom, apparently, I don't even know!" He dug into his pocket again, pulling out a crumpled envelope. "So I checked it against the inscription of the book you brought me, and guess what? It matches. What the bloody hell did you think? That I was some charity case in need of a fictional romance to keep me going?"

"No! I never—"

"You *never,*" he interrupted. "Therein is the key word. You never so much as spoke to me those times I spent with your family, and yet, you felt the need to perpetrate this…this *charade!*"

"No!" she jumped to her feet, wringing her hands. "You don't understand. It was Sara's idea to switch places. I knew all along that I shouldn't have gone with you to the fancy dress party, but I allowed myself to be talked into it!"

His features grew even paler, the darkness of his eyes beginning to burn. "Do you mean to tell me that the two of you schemed together from the beginning to play me for a fool?"

"No! I—it was innocent enough in the beginning. Sara had inadvertently double-booked herself for the evening and she came to me…begging me to help her. To take her place—only for an hour or two," Susan hastened to add. "But then she didn't come…" Her words became husky with unshed tears as she realized the lameness of her excuses in the face of what she'd done.

Sinking onto the settee, she reached out to touch his knee. "Don't you see? I fell in love with you that night…that perfect, beautiful night."

He didn't appear at all moved by her words, so she hurriedly continued. "Then the war broke out, and I realized that it wasn't me you'd courted, but the woman you thought I'd been and—" She sobbed. "It's all so complicated and yet...so simple."

He looked away from her, his jaw hard, the muscle clenching and unclenching.

"When you came back a year later and threw pebbles against the window, I didn't even think things through. I reacted instinctively." Her voice grew husky. "Selfishly." Withdrawing her hand from his leg, she knit her fingers together. "The person who talked to you was me. The woman who kissed you and agreed to write to you was me. Yet it wasn't until you called out my sister's name as you drove away that I realized you hadn't been speaking to *me*. You'd fallen for Sara."

Emotion lumped in her chest so painfully, she could hardly speak, but she forced herself to continue, needing to purge herself of the deceit which had festered in her for so long. "I swore that would be the end of it—truly I did. Until your letters arrived and I...I hoarded them. Unopened. For so long. Until..." She swallowed, reliving that moment when she had sealed her fate. "I couldn't ignore them any longer."

She blinked, tears heavy on her lashes. "Don't you see? By that time, I'd fallen in love with you. And I dared to believe that if I wrote to you...you might learn to love me too..."

The room pulsed in silence even as her heart churned in a bed of broken glass. With each tick of the distant mantel clock, she waited for her happy ending, for the moment when Paul would turn to her and forgive her of everything—because he loved her too. Loved the woman he'd kissed and held. Loved the woman who had poured her heart out to him with every word that she'd ever penned on paper.

But then, he looked at her, his eyes flat and hard, and said, "Get. Out."

He could have plunged a knife into her breast and it would not have been as painful. For the longest time, the words hovered in the air around her before slowly, slowly seeping into her brain.

"Paul?" It was the barest whisper of sound, little more than a puff of air. But he heard it. She knew he heard it.

He didn't respond. He merely turned away from her, staring resolutely out the window.

And in that instant, she knew she'd lost him.

Stiffly rising to her feet, she gathered up her things and took a step past him, two. Three. But then the pain crashed over her in waves and she couldn't stop herself from turning to face him yet again.

"How...*dare*...you," she whispered fiercely. "Yes, I deceived you. Yes, I took my sister's place. But if you had just once looked at me—*really* looked at me—you would have seen that I had ever so much more to offer you than my sister Sara. She was never interested in you. You were nothing more than another of her diversions, another stray. I *loved* you. From the beginning!"

Her voice rose as she became more fervent. "Maybe I am the fool for ever having loved you. Even here, wounded and in a hospital, I come out second best in this horse race. But if you'd truly known my sister, you would have realized that she wouldn't have come to Nocton in the first place. She would have...sent you a blasted card!" She pointed wildly to the note that had tumbled to the floor. "But *I* came. The moment I heard you were injured, I abandoned my home, my brother, my responsibilities, and I came. If you'd given me even a hint of kindness, I would have stayed with you for a lifetime. And I would have been the best thing that ever happened to you during your entire, miserable existence!"

Susan ran from the room then, her shouts echoing behind her, not pausing even when she heard him call out to her. She burst into the cold, dragging her coat over her shoulders, running most of the way back to the Two Horsemen. There, she threw her belongings into her suitcase, settled her bill, and raced to catch the evening train.

As the locomotive lumbered through the worsening weather, she refused to think of anything—her deceit and its consequences or her parting words. She vowed to herself that she wouldn't waste another ounce of energy on the man.

She'd been a fool. A complete and utter fool. She should have known that Paul could never truly love her, even after knowing the truth. Love was a reward for beauty, not for sincerity.

It was past midnight when she stumbled home, following the strips of white painted on the lampposts. As she neared the house, she found the way littered with debris and the air hung heavy with the smell of smoke and damp wood. Heart pounding, she tried to peer into the darkness, afraid that she would turn the corner to find that the block had been leveled in her absence. But it was so dark, she could only pick her way through bits of masonry until she finally reached the front gate and could run up to the front stoop and push her key into the frozen lock.

Frantic, she burst inside, pulling the blackout drape into place over the door and flinging on the light. The moment the yellow glow spilled into the corners, her breath left her lungs in a whoosh. Everything was in its place. The blackout was snuggly drawn, the furniture still sat solid and slightly worn, facing the radio as if waiting for her to turn on a program or the news.

She rubbed her hands together as she moved further into the room. Phillip must have let the coals go out because the air was chilly and curiously stale. Her breath hung in the air in little puffs of vapor.

"Phillip?" she called. "Phillip, I'm home!"

There was no answer and she cursed the Home Guard for keeping him out so late on one of those rare nights without an air raid.

Moving to the kitchen, she made sure the blackout drapes were drawn here as well, then flung on the light. A weak glow emitted from the overhead bulb, lapping into the corners. Feeling hollow and older than her years, she reached for the kettle and set it on the burner, then sighed. The stove had gone out as well.

Maybe Phillip had gone to live with RueAnn while Susan had been away. Maybe...

Her eyes suddenly landed on a piece of paper folded in half and propped in the middle of the kitchen table. Lifting it up, she held it to the light, attempting to decipher Phillip's impossibly messy script.

*Susan,*

*Please don't be mad with me, but I can't just sit around anymore, pretending that there isn't something I can do to help with the war. Matthew had it right when he joined the RAF. I've tried to do my bit with the Home Guard and all, but it's just not enough.*

*When you read this, I'll be gone. I found a recruitment office that believed me when I said I was eighteen and told them my papers had been burned in a fire. Don't worry about me. I've joined the Expeditionary Forces, and they're a good lot of blokes. I'll write as soon as we've shipped out and you can't force them to send me back.*

*Love,*
*Phillip*

The paper fell from her bloodless fingers and the strength drained from her body like so much sand until she dropped to the floor, sobbing.

She shouldn't have left him here alone. She shouldn't have left him. Dear God, why hadn't she done more to keep Phillip safe?

Charlie,

The first time I was forced to handle a snake, I learned that fear has a taste that lingers on the tongue like the sour smell of old pennies. It's a putrid flavor that seeps into my mouth each time I think of that day.

There were three of them. Kentucky Rattlers. Not pets, as many people believed, but wild creatures that my father had found up Dyson's canyon mere days before. Even now, I can picture the way they curled in upon themselves in their makeshift cage—pretty in a macabre way. Like that coveted length of copper iridescent ribbon I'd been eyeing in Mama's notion box for as long as I could remember. Just like the ribbon, the snakes glowed with a pearlescent sheen, deep chocolaty brown in spots, dappled with gold and copper in others. But unlike the ribbon, the snakes undulated, their bodies seeming to pulsate with a palpable threat.

Emotions wound in my stomach mirroring the snakes as they twisted tighter and tighter in alarm. I could understand just how those creatures felt, because I was trapped as surely as they were. Trapped. Angry. Filled with a sickening dread.

And confusion.

How had I come to this point? How, in the space of a few years, could my father have transformed from a stern disciplinarian...

Into a monster. A monster who insisted that I hold one of these deadly reptiles to prove I was among God's chosen followers.

We'd been coming to this church in the hills long enough for my father to assume the role of preacher and for me to know what to expect. Either the snake would accept the worshiper's faith and God would intercede to provide protection, or the serpent would strike. If so, there would be no medical intervention. The venom that surged through one's body would be God's punishment for a lack of devotion.

A chorus of "amens" rose from the congregation as my father held the rough wooden box high for all to see. The snakes hissed in protest, heads rearing, the rattles shaking and adding to the din.

Somewhere from the back, a woman began singing *The Old Rugged Cross*. I could feel the crowd's anticipation swelling, seeming to suck the very air from the room. My knees trembled so horribly I thought I would drop, so I locked them together until spots swam in front of my eyes and I gulped air into my lungs to keep from swaying.

"RueAnn Boggs has come willingly before the serpent to prove the depth of her commitment and devotion to God."

Come willingly? I hadn't come willingly. I'd been threatened and bullied into performing this ritual. I would have been resisting still if my father hadn't promised to throw me into the street to fend for myself if I didn't comply.

Nevertheless, as the box was lowered and extended toward me, I quickly reviewed my options. I was strong. I knew how to work.

But at eleven years of age, I was also firmly attached to my mother's apron strings. To my utter shame, I knew that to leave my mother and find my own way in the world would be far more frightening than any snake.

"Do it," my father growled. "Take up the serpent and declare yourself worthy before God and this congregation."

My tongue stuck to the roof of my mouth, the panic rising like bile. I met my father's gaze, cringing against the glint of obsession and malice I saw there. I watched as his skin darkened in anger, becoming mottled and purple. Flecks of spittle dotted his lips as he whispered more forcefully, "Take up the serpent, RueAnn Boggs. Show your worthiness to God and to this congregation."

He may as well have added: "...and to me."

I looked at the snake then, nausea churning in my stomach as I realized that, regardless of the outcome of this experience, my father might decide I had been found wanting in the eyes of God. If so, I could still be disowned.

Or I could be dead.

One of the snakes hissed at me, drawing taller against the side of the box. It waved its head from side to side, clearly agitated by the noise and the threat I represented.

I tried to pray, knowing it was expected of me. But the words skittered across the surface of my brain like water on a hot skillet. Deep down, I knew my faith was lacking. I didn't know if there was a God—and even if there were, I didn't know if I wanted to pray to a God who believed in ruling His children through fear and retribution like my father. I wanted my God to be like the painting of Jesus on the schoolhouse wall. The one where the Savior sat in a field watching a flock of puffy white sheep. He'd seemed kind in that picture and slightly distracted.

"Do it! Now!"

Knowing my father would probably throw the entire box of snakes at me if I hesitated any longer, I reached out, slowly, carefully. Inwardly, I tried to convince myself that touching the serpent would be no worse than approaching an angry dog. Employing that philosophy, I held out my hand, fingers down, wondering if a snake could smell fear on a person like a canine.

Mesmerized, I kept my eyes locked on the snake's tongue as it darted and licked and hissed in anger.

*Don't bite me, little snake*, I repeated in my head.

Bit by bit, I forced myself to close the gap between us. The tips of my fingers became tingly and numb, but I refused to let them drop. Holding my breath until my chest ached, I slid one hand around its neck, the other beneath the coil near the rattles, scooping the animal into my hands as if it were a baby to be gentled into submission.

The snake hissed. The rattles shook like milk pods in the wind as I lifted it free of the box.

Behind me, the singing continued, joined now by a chorus

of members shouting, "Praise be!"

I dared a quick look at my father, shivering at the coldness that shone from his eyes. But I didn't allow myself to wonder why my actions hadn't been enough to win his approval. Instead, I gently laid the snake back in the box, then turned to make my way back to my seat.

I had barely shifted my weight before I heard a movement and felt a searing pain in my back. Crying out, I fell to the ground, but not before I felt the snake clamp down hard on my skin and a burning ache begin to radiate outwards from the spot. Just like my father, the creature had stolen my acceptance and my willingness to give it love, then had lashed out at me all the same.

"You see!" my father proclaimed loudly as I curled in on myself whimpering. "This child has been found wanting in the eyes of God! He has offered her a warning that she would do well to heed!"

Closing my eyes tightly, I prayed for the darkness, begging God to take me now if I had proven to be so unworthy. But the blackness never came. Instead, I was left to writhe in agony as the poison began its slow and steady journey toward my heart.

It was then that I realized there were far worse things than being alone and I began to plot the moment of my escape.

Your loving wife,
RueAnn

# Chapter Seventeen

The muted jangle of the doorbell reverberated through the empty house. Hours had passed since Susan had found Phillip's note. Her valise still lay at the foot of the stairs and the parlor where she'd collapsed had grown ice-box cold.

Susan had remained impervious to the discomfort. She'd spent the night huddled in her mother's chair, reading and re-reading her brother's letter for some clue that might help her to find him and bring him home. But he'd carefully crafted his words so that she'd been left with no information other than he'd run away to join the war.

The bell rang again, jarring her from the dark cloud of misery and loneliness which had gripped her most of the sleepless night. Pushing herself to her feet, she drew her jumper closer around her neck, moving woodenly to the front door.

If not for that insistent summons, she supposed she would have continued sitting in her mother's chair for hours, staring at the wall. She couldn't shake her feelings of despondency—even though she knew there wasn't a thing she could do to remedy her mood. She couldn't bring her parents or her siblings back, couldn't force Phillip to come home, couldn't make Paul love her.

Swinging the door wide, she froze when her gaze fell on the peaked cap of the telegram delivery girl.

In an instant, Susan was seized with fear.

*No. No more.*

But she must not have uttered the words aloud, because the woman held out the clipboard for her signature.

"Sorry for the delay in the delivery, Miss," she said. "I've tried your home several times before, but no one's been home."

Then, after Susan had scribbled something unintelligible on the paper, she handed her the slick envelope and disappeared.

Even as the delivery girl disappeared into the swirling fog, Susan couldn't move. The cold twined around her ankles and filled her muscles with lead.

At long last, knowing that the news could not be changed, only ignored, Susan slit the envelope and unfolded the slip inside.

Her eyes scanned the message, her brain refusing to make sense of it. So she read the words a second time. Then a third.

Finally, meaning seeped into her brain, and when it did, the paper fluttered to the ground as she whirled into action. Racing upstairs, she gathered her purse and coat, hesitating only a moment to grab something from her dresser and shove it deep into her pocket. Then, she was thundering down the staircase again, slamming the door behind her.

A glance at her watch caused her brow to knit in concern. *Don't let her be too late. Please, don't let her be too late!*

Running to the cross streets, she hailed a taxi. She was sure she had enough in her pocketbook to pay for her fare, but only just.

"Victoria Station," she gasped as she slid onto the hard bench seat and slammed the door.

The taxi crawled toward its destination. With morning approaching—and Londoners emerging from their air raid hidey-holes—traffic was snarled with foot traffic, busses, automobiles, and even horse-drawn carts.

Susan glanced at her watch, feeling her stomach tighten as the precious minutes ticked away, until, finally, the taxi pulled to a stop just past Carlisle.

She already had the coins ready in her palm and dropped them quickly into the man's hand, then darted onto the sidewalk and through the huge brass door.

Weaving through the thick clumps of travelers, she made her way to the platforms. Panic seized her chest when she realized the train had already pulled away from the station. Dodging, she tried to peer around a trolley overloaded with luggage and a pair of porters scolding the newsboys who stood in their path.

Darting around them all, her eyes scanned the last of the passengers who remained—an elderly woman with a hatbox; a pair of businessmen walking toward the exit; a stern-faced woman dressed in the severe green wool of the WVS, issuing instructions to a handful of children seated on a bench. The youngsters looked mournful with the strings of their gas mask boxes slung over their chests, their identity tags fluttering in the cold breeze.

Susan's gaze skipped to a small girl on the end who had been swinging her feet and banging her heels against the bench supports. She tipped her head and a bright red braid escaped from her hat to tumble over her scarf.

Susan stutter-stepped to a halt, her hand plunging into her pocket, pulling out the threadbare rabbit she'd stuffed there.

"Magpie!" she shouted.

In that instant, the little girl turned. Her eyes were the shade of cornflowers, her nose sprinkled with freckles. Jumping down from the bench, she ran full-force toward Susan.

Susan knelt to catch her, offering Wuzzy as the fulfillment of a long-uttered promise. But as Margaret threw herself into Susan's arms, the toy fell to the ground, utterly forgotten.

In some corner of her brain, Susan acknowledged the woman who rushed toward them. She half-heard the breathless explanation of the way Margaret had been picked up by a Liberty Ship—and due to injury and miscommunication, had only just been returned to her rightful family. In time, Susan supposed she would demand more details, but the woman's words soon washed over her like so much noise as she breathed deeply of Margaret's little girl scent and heard her sister proclaim, "I'm home now, Susan. I'm finally home."

## Rouen, France

The early morning air was bitter cold as the small knot of Resistance members gathered in the woods outside the old abbey. Crouching low in the copse of bushes, Charlie counted eleven—no, fifteen people including Elizabeth and himself. These were no farmers with pitchforks. It was clear from the set of their features and the casual ease with which they handled their weapons that these were battle-hardened guerrillas.

They'd been resistant when Charlie had insisted on coming along. But Charlie had been adamant. He'd spent far too long inactive, waiting, praying he wouldn't be discovered. He was itching to strike back, to finish the job he'd been sent to do. The team was going to need as much manpower as possible and Charlie had recovered enough to prove a significant help to them.

Only then would he allow himself to think of the next step: finding a way home.

Mere hours ago, Charlie had made good on his promise to help arm the mission. The radio had weathered its long journey, and the batteries had held long enough for him to contact his superiors and arrange for an ammunition drop. Less than twenty-four hours later, he'd been part of the group waiting in an empty field several miles out of Rouen when the Resistance had set up a pair of smudge pots at the appointed time. Signaling to a low-flying Lancaster with a flashlight, he'd watched the plane circle, fly low, then disgorge a series of parachuted crates that floated to earth like lumpy paratroopers.

England, it seemed, was eager to dispose of the research facility. They'd forwarded more than enough provisions to supply them all—machine guns, extra rounds of ammunition, explosives, and detonators.

The weather was cold, the sky heavy with storm clouds when the strike team gathered for final instructions. Charlie used a stick to draw a map of what they knew about the compound. "There are two entrances." Scratching the sharp point of wood into the dirt, he showed the position of the gates. "Supplies and maintenance vehicles come in from the north, here." He tapped at the opposite entrance. "But here, on the southern end, is the spot where they've been taking personnel."

He gestured to a lean Frenchman with a hooked nose.

"You'll need to take three men and slip over the wall. There are weak spots in their patrols here…and here…"

Charlie looked up and the leader of the group nodded.

"You'll have less than fifteen minutes to set the charges and lay the wires along here…" He drew a line at the base of the outbuilding, then pointed to another pair of men waiting to the side. "You two, will need to set the charges here…in the orchard. There should be two ventilation shafts. One ten paces away from the well, another midway down the center of the row of trees. It's imperative that you set these off within seconds of the first explosion so that we can maximize the damage to the tunnels underneath."

The two men nodded.

"The rest of us," Charlie said referring to Elizabeth, Olivier, and a half dozen others, "will create your diversion. As I've said, you'll have only ten or fifteen minutes at the most once you've made it to the other side of the wall. Our attack needs to be swift, sudden, and deadly. Then we need to get the hell out of there to avoid being caught in the blast."

He peered around the circle. "Is everyone agreed?"

A murmur of assent rose from the group.

"Check your watches. It will be 0345…now." Several of them adjusted their timepieces. "At 0400, we begin. Precisely 0415, detonate the charges."

Within a matter of seconds, the figures had melted into the darkness, heading for their assigned points.

"Let's go."

He loped deeper into the cover of trees where they'd hidden a German transport truck stolen from God knows where. According to the records Elizabeth had seen in Hauptman's files, four prisoners slated for arrival at the railway station would be examined by the physician, then sent here, precisely at four this morning. Another group of men, closer to town, would intercept that transport long before it arrived.

Lowering the tailgate, he stepped aside to let the remaining members of their group climb into the back of the truck. As she took her place in line, Charlie grasped Elizabeth's elbow, pulling her close.

"You don't have to do this. Your role here is done. Head for home before everything blows to hell and back."

Elizabeth shook her head. She looked small and frail with a machine gun strapped around her neck and her hair shoved beneath a tight wool cap. She'd had only the most rudimentary of lessons on how to shoot the blasted thing.

"*Non.*"

"Elizabeth—"

"This is my fight too, Charlie," she hissed under her breath. "I've come too far to stop now."

Climbing up beside her, he fastened the tailgate, then held his watch up to the faint light bouncing off the icy snow.

0400.

At that instant, Olivier climbed behind the wheel and revved the engine.

"Hold on, everyone," Charlie warned.

Olivier pulled out onto the road, quickly building up momentum, going faster and faster, until the truck barreled down the hillside, straight toward the gate.

Peering from beneath the canvas flap, Charlie watched as a guard stepped out of nowhere, lifting his hand for the vehicle to stop. But Olivier was pushing the truck to its limits, moving at breakneck speed.

The guard barely had time to shout and lift his weapon before the truck crashed through the metal gates, sending the man flying through the air.

Olivier careened to a stop toward the rear of the compound just as soldiers in greatcoats began streaming from one of the smaller buildings. But just as quickly, the tailgate to the truck dropped and members of the Resistance stormed into the murky darkness, guns blazing.

Charlie was the last to emerge, his eye sweeping the area, taking in the Germans who already lay on the ground, the firefights which had begun to break out as more soldiers came rushing from other parts of the facility.

"Over here!" he shouted to Elizabeth, gesturing with a jerk

of his chin to a low stone trough that could provide them cover. They dodged behind the rocks just as a volley of bullets strafed the spot where they'd stood.

Elizabeth sat with her back braced against the rocks, panting.

"You all right?"

"*Oui.*"

Then, she was turning, firing at a pair of soldiers who attempted to flank their position.

Sensing that Elizabeth could take care of herself, Charlie began firing as well, the sights and sounds of battle coming hard and fast—the staccato stutter of machine guns, the flare and reverberation of grenades.

Laying his rifle on the top of the trough, he began sighting and shooting, sighting and shooting. Until, bit by bit, the noises became more sporadic and it became harder to find a target.

"*Allez, allez, allez!*"

Olivier was back in the transport again. Gears ground as he turned it in a tight circle, then began heading toward the gate.

Grabbing Elizabeth's hand, Charlie ran to intercept the vehicle, tearing open the passenger door and climbing inside, pulling Elizabeth up and over him until she tumbled into the space between him and Olivier.

Then, grasping his pistol, he began firing out the window, providing cover as other Resistance fighters streamed toward the slow-moving truck and threw themselves into the back.

"Are there any more?" Olivier shouted once they were nearly at the gate.

"I don't see anyone," Charlie bit out in return, sighting in on a German officer who ran out onto the steps of the old abandoned Abbey. Squeezing the trigger, he watched in satisfaction as the man suddenly crumbled. "Some of your men ran toward the hills rather than heading for the truck."

"*Bien,*" Olivier said, mashing his foot on the accelerator.

They were just barreling through the broken gate when a tremendous explosion rent the night, followed quickly by another and another.

The truck skidded, nearly toppling sideways, but Olivier quickly righted it, then veered off the main road to a faint track that wound its way up into the hillside. After a few miles, he stopped, peering into the side view mirror.

Like shadows, his men jumped from the back of the truck and skittered away into the blackness of the forest. Then, shifting again, Olivier altered course, bouncing and bumping across an old rutted wagon road that wound through the trees.

"Where to now?" Charlie asked, peering at his own mirror, searching for any hint of their being followed.

Olivier laughed, his exuberance over the success of their mission clearly palpable.

"You aren't they only one with a radio, *mon ami!*" he chortled. "Nor are you the only person in France with friends in high places. But we will have to hurry, *n'est-ce pas*? The blasts will soon have the area crawling with Germans."

The springs of the bench seat shrieked in protest as he raced down the old country road far too quickly for such a large vehicle. Charlie grew nervous as they drove and drove with no end in sight. It wouldn't be long before dawn began to lighten the sky and none of them could afford to be seen in a stolen German transport.

Just when he was about to demand an explanation of Olivier, the grizzled man topped a rise and brought the truck to a skidding halt.

"*Voilà!*" he said with a sweep of his hand. "You see, *mademoiselle*, I keep my promises."

In the pasture below, unbelievably, miraculously, lay the long, lean shape of a British cargo plane.

"You must hurry, *monsieur*. The British have been so kind as to bring us fresh supplies and six new operatives to help us with our cause. I insisted that—since we will be helping them to plant their spies all over France—they should be so kind as to offer you a ride home."

This time, when Olivier punched the accelerator and the truck jounced down the hill, Charlie could not will it to go fast enough.

Home. After everything that had happened, finally, he was heading home.

At the sight of the truck, the engines of the plane sputtered, caught, then rumbled into the darkness. Olivier stopped by the side door, just as the staircase was lowered and an impatient airman appeared in the doorway.

"Major Tolliver, I presume," he said with patent irritation. "Get your bloody arse aboard before we have the Luftwaffe to contend with."

Grinning, Charlie flung open the door and jumped out. But he'd only taken a few steps when he stopped and turned. Elizabeth stood poised, half in the cab, half out. She jumped down and walked toward him.

"Come with me," he urged. "Come to England."

She clearly hesitated, biting her lip. Then shook her head. "No."

"Why not? You can't possibly want to stay here. Come with me to England where it's—"

"Safe?" she inserted with a note of sarcasm. "I'm no safer in London than I am here. Hitler will bomb your capitol to the ground if he has his way. After that?" she shrugged. "You may be facing your own invasion."

Charlie shook his head. "We'll stop the little Chancellor before he ever gets close enough. If you came with me, at least you'd be away from the Nazis—for however long the war might last."

She sighed. "I would like that. More than you know, *mon ami*." Her shoulders lifted in a shrug. "But I can't."

He took her by the elbows. Until now, he'd never really realized what a little thing she was. She radiated such an aura of strength and determination that she'd seemed taller. More sturdy. He found himself wanting to shield her from the ugliness of war and deprivation.

But she was right. He couldn't promise her that England would be any safer for her than France.

"Please come," he said, trying one last time.

But she merely lifted on tiptoe, pressing a kiss to his cheek.

"This is my fight," she said simply, just as she had before the raid on the abbey. She took Charlie's hand, squeezing it tightly. "You, on the other hand, need to return home." She patted the pocket where he'd carefully stowed the letters. Letters which were once again held together with the frayed pink ribbon which had once adorned his wrist. "Give RueAnn my best regards. Tell her…she's a lucky woman to have been so loved by you, Charles Tolliver."

She touched his cheek, then backed away, returning to the transport.

"We need to get out of here, Major."

Charlie nodded, taking one last moment to fix Elizabeth's face in his memory. His savior.

His friend.

Then he turned and took the steps two at a time.

* * *

"Are you ready, Susan?"

Susan sighed when she heard her sister's voice floating to her from the front of the house.

"Yes, of course. I'll be there in a minute."

Susan slipped into her coat and planted her hat on her head, pausing only briefly to glance in the mirror over the bureau.

It was more habit than vanity that made her check her reflection. She'd been in Scotland for several days now, and she still felt as if she moved in a fog. If it weren't for little Margaret and her exuberance at being reunited with her sisters, Susan would have found it impossible to move throughout the day.

As it was, she'd done her best to explain away the circles under her eyes and her sleepless nights with her worry about Phillip and Matthew. She couldn't let Sara know how deeply she'd been hurt by Paul's rejection. It had taken all the strength she possessed to confess what she'd done to her sister—and Sara, being Sara, had considered the whole situation an elaborate lark.

So Susan had kept her pain to herself, trying her best to join in with the Christmas preparations—shopping, wrapping, and decorating—while inwardly, her heartache burrowed deep within her and gnawed away at her very soul.

"Susan! We're going to miss the services if you don't hurry!"

Susan hurried from the room behind the kitchen, down the hallway, to the knot of people by the front door. Mrs. Biddiwell was resplendent in a refurbished hat and her best fur coat, a Christmas corsage pinned to her ample chest. She indulgently held Margaret's hand while the little girl hopped from one foot to the other, asking if she could open up her presents when they returned from church. Sara, her stomach swelling beneath her own wrap watched with sparkling eyes, her hand unconsciously palming her belly.

"It's only Christmas Eve, pet. You'll have to wait until Father Christmas comes."

Margaret sighed in an affected show of desolation. "Not even one? Just a little one?"

Unable to bear her sister's grief, whether or not it was feigned, Susan tugged on one of Margaret's braids. "Perhaps, if you are very, very good for the sermon, I'll let you open the one from me."

Margaret had clearly expected more resistance, because her mouth dropped in surprise. Then she giggled, tugging on Mrs. Biddiwell's hands. "Then we'd better get there as soon as we can!"

Susan laughed, feeling an easing to the pinch of her heart as she flipped off the overhead light and wrenched open the door.

For a moment, she couldn't account for the shape standing on the stoop, the curiously hunched posture, the royal blue greatcoat and hat. Then, the figure straightened and the moon glow from the snowy street washed over features still recovering from their burns.

Susan felt as if her body suddenly dropped from a too-fast elevator. She stood rooted to the spot, her fingers clenched around the doorknob, her eyes locking with Paul Overdone's.

It was Sara who moved first. "Paul! It's so good to see you. How are you?"

His gaze barely flicked in Sara's direction. "I'm well, thank you." He shifted, drawing attention to the fact that he was supported by a pair of crutches. "I wondered if I could have a word with you, Susan."

When Susan didn't immediately respond, Sara said, "Of course, of course. Come in. You must be freezing." She gently pushed Susan to the side and opened the door wide. "We were just on our way to Christmas Eve services, then a party at the local community hall," Sara continued blithely. "We shan't be home until very late. Very late indeed."

Susan's cheeks flamed in embarrassment, but Sara remained blissfully unaware of her sister's discomfiture as she shepherded Margaret and Mrs. Biddiwell out into the snowy evening.

Margaret's chatter marked their progress down the walk to the garden gate, where they soon disappeared behind the enormous hedge.

Since Paul still stood on the step, Susan motioned for him to come in. After shutting the door, she switched on the light, then stood with her hands clutched behind her back, her heart thudding in her throat.

In the weak light streaming from the bulb overhead, she could see that Paul's burns had begun to heal. The last time she'd seen him, his face had been mottled with yellowing bruises and angry blisters. New skin had taken the place of his wounds, stretching tight and pink over his cheekbone and down the side of his jaw to his neck. Nevertheless, there was no denying the dark circles under his eyes and the gray tinge to his skin.

"You look exhausted," she murmured before she could reconsider her words.

His chin dipped in a quick nod. "I didn't realize I would have to follow you all the way to Scotland."

"Who told you where..." She bit down on the rest of her question before she revealed too much. Just seeing him again had swamped her with a tidal wave of longing. So much so, that she felt as if she were drowning in a sea of regret.

"RueAnn."

"Ah."

Silence pounded around them, stark and frightening and

so completely foreign that Susan didn't know how to proceed. She'd had her fill of rejection and loss and she truly couldn't take any more. But Paul looked so weary that she couldn't send him away, either.

"Would you like to sit down?" she asked, gesturing toward the sitting room. Despite commands to the contrary, Margaret had left the lights on the spindly tree and they gleamed like giant, multi-colored fireflies in the darkness.

"No, I…" he swallowed hard and scooped the hat from his head, mashing it with his long fingers. "I've got something to say to you, and I'm going to say it straight out because I'm just…I'm just too tired to work my way up to things."

Susan found herself staring at his hands, remembering oh, so long ago, when those palms had cupped her cheeks, holding her still for his first, searing kiss.

"Susan, I …?"

She wrenched her gaze away, not meeting his eyes, focusing instead on the jut of his Adam's apple and the faint shadow of his beard.

He offered a short, bitter laugh. "You were right."

Her eyes jumped up to lock with his and she saw an answering misery in the chocolaty brown depths.

"You were right in thinking that if we'd met in another time, another way, I probably wouldn't have given you the time of day. When we first met, I was still in University, young, brash." He took a shuddering breath. "I had my mind set on the usual pursuits—shiny roadsters, pretty girls, flying…" He shook his head. "Dear God, it seems like a lifetime ago."

He threw his hat onto a nearby table, then leaned more heavily into his crutches. "I've told you this before—and it sounds crazy, I know. But I fell head over heels in love with a girl I'd seen in a picture because she was looking straight at the camera and laughing. And the expression on her face was one of such joy…such…carefree exuberance…"

He grimaced. "Then, when I came home with Matthew, I was so hell-bent on making my fantasies a reality, I didn't really bother to look around me. I barely even noticed that Sara had a twin."

The honest statement flayed yet another layer of skin, leaving her raw and exposed. Paul looked up at her then, his eyes moist with unshed tears. "But I should have. I should have recognized immediately that when I was with Sara, things were… off." His voice became husky and so soft she could barely hear the words. "I should have known then that I wasn't in love with a fantasy. I'd fallen in love with a woman. A real woman. One who was kind and giving."

He straightened, bracing his back against the wall. "I know I don't deserve any second chances. I've been a bloody fool to bristle and claim I was the victim in this whole affair, when, in truth, I'm the one who was just too proud to admit that you truly are the best thing that has ever happened to me. I simply hope…in time…you might be agreeable to having me court you. Properly this time. I want you to know I—"

With a sob of her own, Susan rushed toward him, not thinking, not giving herself time to analyze the situation. One hand cupped the uninjured side of his face while she drew him down for her kiss. And in that instant, she knew the words weren't important. All that mattered was that she knew he loved her. *Her.*

His response was immediate, searing. Susan barely heard the clatter of his crutches falling to the floor as he swept his arms around her waist and hauled her tightly against him, hissing slightly when her body crashed into his own. Mindful of his injuries, she braced her hands against the wall behind him, but allowed him to deepen the embrace.

Joy and desire intermingled with a hunger like none she had ever encountered before. The shock she'd felt upon hearing he had been so close to death, and then Paul's subsequent rejection, boiled away, leaving the white-hot ardor that had simmered below the surface for so long. But this time, she met him without guilt and without reservation, her heart so filled with love she could scarcely breathe.

Tearing away, she gazed into his eyes, those rich chocolaty eyes, and smiled. "How long have you got leave?"

He grimaced. "Only a few days, I'm afraid. They wouldn't have let me out of the hospital at all if the nursing staff hadn't intervened in my favor." He grinned. "They persuaded my superiors by saying there was an emergency in my family that needed my immediate attention. They assured my doctors that I would be in good hands since you'd proved yourself to be very level-headed when you came to Nocton."

"Well, then," Susan said softly. "We'd best get you off your feet."

Taking his hand, she began to lead him down the hall toward the back of the house.

"My crutches—"

"You won't be needing them."

"But my hat—"

"You can leave it on the front table."

"But your sisters— "

"Won't be home for ages." She threw open the door to what had once been the maid's quarters and now served as her home away from home.

Paul's eyes widened. "But..."

Drawing him inside, she closed the door behind them, then twisted the key. "I think you need to put your feet up for a while."

He was regarding her with such a mixture of shock and hunger that she giggled.

"You needn't look so surprised, Paul Overdone. I've waited a long time to love a man like this. A lifetime."

She gently pushed his coat from his shoulders, allowing it to fall in a heap at their feet. Then her fingers began working on the buttons of his jacket.

"I don't feel inclined to wait any longer," she whispered, pushing his jacket aside until it joined his coat. Kissing him on his cheek, his jaw, his lips, she made quick work of his tie, then began to unfasten the buttons of his shirt, following her progress with her lips.

He inhaled, shuddering.

"Am I hurting you?" she murmured against his skin.

"Not in the way you're thinking."

"Should I stop?" she asked, a scant inch above his navel.

His fingers twined in her hair, tearing the pins free until the tresses hung about her shoulders.

"No."

The word emerged with such need, such utter adoration, that she laughed, feeling a surge of feminine power flooding through her body, and more...For the first time, she felt completely and utterly at peace with herself, her feelings for Paul, and her role as a woman.

Drawing the shirt from his body, she reached for the buckle to his belt. And as if the heat of her gaze had melted away the last of his resistance, he laughed, his hands eagerly tugging her own coat free before reaching for the buttons of her blouse.

"You're sure?" he whispered next to her ear.

She smiled next to his skin, her hands reaching below the waistband of his trousers to cup the tight swell of his buttocks.

"Oh, yes."

At that, there seemed to be no more need for words. There was only the need to touch and explore, to kiss and to stroke.

Sensing that Paul's strength was nearly gone, Susan pushed him onto the narrow bed, then straddled him, grasping at his warmth pressed up against her most sensitive flesh. Bending forward, she kissed him inch by inch, tracing the recent scars, the fragile skin. Unbidden, she remembered the letter he'd sent where he'd voiced his greatest fear: *Don't let me burn.*

She'd nearly lost him. Not just through deceit. He could have been trapped in his plane or drowned in the channel.

When she looked up, she saw the uncertainty in his eyes, the fear that she would be put off by his scars. Wrapping a hand around the part of him that thrust against her, she dispelled his misgivings as quickly as they had appeared.

"I have wanted to touch you like this for so long," she whispered. "Since the night of the fancy dress."

His smile was slow and filled with an answering heat.

"You will never know how many times I've wished you'd lost control and made love to me up against the tree."

In an instant, control was taken from her as Paul pulled her hard against him, turning them both so that her back pressed into the softness of the mattress and he was above her, straining, his arms trembling with desire and restraint, passion and fatigue. Sensing that his energy was limited, despite his wishes to the contrary, she shifted until he pressed up against her, then wrapped her legs around him and brought him home.

There was a twinge of pain, an uncomfortable resistance. Then Paul slid deep within her, warming her from the very core of her being, sending shivery bursts of pleasure from that intimate linking through her entire body.

Paul was trembling, his features tense and strained. "I can't...I don't think I can..."

"Shh," she whispered in his ear. "Give in. For now, love me hard and fast, just the way I fell in love with you."

He needed no further urging as he drew back, then slid into her, again and again, faster and faster, until she knew that she could not endure the pleasure-pain he inspired in her. And just when she feared she could not take another moment, her body seemed to explode in such sweet spasms that she couldn't help from crying out his name over and over again.

Long, long moments later, she surfaced from a haze of joy and physical completion to find that Paul had collapsed against her, his cheek resting against the plumpness of her breast.

"Are you in pain?" she whispered.

She felt him smile against her. "Not anymore."

Their laughter rippled through the room. Intimate. Knowing.

"Do you need anything?"

Again, she felt him smile. "Not anymore."

His body, which had been trembling with exertion, began to grow quiet. The flicker of his lashes against her breast conveyed his weariness.

"Then sleep," she murmured, kissing the top of his head, twining her fingers into the silken waves of his hair with a freedom that she never would have thought possible.

"But we—"

"Shh. Sleep. We have a lifetime to worry about the details, Paul Overdone. For now…rest."

It took only moments before she felt his body completely surrender to the exhaustion of his wounds, his journey, and their lovemaking. Although she wanted to remain awake and enjoy the headiness of being held so close in Paul Overdone's arms, Susan soon felt the tug of her own fatigue drawing her deeper into oblivion. But for the first time since the Blitz had begun, she didn't rail against the sensation. Instead, she welcomed sleep and the dreams it brought as the weight of her burdens seemed to shift and lighten. Not that any of her responsibilities had lessened. No. She merely had someone else to help carry the load.

It was sometime later when a light tapping at her door roused her. Gently slipping from Paul's tight embrace, she threw on her robe and opened the door just enough to peer out.

Margaret stood in the hall, her eyes snapping with eagerness, "Can I open my present now?"

Susan smothered a yawn. "Of course you may."

Margaret whirled, took two steps, then paused to look over her shoulder. "Wouldn't you like to open one of yours?"

Susan grinned. "I already have."

"Which one?"

"The one from Paul."

"Oh. Has he left?"

"No. He'll be staying a few more days." Susan made a shooing motion. "Go on, now. Open my present, then off to bed so Father Christmas can come."

"Don't you want to watch?"

Susan stifled another yawn. "No, pet. I'm so tired, I'm going to go back to bed. I'll watch you open your other presents in the morning. Sweet dreams."

"'Night, Susan."

Susan closed the door and carefully set the lock. Seeing the pile of clothing on the ground, she picked them up and draped them over a nearby chair. As she did so, something fluttered free from Paul's pocket.

For a moment, she wasn't sure what she was looking at. It was a photo of everyone in her family, save her father who'd been manning his Kodak. She remembered precisely the moment it had been taken, just after her father had been given a camera for Christmas three years ago.

*I fell head over heels in love with a girl I'd seen in a picture because she was looking straight at the camera and laughing. And the expression on her face was one of such joy...such...carefree exuberance...*

Holding the photo up to the dim light of the lamp which had been left on while they slept, Susan realized that this must have been Matthew's photograph. The one that Paul had said he'd fallen in love with even before meeting Sara...

Sara.

Susan looked at the photo, then at Paul who slept soundly, his arm flung out, his body still curved toward the spot where hers had been.

Despite everything he'd said, everything he meant to her, there had still been that tiny aching corner of her heart that had been forced to accept the fact that he'd been attracted to Sara first, not to her. But as her thumb rubbed over the photograph, that last lump of bitterness melted away.

Because the woman laughing up at the camera was not Sara.

It was Susan.

Dearest Charlie,

It's time you know the rest. The whole sordid tale. Because if I don't put the words down on paper, now, I may never be able to tell you the last of my secrets. And it's something you need to know.

After our marriage, there was only one thing that could bring me back to Defiance. The death of my beloved sister Astra.

To this day, the loss of my sweet little sister, my confidant, my own personal angel, is something that I can't bear to think about. I lock it away, refusing to remember. Because maybe, if I'd sent for her, insisted she come to New York to live with me, I could have prevented it.

But each time I begged her to leave Defiance, she refused. Not because she didn't want to go, but because if she came to live with me, nothing would stop my father from coming for us both.

I wouldn't have even known she had died if I hadn't been listening to the radio at the diner while business was slow. A landslide. Forty-two killed including seventeen children at the local school. The school where my sister was the teacher.

So I made the trip to Defiance, going back to the hell of my childhood, knowing well the dangers of doing so. But I had to go. I had been there at her birth. I would see her laid to rest.

My mother and sisters were startled when I appeared on the doorstep. Clearly, they didn't know what they should do. But I didn't give them the opportunity to refuse to let me enter. I was here to say goodbye, and I would not be dissuaded. I'd brought the pistol you took from Gideon the night we were married, and I was prepared to use it if necessary. But the women were so stunned by my presence that I was able to push past them easily enough and make my way to the parlor where my sister's coffin lay on a pair of saw horses.

At the sight of Astra's face, her beautiful, delicate face, the strength left my body. My bag fell to the floor, and I dropped beside it. Sobbing… sobbing.

There are no words possible to describe the utter sense of loss that swept over me. She was my sister…my friend… and in many ways my child…and I knew I would never be the same again. It was Astra who comforted me when I was sad, who tended to my wounds when I was hurt. It was Astra, who taught me to believe in God by writing my troubles to Jesus, then throwing my letters into the deep blue green waters of the abandoned quarry. Because that was what heaven was like, she said. Still and peaceful and deep. And if God was to be found anywhere, he would be there. She was the sole reason I survived living in my father's house and she was gone now. Gone.

I don't know how long I lay there, grieving. But I suddenly became aware of my mother watching me. Looking up, I met her gaze, one clouded with alcohol and laudanum and madness. She squinted at me as if she didn't really know me.

A disturbance came from the front of the house. My father was home. But I couldn't move, she held me so tightly in the grip of her regard. Then she whispered. "You did this to me. You and your father."

Then, before I knew what she meant to do, she bent—and too late, I saw that when my bag had fallen, the butt of the pistol had been exposed. My mother snatched up the gun and turned, just as my father entered the room. As his looming black shape filled the doorway, she leveled the weapon and shot him.

It was the answering silence thundering through the room that I will remember forever. That and the stunned disbelief that rippled over my mother's features as she suddenly realized what she had done.

She lifted the revolver—not at me as I had first thought she would—but at herself. I jumped to wrestle it away from her, just as Gideon stumbled into the room, then dodged to help me.

My mother began to weep then. Weep and laugh and babble incoherently. Drawing her into my arms—my damaged, half-crazed mother—I knew the authorities would take her away. They would lock her in jail or a hospital and she would never really understand why.

So Gideon and I wrapped my father's body in a quilt. Then, with the help of my sisters, we carried him out to the truck. And that night, we pushed him into the still waters of the old quarry.

As the first hint of dawn tinged the tips of the mountains, I took my bag and my gun, and made my way back to New York, knowing that there was only one thing left to do. Retrieve the letters you'd stolen. Letters filled with the whole sordid tale of my family. Because if you'd read them, I knew that you would never want to see me again.

I can only pray that I was wrong. That somehow, you can see past where I come from to the person I've become. Because I love you Charlie Tolliver. Body and soul I can't explain how or why, but I love you with every breath I take.

Yours forever,
RueAnn

# Chapter Eighteen

Christmas proved to be particularly lonely for RueAnn. Although she invited the other boarders for the "feast" she and Edna had originally planned, the spirit of the season had lost its spark without her mother-in-law to preside over the gathering. The holiday came and went, proving to be more a chore to be completed rather than a celebration. The following day, RueAnn packed up the decorations and straightened the house, feeling somehow relieved to put it all behind her.

By the end of the evening, she had decided that if she didn't hear something about Charlie's condition come New Year's Day, she would begin making preparations to return to the United States. She could wait for news there as well as here in the midst of a warzone.

As the days toward her self-imposed deadline marched closer, she felt a bit like a coward about to abandon ship—especially since the Blunts and her boarders would remain to fight the battle. But she had grown so weary. So heartsick. She just wanted to go home—even though she didn't know where home was anymore.

Now, there merely remained the matter of the New Year's dance. She'd agreed to go with Richard during a moment of weakness, one she deeply regretted.

As she began to dress for the event, she vowed that, tonight, she would tell him about her plans to return to the United States so that he would begin looking for another place to stay. Even if she decided to stay in England, she no longer felt comfortable having him in the house. Clearly, he was attracted to her. If she offered him the least amount of encouragement, she was sure that he would begin to court her.

But, come what may, she didn't want to start a relationship with Richard Carr. It was the coward's way out to insist he find new lodgings, she supposed, but the last thing she wanted right now was a confrontation.

She was just placing pins in her hair when the air raid siren began its swooping cry—and conversely, she felt a surge of relief. Now, she had the perfect excuse to avoid going to the dance with Richard.

After nearly a week of no air raids, the bombers closed in upon London hard and fast. Much like an animal being stalked by its prey, she ran out of the house, seeking refuge, barely able to get inside the Anderson before the first of the explosions rocked the earth beneath her.

There had been a time when closed-in spaces had robbed her of her ability to breathe, but after so many hours spent in the Anderson, RueAnn had begun to regard the little shelter as her own safe burrow. As she crouched on one of the bunks, alone, she did an automatic head count of who should be there with her. But Susan had left for Scotland a few days before Christmas so that she and Margaret could spend the holiday with Sara. The engineers had not yet returned to the house and Mr. Peabody preferred the space under the stairs during an air raid. So she was alone, shivering in the cold as hell itself opened up around her.

After so many days of relative quiet, the Germans were determined to make up for the shortfall. Explosions hit so close that the Anderson shook beneath the rippling reverberations and RueAnn could hear debris striking the house. Heat began to seep into the shelter, and fearing another fire nearby, RueAnn pushed the door open a crack to peer outside.

The black winter sky outside was limned with fire and all London seemed to be ablaze. Incendiaries had landed on rooftops, in tree branches, on the ground, self-igniting to spread their devilish fires.

A nearby explosion rocked her on her feet, but RueAnn braced herself against the doorway. Squinting up at the house, RueAnn counted two broken windows, and an ominous dark patch near the attic chimney.

*No. No!*

Fearing an incendiary might have pierced the roof and even now was setting the house ablaze, RueAnn ran across the yard. Pausing only to retrieve blankets from the cubby under the stairs, she raced up, up, throwing open the door to the attic space and dodging inside.

But what she found wasn't a fire or even inner damage to the roof. It was William Peabody hunched over a radio, speaking softly into the headset.

In German.

William Peabody looked up from his radio to see RueAnn staring at him aghast, and too late, RueAnn realized that she had unwittingly been harboring a spy.

As if all of the unsettling pieces drifted into place, she remembered finding him in Charlie's room…Edna's. Then there were the mornings she'd emerged from the Anderson to find that Mr. Peabody was already inside.

Gasping, RueAnn backed toward the door, but Peabody yanked a pistol from his waistband and leveled it at her.

"Where is it?"

She shook her head, uncomprehending, not even recognizing the man who stood in front of her. Gone was his stooped posture, the vagueness in his gaze, the thick horn-rimmed glasses. In the space of a heartbeat, he appeared younger, stronger, and infinitely dangerous.

"Don't play dumb. The list. I want the list of names given to your husband just before he left Washington D.C."

Again, she shook her head, even as a glimmer of recognition wriggled through her brain. The papers. The papers she'd found taped to the back of Charlie's bureau mirror. Could that be what he was talking about?

Peabody drew back the trigger of his pistol. "Tell me where it is!" he demanded more emphatically.

"I-I don't know what you're talking about."

He made a sound of disgust. "I'm not in the mood for games, Mrs. Tolliver," he said. "I was there. In Washington

D.C. I was following your husband when the two of you made contact." He took a step forward. "Who are you working for? The Americans? The British?"

His eyes had begun to blaze with the same fanaticism she'd often seen in her father's. She had no doubts that he would shoot her if she didn't cooperate.

"A-American," she answered, suddenly feeling like an actor who'd been thrust onstage without a script.

"I thought so. Your meeting in Washington just before Jean-Claude Foulard was scheduled to arrive was too much of a coincidence. "What's the matter? Couldn't you get Jean-Claude to hand over the information to you, rather than to your husband?"

She shook her head.

"There'll be no chance of that now. I took care of Jean-Claude soon after he talked to your husband." He advanced toward her, closing the gap between them. His expression grew thunderous and he shouted, "So where is it!"

Without thought, RueAnn dodged out of the little door, slamming it behind her. Briefly, she considered retrieving the gun she'd brought with her to England, but there was no time. She had to get away. Now!

Racing for the stairs, she took them two at a time, even as she heard the attic door hitting the wall. The thumps of his boots were close behind her as she fled outside.

In the time she'd been upstairs, the Germans seemed to have unleashed their entire arsenal so that the world itself was ablaze. RueAnn raced out into the street, dodging bits of smoldering debris and loose masonry. She fought her way through an artificial wind that had risen from the roiling flames, through streets rife with smoke and soot. She was assaulted with noise—rumbling bombers, explosions, and the crackling of burning wood. She didn't dare look behind her to see if Peabody was still following her. She had to...

She skidded to a stop when she realized she'd made a horrible mistake. Rather than heading deeper into the narrow alleys of the business district, she'd taken a side street—only to find it completely blocked by the collapsed wreckage of a hotel. The entire sidewall had been sheared off, leaving a gaping scar—as if a giant knife had cut it in two, exposing rooms complete with beds and furniture and flapping curtains.

Whirling, she tried to retrace her path, but she'd only managed a few steps before Peabody appeared, his form silhouetted in the firelight. In an instant, he was upon her, one arm snaking around her waist to trap her arms at her sides while the other ground the snout of the pistol into her temple.

"You stupid, meddling bitch!" he hissed in her ear. "You're no more an American operative than I'm Papa Noel." He swore fiercely in German. "You should have kept your nose out of my affairs."

The pistol was biting into her flesh. He held her so tightly, she couldn't breathe.

"If you'd just kept a blind eye to things a little longer, this wouldn't have happened. An invasion is inevitable."

RueAnn sobbed, squeezing her eyes shut just as a shot rang out, deafening her.

For several long moments, she waited for the pain, the blackness of death. Then, as a weight dragged against her, she realized that it was Peabody who was falling into her, his body dragging hers to the ground. Screaming, she stared up into a pair of unseeing eyes sunk into a head that had been torn asunder.

Scrambling free from his body, she struggled to push herself to her feet. She leaned against a portion of crumbling brick wall. Wildly searching for the source of the shot, she looked up in time to see a figure limned against the inferno beyond. He stood tall and lean, his arms bent at his side, feet braced apart.

RueAnn sagged against the bricks, wondering if she, too, had been hurt. If this were heaven or perhaps hell. Because she had to be imagining the familiar outline of the man striding toward her.

But as longing swept through her body on the heels of an unfamiliar exhilaration, she began running forward—knowing that if heaven or hell awaited her, it no longer mattered. This was what she had been searching for—not just days, but years.

LISA BINGHAM

She launched herself into his arms, and Charlie caught her, staggering, gripping her so tightly that she couldn't escape even if she'd wanted. His heart thumped in tandem with her own, his breath warm and real against her ear as he whispered her name. Then he was lowering her feet to the ground.

He drew back, looking down at her, and for a moment, his gaze caught and he swallowed hard. Following his line of sight, she saw that the Cracker Jack ring she'd worn around her neck since coming to England hung in plain sight, glinting dully in the fire's glow.

Shoving his pistol into his waistband, Charlie plunged his fingers into the soft waves of her hair, dislodging the pins so that loose curls framed her face.

In his eyes, she found such a mixture of joy and wonderment that she could scarcely believe he was looking at her. *Her.*

"Dear God, how I've missed you," he rasped.

And it was the sound of his voice, that beautiful, husky voice, that caused the tears to well up and fall over the dams of her lashes.

Then he was pulling her tightly toward him, his lips crashing over her own—and it was as if they'd never been apart. Passion swelled between them, filling RueAnn with a heady sense of belonging and more. So much more.

When he drew back, his own eyes glimmered with a betraying sheen.

"I'm so sorry. So sorry," he whispered, but she stopped him with a finger.

It no longer mattered that he'd taken her letters. Nor did she care if he'd read them. In his eyes, she could see that there was no secret, no horrible deed she might have done that could ever frighten him away.

He loved her.

Charlie Tolliver…loved…*her.*

Wrapping her arms around his neck, she knew that there would be a time when she would want him to tell her everything— what he'd been doing in Washington, where he'd been all these months, how he'd managed to find his way back to England. But

342

for now, all she wanted was this moment. This man.

"Welcome back, Charlie," she whispered against his ear. "Welcome back."

She felt him sob against her, felt the wetness of his cheek as he pressed his lips to her ear. Closing her eyes, she fingered the softness of his hair and reveled in the strength of his arms.

Then, drawing away, she wound her arm around his waist and pointed them both toward fires of London saying, "Let's go home."

# Epilogue

RueAnn moved among the rose bushes, pruning them for next year's spring. The yard had taken some work to return to its former glory. The house had too—although the exterior would probably have to wait for the end of the war before it could receive a proper coat of paint.

But RueAnn found she didn't worry about such things. After surviving the worst of the Blitz, she didn't bother herself with such inconsequential matters as peeling paint. She had a home here. A true home. Everything else, as Glory Bee O'Halloran would say, was just gravy.

The sound of a car crunching up the drive caused her to turn and she waved at the tall figure who emerged.

Charlie still limped, even after all this time. But secretly, RueAnn was glad. His injuries had kept him away from active duty. He'd been returned to Washington D.C. Not as an undercover agent, but as a special liaison with America's emerging OSS. But then, she wasn't supposed to know about that. Just as she wasn't supposed to know that Charlie had spent the year before the war trying to organize a series of British spies inserted into American society.

"Come along, sweat pea," RueAnn said, calling to the toddler who'd been playing in the grass. As the wind blew, loose petals showered down on her like a colorful snowstorm and the baby giggled, running through the bushes, her arms upstretched. She had blue-gray eyes like her father. Her grandmother.

Not for the first time, RueAnn felt a pang of love that rivaled only that of the emotions RueAnn felt for the child's father. When she'd discovered she was pregnant, RueAnn had worried that her own upbringing had been so hard, so joyless, that she wouldn't be able to love a child the way she should. But when the tiny bundle had been laid in her arms and had looked up at her with Charlie's eyes, Charlie's coloring, she'd realized that she needn't have worried. She'd been taught how to love by all of the people who'd gathered around her when she'd needed them most. And in doing so, she'd discovered the joy in being needed.

Smiling, RueAnn held out her hand.

"Come along, Edna Louise. Your Daddy is home."

Then she swung the little girl into her arms and made her way to the house and to Charlie.

# Acknowledgements

This novel has been a labor of love for several years. The first germ of an idea appeared when I saw the now-famous photographs of Londoners taking shelter in the Tube. For fifty-seven consecutive days, the Nazis tried to bomb London into submission or surrender. As I looked at these photos—as well as the resulting destruction—I was amazed at the way the British refused to be cowed. Not for the first time, I found myself thinking that a great many war stories have been told of men marching off to the front, but what about the women who were left behind?

What followed was a fascinating journey of research—not just of the women of the Blitz, but of the emerging independence of all females and the shift of their roles in society. Many of the details that I have used in my novel (the naked mannequins, the rationing, and the Anderson shelters) are based on historical fact. However, in some instances, I beg your forgiveness for "dramatic license." The men of the UXB unit would not have been privately billeted, but their role during the Blitz was so important that I felt the story would be incomplete without their presence. For this and any other faults, please forgive me.

I would also like to thank several people who have been instrumental in bringing *Into the Storm* to life. To the gang at Browne & Miller, thanks for all of the encouragement, advice, endless readings, and diplomatic interventions. It has been such a joy to know that my "baby" has been taken care of with such love and diligence. To those at Diversion Books, thanks for bringing *Into the Storm* to my readers. To Nancy and Danice, the first to cheer me on when I was embroiled in writing and rewriting—and the first to celebrate when *Into the Storm* found a home. To my children, who were patient while their mother lost her mind a little bit, and my husband who was willing to wait "just a few more minutes…"

And to my father, who would never share his stories past the boat ride to Honolulu where he served with the Army Air Corp. I was only a teenager when he made the statement, "War isn't all bands and glory." He was so serious and reflective, that the statement made me curious about what "really happened."

CPSIA information can be obtained at www.ICGtesting.com
Printed in the USA
LVOW07s1457300615

444445LV00005B/500/P